AUTOKRATOR

AUTOKRATOR

a novel by

EMILY A. WEEDON

Cormorant Books

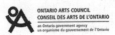

We acknowledge financial support for our publishing activities: the
Government of Canada, through the Canada Book Fund and The Canada
Council for the Arts; the Government of Ontario, through the Ontario Arts
Council, Ontario Creates, and the Ontario Book Publishing Tax Credit.

LIBRARY AND ARCHIVES CANADA CATALOGUING IN PUBLICATION

Title: Autokrator / a novel by Emily A. Weedon.
Names: Weedon, Emily A., author.
Identifiers: Canadiana (print) 20230563139 | Canadiana (ebook) 20230563147 |
ISBN 9781770866850 (softcover) | ISBN 9781770866867 (EPUB)
Subjects: LCGFT: Novels.
Classification: LCC PS8645.E33 A98 2024 | DDC C813/.6—dc23

United States Library of Congress Control Number: 2023949900

Cover design: Angel Guerra
Interior text design: Marijke Friesen
Manufactured by Friesens in Altona, Manitoba in February 2024.

Printed using paper from a responsible and sustainable resource,
including a mix of virgin fibres and recycled materials.

Printed and bound in Canada.

CORMORANT BOOKS INC.
260 ISHPADINAA (SPADINA) AVENUE, SUITE 502,
TKARONTO (TORONTO), ON M5T 2E4

SUITE 110, 7068 PORTAL WAY, FERNDALE, WA 98248, USA

www.cormorantbooks.com

In memory of my mother,
Liisa Kaarina Weedon

We know or should know that every decrease in power is an open invitation to violence — if only because those who hold power and feel it slipping from their hands ... have always found it difficult to resist the temptation to substitute violence for it.

HANNAH ARENDT

GLOSSARY

Autokrator: Supreme Ruler, head of the Triumvirate

Consort: Ruler in waiting, who ceremonially dresses in women's weeds; the child of the Autokrator

Domestic: Catch-all name for female labourers who provide unpaid work and have no autonomy

Hedgerow Mams: Teachers who secretly pass knowledge onto Unmales

Kratorling: Consort in waiting; the child of the Consort

Mams: Honorific among Unmales/Domestics for older women

Orthodoxy: Coded beliefs that support the rule of men and the existence of the Triumvirate

Toolist: Mechanically inclined fabricators, inventors, scientists, and doctors whose areas of study and work overlap and intersect

The tendency with history is to write as though events move inexorably toward a foregone conclusion. The layering of details happens as if by an unwritten master plan that rewards those fittest to lead with their just deserts. It is, however, a grave mistake to assume that events are compelled to follow any one path. A bee sting, foul weather, a mislaid letter, a badly shod horse ... history turns on the smallest of events. The masters we serve today could just as easily have become our servants.

DR. NEREUS GENNADIUS, PROFESSOR OF HISTORICAL
POLITICS, HEAD OF THE DEPARTMENT OF HISTORICAL
STUDIES, POST-IMPERIAL STUDIES CENTRE
from "Introduction to Global Perspectives on Politics of the Autokracy"

1

Tiresius

I AM A GENDER CRIMINAL. I am Unmale, yet I write as though I am a person.

I write this in the 1692nd year of the Autokracy, during the reign of Gentius, from a cell in the Imperial Prison.

What are you, most likely a Male, to make of that?

My readers won't like what I have to write. Whatever is set down in this memoir is suspect, as I am about to be executed. It is very likely my readers will believe that I, an Unmale who writes, lie. My readers are invited to entertain whatever thoughts they wish upon the subject.

But, please, withhold judgment to the end.

I am unmasked. This is a bracing freedom. It compels me to tell the truth, unbelievable as these events might be to a learned, thoughtful Male audience. My Male audience will be disgusted and outraged by my life. I admit, I revel in this fact. More than a little.

The heresy is deeply satisfying. At the time of the events I write about, it was simply the way things were. I sometimes allowed myself to feel it was natural and right that I should be a man of

power and prestige. I held office. I was held in esteem. Even if I
had nothing between my legs.

Call me a liar and feel safe from Unmales. Or believe the terrible
truth and tremble that the order of things may yet change. I have
played my part. I am past caring about the things of this world.

My Mam, the woman who bore me, is unimportant, as all
Mams are. My reader might ask: how could a Mam, being Unmale,
be important? Yet I came from somewhere. I was not grown in the
earth, nor plucked from a tree. I was spawned inside the viscera of
an Unmale, as all my readers were. I understand that it is uncomfortable to be reminded of such horrendous things. I do apologize.
I'd bow were it not for these chains.

I imagine my Mam housed in the Imperial Consiliorum, the
closest thing to being a queen that an Unmale can aspire to. An
unpaid whore — no, make that a serving vessel — to the most
important Males in the land.

Why do I give myself such a lofty compliment? Many of my
readers may be well bred. Some may be incubos, those common
brats conceived in the Public Consiliora. The random obligatory
donation of a Male citizen. To refer to another man as an incubo
in public was, in my day, the crudest possible slur.

I don't look common. My bone structure is very good. My
faculties of reason and debate are sharper than most men. This
leads me to believe that, at the very least, my Sire was someone of
status. For all anyone knows, he could be the Autokrator Himself,
or else Consort. Unfortunately, having come into the world an
Unmale, all I really have are my wits to base my theories on.

Orthodoxy, which comes from the mouths of the earliest
Autokrators, has so much to teach us. The Orthodoxy is pored
over by learned Males, who debate it in august circles. It is written
in giant gold letters that line the Autokrator's library. Orthodoxy
is the foundation of our nation's strength — its backbone and
raison d'être. It tells us what is good and right in our world. It

provides us the comfortable cage we live and fight and earn and fuck and die in. Orthodoxy explains how we got here, why it is that Males are the pure form and Unmales are an abomination. This dichotomy is inculcated in every boy; Unmales come to understand it from the moment they start working.

Orthodoxy teaches that my looks and brains are from my Sire. He bred with a faceless, nameless Domestic, an Unmale whose lot in life is to tend to the needs of Males. That Domestic passed on nothing of herself to me. How do we know this? Orthodoxy teaches that Males create Males, and Unmales are the dumb vessels who carry them. Sometimes, due to a malfunction in the vessel, the pure fetus is malformed as an Unmale. The Founding Fathers decreed that Males are citizens, while a creature born Unmale has no autonomy and owes society lifelong labour.

Orthodoxy is clear: no Male can possibly ungender his own material. Some Toolists — men learned in the technical arts, specialists in the human body — study the role of Unmales in the erratic processing of genetic substance. My own hand signed the Treasury approval granting these esteemed men funds for their experiments and papers. Their research cunningly explains how a Male's seed is corrupted by the Unmale's body, then tragically warped into Unmale form. The author of the paper took pains to bemoan the many possible lives lost in this process: so many promising young men whose lives never happened because filthy Unmales mutated fine and healthy Male seed into mistakes! So the Orthodoxy has it. So the scientific research sought to prove. The resulting work is a disaster of error and assumption — confusing, contradictory, the science warped to affirm Orthodoxy is good. Males are good. Unmales are abominations. I was given a medal for recognizing the study's importance. I allow myself these small moments of personal victory.

What I really believe is this: my Sire, no doubt a wealthy adviser, was probably a sot — doddering, overweight, intellectually unremarkable. The product of hundreds of years of tradition. He survived because of what he had between his legs, not his ears.

My Mam, on the other hand, must have been beautiful. If you'd seen the inside of the Imperial Consiliorum, you'd know this. Of course, few people reading this tangle of lies will have seen the Imperial Consiliorum. Such a rarefied place is closed to all but the members of the Autokracy and the Unmales who serve them. Readers will have to take my word for it when I say that only the most beautiful women in all the Autokracy are chosen for the Imperial Consiliorum. And of the most beautiful, only the canniest survive to lie with one of the Triumvirate. For this reason, I believe all my attributes — looks, brains, tenacity, political acumen — come from my Mam. Does it matter if I say such treasonous things now? My body will be quartered regardless. I can die only once. I heretically state: all my strength comes from my Mam, and I claim nothing from the nameless bureaucrat who sired me.

As for the specifics: the moment my gender was revealed, I was hurried away from the Unmale who bore me. I was not given a moment to lie on her warm breast. I was not nursed. I was not swaddled.

I'd like to think that being torn from my young mother broke her heart and that she longed for me over the years, wondering what became of me. But let's be frank: she likely would have been put back into service at the Imperial Consiliorum as soon as possible. Maybe next time she would get it right and have a son. No doubt she was wracked with guilt over her inability to correctly reproduce. The stakes were high: if she fouled a fetus with Unmale material too many times, she would be retired as defective.

I was wiped off with no real tenderness, the way a prized Male baby would be treated. I was given my first tattoo, with the year and day I was born. It was inked inside the curved bow of my ear.

I was taken Below and given a wet nurse, one I shared with other future Domestics. In their wisdom, Males had determined that Unmales have low caloric needs. I was born hungry and remain that way to this day. I get more done when I am hungry and a little cold and tired. It keeps both the teeth and the wits sharp.

It was wet nurses who named the numbered girl babies: the name we would carry secretly, woman to woman. They called me Deka.

The wet nurse passed me on to a caretaker until I could control my bowels and develop fine motor skills. This is the golden time of an Unmale's life. And from what I can glean from memory and observation, it was pleasant enough. We were held and cooed at. We were as yet wet clay, guilty only of being born what we were. And we had only one another in this world.

At perhaps the age of three, I was taken to a sort of training place. This was where I earned my next tattoo, on my wrist. Domestics carry their résumés there so their skill set is visible at a glance. Too many dots from too many work placements is a bad sign. It denotes insubordination, inflexibility, or perhaps rank stupidity.

Domestics are put to work the moment they show any sort of aptitude. The carpet makers come through frequently, looking for labour. The best workers are young ones with good eyes and tiny, nimble fingers. Young ones make good field labour too, since they are small, and squatting in the weeds doesn't hobble their backs and hold up the entire process. One learns quickly to aim for deftness and accuracy. That way, you get fed. In our slavery, there was a kind of meritocracy. If you showed some promise, you could at least aspire to work inside, out of the elements, away from the shit or unwieldy machinery or heavy loads. In my early childhood, I showed a great deal of promise.

2

Cera

EVA WOKE ME earlier than usual. It was my one freedom in a long, work-filled day, those few moments I lay between sleep and waking.

She was squatting next to me, with her hand on my shoulder. Since I had the earliest shift, my sleeping space was the one on the ground. Other spaces ranged above, carved into the walls on all sides. We all slept in coves scraped by hand out of the soft walls. Over time, the clammy clay dried and hardened. My bed was one of many dug into the walls of a low-ceilinged, dark, earthen room, many stories below the ground. For more than a thousand years, our world of Below had burrowed down, seventeen layers deep — maybe more — into the earth.

Eva was already wearing her shawl. The hood of the coarsely woven dun garment was thrown back.

"Cera, you've got extra to do today."

I made a noise, shaking off sleep.

"They want you Above in the East Wing to clear the grates."

"Eva. Go on. I'm no char Domestic. I'll make a mess of things."

"Adria is gone."

I sat up, completely awake, blood pounding. The news went through me, cold and jarring.

Adria was too loud and big and real to simply be gone, like a meal consumed or a dream that evaporated on waking.

"Gone? Like …"

"The others, yes. From the same corridor." Eva couldn't hide the annoyance in her voice. She'd been up for countless hours already.

"No one should use that bloody corridor," I managed. There were dark corners Below. Some corridors were heavily travelled by many women; others led to obscure parts of the Palace. For several years now, at a steady rate, Unmales had been disappearing.

Eva didn't hide her frustration with me. "Hmph. Then find another way. But get up to the East Wing quickly."

"And if the safer route takes me too long to get there?"

"Come on! You have to go. It's got to be done within the hour." No need to explain. Everything was meant to run like clockwork in the Palace. Each little cog wound along with all the rest, orchestrated to tick out the hours, days, months, years.

After Eva left, I pulled out Mother, my pocket goddess. She was a smooth, grey shape, pleasantly fat in the middle and tapered at both ends. She fit perfectly into my palm. She had little hands resting on her pendulous breasts. Delicate pointed feet. Very faintly, someone had carved a crude face. But to me, a beloved face. My Mother. Most of us had one like it.

They were passed down at birth, though some liked to carve their own. A Mother could pass through the fingers of many women, have many lives, before she was lost or destroyed, her features entirely rubbed off. She was all we had. Mother, goddess, and good luck charm all rolled into one. Mine was worn smooth by years of touching and rubbing it with my fingers. I had no idea who had first given it to me. I kissed her for luck and put her back in my pocket.

My bed was in a maze of passages filled with other sleeping niches that opened up to a communal eating area. The beds were shared, as women from one shift rose and women from another fell into them, exhausted. The adjoining kitchen was one wide space filled with ovens and worktables under low, vaulted earthen ceilings. It was lit by the fire of bread ovens that never went out.

I took a hunk of black bread from an open bin and dipped it in fat for my breakfast. I took the East Wing passage, dangerous though it might be. It was the fastest way, winding upward along the undulating passages that led Above to the world of Men.

The East Wing was dedicated to Hesperius Evander, the Krator-ling. It was a vast expanse of rooms that flowed one into another and sprawled under deeply corbelled ceilings. The wing was the oldest in the Capital complex. A palace within a palace, with its own receiving rooms, courtyards and pools, schoolrooms, and a gymnasium, all built with soaring ceilings, tooled leather walls, and vast amounts of draperies and carpets. In some places, the tall ceilings still bore smoke stains from the days when fires were tended centrally in open pits. The sooty walls had been whitewashed over the years with paler colours, but a darkness persisted. The windows were tiny slits that bored through deep stone walls, permitting only thin shafts of light.

As everywhere in the Palace, the small windows allowed some light but frustrated views inside or outside the hallowed rooms. In the newest parts of the Palace, where electric lights had been introduced to cast a low, ubiquitous illumination, Imperial architects had eliminated the windows altogether. Nothing on the outside was as important as the Imperial lives within.

The former throne room had become the Child's bedroom. It was full of cumbersome antiques and dusty art. One wall, battered with the passing of centuries, depicted Bartolius the Just.

The fabled patriarch of the Autokracy gazed sternly with coarsely outlined eyes. A dour man, he brandished a sword of grim justice. Bartolius was shown seated on the throne. Around him, the mosaic told the story of how Bartolius had discovered his queen's infidelity. She lay with his highest-ranking captain and confidant. Bartolius was shown pulling back the bedclothes from the lovers' naked forms. The artist's style was lumpen. The lovers registered their horror at being found with childish, elongated arms and hands. Their streams of adulterous blood traversed the mosaic in curvilinear forms, glittering with faceted garnet.

Another mural showed the beheading of Bartolius's three sons, whom he took to be illegitimate after his wife's betrayal. Their long, slim hands were crudely drawn, their kohl-lined eyes wide. Their hands attempted to stall their accusers, but the comically oversized axe hung in the moment before they were dispatched. Even then, in the days of old Bartolius, men needed to exaggerate the size of their weapons.

The mural concluded with the stern, just Autokrator reorganizing society, forbidding marriage, forever banishing Unmales to a place of invisible toil Below the feet of men.

These were strange and severe images for a child to fall asleep looking at, but not this child. Bartolius's bloody reign and righteous ire had ensured the line of succession was secure. History ran straight from that man to this child, and this child must understand the basis upon which the entire Autokracy was founded.

The Kratorling was permitted to wander wherever he liked in the Old Palace's gloomy rooms, with a train of perpetual Courtiers and Domestics trailing behind him in case he scraped a knee or knocked over a candlestick or dragged a quill along the venerated portraits. Their jobs were often made difficult by the fact that no one but the Autokrator and Consort was permitted to lay hands on the unruly, spoiled child.

One of Adria's duties had been keeping the many fireplaces in the Kratorling's wing alight. This time of year, only one, lit at night against the damp, needed tending. I felt heartsick to take on Adria's work. It made me feel guilty, as though by making her disappearance seamless, I was somehow complicit in it. The day before, we'd joked about a soldier she'd seen slip in a puddle of his own urine. We'd howled. Her big, deep-throated laugh had echoed as she'd described him thrashing about in his own piss. Now she was gone. Like so many others.

The fireplaces were cleaned and lit from the back by way of a low Domestic gate that led behind the wall in each room. The system had been engineered this way by men so they never had to lay eyes on the Domestics who served them. All the rooms of the Palace were serviceable this way, accessible through a warren of dark tunnels. Domestics could come and go silently, never seen. They took care of the dirty things so the Above world could cleanly function.

Just outside the rear of the hearth were shovels and brushes and pails for the ashes. A waste Domestic would be along presently on bandy, arthritic legs, drawing a cart like a mule on a track through the Palace bowels. She would dump the ashes down a midden chute that bored deep below the castle. At the bottom lay the ashes, the Kratorling's bedpan leavings, table scraps, and rotten vegetables, along with the corpses of Domestics who had died in the night from weariness or childbirth. They all mingled in a great heap of composting refuse.

The rear side of the gate was where Domestics hid their tools. Cleaning supplies, rags, water in pails, vinegar in bottles, dirty dishes from the night before. Beyond the fire grill to my right was a massive, swagged four-poster bed where the boy slept. He looked to be about five years old. From my vantage point, I could see one tender white limb thrown out of the bedcovers.

I crouched over my task, the brass grate across the Kratorling's fire blackened on my side. I regretted having dipped my bread in fat, because now my fingers were greasy and ashy. As I worked, the pail slipped from my hand, and silky grey ash spilled out into the room, marring the carpet. I sighed. Now I would have to enter and clean it up. I moved quickly. A fine brush, a pan, and a dense, soft rag would do the trick.

I bowed low, squeezing under the leather curtain that obscured the Domestic door. The hush on the other side was palpable; everything was upholstered, muffling sound. On our side, everything rang with harsh echoes off bare earth or clay or stone.

I squatted over my task, conscious that I'd managed to get ash into my sandals, soiling my toes. Grime between them, under my nails. How I missed baths every day.

And then I was blinded.

Something pressed against the mesh front of my shawl. I froze. The pressure released, and the Child jumped out in front of me, stark naked and blindingly pale in the angled morning light.

"Boo!"

I bent back to my task, driven. It was forbidden to talk to him.

"Booooooo!" He tugged at the front of my shawl. He tried to peer inside.

"Adria!" wheedled the Child. "Where are you?"

Again, I froze. She'd let him know her name? This was a bad slip. Maybe there was a reason Adria had disappeared. Not disappeared like many women did but hauled off to be put in the stocks. Or hanged.

The Kratorling would not relent. He used both hands and hauled upon the hood of my shawl, leaving me barefaced in his presence. I shot my face down. It was forbidden to look him in the eye. His tiny, pincer-like fingers latched on to my chin and pulled it up. His small face bunched up with confusion and suspicion, eyes squeezed into slivers.

"You're not Adria."

Hazel eyes, pupils peering out from under heavy, slanted lids, thin, mobile lips, a delicate nose with pale cheeks: I was looking at myself. Not many Domestics would know what they looked like, but I had once upon a time used mirrors to fix myself.

"You're more pretty than her. She has a strange nose." He touched my face. "Who are you?"

I looked down. Whispered.

"No one."

"I am the Kratorling, and you have to tell me." His hands were balled on his hips. Imperious already.

"I am Cera," I told him.

The door to the bedchamber swung open, with me knocked on my backside, shawl off. I leapt up hastily. The Kratorling pulled my shawl back down and whispered loudly into my face, "Come back tomorrow."

I swept the rest of the ashes up quickly and passed the damp rag over the carpet to remove the last traces. I got a kick in my backside for my troubles.

"Get out of here, you bloody creature! You should be done all this by now. Filthy."

All I saw were his robes. I scuttled back out through the Domestic door as the man admonished the Child.

"Kratorling! Have I not told you to keep your distance from those wretched creatures? No touching! No talking!"

Two vestment Domestics heaved their way up from Below and passed into the room to help dress the Child. Vestment Domestics held char Domestics in great disdain. I paused on my way out to watch them dress the boy. The Kratorling was worming his arms into a tight-fitting frock coat, shimmying his body in an attempt to pull it on. The Kratorling. The Imperial hope of the future. Whose face couldn't be more like mine were I looking in a mirror.

3

Tiresius

I DO NOT remember creeping about on all fours dressed in shapeless, colourless shawls in lightless corridors Below the houses of men, behind the walls of men. What I do recall vividly is the first book that was placed in my hands by a Hedgerow Mam — a keeper of knowledge among the Unmales. It was a crude book. A contraband book, with rough illustrations of the alphabet scrawled in charcoal on warped parchment.

Perhaps teachers in your school scared you with images of the Hedgerow Mams with their crooked spines and fingers and sooty faces. Your pater might have warned you to be good or a sooty-faced Mam with misshapen teeth would spring out of your fireplace and carry you off to the horrible Below. As a little one, you might have pleaded and cried that you'd be good to avoid being carried off. As an older boy, you likely scoffed that such a thing existed, but you took delight in torturing the littler ones with the idea.

Hedgerow Mams are no fabrication. They do exist — I assure you. They look like any bent and shrivelled old Domestic, shuffling along with a basket of food or a bundle of cloth.

My Hedgerow Mam even had a sooty face. Well, grease and manure, more like. She worked in a dairy, tending the milking machinery. I spent days in that narrow, fetid, vaulted building. The air was dense, filled with straw particles and drifting cow hair, thick with animal heat and breath and flatulence. Light filtered down from windows that spanned the roof. Stalls with cows in them ran the length of the barn, and I tended to endless udders: cleaning, wiping, milking. At night, my Mam schooled me. She was the one who taught me letters and numbers.

Much ink has been spilled over the centuries praising the wisdom of the Autokracy in maintaining strict control over the creation, dissemination, and use of technology and knowledge. The society that resulted was highly stratified by class, race, and wealth. Innovations could only find root if they were compatible with the ideals of the Autokrator. Rigorous control of ideas, especially those that directly affected the Autokracy, flowed out of the central Orthodoxy. The seeds of the future belonged to the Autokracy. Seeds of ideas, seeds of future men. The control of ideas began with the basics: limiting who learned letters and words, numbers and calculations.

Letters and numbers were expressly for Males. The Autokracy, and those who served it, were steeped in letters. Unmales had no business in the intellectual world; it was argued that Unmales didn't have the capacity for thought, and educating them was thought to be a fool's errand.

Hedgerow Mams carried on. They offered impromptu learning circles in corridors and storage rooms under cover of night. Many of my companions spent their time picking their noses or falling asleep over their contraband books. It was natural for a child who had worked for hours to be sleepy. Hunger was ever present, dimming the senses. From an early age, I, too, was voracious, but I was voracious for the letters.

I know the heresy is too much. But many Unmales who toil in the corridors and rooms of men do so while sounding out words, thinking about letters. Many are literate. For the most part, though, Unmales whisper their knowledge to one another while bent over one task or another. They retell their stories in a singsong to the beating of eggs or the threshing of wheat or the chopping of wood.

I was told, when I was old enough to remember being told, that I took to books ravenously from the age of four. I do remember pushing my shawl out of the way so I could better see the words on the page. It was hard enough to see in the dimly lit corridors where no natural light fell (tallow lamps give off a mucky glow).

I remember breathing in the smell of parchment. I even remember licking it, my tongue sticking to the dry page, and the Mam beating me so hard I was unable to work. Books are hard to come by for Mams, you see. One of my earliest memories is the sight of Hedgerow Mams hanging from the rafters of the dairy barn, their precious, illegal books decorating their necks.

The flesh passes, we must remind ourselves. But we Domestics held on to the names of the dead and wove them into songs we taught each other.

I grew. I was moved around, as Domestics constantly are. Kitchens, baths, stables, factories. They put my fingers to many tasks and found them surprisingly nimble.

From ages three to four, I worked in the dairy, where I drank stolen milk and learned forbidden letters. Soon after the appearance of the row of hanging Mams, they cleaned out the shop. I later learned it was a common occurrence. Mams with books meant organized learning, which had to be broken up.

I was taken in the middle of the night, pulled from my nest in the hay next to the cows. I was hauled by a strong Domestic who tucked me under a meaty arm. I was tossed into the back of a wagon with a dozen others. A team of oxen moved the wagon forward; the wooden wheels lurched over miles of rutted roads. Fields furred with grass unfolded under a white moon. I looked at everything with hungry eyes, keen for anything other than the underside of a cow. The air smelled clear and sharp and sweet. I didn't know it then, but I was headed toward the central plain, the centre of the world, where the Autokracy sprawled and industry huddled against its shoulders, basking in the protective glow of the elites, trading crops and resources for goods and miracles.

The hallowed streets where the Autokrator lived were said to be bathed in a golden glow. There they had lights that required no flame, no tallow. It was a place of wonder complete with self-propelled devices, medicines, processes, and ideas beyond the ken of the common masses. Learned men passed ideas to one another under the benevolent direction of the Autokrator.

We came to our destination at dawn, scrambling over the ruts to a long, low, dark series of buildings that hugged dank courtyards. Here was where wool from outer regions came to be spun and dyed and woven into intricate carpets. The stench was unbearable. We were hurried past open pits of stale urine where Domestics stirred sacks of powder into a vile slurry that fixed dyes into wools.

Between the ages of four and eleven, I knotted carpets — my longest work placement. As I worked, I mouthed the syllables the Mam had taught me the night before, shaping the feel of them with my lips and tongue but giving them no breath. Unless I wanted to be arrested, no one could ever hear me. But under my shawl, I could make the shapes. Under my shawl, I could pull faces, even stick out my tongue. Few ever saw a Domestic's face. Why would they want to?

Making faces under shawls tends to lead to deeper heresies. And no doubt the teachings of one Hedgerow Mam after another began to swell my head. I became reckless. I stole from Males. I ate forbidden foods. I snuck in and pissed in a proper, hallowed bathroom. I spoke words aloud. Somehow, despite all signs to the contrary — the way I was dressed, the work I was made to do, the way supervisors used my body — I held an innate belief that I was just as good as any man Above. The thought that they could ignore my good brain to toil in their shit and garbage made my blood boil.

This was the word I spoke, aloud, in the presence of a supervisor: "Ass."

He was squat, with a face like raw beef. How could a man with such greasy sausage fingers supervise a rug facility? I watched, amazed, as his fingers danced over the loom strings like a guitar player. He was of the Common Class; I would soon have as many letters as he did. His currency was experience, oversight, and ownership, a facility passed down from father to son through the centuries. He had no say in his life, unless by some miracle he'd mounted spectacular grades in early school. But one look at his thick face and vacant eyes made it clear that was not so. Nevertheless, he knew his field. He knew the labour of rug making and the ways to exploit Domestics to get the best quality of product.

He was showing me the red pile of strings. He had repeated — for the fourth time, as though I were stupid — that this was the red pile. And then, as though it would fix the notion deeper into my Unmale brain, he cuffed my head, shouting, "Red!"

I knew full well which ones were red and which were not. Of course, given my own hot red hair, I knew the colour. Not that the supervisor had ever seen the colour of my hair. I was neither colour-blind nor an idiot, as Males assumed we all were.

This was what rankled most, what lived sour and hot in the front of my skull: I was no idiot, yet I would serve idiots until I died.

With these sharp, incendiary thoughts running in my head, I turned to the task at hand, carrying the blasted red strands from the table to the workbench. It was then that I muttered the word.

"Ass."

The supervisor's complexion was dark, but his face went the colour of paste. His mouth moved, but he was too outraged to speak. The dark bristles on his chin stood out in stark relief against the pallor of his skin.

He would have beaten me to death there and then had he not been too apoplectic to raise a hand. I surmise in retrospect that he must have suffered an aneurysm or a stroke. He was struck speechless, his eyes bugged, he grabbed at his throat, and he fell to his knees. As he did, I knelt so that I was level with him. His eyes bugged out further in outrage.

I pulled aside the threads of my shawl so I could see him better. So he could see me. And I said it even more clearly: "Fucking ass."

I remained there, hands clasped together inside the stiff folds of my shawl, head bowed, waiting for my next orders. I didn't react when officials removed the supervisor's heavy corpse. They whispered about me behind their shawls. No one saw anything. More importantly, no one saw me touch him.

The next day, they demoted me to stable work. A thankless job for a thankless Unmale, seething behind a shit-stained shawl.

4

Cera

IT HAD BEEN years since I'd been Above, in the rooms of men. Time moved slowly down Below, where there was no sun to clock, and where one day of menial, mindless work bled into another. I'd forgotten the hush of the thick rugs, the pristine cleanliness of the world Above, where your eye could alight on any corner and find it scrubbed, gleaming, free from dust or debris. It was utterly unlike the noisome world below. When I'd lived as an Imperial Consilia, my bare feet had been embraced by deep, clean carpets. Through my pregnancy, I ate proper meals, I rested, I slept: my hands were idle.

My hands were idle; my body was not. My mind was supposed to be idle as well, and I presented myself as mild and pliable. But I thought many things. I wish I could say I'd been clever and plotting, that I'd found a way to work my beauty to my advantage and make a comfortable life for myself. In reality. I was just one of a herd with a pretty pen to languish in.

But I meant something to him. I knew that, at least.

Over the years, memories of us together were my only keepsakes of that time. I wandered through those memories from time to time, reliving.

I recalled how one upholstered wall of my room, my cell, might slide open at any moment. Seeing it crack and then slide, I would feel a rush of anticipation before I could even see him. My mouth watered at the thought of his mouth touching mine. I anticipated the tenor of his voice vibrating in that small room.

I was entitled to nothing and no one, yet I had these memories of him. I kept them folded inside my mind, a cache to luxuriate in.

He always came to me in ceremonial dress. It was a constant reminder of the order of things. Those "women's weeds" were stiff, binding, and oppressive. They were built with whalebone and layers and panels and meant to look like the antique clothes women wore before the start of the Autokracy.

I will never forget the first time I met him. I knelt with four other women. We wore scarves in our long, perfumed hair. It was traditional that our long, winding plaits were piled on our heads and draped on our shoulders. When I was with him, he liked to unleash those plaits into rivers of black, which would sweep the floor. We had tightly cinched waists and draping, folded necklines. We were weighed down by yards and yards of heavy silk. This costume drama was a sight reserved only for the pleasure of the three men of the Triumvirate, made up of the Autokrator and his two successors.

He enjoyed the costume. When we were together, he joked that he liked the laborious process of unwrapping, unwinding, discovering.

I wanted to laugh when he approached, though I'd been trained, harshly, not to. His ceremonial outfit was a finely wrought and slightly streamlined version of what we wore. The fabrics and finishings were more intricate, costlier than mine. Golden thread, honeycomb smocking, meticulously tailored boning, glittering trim seeded with pearls and jewels and gold lace: this was his face to the world. Here in the Consiliorum, we all had a different role to play. The ritual began with us divesting him of the ridiculous women's weeds to reveal the sleekly fitted leggings and shirt beneath. Under every Consort's garb beat the heart of a real man, or so the saying went. The hope was that more than just the heart was truly and fully Male.

While my sisters undid the laces at his waist and ankles and wrists, I pulled the jesses that tethered his collar to his vest. The stiff gold lace attached to the softer, boned bodice. The jesses got caught up in his long braids as I worked. I laughed. Softly enough to conceal it from the others, but my lips were close to his ear. I saw him fix his gaze deliberately on me, peering from the corner of his eye.

We served him wine. We sang. We recited poems they'd made us learn by rote. We lit candles. He was invited to choose among us. When he held his hand out for mine, I went with him to a little upholstered room. I tried not to let myself feel pride.

I was not to let on that I felt anything about being chosen. But I was unsuccessful.

The door slid closed behind us, and he pulled his shirt off.

"You laughed," he said. I nodded. There was no use arguing the fact. "You're not supposed to laugh." The pleased tone in his voice made me brazen enough to smile at him.

That was when he kissed me, crushing me to him, crushing my lips against my teeth. Kissing was not sanctioned.

From that point, the welcome ceremony was moot. He could come and go; I had to wait in that upholstered box. A soft prison. I began to count the seconds between his visits.

I allowed myself to feel successful. Not only had I fulfilled my role, carrying a possible Kratorling, I'd won him for myself. It was utter hubris.

After I'd given birth, I was cast out of the Imperial Consiliorum. This was for the sake of the child's future. A mother could only be a hindrance to a hopeful heir. They lopped off my plaits so my hair hung down just to my shoulders. I felt neutered.

I was sent Below, to the shadows. I refused to eat. I barely slept. I was haunted by the Consort's face, and I panicked as his features became less distinct. I found that I wanted to die. It was a common thing to desire, being an Unmale. The only remedy was work. There was no option to refuse it, of course, and the work was too menial to ever dampen longing thoughts. But the exhaustion did.

Going Below felt like being buried. Though I had steeled myself daily for the fact that they would take the child away from me almost instantly, I was not ready when it actually happened. So my grief and I were buried in a dark, subterranean world lacking light and comfort.

A few weeks after going Below, while I was still recovering from the birth, I was visited by a doddering, fair-haired Toolist, part of some godforsaken medical detail. I wondered who had drawn the short stick to examine the vilest parts of filthy Domestics. I said nothing when he reached out a dewy, moist hand and laid it on my breast. It was shocking to see a Male down Below, but I was new there, so I took the rotund figure of the Toolist in stride. I also took it in stride when he turned me to a wall and palpated my bare belly, then pried me apart and prodded between my legs.

One finger.

I sucked my breath in and hoped he wouldn't take offence.

"You've borne a child some time ago, my pet?" His voice was mild, which gave me hope that whatever else followed wouldn't be too bad.

Two fingers, twisting, probing. He got down heavily on a knee. He peeled up my shawl and peered between my legs, mmm-ing and hmm-ing to himself all the while.

"Be still, pet. I'm a Toolist, after all. This isn't for my pleasure. Domestics need to learn to know when they are being helped for their own good." He said it in a singsong voice, as though he had done so many times. He patted the tattoo on my inner thigh.

"Good girl, good girl. And did you give the Autokracy a Male?"

I nodded, and he unfurled the top of my ear to read my number tattoo. Out of the corner of my eye, I saw him note it in a small book he carried.

"Good, pet! You're a strong one. Good bones. A good, proper vessel. Hurry now, don't be wasting the Autokracy's time."

I yanked the shawl back down my shaking legs, ducked into a nearby tunnel, and squatted there to watch him waddle off. A few feet away, he stopped another Domestic. While he steadied her with a hand on her shoulder, he thrust his other hand casually inside her shawl. "Hello, pet. Open up for me, would you?" I looked away.

Shortly after the encounter with the Toolist, I joined the Domestics' kitchen staff and learned to make bread. In between bouts of proofing and kneading and forming, I nursed Unmale babies. There was always a hungry mouth around. Had I wished it, I could have gone Above and taken a position as a wet nurse in a fine home. I could have slept under the infant's bed when he rested, on a sturdy bedroll. I'd have had nourishing meals. But in my confusion and delirium, I wanted to be far away in place and station from the baby who'd taken root in me and then been torn from my arms. I tried to forget the tiny lodger who had lived inside me for nine months.

I met Adria and Eva near the open hearths when I first started working, along with others, like broad-shouldered Maya and wry Brigid, their faces lit by the roaring fires they kept stoked. It was Adria and Eva who patiently taught me how to be useful in the bakery. Eva was patient and guided my hands, showing me the trick of picking up sticky dough, shaping it, navigating hot baking stones without searing my flesh. Adria yelled and threw things. She curled her lip in contempt when my bread went flat. She threw my hopeless, unrisen dough into waste bins to be taken away for pig slop. Her eyes lit up when I finally made my first good loaves, though, or when she had a saucy tale about a Domestic thrashing her master and running away to live to live another day.

Adria was fiery. She was opinionated and a loose talker, fond of peppering her speech with criminal statements like, "Well, fuck all the men." She was terrifying in her boldness; her zeal was like a tonic compared to all the others who bent meekly to their tasks. Her broad shoulders, strong frame, and big voice filled up a room. She was a fast worker. The churn of her arms would inevitably make the firm, round planes of her face glow with a sheen of sweat, burnishing her from dark olive to deep gold. Her wild hair found a way out of her shawl like eels escaping a poacher's bag.

She liked to tell me about her previous job, before coming to work at the ovens. She used to work with animals. She'd picked up some basic medical techniques by delivering calves and goats.

"What I really enjoyed was castrating the geldings," she told me with a wicked arch of both eyebrows. "Cut the scrotum, reach in, yank out the testicles, let the wound bleed out. I like to imagine I'm doing it to them." She jerked a thumb upward, indicating the world of men. I thought they were lucky she was down here now, far from knives.

Eva was a fraction of Adria's size, but her energy made up for it. She had thick, honey-coloured hair, a round, warmly inquisitive face, and incredibly strong arms. She was small yet looked as though no force on earth could make her lose her centre of gravity. Her brows angled sharply up and were usually drawn together in a look of fierce concentration. Her sharp expression compelled other Domestics to speak truthfully to her, even if her own mind was far away. She had a unique position that allowed her to come and go in the outer world.

The three of us bent our backs over proofing trays and long tables, pulling and kneading like pistons in some great machine. As we worked, Adria told us about the many children she'd had.

At the end of a day, she knew where to lay strong hands on my lower back and pelvis to ease the joints jarred out of place by pregnancy.

"They set up shop inside us and like to knock the framework out of balance," she'd say as she worked my hip back into alignment. "Too bad we can't find a way to stick babies in Males. Knock them around." As she worked the knot in my back with her knuckles, I could feel her gleeful laughter vibrate down through her arm.

When I'd first come down from the Consiliorum, it had been Eva who had known what to do with me. At a glance, she knew what I was feeling. My hair was plastered to my forehead from fever, my breasts rock hard and shot full of pain.

"Your milk's come in," she'd stated. The next time I saw her, she tossed a cabbage at me. I fumbled it, which made her shriek with laughter. She put it back in my lap and peeled two leaves off. She crammed them to my chest, one on each breast like an outlandish purple breastplate. I scoffed, but across the table Eva was nodding approvingly.

"Just try it," Eva said.

Later, with my shawl half stripped off and feeling like an idiot being set up for a prank, I tried the leaves, and they worked so fast, I sat on the floor and cried in relief.

I asked Eva about the bulky, fair-haired Toolist who had groped me. Had he done the same to her when she gave birth? Or after? Did others like him come by to lay their hands on Domestics?

"Him?" She snorted. "Ferrius may be a real Medical Toolist, but all that fatty does is sneak around and feel up Domestics. Bad enough how much access they get to us Above, he has to come Below. Straight to the source."

Eva's role was a strange one; she came and went as no other Domestic did. She ventured out daily to secure supplies for the endless amounts of bread we baked in those giant hearths. From down Below, we supplied soldiers and prisoners and Domestics with bread. Bread for other men was made elsewhere, with finer ingredients. Unmales could make food for Unmales. Cooking for men was done by men. Likely, the early Autokrators had had one too many incidents of poisoning and decided to remedy the situation.

Each morning at about four o'clock, Eva would throw on a second shawl and feel her way up and out to the predawn Above to buy flours in the central market. Whatever was available at the cheapest rate: rye, millet, wheat. She haggled with Unmales who'd brought grain in from the outer regions.

Grain was cultivated and harvested by countless Unmales on old lands held by ancient lords. The oldest Families in the Autokracy were those with the best soil, who had built their wealth feeding the Capital.

Once Eva had brokered a price, Domestics carted the grain back down Below and ground it on massive stone mills. A generous number of stalks found their way into the coarse flours to bulk them up. Otherwise, there wouldn't have been sufficient loaves. Eva oversaw the entire production, proofing to kneading, shaping to baking, cooling and distributing.

When I first came to live Below, after the child, she would bring me little gifts of fruit from the markets — a plum or an apple.

"It will help you rebuild your strength," she'd said.

5

Tiresius

AFTER THE UNEXPLAINED death of the irate rug supervisor, I was moved around a great deal. I think the year may have been 1648, and I was about twelve. They drove us in gangs of Domestics from place to place. A manager would inspect us and keep those he thought useful. After that, we had to present our arms to the quartermaster to confirm our tattoos. We would receive a new tattoo saying that, as of that date, we belonged to such and such manufacturing concern or produce centre. My long collection of tattoos marked me as a troublemaker.

I was good at whatever they set my fingers to. Small machine work, repairs, shelling peas, plucking chickens, soldering, wiring. I needed only to be shown how to do something once, and typically I found a better way to do it. Sitting in a long line of Domestics bent to some task or another, I could see how any process could be made simpler, leaner. Just by placing a bucket here or there to catch the extra bolts or seating the girls within arms' reach to move the product along. It was maddening to see what could be improved and yet have no say in it. The Autokracy was not bent on making the work of Domestics more productive; the Autokracy was bent on keeping Unmales occupied.

The nimble fingers I had developed at the rug factory helped me progress in life, and ultimately, the various tasks men set me to were rungs on a ladder I climbed ever higher. In those days, I never dreamed I would find a place Above. In the dairy, I hauled great canisters of fresh milk, stealing a little from each can, building my strength. I grew strong and might have become an imposing enforcer of other Domestics, or the leader of a gang of heavy equipment operators. I try not to think about where I might have wound up.

It's just as well I didn't: even when I was one, I always thought Domestics on the whole were stupid creatures, little better than the cows they tended, content to plod their way through the world Males had decreed for them. It's true I was the most likely to let a master know if another Domestic had transgressed: it was their own fault. If they were careless enough to slack off, they would catch punishments. Let them learn their own way through the world, as I had.

My final placement as a Domestic was at a school for the sons of the elite, boys chosen to be future military officers, leaders, bureaucrats, and ritualists for the Autokracy. It was far from the Capital, in some craggy, weedy, godforsaken corner. I'd seen the Capital once — its buildings embellished with outrageous phallic structures, its teeming mobs of people. The Capital was a place I wanted to master, a place I thought was perhaps big enough for me. I yearned to walk down those streets, to have a purpose. More: to run it myself. But for the time being, when I passed through as a visitor, I had to content myself with lying in a heap among a disaffected bunch of Domestics, in filthy hay, just outside the city walls.

The school they sent me to was several days' journey from the Capital. I could hope to gain nothing from the place, yet I was stirred by the very sight of it. A massive, ancient institution, it sprawled out among low, rolling foothills. Ruins of the earliest stages of the school were overgrown by soft mosses and vines that breathed an air of antiquity, of august learning. The barracks, the training grounds, the monastic learning spaces built of solid stones, elegantly carved with friezes, spoke of a rational military mentality. It boasted the finest military library in the Autokracy.

The students were almost entirely from noble Families, the sons of leaders who were future leaders themselves. When they weren't being beaten for infractions, they were treated with a scraping kind of reverence for their impending service to the realm. These were the leaders of the next decade, or else its future glorious dead. A few of the students came from common ranks, as well. A boy's best hope was to come to this school. A lesser boy could at best hope to be a Toolist. The rest had to content themselves with the dull lives of commoners, insignificant overseers of artisanal or agricultural concerns.

I worked first in the school's stables. I was quick: I kept the metal polished and bright, the leather supple and clean. My one failing was that I was terrified of the horses. They leaned out of their stalls and loomed high above me, inspecting. Their nickering presence felt strangely judgmental. My hands shook when I grabbed their leads, and I was certain they would crack me in the forehead with their sharp hooves. I loathed the idea of losing my faculties. My intellect was my one pride.

Inside the stalls, the animals pushed me against the stable walls, leaned on me with their dumb weight, squeezing the air out of me. I learned to clean their hooves, digging around the soft tissue to dislodge stones. When I accidentally dug the pick into the soft pad at the centre, I got an annoyed kick. More than once, I was knocked to the ground. Ultimately, I did take a hoof to my temple. When the bright crown of pain subsided, a deep resolve remained. I pushed back. I mastered them out of grit and spite. Secretly, at night, I practised saddling them. I mounted them; I fell. I crawled up again, careless about pulling on their manes. I recalled all the shouted instructions I'd heard the captain drilling the boys with during the day.

"Up straight!"

"Eyes front unless you want them to veer!"

"Heels down. Heels *down*! You little shit!"

Inside my head, I shouted at myself louder than any of the instructors. I rode in the enclosure at night. My long legs were well suited to standing in the saddle and my hands to wielding weapons. I whipped the horses into canters and gallops with a heavy hand so they would give me respect whenever they encountered me. I found their cowed submission enjoyable.

Boys began their training at the school when they were just a little younger than I was at the time, and they stayed until they were old enough to enter the highest colleges and guilds in the city. At age eleven, they were expected to be riding and learning weapons: archery, combat, hunting. Because I was tall and strong, I assisted with heavy equipment: holding swords, cleaning and sharpening them, hauling mats, spreading fresh straw in the arena when it became mired with blood and sweat. Martial exercises could be fatal. It was rare, and the school administrators wished to avoid it. Whenever it did happen, I was the one with the stomach to pull the boy's corpse from the arena. Between tasks, waiting for my next order, I squatted quietly on the edges, observing the way the boys fought, memorizing the strokes and manoeuvres, studying the bodies of the winners and the vanquished.

The boys came from all over the Autokracy. They ranged from flaxen haired and albino white to inky black, and every shade of pink and brown in between. Domestics were similarly mixed, as their Sires and nameless Mams all came from somewhere and mingled in the Imperial city. I found myself fascinated by one boy in particular. He had fiery red hair, close cropped as all the boys were, and a spray of freckling across his nose and cheeks. Domestics had no possessions, including mirrors, but we did get to steal glances in them from time to time. This boy and I had the same freckles and red hair. For all I knew, he could be a cousin or a brother, though no man would admit to being related to an Unmale.

I felt no kinship with him on account of our shared looks. There were no soft feelings or yearnings toward him, either, though sometimes young Domestics allowed themselves to develop feelings for their masters. The only feeling I had for him was disgust. Like all the other boys his age, he was beginning to indulge his filthy urges. And like all the others, he freely and openly abused me. What was remarkable was that I resented it. I churned with anxiety, steeling myself against the next ingress, and bore the defiling with gritted teeth. Worse, I meditated on the attacks long after they were over in a way that the other Domestics told me was unhealthy. Why fight the order of things, they said fatalistically. They urged pacification and acceptance. But I fought, even that far back. I fought in my mind, with every traitorous notion, with every flicker of rage.

On the terrible day, it came as no tragedy to me when the red-haired boy lost his mount. He bungled his stance; he was proud and lacked focus. He was showing off, grinning maniacally. He lost his footing. He did two complete circuits of the arena dragged by his heels by an enraged horse. When he finally managed to pull his foot from the stirrup, screaming and yelling, sword flailing, he landed square in the path of the animal. The horse reared and came down upon him with plate-sized hooves. Even I winced, hearing the crunch.

His skull was crushed. The instructor looked angry rather than saddened. The horse would have to be put down and a new one acquired. There were muffled sounds around the arena as the other boys froze. One or more of them was crying, working hard to stifle it. The sobs ceased as the instructor swept his gaze over them. He called for assistance, and it was I who was closest at hand. The instructor waved in the direction of the infirmary, where there was a small morgue.

I carried the corpse of the boy over my shoulder. He was dead-weight, but my years of labour had made me strong. I heard the last air go out of him as he bounced against my shoulder. I hurried; my moment, my one opportunity, had come.

I laid him in the morgue, splayed on the table like a life-sized doll. I pulled open his leather top, stained all around the collar by his mortal wound. His one good eye stared sightlessly. I stripped him naked.

The horse hadn't only crushed his head, it had also flattened his pelvis. Had he lived, he would never have grown to sire children.

He wore a rank, sweaty leather undergarment. Now, it was covered with gore. I held it up. I was still flat-chested; the one great difference between us was what we had between our legs. I lacked what he had, knew it keenly. For the moment, I put it aside, but I already had a temporary plan in my mind. I pulled on his soiled undergarment, snug against my skin.

He was slightly shorter than I. I rolled up his leggings to make them fit closer. I hoped that this was a detail that others would miss. His boots, when I donned them, were greasy inside with sweat. My sandals were a little large on him. But would anyone notice the fit of my footwear?

I regarded myself, wearing his boots and leggings, shirt and belt. Only a few details remained. My red hair fell to my back in one braid. I found shears in the infirmary and cropped as close to the scalp as I could. If I nicked myself, it only added to the ruse, so I took the bite of the metal. I shoved the mass of hair in the midden and felt strangely liberated. I pulled my shawl over the dead boy. This would have been an unthinkable mutilation to his Family. To dress him in women's weeds? Horrifying. Almost worse than having his balls stomped on by a horse.

I dragged his body out to an alley and piled straw and dung over it. At first glance, he looked like a Domestic enjoying a forbidden nap when she should be working. Perhaps they would investigate the wound between her legs. They might only see the blood and make assumptions. Miscarriages were so often fatal to young Domestics. Especially if they attempted a termination by themselves.

I hurried back to the infirmary, heart beating against my ribs. Grim work remained. I gathered tools and climbed on the infirmary table. I'd chosen a large bedpan and several instruments I required to carry off the rest of my ruse. A sharp blow from the bedpan gave me a plausible bruise in the centre of my forehead. A sharp blade would do to remove the strip of tattoos on my left arm. Shears for the ear tattoo. Another wound, grislier yet, was required to imitate that of the dead boy, and to cover my shame.

The ear was quickly done. I lined up the blades, averted my eyes, and squeezed the handles together. I wasn't expecting the rubbery skin to make the shears jump and overlap. Instead of a clean slice, I was left with an ugly, ragged line. Better, I thought, even though it glowed red hot with pain. It looked more like my head had been raked by a hoof.

I started with the wrist. Having seen Domestics kill themselves by deeply slitting the veins up their soft inner arms, I knew enough to stay on the surface. I took my time, digging the tip of the blade into each tattoo I'd earned over the years. The pain was strangely bracing, hot and sharp like alcohol on the tongue. This act of rebellion, effacing my history from my skin, brought with it a kind of stinging euphoria. Blood dripped from my wrist and pooled on the metal table below. Teardrops slid rapidly down the plane of my cheek and splashed into the red pools. But I kept my mouth shut. As an artistic flourish, I tore a few strips between the gouges; it wouldn't do to have such regular divots. Someone might guess what had been removed.

I bound the wound tightly enough to numb my fingers. I would be certain to cast off the bandage before I was done, but I was not interested in bleeding to death.

I rinsed off my blade and spread my legs. I regarded my own sex, already the source of so much pain over the years by dint of its very existence. I surveyed the area. I needed to simulate the mutilation the boy had experienced enough to convince anyone who peered at me and to create the ruse of being a castrated boy.

No bracing sensation of freedom helped me now. I was aware of my own voice growling in the base of my throat. I let my vision gloss and blur over the sheets of blood that flowed between my legs. The volume surprised me; it ran off the edge of the table and onto the floor. Though my hands shook, my vision wavered, and the pain threatened to overwhelm me, I knew I had only moments until someone came into the infirmary.

I heard them before they arrived, clattering down the hall, no doubt alerted to the events in the arena. I tore off the bandage with my teeth and spat it out. I hurled the blade so it skittered and slid under a low metal shelf. I let my head sink down to the table and curled in a fetal position around the gushing wound I'd inflicted. I allowed myself to acknowledge the pain. I howled like an animal.

6

Cera

I RAN, HEART knocking my chest, away from the Kratorling's rooms Above. I was late for my usual duties and panicked by the loss of time. More than that, the encounter with the Child had unnerved me.

Eva was resting with her feet up, nearly done her night shift and ready to sleep part of the day away. She eyed me, alarmed.

"How did it go?" And then, observing my expression, "What's wrong? What happened?"

"He is the right age." My mouth and chin twisted involuntarily. She dropped her heels heavily to the ground, wearing an angry look on her face that I knew well enough to read as surprise.

"I was afraid you would think that." She leaned on her bread table.

"Eva. It's like seeing my own reflection."

"You know you don't get to think like that."

I was already moving about my work. I added portions of starter to the dark flour from a hopper. The dough grew denser and came alive under my fingers as I kneaded. I worked in rhythm as I spoke with Eva.

"I can't be the first one who wondered."

"No, but you might be the one who keeps quiet about it and lives. No good comes of pursuing the matter."

"Am I to go again tomorrow?" I asked offhandedly, not wanting to seem too eager.

Eva sighed. "Yes. Adria is gone."

"Gone-gone?"

"Her pouch remains in her bunk. And her pocket goddess. No one leaves those things behind unless …"

"Unless they've stopped needing them," I finished the thought for her, bitterly. "How many is it now?"

"Dozens now. And they expect everything to march on regardless." She jerked a hand upward and lowered her voice. "I think it's the soldiers. I think they take them for sport. Sport no one lives to talk about."

I worked the dough, feeling it grow elastic in my fingers, fighting back with tensile strength. I didn't want to think about what was happening to Adria. Or what had already happened. "I'll take on her work."

"Good. But remember I need you here. So don't do anything stupid." Eva stood and stretched. "I am not taking my rest here today. I've things to do Beyond. Market and all."

Beyond was a word seldom used between Domestics. Life was measured out in the tedious world of either Above or Below. Few Domestics were allowed to venture from where they were stationed.

I nodded in reply to Eva. I did wonder how she had managed to carve out for herself a life so changeable and free while the rest of us remained mired in rote repetition.

"Walk watchfully when you go alone," Eva murmured. "I need you here, Below, my girl. My best bread comes from your hands."

The next morning, I left many hundreds of fat, dark-brown rolls to rise. I felt my way Above, through the winding labyrinth of low corridors, to the Kratorling's wing with a tin pail of warm embers and an armful of kindling. It was a steep climb in murky darkness, up from Below.

I approached the Kratorling's bedroom from behind the hearth. Looking across the grate and the cold ashes of the fireplace, I could see the massive space where the Kratorling rested. He was tucked into a bed big enough to fit twenty people. It was a veritable hill of costly fabric and pillows. His eyes were closed; the lashes lay against the smooth rise of his cheeks, which bellied out from the corners of his eyes to his round little chin. His flesh and his lips were smooth, tender as risen dough, flawless. The sweetness of baby still clung to him, and the sturdiness of boyhood was starting to shape his limbs. His eyes opened, and he watched me through his lids, pretending to sleep but betraying himself by the gleam in his eye as I built a mound of kindling. I slipped warm embers through the slender pieces of wood with tongs and blew. They breathed with me, growing brighter. The heat hit my face, and I knew it was penetrating the wood. It yielded to smoke first, and then to a bright red light, and finally a cheerful yellow flame. I guarded the little fire as it grew in strength, stretching its tendrils, first tentative, finally hungry. When the larger pieces of ironwood caught, I sat on my haunches and looked across the flames at the Child.

I realized that I had an inexplicable need for him, greater than food or water or sleep. It defied belief. This spoiled, coddled creature who wanted for nothing, whose life was nothing like mine, inspired an irrational yearning in me.

"Will you tell me a story?" The voice from the bed was very small, not the bossy tone I'd heard him use before. I turned to look at him through the shawl.

"Please? The old Domestic used to. She made up stories for me."

I waved my hands slightly, pleading no. I wasn't allowed to speak. But neither was I allowed to refuse a better.

"You can whisper them. Here."

He pointed to a spot on the floor, near his pillow. I gathered this storytelling had been going on for some time. "Here, you can even sit on a pillow." He dropped one on the ground.

I remembered pillows. My cell in the Consiliorum had been stuffed with them. Just looking at the soft bedding the Child had casually tossed on the floor made my stiff legs ache with longing. I crept near, but I did not sit on it. I would have soiled the pristine fabric with my filthy shawl. Instead, I knelt on the deep carpet.

He reached for my hood again, and I instinctively shrank back. It was forbidden for Domestics to touch men. The same was not true in reverse, of course. He put a small hand — warm and chubby — on my cheek.

"Very beautiful," he declared. "Big one and little one the same." He pulled my head close to his and squished it so that we could see ourselves together in a looking glass by his bed. "See?"

What I saw stirred me. His was the same face as mine, in tender, rounded miniature. He looked back through the glass with the same eyes, the same tilt to their corners, the same angles to the cheeks. I knew, and I couldn't unknow, though it was forbidden to even think it.

Orthodoxy was clear: according to the word of the first Autokrator, the Kratorling was born not of some mere Unmale but by a divine miracle, cooked up by Court Ritualists and carried to term by the Consort. The entire Autokracy was built on the idea that Unmales had no role whatsoever in the chain of succession. This bit of backward thinking had been created to explain how a perfect man could be born from a perfect man who had never touched the flesh of a woman. It was a monstrous, spiritual birth — a mystical birth. This child was destined one day to rule, and one day to be replaced by his own magically born, divine child. The Consort replaced the traditional queen and wife of the early kings. Orthodoxy dictated that the Kratorling was "born" to the

Consort; since the kings were, from ancient times, semi-divine, why shouldn't they be capable of such miracles? Orthodoxy prohibited the idea that such a thing was preposterous. The select few of us who laboured in secret to actually carry and bear Kratorlings were unseen and unheard, so who was there to argue?

He lay his head down beside me.

"Go on."

I had no stories. I had a few love poems they'd taught me to recite in the Consiliorum. Those were inappropriate here. I told him about some chicks I saw once, when I was very small. An old Mam was carrying them in her apron. The Domestic charged with looking after me and several other young girls stopped her, and she let us play with them. I told him how the chicks would peep and peep and peep until they fell right over, exhausted. He giggled when I told him that I saw one fall face first in its own excrement.

We talked for a long time. To amuse him, I pulled my pocket goddess out and let him handle her. His small fingers traced her features.

"It's a lady?" Which guilty Domestic would have taught him this forbidden word, I wondered. I snatched her back.

"You shouldn't hold her for long. She's too powerful for little boys to play with."

We drifted into a comfortable quiet until I thought he had fallen asleep, but he popped up with more questions. Eventually, sleep took us both. I did not wake until I felt myself yanked up by the collar of my shawl.

I couldn't see my assailant in the dim room, but he had a pitchy, grating tone. He spoke with great self-importance.

"You dare!" He was apoplectic. "You dare bare your head to the Kratorling? You dare rest on furniture? You *slattern*."

I was dazed, fighting for breath in his grip. I hung in the air, my toes pedalling for the floor. My collar dug into my throat, cutting off my air.

"Stop! Stop it!" shrieked the Child, woken by the man's shouts.

"As you wish, Kratorling." He dropped me into a heap on the floor, where I gasped, hands clutching at my bruised neck. I did not forget to pull the shawl over my head, nor to huddle on my knees on the floor. Under the hood, tears slipped down my cheek onto the carpet. I could not imagine the punishment I would receive for this.

"I wanted her to stay and tell me stories," the Child explained.

Even in my frightened state, I was impressed he knew it was his place to command.

"Kratorling, you know it is forbidden for Domestics to remove their shawl without permission."

"I pulled it off."

"As you say, my lord, but the punishment must fall." He spoke to someone I could not see. I knelt, head down, staring at the floor, and did not dare raise my eyes.

"Take her."

A hard shiver raked me. I thought I might be sick on the carpet. I peered through the shawl at the dim view the cloth allowed. The Domestic door was close. The man stood by the Child's bed; I was closer to the door than he. I had a chance, so I took it.

I bolted.

I heard his body land lengthwise on the floor as he leapt behind me. I scrambled out through the low, narrow door. As I did, I felt his hand grip my ankle, squeezing tight and yanking me back. I kicked at him with my other foot. Then I grabbed at the fire tongs hanging just outside the opening. The metal smacked his hand, thudding against soft tissue in a satisfying way. My ankle slipped out of his grip, leaving him with my slipper and me away. I fled, feeling my way with my hand, debris under my one bare foot, down the pitch-black pathway.

7

Tiresius

I SHRANK FROM the clammy touch of a Domestic. One whom I did not know. She tugged at my clothes with spindly fingers.

"Keep your filthy hands off me," I spat at her.

She leapt back. I was surprised how easily the words sprang to my lips. I'd heard such threats myself over the years. Wielding power felt better than cringing from it.

One of the school's Toolists came in on the heels of the infirmary Domestic.

"There now, Lord Tiresius! Easy," he said soothingly.

I turned away, my knees clenched shut.

"There now, I'm a Toolist, lad, you can let me see!"

"I don't want another man to look!" I shrieked. It was a reasonable request to make under the circumstances. Being unmanned was a fate close to death. It was an unthinkable sentence to bear for any Male. "Let the Domestics do it, please!"

The old man's hands were stronger than they looked. He pried my knees apart and gave a perfunctory glance.

"All right, lad, you'll live. That's the important thing. You, here." The Toolist directed the Domestics who stood mutely nearby, waiting.

"They might be animals, but these ones are nimble," he said to me. "We'll get you sewn up."

"They will think I'm Unmale," I cried.

"Who will?"

"Everyone!"

"Tiresius, lad, calm yourself. No one will do any such thing. This isn't the olden days. And anyone who gives you grief can answer to me about it, you hear? Now relax. Here, they've brought the sedatives and numbing gel. You had a close call, you did. Easy now. Lie back on the stretcher. You can't be too careful with a head wound like yours, son."

I marvelled at being treated like this. The warmth in his tone sank into my marrow. The indulgences he gave me — lifting my head to have a sip of water, smoothing my hair. This was treatment I'd never received. I had been fashioned into flint years before, but even I softened inside to be coddled so.

The old man turned away to make notes on his chart, and the two Domestics crowded between my legs. I saw the first one start a little as she approached with a swab. Her eyes met mine, and the accusation was clear: my mutilations hadn't gone far enough to convince her. I grabbed her wrist in a vise and hissed at her, "You stitch me up so no one can tell or so help me I'll see to it you're crucified for gender crimes."

On the other side of her shawl, her eyes blinked. With the Toolist fooled enough to call me Tiresius, only my word counted.

"Make it look convincing," I hissed low so only she and the other Domestic could hear. They nodded fearfully, and I lay back to be remade as Tiresius.

I convalesced in a large infirmary lined with cushioned beds. Domestics and Toolists with hushed voices and soft hands worked on patients in this room. There were window boxes fringed with creeping flowers and curtains swayed by gentle breezes. The bed took getting used to after sleeping on the floor my whole life; the plush mattress suffocated me with its softness. To this day, I am thought peculiar for my austere love of a hard board with only the thinnest of mattresses. The linens, however, must be of the best quality.

I was waited on by a retinue of Domestics who washed my face and combed my hair. With their eyes averted, they wiped the urine off my legs when I was unable to aim for the pot they provided. I perfected my aim over time.

When the Domestics thought I was asleep, they murmured among themselves. This was how I learned that they had found the maimed body on the refuse pile at the back. They spoke sadly about how Deka must have died. The story ran that I must have gotten in the way of the horse and been fatally trampled.

"How did it happen?" asked one girl, with that strange fascination people have when asking after something grisly.

"I heard she was changing the horse's shoes and it kicked her," her companion replied.

"I heard she was used as a target in the ring because she was slow bringing the straw bales."

"I heard the hoof and the shoe went right through her skull so you could see the brains inside."

"It's true. I saw the body, and the whole head was a mess. Completely unrecognizable."

"Horrible. We burned her last week."

"I hope they don't put me in the stables. I'm scared of those horses."

"You're scared of bees."

"Well, serves her right, I say. She was always a bitch to me."

"You know, I didn't want to say anything, but she was always tattling. Always thought she was better than everyone else."

"*Always* tattling. And thieving. And a bloody know-it-all."

"A bully. Always slapping and pinching and shouting and bossing."

One of them mimicked my high-pitched voice: "I once worked in the Imperial dairy, and I know what those cows eat. I know how to read and write because my brain is as good as any Male's. La la la." It was something else I noted to correct about myself.

It was interesting how quickly they went from sorrowful to nasty and back again. When one of them admitted saying a little prayer as my body burned, I scoffed at the sentiment. Who wastes their breath saying a prayer for someone who has terrorized them? I made a note to myself to find ways to make both their lives unbearable as revenge for the witness they bore to each other about my character.

The head injury provided an ideal cover for my relative illiteracy. As proud as I was of the letters I did know, I was behind my new Male peers by a long way. Due to the head injury, I was given a tutor — a patient, kind old man who walked me through letters and words using baby books. This went on until I was declared mentally fit and able to read at a level befitting a young man my age.

Once I convalesced, I was moved into the boys' barracks. This came with no small amount of panic. The night before they moved me, I lay awake, wondering how long it would take for them to discover my duplicity and out me. But the deliciousness of deceiving them for any amount of time was too great. And I reasoned that if I were killed tomorrow, I had at least had a little vacation from work, and that was worth any suffering to come.

Curfew was early, as was our wake-up call: we rose and sank with the sun, and all the hours in between were prescribed. It was a solemn life of eating, exercising, training, reading, lectures, and punishments large and small. At times, I wondered if I hadn't actually lost some of my freedom in switching sides. My years of menial labour helped me adapt well to regimentation, though. Some of my peers were still soft boys, minded by cooing, indulgent house Domestics.

That first night, I stepped into the echoing barracks clutching a few items to my chest. When I paused at the door, my heart accelerated in my chest. A sea of boys, half of them rank, gangly adolescents, ranged about the room tidying their belongings before turning in.

"Bed down, Tiresius. Move." A monitor shoved the back of my head in the direction I was supposed to go.

I moved a few steps and then faltered, only to be cuffed or shoved further along.

"Not here! Keep going. Down to C range!" a burly cretin spat at me.

A tall, thin boy with a morbidly fascinating landscape of boils all over his face sneered, "Get your filthy southern feet off my blanket."

Finally, at the far end of the room filled with twelve-year-old boys, I found the empty cot that had belonged to Tiresius. It was eerie to see the bedroll and cover neatly placed on the cot. A table nearby held very few items. Boys were expected to focus on their studies. The moment I found my place, the lights dimmed, so I scuttled under the covers, still clutching my bundle to my chest.

I didn't sleep that first night, though I was exhausted from the panic of the night before. At any moment, I expected to be woken from my sleep and outed as a gender criminal. Every cough nearby, every rustle made me jump. How long before someone came by and tore the blanket off me to expose my true nature? Just when my eyelids grew heavy, I would hear footfalls. Someone was taking a leak in one of the communal piss pots.

Was I mad? All these boys would grow, their limbs would fill out, they would sprout beards, and their voices would deepen. What would become of me? How would I pass for Male? My eyes prickled, and my throat swelled with self-pity at the momentous, idiotic path I'd chosen. But I would not allow tears to gather and fall. I held myself rigid, grinding my teeth together, flaring my nostrils until the feeling subsided. Without height or breadth, or a cock, I would have to best them all through wit.

The barracks were watched over all night long by a soldier and a boy in training. Talking and horseplay were prohibited. No doubt kept awake by my own tossing in the dark, my neighbour signed something to me. He repeated the motions several times, and, when I continued to look blank, he gave up in frustration.

"So the horse's kick made you an idiot as well as a eunuch," he whispered. He turned over in disgust, leaving me there to stare at the peeling frescoes of martial glory painted on the ceiling.

In line for food the next morning, I had an opportunity to speak to him. He was far less patient than my reading tutor. When I asked his name, he slapped me on the head.

"Idiot. I'm Andrius. Do you really know nothing anymore?"

"The Toolist said it would take time for me to regain everything."

"Well, this is a sticky bun," Andrius hissed, throwing the pastry at me. "It has custard inside. Like your brain."

He was a few inches shorter than me. I gauged my next move carefully. And acted. I shoved the sticky bun into his mouth, pushing it hard, past his open teeth and up into his palate. While he was choking, I bent one of his flailing hands behind him until his back arched. I was copying a move I'd seen the military master use on the boys.

"Maybe when your mouth isn't full, you'll find more pleasant things to say to me," I growled. "After all, Andrius, I am a lord, and you should respect my position. You should be thankful I've included you in my circle at all." I shoved him for good measure, so that other boys in the line noticed him stumble. Most of all so they noticed him wipe away an angry tear. "Now be civil, and you'll find me the same."

I walked alone to the rows of benches and tables. I sat with my back straight, chin out, and knees spread wide. I clutched utensils in my fists and ate staring straight ahead. I could feel the eyes of the whole room upon me. There was an electric bristle as I was noticed.

I sensed my error. I should have put my years of being invisible to work. I should have become the boy who curried favour and got things done economically. I should have found a bigger boy to idolize and made myself his toady. God knows I'd learned enough about pleasuring them, despite my distaste for them.

But I'd already chosen a path. I'd felt the lick from power's flame: it burned. When it passed through me, incinerating what was left of my kindness and softness, it cleansed me. I wanted more. I would be invisible by becoming ever present. I would make them kiss my ass. And I would luxuriate in every heretical minute of it. I did not expect to last the week.

A boy slid me a bun. It entered my vision sliding along the table. I understood it was a peace offering, made with fear. I looked neither left nor right but nodded, almost without moving my head. I could feel the other boy relax, could sense his guard go down. He felt safer, because I had allowed him to.

I chewed and stared ahead.

Inwardly, I rejoiced.

8

Cera

BREATHING HARD, IN full panic, I sought Eva near the ovens and drew her away to the sleeping quarters. With our shawls up over our heads, there was at least a chance that fewer people would notice us right away.

"There you are," Eva said. "We needed you this morning. I had to have the kneading done by ... What is wrong?" She saw my pinched face.

"He took the shawl off my head."

Eva grabbed my hands. "I told you not to do anything stupid."

"It was the boy who did it. But it doesn't matter. Some official saw me. I ran. They're coming for me." Despite myself, I was crying. "Eva, he's mine. I know it."

"Who is?"

"The Kratorling."

"Shut your blasphemous mouth, Cera."

"Even he said so."

"You can't —"

"He's so lovely —"

"You can't think like that. It's a sin to even insinuate a relationship."

"So lovely. So soft. I just wanted to touch him."

"Cut it from your thoughts. What is wrong with you? I can help you. But if you want to live, you must swear yourself to secrecy." Her look was fierce.

She was right to be angry with me: one infraction by a Domestic often led to punishments all around.

"Of course."

"If you betray me, I'll kill you myself."

This was a new Eva.

"I won't."

Before she could acknowledge me, we heard the heavy clank of armoured men and the grinding of the lift cables. The lift was reserved for the few men who came down Below; it was almost never used. A barking voice on the overhead called my Domestic rank and number.

I pulled my hands out of Eva's to slink away from her, but she held me in place. She held me at arm's length, as though measuring me with her eyes. She seemed to come to some conclusion.

"Keep your shawl up and follow me," she said.

Still holding my hand, she hurried me out of the sleeping area and into the kitchens.

Men approached, clattering swords, shouting orders. I retched as we ran, eyes watering from the effort to keep my stomach down.

We headed for one of the pitch-black tunnels that wound underground like ant trails. Eva knew the way, and I had to blindly trust her to lead us, my one bare foot tripping the entire way. The pathways became steeper as they got closer to the top. My breath strangled at the base of my throat, and my legs ached against the climb.

The tunnel sloped up and up, the ground grooved and studded, the walls rough. The air grew sharper and cooler and hit my face, unexpectedly fresh. A moment later, we emerged from a low, wide leather Domestic door into a blinding light.

All the smells in the world cascaded over me. It was the first time I'd been outdoors in more than a decade. I had a sudden urge to cower against the side of the building, to crawl back into the embracing dark. Out in the open, I felt naked and exposed to a harsh and dangerous world. The sky overhead felt like it could crash down upon me. I reached into my pocket and rubbed my pocket goddess, turning her curved body over and over in my fingers.

We stepped directly into a narrow street thronged with people, almost entirely men. We hugged the wall. The bright sky made me half blind; I had to feel my way along like a mole. We were jostled by burly crowds. At times, we had to throw our bodies flat to the wall to avoid touching men or being crushed by carts and animals and palanquins going by.

I was overwhelmed by the noises and smells of people, animals, tanned leather, wet stone, and damp hay. Rooftops leaned together, like old men conversing. The sky was a bright ribbon of blue shimmering high above. Only the clouds were oblivious to the hurry and bustle below.

The din of men's voices shouting and bodies jostling in the streets crowded my brain. Soldiers wandered among the crowds, for good reason. Brawls were frequent; men sparred openly in the street with fists and weapons. The patrolling soldiers tended to let the assailants cancel each other out and only got involved when the violence threatened properties and businesses.

The city sprawled out from the ravine surrounding the Palace walls. The nearest buildings were palaces in their own right — august business and civics buildings that soared high above the melee in the streets and ringed the Imperial city. The next consecutive ring housed wealthy patrons and merchants. The individual structures formed an architectural pie, with a sliver cut in the centre to allow one common Domestic door to access all of them from the rear. The facades of shops and houses looked out through ornate doors and wide glass windows to the streets. A man could live his whole life in the city and be so overwhelmed with its size and grandeur and pursuits that he could forget there was a massive empire beyond.

My wonder at the tall buildings and the sky was short-lived.

"This way." Eva's strong grip tugged at me. A dark, narrow alley led down and away from the high street, along a twisting flight of worn steps that wound tightly between buildings. Finally, at the bottom, another low Domestic door appeared. We crawled on hands and knees through a short, lightless passage until we emerged in a taller place, a rude central vestibule leading to six different painted doors.

Eva led me through a yellow door, and we emerged in a tiled room. We found ourselves in a tall, narrow kitchen, hung neatly with pans, high shelves stocked with staples and preserves and a ladder on wheels to reach them. The air was thick with the familiar yeasty smell of baking. It was a commoner's home, neither crude nor opulent. I had never seen anything like it; it seemed marvelous to me. This tiny, self-contained world had the elements of the Palace, but in miniature. A small kitchen to service only a few people, modest bedrooms dedicated to one person apiece. In place of thrones and gilt, there were cozy chairs and a nook to read in, all the items a person could need close to hand. Above all, a door to close against a troublesome world. It seemed like a heaven.

As we stood there in that snug kitchen, Eva grabbed my hands again.

"You swear to keep my secret?"

"Your secret?" I was confused; I thought I was the one with a secret.

"Tell me you swear it."

"I swear it, Eva."

She let go and stood up straight. Then she threw off her shawl.

"This is mine. This is where I come when I am not on official business. Look: my own baking corner. My baking stone. My hearth. I set it up just so." Her pride was apparent, and foreign to me.

My stomach lurched to see her bare her head like that. Even down Below, we kept our pale, grimy faces covered almost all the time. Barefaced, she stood there and then threw back her head and called a man's name out loud. Bearing witness to this blasphemy, I felt queasy again.

"Vincius!" Eva looked about and listened for a response. "I'm home!"

"I'm here."

When a man entered the kitchen, I shrank to the floor, terrified. I knelt with my forehead to the ground and felt the cool tiles against my skin. I was amazed that I had made it this far without getting caught. I had known the entire time that punishment would come eventually. I braced myself for the blows.

9

Tiresius

"WRONG PRODUCT OF the sum!" The instructor's pointer hit my desk with a smack.

"Make the tail of your letter longer!"

"The White Period, not the Grey! Page three hundred!" This time, it landed on my back.

I could stand being an outsider, studying alone in nooks and during free times while other boys jostled and bonded. I had no interest in letting them get too close. What I could not stand was being made to look foolish when I was called on and forced to stammer because I had no idea what I was being asked. So I read, every stolen moment that I could, to catch up to my classmates. No, not to catch up. To surpass.

I was amazed how long the Autokracy had endured. The notion of a deeper time than fading yesterday and tenuous tomorrow was enticing. If there was a deep past, then there was a deep future. For the first time in my life, I began to wonder how far forward through time I might travel and what I might do, given the chance.

I discovered that, for more than four thousand years, some version of our realm had existed, called sometimes Fatherland or The Centre. It had begun as a ragtag association of petty kingdoms and unclaimed territories that grew into a republic tugged between warring kings, which finally took shape as the Autokracy. I myself was attending school in the year 1651 of the Autokracy — under the sixty-fifth Autokrator, Rufus, known as the Technocrat. In those days, Gentius was Consort, and he was as eager to grasp his future as I was mine.

The central kingdom began as a small, unimportant regency that gradually gobbled up its neighbours, devouring cultures and resources as it went. The borders swelled to the coastal regions. The Autokrator built fleets of ships to venture across the seas.

I discovered that my unruly red hair came from some land many leagues away and that many who looked like me had arrived on our shores as slaves. In those days, the work of the Autokracy was carried out by legions of Domestics as well as unfortunate slaves stolen from other lands. Eventually, Males of any origin were considered free. It was the Unmales who laboured on, yoked.

My adopted Family had gained their freedom from slavery by various acts of merit and courage. By the time the first Autokrator ruled, they were no longer viewed as transplants. My Family were among those who helped cleanse the realm of pernicious Unmales and set things right. They were rewarded for this with land and titles.

The school was far from the Capital and the machinations of the Imperial city in what was deemed healthy agricultural hinterland. Here, the young future minds of the Autokracy were moulded into fealty to Orthodoxy, nation, and martial might. The marching grounds and training fields, playgrounds for strength and tactics, were laid out in rolling fields near well-to-do farms that fed the land.

Here, the simplest peasantry of the Autokracy lived quiet, respectable lives.

They ran large farms and had many sons to carry on for them. They kept droves of flocks and Domestics. Many sons ensured that there would always be keen managers to oversee Domestics, animals, and crops. No matter how many sons were plucked by the Autokrator to serve in his teeming armies, the work could go on.

A boy who failed school would be a farmer if he showed an aptitude for calendars and timing and the change of the season. If he mastered simple sums and had a head for making money, he would become a merchant. If he was factual and object-oriented, he would oversee Domestics who fished, razed forests, or pulled metals from the ground. If hardy and physical, he became a soldier.

Unmales were divided in much simpler ways. An Unmale's work included carrying children along with any other household or menial task. Throughout the Autokracy, Domestics did the washing, cleaning, serving, sowing, reaping, threshing, cutting, shearing, fishing, mining, and bricklaying. The resources of the Autokracy flowed back and forth by dint of their shoulders and feet and hands.

In the second form, successful boys had five additional years of school and entered guilds as lower-rung Toolists — fabricators and inventors. They could be recognized by their colourful scarves, which denoted their vocation.

Passing the third form secured a boy a place in the highest industries and brought them to employments inside the city itself: engineering, politics, math. Boys that passed at the top of these fields entered the machinery of the Autokrator's bureaucracy.

The higher the tier a boy achieved, the greater attention the Autokrator paid to his patents and ideas.

We learned in our civics classes that careful planning of society under the Orthodoxy involved harmonious competition for the good of all. We accepted that daily life for many souls remained agrarian. Life in many parts of the Autokracy moved at the pace of placid animals.

Civics was interesting, but classes in the state religion, the worship of Fallos, were more amusing. The religion centred around a god with an enormous and eternally erect penis. Who but men would have made such a deity? The boys around me stroked themselves so often it was clear where the fixation had come from. What truly drew me in were the history lessons. I loved the gore-soaked twists and turns of effort and fate that led inexorably to the moment at which I sat at a desk, reading about it.

I enjoyed ancient history, when bloodthirsty kings tried to outdo one another in gory bloodbaths. They boiled their enemies in vats, or skinned and roasted them. They slaughtered children and fathered new ones. There was a dizzying succession of rulers, with some reigns lasting as little as days.

Despite the carnage, technology began to appear. Early Toolists, as they called inventors, mechanics, and craftsmen, were busy creating all manner of inventions. They conceived of ways to roll wheels using nothing more than steam. They fabricated the means to duplicate printing by machine rather than hand. They found ways to light the night without needing fire.

Straddling the transition from ancient to modern history was the man for whom the next age was named: the Age of Bartolius, the first Autokrator. He was his father's fourth son, the only one to survive sickness and murder. His oldest uncle had been crowned king after a leaderless period of civil war. Bartolius's father took the crown only fourteen months later, seeming to herald an era of calm. Midway through Bartolius's reign, he discovered his wife's adultery with his captain. In a rage, he murdered his own children, tortured his wife, and banished all females from his sight. In his fiftieth year, he declared himself Autokrator over a glorious Autokracy free from the scourge of sinful and maligning Unmales. This became Year 1 of the Autokracy.

Under Bartolius, the Autokracy suppressed technology and modernization. The fear was that if labour were freed up by faster transport or steam power, the idle legions could rise up, if only because of their sheer numbers.

The Autokrator looked after all his subjects and doled out industrial advancements only when it was clear the Autokracy would not be imperiled by a future rife with idle Domestics or unemployed Males.

Once Bartolius cleansed the Autokracy of Unmales, calm ensued and peaceful transfer of power was ensured. The first thousand years of rule were almost completely free of fratricide, patricide, and plotting. Best of all, succession no longer depended on the viability of one sinful queen's womb. Maternity was unimportant. A crop of able, healthy boys bearing the Autokrator's lineage was all that mattered.

As time went on, power-hungry Autokrators clung to power and life for decades before they died. A new law dictated the maximum age of seventy-five for all Autokrators. This was the work of crafty advisers who benefited from a regular turnover of rulers. How was a Male expected to give up absolute power willingly? Most Autokrators were convinced to retire with enormous stipends and glorious palaces in municipalities far from the Capital. They lived their days near tinkling fountains, gazing on majestic mountains.

Of course, not all Autokrators were willing to go. In some cases, they sought to murder and replace their successors, regaining power for themselves. One enterprising fellow killed a Consort and took his place, painting his face with thick makeup to conceal his age.

It was Bartolius who invented the intricate ceremonies and rituals around the Autokrator's coronation. It was he who decided a boy would be Kratorling for twenty-five years, then Consort for twenty-five, and finally rule as Autokrator for twenty-five.

Initially, Bartolius's casting out of Unmales was seen as a natural consequence of his traumatic cuckolding. Later, it was elevated to the status of divine fiat. The god Fallos had come to Bartolius in a dream and told him to banish the Unmales. In a strange piece of theatre, Bartolius decreed that his Autokrator-in-waiting should spend his twenty-five-year tenure dressed as a woman. This indicated his subservience to the will of the ruler and probably reflected Bartolius's odd sense of humour.

Through Orthodoxy and repetition, a belief emerged that the Autokrator as head of the Triumvirate, also called the Holy Family, was spawned without need of Unmales altogether: the Consort was somehow divinely able to produce a child — the Kratorling — by some mysterious transmutation of his body.

A puppet show played out at each succession. Upon being crowned by his own sacred hands, the Autokrator pointed his sacred staff — of course it was a stylized phallus — at the former Kratorling, by now a strapping twenty-five-year-old man. Behind a ritually raised curtain, attendants stripped the outgoing Kratorling of his garments, burned them, and reclad him in the dress of his new station. The garb of the Consort came to be known as women's weeds.

Seated at the right hand of the Autokrator, with much fanfare, and at the appointed time, the newly assigned Consort produced the next Kratorling from under his skirts. Via theatrical sleight of hand and an ingenious system of trapdoors and pulleys, a newborn wrapped in the Imperial colours appeared and lo! the miracle came to pass. It was seen as an infinite improvement on the disgusting reality of flesh and blood and sweat and complaining that traditional labour entailed.

The infant was placed on the left of the Autokrator in a gilded bassinet, the Consort on the right, completing the Holy Family, the august Triumvirate. Power was seamlessly cemented for the next twenty-five years.

As time passed, Bartolius came to be considered semi-divine — his reign perfect, his mind unassailable. He took his place alongside Fallos and was worshipped after his death. His proclamations were considered the Sacred Word, collected in vast tomes known as the Solemn Orthodoxy of the Autokrator, colloquially called the Orthodoxy.

The Kratorling was chosen from ranks of preselected healthy infants born in the Imperial Consiliorum, sprung from the seed of the Autokrator and incubated by specifically chosen Unmales. The Autokrators and Consorts from the earliest times had preferred long, dark hair. Black hair was regarded as Imperial colouring. They had also preferred high cheekbones, plush lips, and almond eyes.

I devoured all this knowledge and began to form an image of myself wrapped in silk robes, bowed to by almost all, holding the sceptre or crown and officiating at the coronation of a future Autokrator. I had come a long way from a simple dairy Domestic. And knowing I had far yet to go, I dove into the tomes detailing the secrets of the workings of the Autokracy with relish.

10

Cera

I KNELT ON the floor, trembling, waiting to be beaten. To my shock, the man standing above me did not strike me. Instead, he picked up Eva by the waist. Not to punish: he beheld her, laughed, and pressed his face to hers. Incredibly, he kissed her lips and clasped her to him.

"Welcome." His voice was warm; he seemed happy to see her. "Welcome, wife."

Wife?

It was a word I'd never expected in my life to hear. Eva laughed at my expression.

"Remember your promise," Eva warned. Her face was light.

She tugged off my shawl, and, instinctively, I tried to cover my face with my hands. She pulled them away.

"You are safe here," she said. "As safe as in the kitchens. And free." She drew me boldly along with her into the next room.

It was modest, without decoration or deep rugs. Yet it was not lightless, nor were the walls made of mud. Tiles covered the floors, and high shelves climbed the walls. There was an austere quality to the tall, narrow place. There were a table and chairs, and another door in the far wall, through which I could see several more rooms stretching away, each leading on to the next like a chain. Eva pointed to a chair. I nodded.

"No, don't just look at it," she said with a smile. "Sit."

I bent my knees to sit, unfamiliar with the experience.

"This is Cera," Eva said to the man. "Cera, this is my husband, Vincius." She stressed that illegal word, *husband*. "He is an independent Toolist."

I nodded.

"Please," she said, "remember your oath to me. And try to get accustomed to the idea of freedom. We nearly have."

"Nearly," agreed Vincius.

"Be easy."

I nodded dumbly. I did not know how to be easy. Eva gestured for me to wait where I was and went to the kitchen, leaving me alone with the man Vincius. He put his hands on the table. I did the same.

"You're in trouble," he said flatly. It was a statement, not an accusation, though his voice was serious. "Eva has never brought anyone here before."

I expected at any moment to be thrown out.

"Well, now that you know about us, you are a party to treason. I guess that makes us nearly equal."

In the rush to escape the Palace, it hadn't occurred to me to wonder why Eva might risk her own life to help me, but I was beginning to understand. She was living in Unorthodoxy, married to a man. Eva and Vincius were greater criminals than I.

Vincius gazed steadily at me. He had a wide, almost round face with an open expression, a dark beard, and dark hair that curled at the top and temples. Without the shawl over my head to hide my face, he could see me looking back at him. I dropped my gaze to the floor. It was all too much to take in at once.

Eva reappeared with drinks and bread, which she set on the table before sitting. She chose glasses that supported themselves, not the vials Domestics held for men when they drank. I picked one up. Vincius helped himself to the food. He even offered some to us, with his own hands. Unmales who sat like equals at his table. I could barely hide my shock.

"So. What do you want to do?"

I should not have had an answer. Domestics don't plan; Domestics don't want. But I did. My response came all too easily.

"I want to see my son again."

Eva stared. Vincius looked surprised.

"Cera, be serious," Eva said. "Vincius wants to help you. We both do."

"He asked what I want," I said.

Eva scowled all the same.

"I don't understand it, but it's what I need to do," I said, the words sounding even more plaintive to my ears than I'd expected they would. I felt as though the child was tethered to me with sharp hooks.

"We need to make a plan," said Eva. "Maybe find you a placement outside the city. You can stay here a while, but someone will notice you're gone before long."

It was true: various guards with different functions marauded throughout the realm. Some knocked on doors by night, making sure common people in their little houses were living in Orthodoxy. Roaming guards of a lower order stopped Domestics in the street and recorded the numbers on their tattoos. Errant Domestics were soon noticed.

I ate hungrily. I hoped my hunched shoulders did not make me seem ungrateful, but my stomach was roiling. Despite everything Eva had said, I could not stop thinking about my child. Leaving the city meant never seeing him again. I could not leave the city.

After our meal, Vincius said the traditional thanks for having eaten and pushed back his chair.

"I will show you the house," he said to me. I followed.

"This house has been in my family for many, many generations," Vincius said as he led me from the back rooms to the font
of the house. "My great-grandfather was an Imperial Toolist. He
fell from grace, and we have been independent since then. I fix
some things. I make some things. I hope one day to re-enter the
Imperial fold."

We passed through sleeping quarters, separated from one
another by curtains. Only a little light leaked in from windows
on the ceiling.

We reached the end of the long corridor, and Vincius pushed
open a set of ornate double doors. A flood of light welcomed us
to the workshop and street-front shop. Crowds bustled by on the
high street outside the windows, occasionally peering in at their
own reflections.

The workshop was filled with a confusing tangle of long black
cables and tubes snaking down from the ceiling. Some fed a collection of pouches and flaps as plentiful as leaves on trees hanging
on one side of the room. There was the constant hiss of flowing
liquid and tiny billows of steam pouring from bizarre machinery
and tools. I could only guess at the function of anything. Some
machines bore representations of the human body, with their
abdomens shaded.

Some areas of the workspace were sealed off. Every surface
gleamed.

"Much of my work is in medical research. Engendering. We
pride ourselves on our research machines and tools. We have a side-
line of fabrication for hire, but the main work is the engendering."

"We" was Vincius and Nelius, his natural-born son by Eva,
who hoped to one day follow in his path. We came upon Nelius in
the workshop. He wore a leather smock and had pushed his dark
goggles up on his forehead. He also wore a black kerchief around
his neck — a sign that he was a deeply observant follower of Fallos. It meant he would never have failed to attend rites throughout

the year honouring the god. It meant he prayed several times daily to Fallos, who demanded absolute fealty. It meant he had a special hatred for Unmales, whom he would consider utterly unclean and hateful. And yet he lived under the same roof as his mother.

He was lanky, with a closed face, narrowed eyes, and firmly shut lips. The patrician cut to his features gave him a permanent look of disdain. He stared at me, and I shivered. Though he was quick to try to hide it from his father, I recognized the disgust in his eyes. One thing was clear: despite Eva and Vincius's hospitality, Nelius seemed murderously unhappy that there was another person in his home — an Unmale, at that.

11

Tiresius

I TAKE THE time now to think back. It will appear to my guards I am pondering what to set down next in my confession. In fact, it is a moment of wonder I give myself.

I once openly lived with boys and enjoyed all their entitlements. These boys were a tangle of limbs stretching like putty, skin roiling, feet growing, oozing into adolescence and constantly tugging and rubbing and checking erections that never seemed to fully fade. Truthfully, they disgusted me. But then, so did the mealy Domestics with their constitutional meekness. I wanted nothing to do with either. While boys in cots all around me dreamed their sweaty dreams, their pods bursting with foul-smelling pollen, I dreamed of gaining ground and holding sway. I dreamed of arming myself with enough power that it didn't matter what was under my clothes.

I was spared tribulation, I think, by a combination of disgust and pity. I was the boy with the missing penis, too freakish to even tease. Think about it too hard and your own might fall off, I could imagine them saying. They played with their magic wands endlessly. But in a strange way, I was the magical one, moving through their world despite my lack of a dick. I think it would have been less strange to them had I lacked a head instead.

Over time, I learned about my new identity. I pieced myself together from the way boys behaved toward me and from regular mail I received from home.

Tiresius: Greetings

I write on behalf of your pater, who is occupied with too many things to undertake this himself. He declines to come and visit you in your convalescence as he feels such coddling will only make you weak and look for more of the same.

Your first correspondence since the injury indicates that you have suffered a severe blow. Enough to make your writing, which has always been bad, even more of an embarrassment. The school's Medical Toolist assures us that you are not a complete idiot as a result of the injury. As such, we insist that you remain at the school and learn to apply yourself and try not to bring additional shame on the Family Marnius.

Marnius Second

It was penned by my pater's Second. Judging by his handwriting, he was no academic either and was not inclined to write to me at all. The fact that my pater had declined to make the trip to visit me during my convalescence was lucky. It gave me time to assume my new role and prepare for that scrutiny. It appeared that the real Tiresius had been at the school for several years without seeing his family. All the better. Who could say what I looked like then?

Tiresius: Greetings

Your midterm report card shows that you still function as a halfwit in various areas, but we are pleased to see that you are improving in the areas of History, Civics, and Science. Your family will not attend the annual holiday gathering as the trip is arduous and many things occupy us here. The absence will make you a stronger man, better able to withstand privations in life. As a result of a poor crop and fewer monies coming in and greater taxes being levied, your allowance is to be cut in half to two Crowns. Spend your money wisely and do not indulge in idiotic frivolities.

Marnius Second

The old Tiresius was inclined to be completely slack at his studies. He was good-natured, quiet, and seldom spoke against others. His Family held him in some disdain and despaired that he would make it through his studies. These were all things I aimed to reform. School and Family would be delighted, in the future, to find that the accident Tiresius had endured wound up tempering him into a better student and citizen.

Tiresius: Greetings
It appears that you have turned around your studies completely, which comes as a surprise to your pater, who long thought you would amount to nothing. It appears that you will finish the term better than hoped for. Your pater received the request that you train for a position in a Portfolio and replies: no.

These letters from "home" frequently harped on the issue of my missing manhood. It was a great trial to my pater and his Second that I wouldn't be able to directly add to the lineage of my Family. Nor did they encourage me when I spoke of being a Portfolio, a Minister in service to the Autokracy.

Families were large groups of men organized under a single patronymic. Many of the patronymics had originated in the regions of the Autokracy — the North, the East, and so on. They were ranked based on prestige, which was linked to the relative age of the Family. Since new blood was continually brought into each

Family through adoptions, there was no genetic cohesion. Instead, fathers and their adoptive sons carried on familial traditions, business acumen, academia, military interest, and so on. Acting out of keeping with one's Family was considered a grave taboo.

Other topics of disappointment — reports about my short stature and puny chest — invited endless suggestions for exercises and recommendations about which foods to eat in what measure (gallons of milk, cow fat, bull testicles, wild game, especially organ meat). Whatever my Family ordered the chefs at the school to prepare was made. I ate it dutifully and still did not grow.

It became clear over time that all the letters I received were hastily dashed off by the Second at my pater's insistence. The Second took pains to say that neither he nor my pater saw much value in corresponding with me. There were no accolades for high marks, no gushing hopes I would soon come home. There was only a stream of disappointment and proscriptions. I learned to hate the Second through his barely legible scratches long before I met him myself.

I kept all those letters and reread them whenever my ambition failed. Motivation came from the insults about my slight build, my puny hopes, my certain future as a backwater petty noble.

In time, I would show them.

Still, there was a ruse to keep up. As all but a few truly pathetic runts grew and swelled around me, it was clear that a lack of genitals was not my only problem. I was small and slight no matter how I applied myself to exercise. I needed augmentation.

I started my search in that holy of holies: the library. The first moment I set foot there, I had found my place. It was a rarefied space that echoed with my footfalls. I spent every moment I could steal there. And gilding every moment was how forbidden it was that I, an Unmale, should be there, growing fat with their knowledge.

The Toolist books on medicine, with their sterile language, led only to frustrating dead ends. But why? Then it dawned: what I wanted to know was strictly Unorthodox. I could not ask for help from the librarian for my research was about forbidden things. How to make an Unmale appear Male. It was heresy. What might make Unmales look more masculine was an unclean thought worthy of punishment.

I framed my question to the librarian as an inquiry about Domestics from a budding historian. Had there been a time when Elders thought they could breed them stronger and taller to carry out more manual labour and be less susceptible to disease and fatigue? Could Domestics rise up if they became too strong? Was this something that could be guarded against?

Sitting hunched in his enormous chair, the librarian sniffed at me.

"A ridiculous question. You don't want to go giving rank Domestics traits like that. We'd have to put them all down if you did. Be careful, young lord. Watch how close to Unorthodoxy your query travels." But he waved me to the annex where the outdated texts were kept anyway.

In a bound sheaf of papers that focused on the properties of plants, I found a few scattered hints about what certain herbs could do for me. Some were supposed to be able to grow hair on bald heads. Some increased virility. Some deepened the voice or added muscle depth. But there was no indication of amounts, distillation processes, or effects. So for once, I was thankful for where I'd come from; I could find answers from a more direct source if none were available in books.

I walked through the main door to the kitchens. I knew the way from the Domestic passage, of course, so it was odd to pass through to that side of the building as a Male. I was immediately barred by a broad cook with a hot, leathery face. He crossed arms over his uniform.

"Kitchen staff only." The lowly cook puffed his chest and barred the door. I was developing a sense of entitlement about my stolen place in society. It was a reach for a mere cook to speak like this to a future lord. It was a lowly profession, and the men who took it often carried themselves with extra bravado — overcompensating for having to work close to Unmales.

I cut a courtly bow, which took him by surprise.

"My master in the library sent me to seek herbs from the pottage garden for identification in Toolist class."

"They could have sent word first." He huffed and leaned in, breath hot. "But the up and ups never think to ask the little men for permission, do they?"

"It's ill-mannered, I agree. I'll be sure to mention it to the Master."

The portly man stared me up and down. My words softened his edge, and he made way, only slightly, so I was forced to brush past the buttons on his belly. I could feel the heat emanate from his collar as I squeezed sideways between him and a doorframe.

He pointed with his spoon toward the scullery in the back. I waited for him to waddle off before I ducked under the stained leather blind that hung over the Domestic opening. I seized an extra shawl from a hook just inside and threw it over my student uniform. My shoes showed out the bottom, but I planned to be too quick to be seen.

The scullery was a long room that let light and water in high up at one end. The cold water rushed down a chute and along a channel against the wall. Domestics stood in a row along the chute with the hems of their shawls gathered up, bare feet shrivelled with moisture from the greasy pools on the floor. At the far end, the soiled water drained away. I knew this place — it had been my first station in the school, scraping thousands of pots and plates into the fetid water. The scraper handed the plate left to those working further up the line. The last one in the line rinsed the plate in the cleanest water, and back it went to the kitchen to be filled anew. The cycle was endless.

Aside from the pruned fingers, nicks from knives, and the grease that clung to everything, it was a good job — an opportunity to supplement nutrition if you were sneaky about it. The noisy rush of water allowed Domestics standing side by side to converse a little with each other.

Outside, more Domestics scraped the slops from the scullery into pig troughs, and the pigs' droppings were ferried in baskets over a series of fences to the pottage garden, where Domestics tended most of the school's greens. Another low door at the back led there.

That was where I found the Mam I sought. Wise about plants, she took care of the gardens. She was squatting by a canvas sheet on the ground where she sorted and bundled herbs. I brought a treasure with me, as one must when asking a Mam for her guidance. She had access to fresh greens in her line of work, but she likely had less opportunity for protein. I'd brought her a fine, soft cheese. One that could easily be chewed, even without teeth.

I'd never spoken with this Mam, so it was a surprise to see her hold out her hands and turn up a face with blind eyes.

She felt my face with sandpaper-rough hands. I cringed from the touch; her fingers were grimy with soil. She felt the cheese, smelled it, then pulled open the wrapping and bit into it.

"What do you seek?"

Wise old Mams were often abrupt. Their wisdom was sought in haste and secrecy.

"Herbs to grow into a Male, Mam."

She snorted.

"Why would anyone want to be a Male. Unhinged. Unconnected." She clucked her gums and shook her head absently. She was senile. Absent. I worried nothing useful would come of this.

"I was sent by a master, in secret, so he could … change an Unmale child."

She frowned and paused to sort another handful of herbs by smell.

"They can't bloody create, so they want to change." She shook her head again. "Can't be done. Not without trouble. Not without sadness. Not without sickness."

"The master is insistent."

"Tell this master that fenugreek and panax root will stimulate the muscles. Flax and withania will bring stamina." While chewing the soft cheese, she reeled off the names of several mushrooms from far corners of the Autokracy, roots from the ground, weeds from the sea. I used a pen to scratch the names shorthand on my arm. "But be careful," she warned. "Unborn children will grow two sets of genitals, or none at all. To an Unmale, the skin will grow hair, the voice will deepen, and the muscles will grow, but these things can cause nausea, insomnia, uncontrollable growths, madness, and even thoughts of suicide. With great change, there can be great danger."

"We can make ourselves as we wish," I muttered to myself. Her hand shot out and grabbed my wrist.

"You cannot escape your fate. You will be found out. Tell that to this master you claim to have."

I shook off her bony grasp.

"Keep your filthy claws off me. I seek only the information."

She turned to me with a long, level expression, unperturbed.

"The information without the advice is useless. Try to enjoy what you have, while you still have it. Good cheese." She waved me off.

12

Cera

WITH EVA GONE, I felt like a prisoner. Setting foot outside was out of the question, so I spent long stretches of time in Vincius's home alone. Eva gave me tasks to do while she did her shifts in the kitchen Below. I cleaned the house, putting linens and clothes in order, taking out refuse, preparing meals, all the things a Domestic would typically do. I was glad to make her work here lighter, in gratitude. And to take my mind off the things that plagued me: fear, loneliness, and longing.

Every sound from the street echoed over the long stretches of dark tiles, and every clink of harnesses or shout of a man outside made me jump. I expected to be discovered every day. That they'd kick in the door and arrest me. Take me to something I couldn't even bring myself to imagine. My hair came out in clumps thinking about it.

When I wasn't thinking of my arrest and capture, I pined for the sweet, innocent soul playing alone in his room. Never mind he occupied a royal chamber. To me, he was only flesh and blood, of *my* flesh and blood. I held on to glimpses of the child in his white shift, with his glossy black hair, his chubby arms reaching up for me. I had only a vague memory of the first time we met, of those brief moments before they took him.

His naked skin was red and tissue-paper thin. He had puffy, unseeing eyes, two impossibly small hands, and tiny, sharp nails. I remembered his grip. Each of his hands had clutched one of my fingers relentlessly. To relieve my hunger for the child, I fantasized instead about going back to the kitchens and toiling in anonymity with the others, rather than pacing alone. But my anxieties dredged up what would come if I did so. I tried to hide from grim thoughts of how I might be put to death by constant toil. But the days were long, and my anxieties were colourful.

I broke my days up into sections of chores, punctuated at last by Eva returning with news from the kitchen and snatches of her telling how she'd come to be with Vincius. She had begun as his personal Domestic.

As a matter of routine, he'd picked her up from one of the depots where unassigned Domestics wait for new orders. His previous Domestic, old enough to be a Mam, had died in the night. In a rush, sight unseen, he'd signed for Eva, paid the fees, arranged for her new tattoo, and presented the overseer with a serviceable shawl to replace the one she'd been wearing.

For years, they'd lived under one roof, separate, as Males and Domestics do. He worked, she served. They crossed paths only inadvertently, accidentally. They had intercourse — this was an expected outcome of a Domestic living in close quarters with her master. It was anonymous sex for him; Eva was unknown under her shawl and had no name. She offered a collection of services, of which sex was only one. It wasn't personal. Not at first.

In time, Eva knew him as only a wife could know a husband. She knew how he preferred his clothes folded. She knew when he slept, when he rose, how he took his hot drinks. She kept an eye on where he put his favourite writing utensils, or his safety glasses, and made sure they were close to hand before he even knew he needed them. She knew what small comforts made him feel most cared for when he was sick. And she came to learn when he preferred that she stay in the same room as him, working at some task, out of the way but not far. It was normal for a good Domestic to get to know these things.

But, knowing his routine as did, she took a liberty one day. And then another. Soon, it became a habit. When he left for long stretches on the second day of the week as he always did, Eva sorted the kitchen. She gave the sink an extra polish. She filled it with warm water, appreciating the way the light caught it, just so, this time of the morning. She threw back her shawl to let the warm, white light hit her face before she washed it. Then she unlaced the neck of her shawl, letting it slide to the floor, and bathed her body, using soap meant for the dishes. It was an outrageous act of luxury.

One day, Vincius came home early.

There was nowhere to hide. She stood dripping wet in the kitchen, her shawl pooled around her ankles. And so, rather than flee, rather than flinch, she stood her ground and looked him in the eye, daring him to bring his worst punishment.

He admitted to her (much later, of course) that he'd had an immediate reaction to the sight of her. Secondary to his physical reaction, he'd thought to himself: *Oh. The Domestic is very attractive.* It was an Unorthodox response to outrageous behaviour.

Somehow, the master of the house, there in the shadow of the deep doorway, was reduced to a stammering fool.

"My ... my ... ah, my ..."

"I'll be done in a moment," she said to him quite casually.

"Yes ... Of course. I had misplaced my ... pen." He was bright red.

"It's in the top left drawer of the writing desk."

"Of course. It appears I would be lost without you," he said sheepishly. A very slight lift of her eyebrows seemed to suggest that she agreed. He would.

From that moment onward, a series of "accidents" on Vincius's part meant that he spent more time working in rooms wherever Eva was. His enthusiasm for the Public Consiliorum waned. Strangest of all, he wanted to see Eva when they had relations. He wanted to look upon her. At first, it was only at the moment of climax, which could be excused, almost, as a reflex of that helpless moment when people make sounds and motions that can't be rationalized. But it was clear something else was happening when he began to seek her nakedness, with his, before anything else. When he needed to touch her face. When he needed to complain about the small hurdles of his day and the depths of his dreams at night. When he needed to keep her close after they'd laboured together.

Would Eva have loved him the same way on her own, in another setting? It's possible. But what happened was that this illegal closeness and this utterly uncharacteristic intimacy bound her to him completely. He loved her. He told her so. She loved him too.

13

Tiresius

I LIVED IN perpetual fear of being found out. I knew I would have to take drastic measures to guard my secret. The incident in the lunch line had taught me the benefit of taking the upper hand early.

When I was "re"-introduced to the general population of boys, I knew I needed to work the benefits of having a serious head injury and a trauma to my male parts in tandem. The most effective mode was to manipulate the mystery and shame of the two injuries and to capitalize on the extra time and care the injury afforded me. The mystery would inspire curiosity, and sooner or later, there would be a reckoning. When questioned, I would over-react with shame and make a clear example out of my victim. If I did a bad job of it and was found to be an Unmale, I'd be dead within minutes of the revelation. The simple binary nature of this fact appealed to my rational brain. It gave me the courage I needed to carry out my plan.

My opportunity came on the first day I was in the changeroom. We arrived in an orderly line, ferried along by a schoolmaster down the dim lower halls. But once we were allowed into the changeroom, all order evaporated. Boys bounced off one another, all elbows and knees and slaps to the back of the head, racing each other

to their lockers. I was sick to my stomach. I'd never been inside
a boy's changeroom. Nakedness would have to follow since we
were supposed to change from school uniforms into drilling uniforms. I had to look for my locker, an open wooden box with my
things hung on a hook, by reading the nameplates above.

Everyone else was half stripped by the time I got there.

"Antius says you don't have any dick left at all."

The bully was larger than me, which would work either to
my detriment or my benefit. But he was thick-skulled and, as I'd
observed about him in the past, not fleet of foot.

"I guess you must be a man lover since you're so keen to
know." I made sure to speak slowly and with great derision.

He puffed up proudly at the accusation. "I am," he retorted.
"Just like my father before me."

"Well, I'm no man lover, so what my dick looks like is none
of your business."

"I think you have no dick left at all and you don't want anyone to see it. I think all you got left is a gash. And that makes
you an Unmale. That makes you a *woman*." That last word was
a particularly distasteful one in polite circles, and he enunciated
it slowly. Laughs came from the growing circle of boys forming
around me, some naked, some dressed. I was bare-chested; I could
still get away with it then. "I think you're afraid they're going to
send you Below."

The last word wasn't out of his mouth before I had him down.
I grabbed his wrist and bent it back, forcing him onto tiptoe. Once
he was off balance, I swiped his ankle with my foot, and then I
was sitting on his chest, with a knee pressing hard into his trachea.

"Perhaps you'd like to know what it's like, firsthand, to have
half a dick?"

His eyes bulged, and he gasped for air, turning a deeper red.
He managed a slight shake of the head. But for good measure I
made a fist, the way I'd seen various instructors teach the boys,

with the two first knuckles pointed, thumb tucked, and I heaved it at his eye socket.

I broke my knuckle against his orbital bone, and he howled, curling into a ball. While the boy lay cupping his eye with his hands, I stood up. Blood dripped from my torn knuckle.

"Does anyone else want to see what that horse did to my dick?"

No one else stepped forward.

"Good. Maybe now we can go practise knives."

I strapped on a protective cup and finished dressing. (In time, when my monthly came, I had an excellent excuse: the wound in my pants never seemed to properly heal, necessitating many medical interventions over the years.)

The boy had a black eye for weeks, a constant reminder to him and the others that I'd taken the upper hand.

Years later, I sought a rural Domestic unconnected to anyone in the Capital who saw to my medical needs. I had to pay her dearly to keep my secret. She knew how to treat my ailments as a "Male." She taught me many valuable ways to cover up the truth and live with the complexities of my anatomy. I was both Male and Unmale. I was neither.

I attended the years of education required for a boy of my rank. I caught up to and easily surpassed my classmates, finishing as Top Boy — a fact that gives me great satisfaction to this day. Great, sacrilegious satisfaction.

It soon became clear that I was not going to fill out and up like the other boys. I was taller than most of them that first year and into the next, but they soon outstripped me. While I plied my fists as often as my mouth initially, I knew I would have to find another way to protect myself. It was a military school. The boys, awash in hormones, were taught to fight. Every slight, every pointed look, misplaced word, or accidental brush was provocation for blood and bruises. The instructors laid down rules and mores, often underlining the lessons with marks in our flesh to help us remember them. The school was a microcosm for the feuds and machinations that ruled in the larger world.

Several dozen Families made up the ranks of the noble elites, and they forever jockeyed for position and the Autokrator's favour. The Triumvirate benefitted from a world constantly heaving with compacts made and broken, with battles, brawls, and assassinations. Many Families worked for years, even generations, to buy their way into influence, only to have another jealous Family with deeper pockets and unscrupulous ambition depose them.

All the Families were represented at the school, but despite the pretense of unity promoted by all institutions, members of Families kept to their own groups. They chose bunks near each other, they arrayed themselves into teams, they worked among themselves to promote from within and crush those on the outside.

The first time I experienced rivalry from a different Family began with a simple accident. Antius and I fought when I sat in the wrong seat at mealtime. The encounter left me with a forearm fracture. But as Antius was in my Family, if I told my instructors how I really got the break, it would only yield more beatings — first from the Family boys, and second from instructors disgusted by my disloyalty. So I lied to an instructor about the break.

"The boys in Second Militia left pikes in the lower access. I tripped. I put them away as best I could before I came up."

The plausible lie implicated boys from a different Family of a serious charge. Treating weapons and armaments carefully was a serious duty. I was excused. Antius was never suspected. The boys in the other Family lost privileges and received straps on their palms during a school assembly. Antius and the others in our Family jeered as they took the blows.

At mealtime, our table was agog.

"Did you see Perius's face? Crying like a baby."

"He wasn't crying about the strap. It's because now they won't be flag bearers for the Charge."

"He's a prick anyway."

"No one left the armaments out. I saw them locked up, just this morning."

"They *were* locked up," I said.

Antius eyed me coldly. It was rare for me to speak up in those days.

I continued, "I saw them locked up myself. But that's not what I told the instructor."

Antius looked at me, surprised. And then he clapped my back. "One little tattletale gets six incubos taken down a peg. Well done."

It didn't put an immediate end to the casual violence. But between careful observation and "tattling" and allowing boys in my Family to copy my excellent study notes, I found my niche.

I was encouraged by glowing academic reports and approving instructors to attend further studies. A military career was out of the question with my puny stature, but I had a taste for stirring things up, which I knew would work well at the highest levels of politics.

I entered economics, along with a secondary specialization in ritual. This was the time-honoured path of the high-functioning bureaucrat and a future Cabinet Minister of the Autokrator Himself. My pater, whom I'd "met" through the letters his Second scratched out on his behalf, was pleased with my grades. He wrote often to tell me that I should focus on skills that would actually benefit the management of my family home. He wrote of the influence I could expect there if I continued in my studies. Influence, I assured him, when I took the time to write back, was something I dearly coveted.

From the letters, I learned that I would one day inherit an upland estate, one of the oldest keeps on the perimeter of the Autokracy, prestigious in lineage if not actual income or rank. I was as yet only Heir apparent, below a senior Second who managed the estate. My pater owned it, ran the purse, paid taxes, and set the local laws. A boy who hailed from my Family assured me that the place was a rotting pigpen with an adjoining stone tower.

A pigpen with a tower ... but mine one day! I admit, there were times when I was young that I tried on the role of lord in my head. I could have a comfortable life, be my own man, with my own funds, on my own land. Me. An Unmale. I had fantasies about living out a lifetime only to announce myself and my crimes in fantastical ways — exposing myself at a banquet, shouting my real story from high balconies to astonished crowds of Males. Crowing about how easily duped and overcome they all were.

In truth, even back then, my goals were loftier than my Family. My sights were on the Capital. If I was going to fool them, I intended to fool them to the rafters. Pulling the wool over the eyes of rubes was no feat. As time went on and I was not found out, my desires grew fat and wanton. I wanted the power to make others scurry in fear and intimidation the way I had.

I wasn't interested in a provincial life, so from that moment on, I embarked on a different trajectory. My injury and convalescence were hailed as a miracle; so was the turnaround in my grades. I lost the strength of limb I'd been known for, but my archery and horsemanship "improved." I was, quite literally, a new boy.

With my improved academics, I reversed a long decline the Family had suffered intellectually, falling further from the Capital, descending lower into military ranks. Not for twelve generations had a member of my family aspired to the rank of Cabinet Minister. By my "newfound" wits, I would reset the Family's status, and fortune would pour into the coffers; the local school would be repopulated, bringing even more money. I was sent several gold pieces as a reward for my term marks. Even with the bribes and favours I dispensed, I wasn't able to spend it all before I graduated.

All boys learn songs that layer verse upon verse of respect and love for their school. As grown men, they get misty-eyed over drinks with one another and sing about these glorious old days, glossing over the thrashings and abuse. When we graduated, they played these songs with grating brass instruments and showered us with flags, flowers, and confetti in a pseudo-triumphal march. We received gold pieces sent straight from the Autokrator's Treasury in recognition of our academic accomplishments.

We gave speeches in class about our future aspirations. I spoke of mine to enter the Imperial Treasury, which elicited only bored groans from my peers. It was true that the Treasury and economists were hardly well thought of. Nothing as exciting as being a dashing officer or a governor. *Let them groan*, I thought. *I shall be vastly wealthier than them.*

While I spoke, I thought of the ancient Capital. In my dreams, I'd walked through the place I'd read about. The Imperial Palace sat glittering atop sheer limestone cliffs overlooking a wide river, built over the ruins of previous dynasties. Ringed with ravines and moats, it was an impenetrable structure that had never been breached. It was one I aspired to conquer.

All around me, boys hugged and wept (it was one of the few sanctioned moments for such displays of emotion) and laughed and promised to stay true friends and brothers in arms. I walked away without a backward glance.

As the halls emptied and boys met with fathers and brothers in the hall, I sat in my usual place, bent over my books, until the school porter told me that my Family had come.

In fact, they had not. My Family had sent a retinue of scruffy, hard-looking men with lean horses and empty packing chests for me. I was pleased that of all the horses, at least the healthiest looking one was to be mine. I was pleased, as well, that I rode at the head of the band beside their leader. And that I was *his* leader.

I saw their eyes dart surreptitiously to my groin, and I drew myself up with inner pride knowing that despite what I truly was, I ranked too high for them to openly question me. The swirling elation went to my head faster than wine. This was better than a goal met, lauded for excellent deeds, a windfall, a day off. This was the most potent thing of all: bending the will and actions of others to mine.

It was both a happy day and a reckoning when I took the winding road up to the archaic keep of my "ancestors." Modern, gracious buildings in the South might be wood with peaked roofs, or brick with clever patterns and many chimneys. This keep was rugged, built out of raw stones pulled from the ground. The wind whistled through the spaces between them.

My schoolmate's description was apt. The only thing that grew in that rocky land were hard, spiky thistles. Vines grew around the main tower like calcified veins, pulling out the mortar in chunks. Hay lay in the fields in rotting piles. Animals looked diseased and underfed. Men sat about hunched over their paunchy bellies, holding dull weapons in thin, flaccid arms. Fate had given me an ancestry that would be easy to rise above. I should say: my unfortunate predecessor's ancestry. I have a bad habit of forgetting who I once was.

From humble roots as farmers and soldiers, my Family had charted a brilliant climb. An early ancestor became a general, killed many of the Autokrator's enemies, and won a title. His descendants consolidated holdings across much of the North. But after two hundred years of ruling their fifes, they fell into drink, neuroticism, and infighting. Neighbouring lords picked them off, reducing them to halfwits presiding over a keep little better than a farmhouse. I brought new honour and prestige to them, when they had long ago submitted to being political nothings, living out their lives in a hinterland. Of course, this would never have made up for the shame of being led by an Unmale. Ill-gotten or not, my industry brought new life, new money to an irrelevant line. I had to content myself with knowing what I was able to do, despite my many shortcomings.

In life, I've found, one can't have everything. Take, for example, the first time I met my pater.

14

Cera

EVA JOKED I was becoming her wife when she returned from the kitchens one evening and I fed her. Her eyes lit up at the offering.

"It takes forever to get out of the kitchens now," she said through her food. "They set extra watches, they question everyone, pat us down more than usual. I have begged for additional kitchen Domestics. Refused, of course. Everyone is shorthanded. Trouble is, now they talk about the loss of Domestics Above, that it must be due to runaways. They claim there's rebellion in the ranks."

"They'll start purges and executions," I said.

"They'll want to do that. But then who would be left to wash and feed them?"

We let the moment hang. I imagined what an uprising could possibly look like. Wooden spoons against swords and pikes. Then again, we had access to pitchforks. Axes. Had it ever been done? Had Domestics ever thrown off their yokes? I scoffed to myself. To think of rising up was preposterous. One cuff and I'd be down.

"Do the others think me dead?"

"I haven't told anyone otherwise. You are missed. In the kitchen most of all." She pressed her hand to mine on the table.

"But you are greatly appreciated here, 'wife'!" We both laughed at the blasphemy.

Eva told me how Vincius had warmed to her, and that she'd begun to leave her head uncovered all the time in his house. They'd talked in the evenings. He took her to his bed each night and asked her to stay with him until morning. They touched hands. He carried things for her, rather than the other way around. They created nonsensical pet names. They ate together. They exchanged nonsensical chatter. They ran the risk of being discovered but felt invincible against punishment in their happiness. In time, Eva had realized she was carrying a child.

Though they felt joyful, her condition made life perilous. All babies fathered by commoners had to be surrendered to the Consiliora; they were the property of the Autokracy. Boys were placed in nurseries Above where they all found homes as the adopted sons of Males. As long as he could support them, a Male could adopt as many sons as he liked. Unmale babies were sent below and handed from Domestic to Domestic, communally cared for, until they were harvested for work placements.

If neighbours noticed that Eva carried to term and that Vincius immediately had a child, both would be suspect. Both could be executed. So she hid her pregnancy and had her child secretly.

After the birth, Vincius used connections at the Palace to find work for Eva in the kitchens rather than in his home. He hoped her new position would remove any suspicions that her secret pregnancy had created. Each day, years before I came to work with her, when she was supposed to be Above procuring yeast and rye, she returned to Vincius's house to nurse her child.

Vincius had forged Consiliorum papers for the child, drawing on his access to genetic equipment. He made a public show of bringing home the child like any self-respecting pater might, so no one would know he had been born at home. That way,

Nelius could be enrolled at a school and raised in the normal way.

I continued to help in the house kitchen, kneading as before, filling every available space with rolls and tending to the starter dough.

At night, lying in the bedroom Eva fixed up for me, I could sometimes hear them, muffled through the walls, in their room. They slept together, sometimes chatting, sometimes laughing, and, very often, having intercourse. It seemed that she liked it as much as he did. Aside from the affection they showed each other, it seemed to be another reason they risked everything to live together. I tried not to think of affection. Having it for someone. Wanting it for me.

Hearing them brought back old memories. My stiff ceremonial shawl. The blindfold I was supposed to wear to shield the Male from my eyes. The small, dark, padded room, and my visitor. I wore the blindfold initially. I recognized his face with my hands. I knew where the muscle overlapped from shoulder to chest. The flatness of his sacrum. The sharpness of his hip bone. Eventually, I knew the tenor of his voice.

When we spoke, he asked me about my world. About how things were made and manufactured, about where Unmales slept, whether we had leisure at all. Most of what I told him was doctrine. For example, talking about Mams was not doctrine. I did not betray the many Hedgerow Mams I'd had by admitting they were real to him, then. Or the thousands of small acts of sabotage carried out in the course of a day. Those I kept quiet as well. He wondered, clumsily, if we had thoughts, as Males did. Did we have aspirations? Did we have dreams? Did we form friendships? Did we understand that there were such things as culture, poetry, literature that served the highest functions of Males' minds? He'd been raised to believe these things were inaccessible to Unmales. Yet, as he asked the questions, he realized how ridiculous they were. The world he'd been taught to know fell apart talking with me. He grew contrite.

He was amazed to learn that we sang little songs, passed lip to ear for who knows how many generations — and that we learned many things this way. Joked this way. Mourned this way.

I didn't fully comprehend who he was, then.

I didn't know whose child I was meant to conceive.

Tattoos on my wrist described my various stations. My Palace Domestic tattoo was intricate, finely made, with a miniature Seal of the Autokrator and a cartouche surrounding the date of my acquisition. My baker's designation, by comparison, was just a crude blob with blurred numbers. The first mark in my ear was from the day I was born, a number.

I was born an Imperial Consiliorum child, but Unmale. It was a forbidden thought, but I could have become ruler myself, if I'd only had the right parts. Instead, I was selected, based on my looks and good lineage, for the most prestigious thing an Unmale could do — bear the Autokracy sons. I was bound for the Imperial Consiliorum as soon as my monthly started.

Compared to most Domestics, I was lucky. I had a lovely childhood. I was fed the best food. I was spared physical labour. I was instructed on how to speak well, to look appealing, and I was taught to recite poems. I had to be a delight to the royal patrons.

Looking healthy and well-groomed was a mania in the Consiliorum. Unmales looked so alike it seemed we might be sisters or cousins. Historically, Autokrators favoured long, straight, dark hair, almond eyes, and noses with a certain patrician line. As Unmales grew into their bodies, they were weeded out from the Consiliorum over things as insignificant as lashes ever so slightly too short, an ugly second toe, a blight of acne, or too much natural body hair — not that they didn't manically shave us. There was an ideal height, weight, bust, and waist. The fixation had spawned an entire class of Toolists who studied the ideal ratios of the Autokracy's favoured aesthetics and the most likely to be able to procreate.

The ways of formally receiving a noble visitor in mind and body had been drilled into me. But we conspired, he and I, to act Unorthodox.

His first Unorthodoxy was that he told me his name.

"My Family is Evander. They say we go all the way back to Bartolius Himself."

"So you are someone important, then?"

"Do they not tell you I am the Consort?"

"Almost everything I know is despite them. What is a Consort?" I ran my finger over the bones below his throat as we talked, tracing the way the skin clung to his frame.

"I am the successor to the Autokrator ..." He found a blank look on my face. "The Autokrator is the supreme ruler, and he lay with an Unmale in the Imperial Consiliorum to get me ... Wives, as you must know, are forbidden even to the nobility."

"That is known to everyone. How do other Males get sons for themselves?"

"Common Males go to a Public Consiliorum. But they don't talk. They just ..." He paused, a little embarrassed. "They just deposit. There are many Unmales there ... lined up like ... well ... lined up rather like animals. It's a breeding pen." No one had told me about this. In my early adolescence, I assumed that my life was much like any young woman's life.

"Why did they make wives forbidden?"

"Do they really teach you nothing about history? You know about Bartolius the Just?" I laughed at the notion.

"The 'Just.' Tell me about him."

"Bartolius was the first Autokrator. He discovered that his wife was unfaithful, so he tortured and killed her. I am his direct descendant, Caelius, in line to be the sixty-seventh Autokrator. You do know about the Triumvirate?"

"Tell me about it. I imagine it's very important."

"I think you are teasing me now. The Autokrator is pater to all, really. The Consort is his direct Heir and functions as a second-in-command. The Consort learns to rule at his pater's side, and as his flesh and blood, and as a Male —"

"As a Male, he won't betray the Autokrator like an Unmale would."

"So they say. But the tradition was that the Consort takes on the role that a wife used to have. Bound by vows. The weeds stuck." He poked at his cast-off garments nearby. "Would you call me Caelius?"

"Caelius."

"What do they call you?"

I turned my head and showed him my ear. He traced the crude tattoo. From there, his fingers laced through my black, bone-straight hair. He was always finding my hairs, stuck to his chest, in his mouth.

"You can't be called a number. Can you?" There was doubt in his voice.

"When we are little, they call us something. They called me Cera."

He twirled my hair around his finger. "Cera. Tell me about your days before you came here."

"I have been trained in the Consiliorum since I was very young. There are a lot of rules and ceremonies to learn." I raised myself up on an elbow. "I remember being very small. I don't know what age. I was outside with other girls. We all looked so much alike we called ourselves sisters. We had a walled garden we could sit in. And it was spring. There were petals in the air. On the ground."

"Mmm. Sun on your face."

"Wind against the little hairs on your neck." I traced my fingertips against the nape of his neck.

"The hair on the very top of your head hot with sunlight. They rarely allowed me out either."

"The smell of rain on leaves. Blossoms. The ground when it was wet. Worms, inching through the earth ... I remember a baby bird. Naked. Featherless. It was on the ground. Its eyes and beak looked too big for its weak little body. You could see its pulse. See it trying to lift its head. We wanted to look for the nest to put it back. But our Mam wouldn't let us. We had to leave it lying there. She told us another bird would come and peck it to death and that would be the end. She was horrible." We lapsed into a silence, and in the darkness of my cell, all I could see was that blue and purple body, powerless and exposed. I had to find a way to lighten the mood. It was expected of me. We were to offer comfort to them.

"Do you ask all the other Domestics their names too?"

"Of course not!"

"I bet you do."

"It's treason to accuse the Consort of lying." He whispered the words against my mouth.

"You're lying," I breathed back. He bit my tongue.

"Not in this instance, I'm not."

I proved not to be a waste of resources.

His nightly visits, despite the aberrant conversations, were fruitful. I viewed the resulting pregnancy with the detachment I'd been instructed to practise. You are the vessel. You are the vessel. You are only the vessel.

I was young and springy. Pregnancy could be hard for some. I took for granted how easily it came for me. I didn't expect to feel the child moving around, dancing on my insides, tickling me. Nor did I expect the strange feeling of slow strangulation as air became harder to come by. With my lungs pushed aside as the baby grew, I had to learn to take sips of air. But other than this, I was fortunate. I was also lonely. Once an Imperial Consiliorum girl is fertilized, she is taken out of the pretty, silken boxes and placed in a smaller, rougher box, and she is not visited again by her lover. I heard him once, moving around in the hallways beyond reach, asking for me. He was soothed by many hands, and they attempted to seduce him with other girls who had my kind of looks. It was his duty to keep getting as many sons as he could. The Consiliorum was a veritable factory of babies potentially destined for greatness.

I remembered the beginning of labour. I had sat for endless dull days in my confinement, paying attention to nothing but the shifts in my body. As months went by, it became harder to breathe. I had to lie half sitting up toward the end, taking frantic sips of air as my chest was ratcheted tighter. Labour began with pain in my back for days that would not relent. When I mentioned it, Mams began to visit me more often.

I wept between their visits and willed the child to stay inside me. Their beginning would mean the end of my life as I knew it. Who knew what lay beyond? Backaches gave way to early contractions. Slow, dull aches that pulsed through my lower belly. But these were only show. The real contractions came later. They were shuddering clenches that started at my spine and radiated out to the ends of every hair on my head. It was as though my body were a fist closing tight for minutes at a time. They grew in intensity over three days.

The feeling of being unable to breathe finally let up when something shifted. At last, I could breathe freely. A Domestic rubbing my belly told me the baby had fallen lower inside me. Almost ready to come out. More Domestics came rushing to my padded box and bent over me, touching me from head to toe — mouth, eyes, breasts, belly. They knew almost as soon as I did that the time had come.

But then the labour stopped. The fist no longer clenched. Panicked, I looked at their faces for answers. Was the child dead? What now? They broke my waters and rendered me unconscious.

I woke in a dim room. I was cold. My belly was no longer burstingly turgid. I looked almost exactly as pregnant as before but knew, unmistakably, that I was not. My mouth was dry. I ached. No, not just ached — sharp pains spoke to me from all over my body. I passed my hands over my belly and felt, at the base of my abdomen, a long, rough wound. I was an emptied vessel.

I was instructed by Domestics around me not to think of the child. But the thoughts always returned. And my mind reeled with the magnitude of what he might become. It was the Consort-in-waiting who had lain with me all those nights in that small, box-like room. It was he had who inquired about my health and my feelings, as though those things mattered.

Those days in the Consiliorum seemed so long ago. And though I had hated much of my time there, there had been some sweetness to it. There had been him. Now, I lay in the house of a Toolist, in a little bunk.

Through the walls, I listened to my hosts' pillow talk and wondered at their easy closeness. My thoughts wandered back to the child. The boy. I only allowed myself so many of these thoughts. They tended to break me from within, and I would lie for hours with a steady stream of tears and grief gripping my throat.

I kept my memories and thoughts to myself, though, and did everything Eva asked me to do. I tried to be casual about sitting at a table. Sharing a meal with Males. Like equals. As though it were the most natural thing in the world.

15

Tiresius

MY PATER'S ANCESTRAL home lay at the end of a narrow road carved into rocky, sea-sprayed cliffs. I travelled there full of apprehension. Had I let my apprehension get the best of me, I would have slunk away, headed to the Capital, and lived some other clandestine life. But I was young and increasingly cocky, and I marched to my fate with a grim resolve to see things through.

It was a bleak place at the northernmost reaches of the country. The soil was thin, and the coast was buffeted by the cold, damp winds. Apparently, my Family's decline had started with the very land they occupied. The founder of our Clan was a gullible younger brother who drew the short straw for these barren highlands. The story went that the older brothers conspired against my ancestor. They took the rich lowlands for themselves and became fat with wealth and grain while my ancestor's land grew only rocks.

I arrived through the crumbling gate, expecting to be celebrated as the young Heir of the house. Instead, they hauled me bodily off my horse and marched me at a quick pace inside the clammy main building, giving me neither rest nor refreshment.

Cold clung to the thick stone walls built as one of the early defence towers of the kingdom. It was a lightless keep, not a pleasure palace. The deeply arched and narrow ceilings were stained with time. Moss and lichen ate away at the cracked flagstones, softening every contour.

My pater was a tall man whose body hung from his broad shoulders like a scarecrow tilting in the wind. I recognized his long, drooping nose in the face of his Second. Unlike gentrified men of the city who sheared their hair close, they both had long hanks of hair, although Pater's was white. He sat at the head of a long table, surrounded by paperwork. He did not stand. He did not open his arms to me. He looked me over from head to toe. His disgust at my size was apparent. I bore the examination with a bland face, though inwardly fearing discovery. After a moment, he spat on the floor.

"Why did no one tell me he was so puny?"

He asked it of the Second. I didn't even rate being addressed directly.

The round-shouldered Second whispered to him.

"They say he never grew proper after the horse unmanned him. But he finished top academic in his class, for all that." It was the Second who'd read the many unanswered letters I'd sent over the years.

"He'd better have finished top of his class, to be so bloody puny. How does he expect anyone to take him seriously as a leader when he's built like that?"

No one had an answer.

"If my pater wishes to try and get another Heir, I'd be content to leave and find my own way in the world," I ventured.

The Second's eyebrows shot up. Heirs didn't talk back. Heirs most certainly never offered to walk away from the duty and power they were to assume.

"If a pater finds his chosen Heir wanting in any way when he achieves the age of majority, he may apply to the Triumvirate to have the Heir released and may choose another child to rear in his stead." I spoke from memory on civic law. It was by no means a completely obscure piece of legislation, but it was rarely necessary.

"You're that confident of yourself, boy?"

"I'm confident you would waste your valuable time raising a new Heir, and that you'd never do as well as me, intellectually. What's more, I'd be willing to pay you back whatever you spent on my schooling were you to release me."

My pater's eyebrows disappeared into his hairline. "You're cheeky. I'm going to see to it that we knock that out of you." He sat back, chewing his own cheeks.

"No. This place has gone long enough without an Heir to come under the Second. If I were to croak tomorrow, this place would go to shit." Glancing around, he corrected himself, "More shit, in any case. Tell me what you plan to do with yourself, boy."

"It is my wish, honoured Pater, to learn all that I can about leadership at your knee and then, one day, to join the Treasury in the Capital as a Portfolio to honour the legacy of this house and my Family."

He chewed this over, looking at me through the wisps of his bushy eyebrows. I was dismissed with a jerk of his head and a curl of his lip.

"A Portfolio, serving in the Treasury. To honour the legacy of this house." He aped my voice unkindly. "You've got an ego. This house has had no legacy to speak of for three hundred years. You've got another thing coming if you think I'm going to start curtseying around and playing favourites with the Autokrator just so you can find yourself a position in Parliament. This is where you're needed. They can all fuck themselves. Second!"

His Second stirred to a somewhat more upright posture.

"Get this whelp down to the kitchen. He can start by slopping out the pig shit and taking it to the field." He turned to me, pointing a crooked finger. "While you're at it, you can take your lunch with the pigs until such time as I determine you're fit to eat with us." Inside, I seethed, but I kept my expression as bland as possible. This didn't wash well with him; all bullies like to see results for their efforts. "And make sure you give him a good whipping off the top, to get him in the mood for knowing his place." Still, I didn't allow one flicker of fear to betray me.

All the fine ideas of strategy and rhetoric and mathematics they'd crammed into my head at the military school were clearly going to be of little use in this sorry outpost. The buildings were crumbling, and half of them had only partial roofs. The crops were scanty, the livestock weak, and the Males more so. In my first year acting as de facto maintenance manager, I directed Domestics in the removal of shit, the repair of broken masonry, and the decent preparation of food. It felt like being a Domestic all over again, only with the aspirations of an educated Male. I was going to use every hateful minute of it to plan my revenge.

16

Cera

NELIUS WAS ALWAYS cold to me. His looks at me were long and full of hate. He didn't directly address me when he spoke. When we passed each other in the hallways, he walked down the centre so that I was forced to shrink close to the wall while he strode by.

One day, he found me in the kitchen. I gave him a tight smile and bent back to my work scouring a dish. He leaned on the counter for some time, watching me work but making no effort to converse. As I moved on to making rolls, he pierced the flesh of an apple with a small knife. I jumped at the sound. He cut into it and ate pieces off the blade, chewing with an open mouth. I could see his teeth grind the morsels.

"You do realize you are a liability here. To all of us." He said it lightly, as one might ask about rain.

I turned away from the work, hands mucky with clumps of dough.

"I am indebted to your family. To you."

"It would be so easy for someone to let slip that you were here. Acting like … this. And then *phup* … gone."

"I am constantly aware of it. And thankful to all of you for a place to lay my head."

He laughed. "Indeed. Our strange, illegal little family. Since we're harbouring you, your goal should be to make yourself useful. In fact, if I were you, I'd concentrate on becoming utterly indispensable." He casually rubbed at his genitals. Something between a scratch and a stroke. It was a common enough gesture, but I stiffened.

He noticed the line of my gaze and stood up straight.

"Please. Don't flatter yourself. I'm not one of those *animals* that prefer Unmales."

This was not a relief. No Unmale was safe from Male advances. It was as common as beatings, to keep us heeled.

"You're capable with mixtures."

I nodded at his assessment. He meant that I was good at measuring and calculating — precise and careful.

"I have urgent business outside, but Vincius requires samples to be prepared. They're simple enough that I think even you would be competent with them. Leave that. Come." He left without a backward glance. I wiped my hands hastily and threw a towel over the half-kneaded bread. I wasn't about to argue with him.

The workshop was between the living quarters and the street, easily the largest room in the house. Most of Vincius's money came from novel treatments he offered to men and their sons to increase their virility or fertility. In some cases, this involved treatments or serums. Sometimes it involved procedures. No one wanted to go to the Public Consiliorum and make no donation. It was considered one of the worst failings a man could have. The easiest way to save face was often to buy a sample of semen. Vincius did a brisk black trade in hermetically sealed vials of bought or donated semen. He used the money he made in his shop to fund his personal research in fertility and procreation. His papers and scale models and beakers and vials full of mysterious contents populated the workroom. I was ignorant of how they functioned, as well as the purpose of the various mixtures Nelius was charged with making, but they appeared to be growing things in beakers and tubes. The gentle whir of a machine that spun around in circles kept a constant hum in the room.

It was clear from the chaotic state of Nelius's bench that he was ill-suited for the work. Jars were carelessly stored, and paper and writing utensils littered the area, mixed with plates of half-eaten food. Some kind of fluid had spilled over a journal, sticking the pages together. Where his writing was visible, ugly, hasty scrawl overflowed the margins, as though he resented having to make the notations in the first place.

"This one is the simplest. Even you can manage it."

He showed me a jar of finished compound. He showed me the measuring instruments and the various ingredients. "Five." He pointed. "Five again. Seven of these and eight of these." He indicated the ingredients imperiously. "You must make fifty jars. They need to be done in the next two hours so the solution has time to react. I will label them when I return." He left, and I set about the work. The sooner I finished, the sooner I could get back to what Eva had assigned.

As a baker, measuring was second nature to me. The jars were soon lined up, and I waited for his return. When he did not come, I examined the label on the example jar. I thought I could try copying it, so he would have them to use, or to throw away if they were wrong.

My first attempts were a disaster. I kept losing my grip on the pen, looking for purchase on the slight thing. It had a tendency to run off at angles that didn't match the figures I copied in the least. Slowly, I was able to make the pen move as I wished. I followed each line religiously until I had a tight copy of the original.

When I was finished, I neatly stacked the labels, the unused paper, and the jars. Nelius didn't return for some time, so I tidied the rest of the workbench and returned to the kitchen.

Later, Vincius returned. As I listened to him bustling in his lab, I squeezed the dough I worked with anxious fingers. What he would think if he knew about the tasks Nelius had set me to?

17

Tiresius

WHEN PATER CALLED me to an audience, some months after my return home, I imagined he wanted to give me guidance or praise about my work. I was wrong.

"You're taller." I bowed. It was the best way to agree with him, and often staved off a backhand to the head. "You have no dick."

"Sir, I ..."

"You have no dick because of that accident."

I bowed my head. I was acknowledging the uselessness of disagreeing.

"We will have you seen by a Medical Toolist."

I was immediately on edge; I had not considered this. Anyone investigating my lack of parts would find I was a gender criminal.

"My lord, I've come to accept th—"

"There have been many advancements. I prefer to see you sire a boy and contribute meaningfully to the Family if at all possible." He signalled, and a tall, sallow Male in long robes emerged from the antechamber. From his uniform, it was clear that he was the Medical Toolist.

"Your Heir is at your disposal," I told him, bowing. My pater waved the two of us off. He was certain he was about to gain more of a son. I was certain I was about to rob him of what son he thought he had.

The Toolist walked with me to a room set up for him. Bending deeply at the waist, he held the door for me.

"After you, Heir." He turned to latch the door behind him. "If you will, please remove your breeches, and we can take a look at —" He swivelled around, his strange, waxen face marred with surprise when he found my blade out.

He held up his hands. "I assure you, there is absolutely nothing to fear, Heir!"

I pushed the edge of the blade against his trachea. He was much taller than me, but the point against his throat mitigated that. He rose on tiptoe to stop it from poking at his Adam's apple.

"You will not perform procedures on my person," I hissed at him.

"I've seen everything you could possibly imagine, Heir." For someone in his position, his voice was surprisingly smooth. "I've seen terrible diseases of the genitals. Amputations, mutations, even ..." He lowered his voice. "Abominations." He rushed his trembling fingers to his lips as if to shush himself. He meant those sad creatures cursed to appear Male and Unmale at once.

I eased pressure off the edge of the blade. A little.

"Indeed, Heir, whatever, *hem*, condition you find yourself in, it can be mitigated, or perhaps even corrected, with Imperial technologies, in ways that are quite miraculous."

"If I were to submit to such miracles, what hope could I have that I could find a Toolist who would protect my privacy?"

"But you will find me utterly discreet, Heir —" Again the point, again his tiptoes.

"Whatever my pater paid you, I will double if you find me a competent Toolist in your place. One who will never know me, who will never tell of what they found."

I heaved a small purse from my cloak. He took it with long, folding fingers.

"All things are possible, Heir."

I re-sheathed my blade, with a firm click, to keep him conscious of its presence.

"Good. You tell my pater that you find my condition treatable, and that I will go with you to your lab to have it addressed in a month's time."

"Depending on the actual condition, the process might be lengthy." He began to complain, but I handled the covered blade conspicuously, and he was quick to add, "My will is in complete accordance with your wishes, Heir." He made a satisfyingly deep bow. And he produced no more smirks on his thin lips. He offered me a sachet.

"Take these — since your accident occurred at such a tender age, no matter what corrections are needed, these will help adjust your inner physiology. You should find an improvement in size and strength. Tone of voice should deepen. You may grow facial hair." His tone was soothing. "Though I warn you, once begun, the regimen must be adhered to for a lifetime." He slipped out the door, keeping his eye on my sword hand.

My pater invited me to dinner with him that night, at the same table, along with the Second. He believed deeply enough in the Toolist that I had become more of a Male already, I supposed.

He waited for us in the "great" hall, a cramped room with uneven floors and strewn with filthy hay. The Domestics weren't kept in hand and didn't take their work seriously. Pater sat at the head of the time-scarred table. The Second, in his ceremonial women's weeds, unkempt hair, and a week-old beard, sat at Pater's right hand, hunched over his food.

Pater had business to discuss.

"You spoke of one day going to the Capital, to serve in Parliament."

I looked up, eager. "Nothing would please me more than beginning my journey to the Capital." And to power, I added to myself. Power over Males.

Pater spoke between mouthfuls, with no expectation of interruption. "I will not sanction your delusion to go to the Capital. I need someone passably capable, as you are, to stay here. I've suffered with that lout of a Second for long enough. I had hoped he would grow some kind of wits. Instead, he fattened up on my food and grew stupid." The words bubbled out between lips thick with sauce. I was hardly surprised. The trope of the warring Pater and his grasping Second who bicker endlessly while being completely dependent on each other was an old one. "Besides which, the Capital is full of fawning idiots who waste their lives trying to get close to the Autokrator."

"Foolish men chase the Star / Wise ones fill the firmament." My quote from the old poets stopped him in mid-chew. He nodded, pleased. It helped that it was a Northern poet I'd chosen to quote.

"Indeed. You'll shadow the Second. And, one day, if you're lucky, be the lord of all this yourself."

Screaming crows burst in a flurry from their nests in the rafters and punctuated his grand offer with globs of green shit. Lucky indeed.

In truth, succession was not a hereditary right: a man could elect anyone successor in the case of his death. Typically, though, when a man chose a boy and educated him to follow in the Family footsteps, it was a given that he was the most likely to succeed. Then again, my Second could die before my lord did. I could succeed directly. Perhaps that was why he often shot such daggers at me with his reddish-brown eyes.

"The Heir is going to have a lot to unlearn before he'll be any use to me," spat the Second between mouthfuls.

My pater shrugged.

"You should add the middens and jakes to his duties. That'll straighten him out." He smiled cruelly and bent back to his soup.

"A good plan, Pater. I appreciate the foundation you're building in me."

He gave me a sharp look. He wasn't expecting his insult to be met with praise. He started chuckling, but the chuckle developed into a wracking cough. The Second and I watched him turn beet red, veins popping out of his forehead. When the coughs grew violent, he retched up some of the soup he'd already consumed. The Second and I shared a significant look and politely ignored the laboured breaths he took as his normal colour returned.

I smiled at the old man while he talked about his plans for the blighted house and lands. Inwardly, I fumed. The old man had another thing coming if he thought I'd stay in these forsaken lands for long.

18

Cera

"HAVE YOU BEEN touching things in the lab?" It was a few weeks later, when Vincius approached me with a stormy face. From habit, I shrank to the ground, shaking. He pulled me up by the shoulders, his demeanour suddenly softer.

"Cera, forgive me! I only mean to find out if Nelius has been shirking his work. I'd recognize his handwriting anywhere." He held up a jar. "And this is too neat to be his."

I'd learned my letters from a Hedgerow Mam when I was very young. In between her chores and ours, she would sit with us in dark corners and teach us lessons in whispers. She traced her finger in the dirt to acquaint us with the letters. Almost everything the Hedgerow Mams knew was handed down, Unmale to Unmale, by mouth or by scratching in the dirt.

Between sickness and overwork, few Domestics lived to old age. Those that did were able to slow their service and be Hedgerow Mams to the little ones. In thanks, we all shared our bread with them. It was considered a sin to pass a Mam without inquiring whether she needed anything and giving from what one had.

It was a risky undertaking. I myself once saw a Hedgerow Mam dragged off in the midst of giving a lesson. I remember her kicking feet marring the figures she'd just written in the dirt.

I had picked up my letters fairly quickly, but there had been little reason to exercise the muscle. There was always work to be done. Inside Vincius's shop, though, words were everywhere. They were on labels and machines, on diagrams, books, and bills.

As soon as Nelius had discovered the labels I had done, a mountain of work had followed. Labels, lists, notes, paragraphs, abstracts ... He had rough papers for his Toolist degree that he needed to turn to fair copy; he had work to complete for Vincius. Bit by bit, I had become his full-time secretary, and soon I learned I enjoyed not making the letters but rather understanding the content that they communicated.

As I'd embarked on learning the specialized Toolist vocabulary, I began to understand the purpose of it all, and I found myself both awestruck and horrified.

Vincius was experimenting with storing and duplicating Male and Unmale cells. He regularly sent Nelius out to fetch samples. From time to time, he had Domestics brought to a screened-off area in his lab. He kept the Domestics there for a few days and didn't let anyone else in, except me. I brought supplies to him while they convalesced after procedures Vincius kept secret from everyone. Food, water, bandages ...

"Why does he bring them here?" I'd asked Eva. She'd thrown me a look to say, *Don't ask any more about it.*

He was trying to combine the cells in test tubes to make off-spring. And beyond that, it seemed like he was trying to find ways to make cells combine to reproduce without the Unmale cells. Much of his other work was about trying to perfect a medium in which his creations could continue to grow. His notes were littered with sketches of strange bags and vats that incubated fully grown fetuses ready to be liberated.

I felt bad for Vincius. As his apprentice, Nelius was expected to carry on his work — but the countless botched experiments Nelius carried out were costly. He would make a poor Toolist when he graduated — especially if he relied on my notes to give his Dissertation.

Nelius was making more and more use of me in order to give himself time off. He had Family boys and other companions to meet up with. He would return in the small hours, often stinking of resin and so intoxicated he was incapable of undressing himself.

"So Nelius ordered you to carry out experiments? To handle specimens?" Vincius pointed out the workstations in the lab as he spoke. Evidence of my neatness was everywhere.

"Initially, it was just measuring and mixing. But he found I was good at copying and writing."

Vincius clapped his hand to his head and shook it. "How long?"

"A few weeks after I arrived."

He sat down and rubbed his hand hard over his forehead.

"It's one thing to have another Unmale here in the house. But writing now? Reading? Doing Males' work?" His black expression made my stomach coil in fear.

"I'll understand if you want to send me out."

"Then who will do the work around here? Here I thought Nelius had turned a corner, and instead I find the only reason we're caught up is because a Domestic is doing his tasks. Damn it!"

He paused, looking at one of the beakers I'd used to carry out Nelius's work.

"The Imperial Dissertation is next month. There are so many things to document, to prepare." He stopped pacing about the room and looked at me. "It must be difficult working with the shawl on."

"I'm used to it."

He shook his head and stormed down the hallway.

I could hear him berating Nelius, his voice booming throughout the house.

"How many times have I asked you to just carry out a few simple tasks? Time and time again, you assure me that you're doing them, and instead, I have to find out from a Domestic that you're lying to my face. Do you have so very little respect for your own pater?" There was a pause during which I imagine Nelius muttering some kind of weak response.

"Do you know what lengths I went to keep you as my apprentice, Nelius? I could have lost my standing. And what thanks do I get? Lying, sneaking around, taking resin every night. And why did I do it? To raise my own seed as my own son. To have his own mother tend to him ... I don't care if you didn't want it. It was what I thought best. In the end, your best work was easily done by an untrained Domestic. Go ahead, scoff. I'll have you know she's infinitely more reliable than you. You're lucky I don't put you in the street for this. Go join the army for all I care."

A door slammed, and Nelius sped past to his room, trailing the reek of resin. Vincius came through the door.

"Here. Get changed," he told me. "If you're going to do Nelius's work for him, you should dress the part. We'll call you Dominius. It was the other name I had picked out for a son."

Eva appeared, looking peaked and wan. Nelius came back from his room.

"What is the matter?" she gently asked.

"Shut up, incubo!" Nelius shouted at her. She staggered back at the insult and looked heartbroken.

"You dare!" roared Vincius. A sneer blossomed on the youth's face.

"I don't care to live in this Unclean place." He said it lightly, knowing the insult would burrow deeper because of his casual tone.

At the front door, wrapping his scarf around his neck, Nelius looked up at me on his way out. His face was black with murderous contempt.

19

Tiresius

"WHERE IS MY Seal?"

"I'm sorry, my lord?" I asked.

"The Seal! It was here at my place." He fruitlessly rifled through papers on the great table. If the large Seal were there, it would be visible even among the great stacks of paperwork we needed to get though.

He continued grumbling to himself as council members filed in. A Domestic arrived with his midday meal. He ignored the council members and the Second, who arrived late.

"Where's the damned Seal!" he thundered. Covertly, the council members eyed him. The Lord was known for throwing things.

"The Seal is gone?" The Second appeared panicked. And for good reason. Without the Seal, no goods could be requisitioned, no deliveries made, nothing enforced. It was the sole charge of the Lord to keep the Seal safe. The Second paid the consequence if he allowed the Lord to fail in his duty.

"Your soup, my lord," I murmured, handing him his bowl. I made sure to stir it for him. I even tasted it. "They corrected the salt as I asked."

"Hmph." He continued his frantic search.

As I leaned toward him with the tray, I made a "discovery." I surreptitiously pulled the Seal out from my inner pocket.

"Lord, what is this here? I believe you must have misplaced the Seal." I spoke in a calm, helpful voice.

Council members' heads swivelled as the Lord looked about, dumbfounded.

"But it wasn't there just a minute ago!"

"Lord, your burdens are many," I said, soothing his concern. "It was overlooked among these piles. You must not have seen it. No matter. Here it is now. Sit. Take your meal."

He sat and ate some of the soup, his gaze distant.

"The taste is off," he complained.

"It's because there is less salt," I soothed. "It is for your health."

Pater shuffled off at the conclusion of the meeting, barely getting through his closing statements. I grabbed the Second's arm after he'd left.

"Does our lord not seem terribly fragile of late? I worry for him. It's cruel to finally spend time with Pater, only to fear he will be snatched away by old age ..."

"Indeed," the Second agreed, but he looked cagey.

"What a shame it would be if he had to step down sooner than expected. What a burden it would place on you, Second," I mused. "But then, were you forced to take over for him, assume the role of Lord, I imagine the estate would run smoothly."

"I think it would."

"Smoothly enough that I could, perhaps, consider going to the Capital. If I stayed ... I'd just be in your way."

"Just so." It was pleasant to agree on so much together.

Not long after my pater misplaced his Seal for the first time, he became seriously ill. The curious disappearances of the Seal were put down to the onset of this illness. He doddered around, needing to grip the wall to move about the place. He went to bed early in the evening and slept late in the morning. Finally, one day, in the midst of a meeting, he suffered a medical episode of some kind. He vomited and flung himself forward on the table before falling onto the floor, where his eyes rolled back in his head and one side of his face drooped. He was carried to his bed.

Day and night, he was flanked by Medical Toolists, infirmary Domestics, and other attendants. The Second and I did our best to run things in his absence. I deferred in all matters to the Second, who took to the position with relish. Despite the best efforts of the Toolists secured by the Second and me, Pater's condition worsened.

I made sure to personally bring his soup to him, as a dutiful son. Now that he was further weakened, I spoon-fed him, wiping his chin after each mouthful.

"You've grown accustomed to the taste with less salt, have you not, my lord?" He nodded. His face was even slacker now, after the brain attack. Some of the angry folds in his skin had smoothed out — in fact, he appeared more genial.

"Not to worry," I told him. "The Second has risen to the task beautifully. He holds meetings in your stead, and the household runs as smoothly as it ever did under your hand. He has had to reach into the Treasury for a number of long-overdue disbursements, but now the accounts are paid, and the books are balanced." Some of these disbursements had been made to me, since the life of a petty aristocrat had inescapable expenses. But the Lord hardly needed to be bothered with this information. "Another spoonful?"

The Lord tried to say something, but alas, his tongue was not inclined to form intelligible words.

"Easy now. Don't overexert yourself, my lord. It's harder to speak, no?" He nodded weakly. His eyes looked watery and distant as they roved about the room.

"And now, you find, it is even difficult to nod or shake your head?"

He lifted his eyes up to me — there was a look of loss and deep sorrow in them.

"Indeed, by now, I expect you'll feel almost nothing at all in your body from the chest down."

Another sad nod.

"That will continue." I gave him this news as gently as I could. He finished the last spoonful of soup, sucking it up noisily. I wiped the grease from his slack mouth.

"It's the soup, my lord." I gave him a little smile while I tidied away the dishes.

"Bit by bit, you've dutifully eaten your soup," I told him, pulling the cover up for him and smoothing it around his useless legs. "And bit by bit, the paralysis has set in. Another day or so, and it will be complete. Indeed, likely by this evening, the only thing you will be able to move at all will be your eyes."

Those eyes found me, tinged with panic.

"Your brain, of course, remains as sharp as ever."

A firmer nod.

"Unfortunately, the cumulative effect of the ingredients you so dutifully ate is that your mind will remain intact, but you will be locked inside your body until it crumbles away at last."

His eyes remained fixed on me as I moved about the room.

"You should last a decent amount of time. Years and years, as long as your care is good. Yes, my lord, you can look forward to lying here, in this bed, in this room, until they carry out your corpse." I smiled warmly. "I'll be sure to send you updates from the Capital, for the Second has graciously agreed I should go there to pursue my vocation in the Cabinet and one day become Treasurer to the Autokracy." I rubbed my hand on his knee. "A pity it had to come to this. Had you simply let me go, you could have enjoyed your lordship in health for years to come. But you see, I have so very little time, my lord, and so much left to accomplish that I couldn't wait to win you over by charm. This way was much easier."

He watched me, hawkish, as I stood.

"And since I'm being so confessional, my lord, I feel there is something else you should know, before I depart for the Capital for good."

I unlaced my overcoat, unwound the long belts, unhooked the many fastenings, and held my garments open so that the light glanced bright over my naked breasts.

His outraged eyes took me in.

I put one leg up on the side of the bed and let my fingers run along the length of it, tracing from kneecap to inner thigh. I wore a rudimentary prosthetic that dangled from a heavy leather belt, thanks to the Toolist my father had found me. It was an ugly thing — the wrong colour, and slightly lumpy — but it was sizable. I undid the belt. The heavy piece landed with a soft thud. I eased my knee open wider so Pater could assess for himself the true nature of my "wound." I grazed my fingertips back and forth along my thigh, teasingly, enjoying the tingling warmth and the spring sun pouring through the window.

"I thought it important that you know what kind of son you find yourself with, my lord. You see, your boy died seven years ago in that accident with the horse. There is no wound here. There never was. I found your son dead in the arena. I dragged him to a garbage heap and took his place. And so, you see a humble Domestic."

I pulled my clothes back together. "It's a pity that you won't be able to tell anyone that an Unmale found their way into the very bosom of men." I smiled, brushed his whiskered hollow cheek. "A very great pity."

Later that day, I packed horses and provisions for the long trip to the Capital. It would have been so much easier if the Autokrator would simply allow any Males to move freely about the land with self-powered vehicles. But, of course, doctrine decreed that technology like that belonged to the court alone.

My journey took me first along a coastal road that had fallen into disrepair. Sections of cliff had fallen across it, and there was a constant spray from the bitingly cold North Sea eroding the soil.

After one week of travel, my path turned inland; a day's climb up away from the coast and the road gave way to a flat plain where the climate was more temperate. I was below the string of mountains crowning the top of the continent. The Capital lay three weeks to the south. But first, I had an important stop to make. One that would considerably reduce the load of gold I had liberated from the Marnius Family treasury.

20

Cera

EVA CUT OFF my long, dark hair over the sink in the kitchen. While she worked, I played with my pocket goddess, spinning it by the thread that passed through a small hole in its crudely formed topknot. Turning the rough texture over and over in my fingers was a nervous habit.

"Vincius said you should put that aside. What might happen if someone were to see you with it?" She was right. With a trembling hand, I handed her over.

"I'll find somewhere to hide her. We'll keep her safe." Chopped hanks of hair soon covered the sink in long, ropey coils. Eva switched from shears to a razor; the cool blades ran unfamiliar against my skull. She left a long front forelock, traditional for apprentices. Anyone would assume at a glance that I was a young man, well into his studies.

As she worked, she said, "Maya has gone."

I saw her lips form the words before I completely understood. I started at the news, but she kept my head still with her hand.

"When?"

"Not certain. Her position allowed her to come and go, but no one has seen her for three weeks now." My eyes burned with sharp tears. Maya, with her broad shoulders and muscular legs, moved through her life like a tank: unstoppable and seemingly impervious.

"How many is it now?"

"Too many." She finished shaving my head. "There. Now you'll pass for a young man, if a pretty one ... And if anyone were to see us now, it would look like a young apprentice being tended by an ordinary old Domestic." She pulled out a pan scoured many years on one side to give a muddy reflection.

I looked at my naked head and ran my fingers over the sharp ends. I felt the air against my scalp where the hair was shorn. I looked like a pasty, unhealthy lad who had yet to fill out with testosterone. A young boy.

"It brings out your bone structure." Eva ran a finger along my jaw. "Easy to see why you were in the Imperial Consiliorum."

"Oh, I know. Such an honour," I said rolling my eyes. We both laughed but were soon cut short.

Nelius appeared, lanky and sullen, in the doorway.

"Have you returned to us?" Eva asked mildly. I could tell she was trying hard to make sure nothing set him off.

"Obviously," he spat. "Cut her hair, I see. You really don't have any respect, do you?" Eva said nothing, and after a moment, he strode across the kitchen, heading for his bedroom. Eva watched him as he went past. I could feel her longing for him. And her fear.

"He's wearing the kerchief all the time now." She said it low and even. I didn't understand. "The Fallos cult. They're ... rabid. They believe Autokrator Bartolius will come back one day to punish the unrighteous." She paused. "I have to talk to Vincius about this. I don't think you or I are safe if he keeps that up. I just wish the boy would mind his pater and do his studies. I think he has a good heart, but I worry about him so."

I knew about Fallos generally, of course. There were statues dedicated to the god standing at virtually every corner of our city. But this Fallos cult was new to me.

"Dominius." Vincius appeared in the doorway. Nelius lingered behind him, arms crossed. "I want you two to run errands. I'm behind in my work, and I need many things."

"You make me a party to this blasphemy."

"I'll thank you not to get in the habit of talking back," Vincius told him.

"I just don't particularly like the idea of being executed. You might be Unorthodox, but I'm not."

"And while you live here, I am your pater, and I am master in my own house."

"Certainly, Pater."

Vincius narrowed his eyes at his son. He could tell this was a passing acquiescence. When Vincius left, Nelius turned to me. "Time's wasting."

Rushing, I fumbled with a scarf and cap. Nelius gave the scarf a disapproving look.

"No one does it like that." He fiercely pulled one end out and rewrapped it, tight against my neck. "You want to get us both killed?" He pulled the cap down low, ensuring the forelock was still visible, and hustled me through the house.

He pulled open the large glass doors, and for the first time in my life, I walked through a Male door.

On the high street, buildings soared up toward a bright, clear sky. The faces of buildings were deeply etched with images retelling the glorious history of the Autokracy. They depicted men who were titans ... philosophizing, exploring, fucking, governing, vanquishing. The Autokrators of old were popular subjects and were portrayed with exaggerated muscles and enormous phalli. The oldest buildings featured monumental pillars shaped like men, holding the weight of the world on massive shoulders. Architects called these types of pillars Bartoli, after the good king.

Men strode through the streets, some in fine, richly coloured robes. Wealthier men rode high above the rank and file in litters. They went about their business, talking as they walked. They stood in doorways, negotiating. They lingered at tables, arguing over beverages.

No one paid me any mind. I was just another lanky new boy in the Capital. To me, I felt so obvious, so plainly Unmale, that I might as well have been walking naked. I slunk along the walls, trying to keep out of sight.

Nelius pulled me along by the ear with an unsuppressed growl. We stopped at dispensaries, where he barked orders at unctuous compounders. He ordered steel and glass and plastic parts from a foundry. He ordered me to carry the parcels as they accumulated.

He stopped on his own personal missions, as well. I loitered against a wall, staying out of the way of random brawls and hurled bricks while he paid a scruffy-looking man for a pouch of resin.

"You should cover the smell of it with lavender and rosemary," I told him. "I can smell it from here."

He grimaced at me. "Keep your advice, incubo."

The resin itself wasn't illegal, but the pipes were. While I nursed a hot, bitter drink, I watched Nelius under the brim of my hat. He poured the syrupy resin into a glass bowl, which he warmed with a candle. He hid his business under the edge of the table. The hot bowl vaporized the resin, and with one swift inhale, it was all gone.

He sat, feet up on the edge of the table, balancing perilously on the back legs of his chair. He shoved his hands into his belt, looking more smug than usual. I hadn't thought that possible.

"A fine day, by Fallos," Nelius said loudly. Someone at another table snorted.

"What's so bloody fine about it," muttered a surly man without turning around.

"A fine day, Fallos willing, for the Autokracy to turn back to the way Bartolius wanted it." Nelius pronounced it with a righteous quaver in his voice.

"Have you eyes in your head, lad? The whole place is going to shit. Can't find a Domestic handy when you need one, can't get them to do their work straight when you do. Taxed up the ass and tithed to the balls."

"They say the Consort plans to raise the taxes even higher when he throws off his women's weeds." Nelius let indignant ire colour his tone.

"Well, I've heard that incubo plans to outlaw your pathetic Fallos cults," replied the man, turning in his chair. He was broad. And he was angry.

"I'd be careful putting words in the mouth of the Consort," Nelius muttered. The man pulled his jacket aside and showed that he wore the scarf of the Guard. A career soldier. The type that enjoyed fighting.

"Let me enjoy my break in peace." He stood, feet wide, arms crossed.

Nelius rose in a hurry, his chair clattering to the ground. By this point, his eyes had begun to dart back and forth. He rubbed at his own knuckles in a ceaseless motion.

"Up, you!" He yanked me up by my scarf and moved down the narrow alley with a tight-hipped walk that was almost a run.

Seconds later, he was snickering nervously. The resin had taken hold, giving him a manic air. He moved with greater purpose after he'd partaken, so at least our work went faster.

I struggled along, weighed down by various items. He snaked us down a steep, winding alley where the clustered buildings blocked all the light. He brought me to the stone doorway of yet another resin den.

But we were barred in the alley by a long, black, velvet-clad leg.

The owner of the leg picked at his nails in the dim light of a thick stone doorway. Like Nelius, he wore a black kerchief.

"You've been long absent, Nelius," remarked the curly-haired youth I judged to be the same age as Nelius.

Nelius playfully launched a fist at his shoulder.

"You're looking well, Maxon."

"And you look like refuse. It's all that resin." Maxon waved a hand in front of his nose at imaginary odours.

"Let us through, then. I'm on lab business, got to keep a clip."

The youth plowed an unfriendly fist into Nelius's face, throwing him against the opposite side of the doorway.

"You left without paying the other night, Nelius."

"I thought we were friends. I thought we might be more." Nelius smiled a genial smile through blood-smeared teeth. His lip had split and swelled. He put a hand on Maxon's leg, cloyingly.

"I've told you, we are not. Nor will be." Something in Nelius's eyes died when the boy said that. But he made it seem like he rallied.

"All the drinks and resin will be on me soon enough. The time is nearly right." Nelius's tone was glib. But the youth grabbed his collar and pushed Nelius harder into the wall.

"I wouldn't have you in my squad, Nelius. Not for any amount of drinks nor money."

Nelius groaned, face pressed to the wall.

"Dominius, get a move on, you incubo," he called to me, as though I were the one procrastinating. "We should be going." I was cowering against the far wall of the alley, as far from the two of them as space would allow. But now, I nodded, and we hastened out of the dark alley.

Some distance on, Nelius stopped me.

"You won't speak of that. To anyone. That ingrate doesn't know what he's missing, spurning me like that. My Family is better than his. I've paid him endless compliments. I've bought him gifts. And still, he refuses to lie with me." He spat. "A boy like that who didn't even make it out of first form should be so lucky to lie with me. Come on. Stop dawdling." He cuffed me and set off, leaving me behind, puzzled.

A little further ahead, our way was blocked by a small crowd of men, shouting and jeering. Someone had set a fire.

"Come on." Nelius pushed through the men, making a pathway. At the centre of the crowd was a dismantled Mother shrine and two Domestics, huddled with their heads to the ground. The men were pelting them with anything that came to hand. I recognized the parts making up the shrine. Flowers and fruit for fertility, tallow lamps representing hope — all of it being torn to pieces or smashed. The Mother herself was a broad, squat shape with massive hips and breasts.

The men were hacking at the clay figure, breaking off chunks.

After Nelius had gathered everything on Vincius's list, we arrived at a pedestrian intersection that met the high street. We passed beneath an arch formed by two thick, towering phalli that met in the middle. Down several well-worn steps, we came through a crude lesser arch.

"Where are we going?"

"That's for me to know," Nelius spat. He had a small tic below his eye, which had set in after taking the resin.

We joined a steady stream of Males going down the steps; an equal number leaving formed to the left. There was a constant chatter.

Inside, men gathered at panels, punching in choices. One by one, they were issued a card at a window. Nelius approached the window with no card.

The man there recognized him. He nodded but narrowed his eyes at me.

Nelius told him I was a new apprentice. He appeared hesitant about it. My stomach was squeezed in knots, but I hadn't thought

Nelius might be nervous too. The man was oblivious to our anxieties. He nodded and buzzed us through a curtained doorway.

A dim, cavernous room made up of aisles and stalls stretched out before us. The air was thick with musk and sweat, almost unbreathable. There were two hundred or so Domestics chained up in the stalls like livestock, bearing the thrusts and grunts of rutting men. My days in the Imperial Consiliorum rushed dizzyingly back to me.

The Domestics of the Public Consiliora "serviced" any man who chose to stop by and do his duty for the Autokracy. There, in plain view of one another, men copulated with healthy, sturdy Domestics chosen for their wide hips.

The steady stream of men entering the Consiliorum found their way to a stall. Likewise, a steady stream of Domestics were led to the stalls.

From my time in the Consiliorum, I knew they'd be positioned with their legs up, then tested. Their blood would be referenced and catalogued, hormone levels checked, vitals monitored. Once it was clear there'd been no conception, they'd be sent back to the stalls.

Mine had been a lonely existence, left in a dark room with no other Unmales to talk to, waiting for the Consort's attention. Still, I wouldn't have traded that for this barn full of animals.

I was overwhelmed by the sheer size of this place, the number of Domestics, their mute attendance, the rhythmic clanking of neck irons and the chains around their wrists. Their legs were unfettered so that the men could arrange them in different positions. I wanted to retch. I wanted to weep.

Nelius stopped at an intersection and folded his arms, like he was appraising a heifer. He noticed my agitation and smiled crookedly.

My eyes fixed on the rafters or down to the filthy, slippery floor. I tried not to take in the sights and sounds, but my eyes found digital displays above each stall spewing information on the Unmales' vitals, their barcodes, and their viable offspring.

"Never been here?" he asked mockingly.

I shook my head.

"I'm surprised. You're good-looking enough."

I had no intention of telling him my past. I kept the Imperial Consiliorum tattoo on my inner thigh well hidden.

"Why are we here?"

"Worried? Afraid I might disobey Pater and sell you off to the Consiliorum?"

"Why would you say that out loud?" I hissed at him.

"You'll see." He seemed very pleased with my discomfort. I shrank against the wall as a plump middle-aged man waved at Nelius from across the room. He bustled over with a small plastic box filled with vials.

"I'm sorry. Run ragged today," he huffed. He handed over the vials, which Nelius set in his satchel. "Not staying this time?"

"Breaking in an inept apprentice." He gave me a theatrical cuff for good measure. "I'll do my duty another time."

The man waved him off genially.

We emerged into sunshine and fresher air.

"A young man should be walking out of the Consiliorum with more of a spring in his step," joked Nelius.

I wouldn't be drawn in. "What's in the vials?"

"Vincius's work." He spat the name out, then, thinking better of it, corrected himself. "Oh, do forgive me, I mean *Pater's* work. He's using it for his presentation at the Palace. Gene separation. Replication. Recombination. He'll win a place in the Palace lab if he's successful."

I nodded. Much of the work in the shop focused on blood work and cells.

"You're lucky you were with me. Otherwise, they might have carded you."

"And?" I asked, sick with fear.

"If you had a card, they'd make you perform your duty. Every man has to at some point, even if he's exclusively a man lover."

"And without a card?"

"They would have found you out pretty quick if they'd given you a closer look."

The rest of the walk, I kept my eyes to the ground. It was nothing new — as a Domestic, it was where one tended to look anyway.

21

Tiresius

I'D LEFT MY adopted ancestral home with a light heart. I had never been welcome, and I had set my sights higher than being some provincial lord of nothing. After I left the road that hugged the sea, I reached a crossroads marked by a Fallos statue pointing the way to the Capital. It had been defaced; its erect penis had been crudely lopped off.

It tugged at my heart to have to do it, but I took a different path. Even though I'd felt the nip of destiny at my heels rushing me toward power and the Capital since I was a child, this detour was vital to my future career.

This path led into barren, steel-coloured foothills and meandered between rock falls. It took me past foul-smelling hot springs sputtering thick, yellow water and scattering calcified deposits all around. It was these springs that had first drawn the Medical Toolists of years past to establish their renowned, far-distant clinic. Later, the nearly secret location encouraged them to offer more esoteric treatments. Men came from all over the Autokracy to find cures for embarrassing and unmentionable ailments.

The Toolist my father had summoned to examine me lived and worked here. I'd sent messages and gold ahead, and he knew to expect me. He also expected even more gold. The more secret the condition, the more costly the treatment.

I was met at the foot of a steep hill by several stooped figures. As I approached, I could see that their eye sockets were sunken and scarred over. The purpose of their blindness was clear: patients expected complete secrecy, so their identities had to remain unknown to the staff. And even to the Toolists themselves. But I wondered what benefit they were offered for the removal of their sight.

"Welcome," offered one of the bent men before me. "Allow us to stable your horses." He held out long, spidery fingers to receive my harnesses. "We also ask you to put up your weapons, as this is a place of healing."

I made a big show, clanking about, gathering various blades, naming them aloud as though in inventory. I was careful to slip one long, narrow knife inside my boot. It was essential to my plans.

He offered me a guiding hand as though I were a small child. He walked briskly, leading me up a rocky path set into the hill. He tugged slightly to quicken my pace.

He led me through a dark archway, where a tall tower rose sleekly out of the rocks. Plunged into disorienting pitch after being in the bright daylight, I stumbled and put my hands out, but he moved confidently ahead. I heard the echoing clip of my horses' hooves as they were led away to the right. We bored straight ahead. Smears of flame dotted a long hallway that came into focus as I squinted. Many grand doors let onto smooth onyx floors.

My guide selected a door that opened to a handsome antechamber. He busied himself stowing my things in closets and chests.

"The suite serves as a private operating chamber as well as a convalescence room, so you need never worry that others will see you here," he explained. A richly dressed bed occupied an alcove on one side, but in the centre of the room was an imposing table with levers and sections, flooded with both natural and artificial light.

"The Toolists and assistants use this door to come and go — they only see the parts they work on. During any procedures and consultations, your face remains curtained so none can know your identity. In addition to the level of surgical expertise practised here, we pride ourselves on our secrecy. It is the sacred vow of our Order and Profession that all who come here are protected from discovery. So you may rest easy about your fate. Someone will attend you shortly. If you would, disrobe and cover yourself with the sheet on the raised bed."

He gave a slight bow as he departed. I did not rest easy then, nor at any time in that place. Despite the pledges of secrecy, I knew that my life was at imminent risk. With shaking fingers, I undid my clasps and buckles. I pulled my foot slowly out of my boot, careful not to graze the hidden blade. I stuffed a scarf into the neck of the boot to conceal it and left my clothes near the ornate bed in the alcove.

I slipped naked and shivering under the crinkling sheet, but I had brought a heavy bag of gold with me and left it conspicuously on a side table. I lay down with the curtain just above my incriminating breasts, thinking this could easily be the end of my adventure posing as a Male.

Presently, I heard voices at the door, which opened with a breath of cold air.

"Good day." I recognized the strained voice of the Toolist who had examined me at my home. Nonetheless, my skin prickled, and my breath quickened. Through the cloth, I could just see the slight outline of two men, distorted by shadow.

I still wore my rough prosthetic, as though it would protect me from being found out. It should have been removed with the rest of my clothes, but by now it felt almost as familiar as my own body.

I was at their mercy. They might out me and send me to a quick death, as was the right of any man when presented with evidence of gender crime. On the other hand, my gold might inspire them to keep the secret. In either case, my life as an Unmale had to end.

Both men approached, and I felt their hands on my flesh, prodding the rough scar from my self-mutilation. "As you can see, the young lord still carries the scar of the original mishap." I looked hard at the ceiling and tried not to curl into a ball. Then I heard the subtle clink of coins.

They were counting the offering I had brought.

"Five hundred pieces of gold."

"I have more, should it be necessary." I tried to keep the quaver I felt out of my tone. "In fact, I'd be honoured to make an additional payment once the procedure is complete."

"The young lord is too kind," demurred the Toolist. It was impossible to tell if he'd taken offence at my attempted bribe.

The Toolist dropped his voice. "Our task is to overcome an extremely cruel twist of nature — our young man was born with two sets of organs, through no fault of his own. Without a proper member, he is, of course, desperate to restore what he lacks as well as excise what offends nature."

The other Toolist cleared his throat repeatedly and prodded underneath my prosthetic. My heart hammered in my throat as he moved my flesh about, lifting, parting, exposing.

"Is the second set fully ... functional?"

"No, no, of course not functional, but it is a most unhappy thing to have to bear in addition to the mutilation he suffered. The young man detailed his symptoms to me in several letters. You can imagine his distress."

"Quite." He cleared his throat again. The hands, warm and baby soft, migrated to my abdomen. I breathed a little easier now. He pressed deeply in the crease of my thighs and near my navel.

"So a complete removal of the second set, internal and external, is indicated." His voice was flat, factual.

"He is eager to have something replace ..."

"Yes, yes. A separate procedure. And extremely involved. We harvest muscle from here" — he jabbed my thigh — "and here" — he jabbed my buttock. "Of course, it is beyond anyone's scope to create a fully functional member. But I think the young man will be pleased with the aesthetic and find that his deficits and his self-image will improve greatly."

"My lord, have you eaten yet today?"

I assured him I had not.

"Good, have the assistants prep him. We can begin with the removal right away."

"My lord." The first Toolist bid me farewell from the other side of the curtain and disappeared silently out the second door.

There was no indication by his tone that the pronoun he used was snide or ironic. I was accepted as a Male with an unfortunate condition, and that was the way he treated me. Still, I wondered how much of that was gold and how much was professional oath.

There was virtually no time to consider it further. The room was soon filled with assistants on padded feet who set about preparing me with quick hands. I felt warm liquid spread over me. It was mopped up, but it cooled quickly, covering me with gooseflesh. At the same time, a hand bearing a cloth slipped under the curtain shielding my face and was put over my mouth and nose. I was aware of a sweet smell and the cool roughness of the loosely woven cloth. And then I was aware of nothing at all.

My first thought on waking was to wonder how I'd gotten to the other side of the room. For I lay now on that beautifully made bed in the alcove, with a window casting light around my head.

My second thought was for the pains that wove their way all over my body.

I had no idea how much time had passed. With an enormous effort, I willed my fingers to move — which they did only reluctantly — and slipped off the loose tethers on my wrists.

Instinctively, my hand groped my belly, where I felt a sharp burning. An angry raised line protested at the touch, but I felt on. The incision ran across the base of my belly. Below that, I felt the scar from my mutilation, bumpy but familiar. Even further down, I could feel something was different, though I did not know the full extent of it. I picked at the dressing, working the sticky tape with my fingers, wincing at the pain from the fresh wound. Once I had worked a corner flap free, I could feel the newly sutured skin. It was puffy and strangely flat.

Below where I made water, where the folds of my "second set" should have been, was an alien smoothness. It was walled up. No longer an opening.

I lay back, exhausted by all this, and several attendants hurried up on their silent feet. They too were blind, which explained why I was no longer curtained off. They ran their hands over me, briskly checking tubes and tethers and dressings. A frown passed over the sightless face of the one who found my mangled dressing, and I was quickly redressed. A huge sense of relief flooded my being. I had ceased to be recognizably Unmale.

To the untrained eye, at least.

22

Cera

I KEPT MY cap down and became Dominius, a swift errand boy and shadow for Vincius. I watched him work, observed his habits, and copied the motions of his hands. The fraudulence never once left my mind. Each time I set foot out the door, I broke into a cold sweat and could take only quick, shallow breaths. And in the midst of it all, I thought often of my child. He was woven into my every waking thought and even my dreams. Some days, I feared that I might never lay eyes on him again, and on others I dared to hope that if I worked hard enough, I might earn a way to get close to him again. Mixing in the company of men might somehow get me back to him.

Nelius dawdled and was often hours late if he fell into a resin stupor with friends at some back-alley flop. Every time he didn't come home, I was there to attend Vincius and learn.

Vincius had started out as a Toolist interested in animal husbandry. He'd come to the attention of the court as a young man by creating ever more precise methods of artificially inseminating cattle in order to increase the yields of offspring. He was also studying how to select the best breeds for strength and robustness. He knew male reproduction was of particular interest to the current Autokrator. In fact, it was a mania of his, and money had flowed from the Imperial purse throughout his reign for pursuits such as Vincius's. He wished to find a way to control, perhaps at will, the engendering of Imperial babies.

"Pure bollocks," Vincius told me, laughing at the notion. "Orthodoxy likes to think that Male seed can spring into new Males by itself. It's utterly beyond our ken, but it doesn't stop him from wanting it. I'm just trying to do with human material what I did with cows. Introduce Male and Unmale genetic material. See how they react to each other. I like to think I've come quite a ways. And if we are diligent, by the time the Imperial Dissertation is held, we can show a rising positive yield." He indicated an array of beakers and vials. At the time, I didn't really understand what he meant, but it required endlessly mixing minute amounts of the material he kept sending me to the Public Consiliorum to gather.

"Maybe one of these days we'll borrow some material from you!" I think he was joking. "After all, you've successfully produced a boy. And a well-heeled one at that. In animal Toolism, you're what we call good stock."

I was surprised Eva had told him about the child. Perhaps I shouldn't have been. I'd said all kinds of things when my head was on a pillow close to the Consort's all those years ago. But we'd both had secret Unorthodoxies, which had formed a bond between us.

Vincius had marvelous tools, like machines for instant cooling, minute droppers, fine syringes, and a glass that magnified things that were too small to be seen at all.

He allowed me to look upon a universe living inside drops of water. I was unnerved by the creatures that swam in even the cleanest of water.

"How can we drink these?" I marvelled.

"You're made almost entirely of such organisms. We are conglomerations of many tiny animalcules. Our ancestors thought we were animated by spirit, but perhaps we are instead animated by uncountable tiny creatures living inside our very blood! Observe!" he told me. "This is my field. Male genetic material. I've refined the sample and removed what is inert from what is alive. You see these animalcules — these little soldiers are the Male material. They are tinier by far than any grain of sand. And there are millions of them in a few drops. I've made a study of them and published my drawings to the Imperial Toolists. A drawing in my own hand is framed in the Autokrator's personal library. It suited a bunch of old fools to assume that they are tiny homunculi — indescribably small men propelling themselves with some kind of tail or paddle. I have observed that they do have heads, like tadpoles. They swim. They link tails. They fight. They falter. And after a time, like the men who gave them life, they die. If you freeze them, they stop moving. If you heat them, they move faster and then die quickly.

"Orthodoxy says all they need is a good bed to be seeded in. But I know they require the Unmale egg. Somehow, I need to show the creation of life in beakers. Without the woman. And I must downplay the need for the Unmale. Impossible, of course. But I seek to find a way to make the material divide, as is known to be the case with twins. I have imagined that one day, the whole process could take place in giant beakers."

It made no sense to me. Just some sleight of hand in glass jars. I knew that the only way one produced children was by a man and a woman lying together. Though we Domestics had often joked that if men could get more men by lying with one another, they'd have done it long ago.

We worked continually, with the day of the Imperial Dissertation circled on a calendar. Initially, it had been months away. But the days bled into one another. I worked from dawn until dark, sleeping like a stone, and even so I slept less than Vincius. Those days, though he tried to shirk, even Nelius was bent to the task.

A successful Dissertation would ensure Imperially funded work for Vincius and graduation for Nelius. Success meant his freedom from the household — freedom that doubtless meant getting lost in resin dens. More than that, it meant he could live a cleaner life away from Unmales.

23

Tiresius

I HAD PLENTY of time to worry what my next steps would be while I was in recovery. I was uncomfortable leaving anything to chance, but I knew so little of the world then, and it was necessary to wait. Since then, I've learned that sometimes, the most effective strategy is to do nothing. Some events have a way of playing themselves out so that one never has to dirty one's hands. It's a ploy that has often served me well.

Over several painful procedures, an inert but reasonably recognizable member was fashioned between my legs. After I woke from the final procedure, I explored around my bandages, finding that they had harvested strips of flesh from my breasts to create the effect of a phallus. A useless one, but still. I planned to make up for whatever I lacked with attitude.

The Toolist himself visited me in the final days of my convalescence. When the attendants left, he very familiarly moved aside the curtain that shielded my face. I'd forgotten how sallow and thin-lipped he was, like some kind of tropical frog.

He smiled through those thin lips and took a seat near my head.

"You are healing remarkably well, my lord."

"Thanks to you and your colleagues."

"Nonsense. Every good Toolist knows all he can do is guide the patient in the right direction. All healing comes from within." He ventured a good-natured chuckle. "But perhaps from without, in your case."

I smiled tightly. His casual reference to my changes were uncouth.

"So from here straight to the Capital?"

"If my brains are as good as I told them in my letters."

"Of course, of course. No doubt you'll be fast-tracked for the Parliament. They'll be lucky to have you."

"You know the bureaucracy there?"

"Oh, in my youth, I had dreams of working in the Capital myself, closer to the Triumvirate, closer to the money. But it wasn't to be. And working here, even with generous clients, it's a mean living."

"I can imagine that it's stultifying as well, here in the outer reaches."

"You've no idea what decades can do to a decent brain, young lord. But I have good reason to think that is all behind me now." He took my sharp look as a reason to continue. "You've amassed a decent sum to take you to the Capital, and naturally I only expect a certain portion to begin with, but I think a percentage for life, commensurate with your rise up through the ranks, should be enough to keep everyone quite happy. Chiefly, me."

"I'm sorry, I don't think I follow. A percentage? Of what?"

"For lack of a better way of putting it, young Tiresius" — he used my name with an emphasized crispness, even though the uttering of names here was forbidden — "a percentage of your income. One equal to carrying the great burden of your secret." He played with the covers and the vials of medicines and spoke casually. As though we were discussing nothing more than how well I was passing water. "I hope one day, soon, to leave this place. I'd always

dreamed of going to the Capital. Being a gentleman of some leisure. With your certain success to come, I finally can."

I stared at him. I had been an idiot to think that a single
payment, no matter how large, would have been enough to buy
permanent secrecy. He meant to feed on me for as long as I lived,
which would be no time at all if he chose to reveal my secret. It
was brilliant, a different kind of servitude than I'd known before,
and I made a note to make use of it someday.

But I had not suffered daily beatings in the military school, the
bleak incompetence of my pater, or these painful procedures to
stop here.

"Do you think me well enough to leave here shortly?"

"We can begin your discharge today, if you like. Your wound
care instructions are in a dossier you may take."

"I wish to begin my work, begin my earning. For both our
sakes." I said it collegially — so we could both enjoy a little laugh.

He nodded eagerly, licking his lips with gusto at the thought
of the earnings that would come his way.

"But perhaps you'd be better pleased with another portion, in
advance, with my sincere thanks."

"It would ease my burdens greatly, young lord."

"Be so kind as to hand me my boot, the left one. I hid another
purse there so as not to be relieved of it by curious attendants."

"Clever lad. Very generous of you, indeed." He fetched it for
me.

I made a big show of unfurling the scarf from my boot. His
eyes glinted with expectation. I beckoned him near, and he closed
the gap between us.

With a fluid motion, I used a technique often demonstrated at
the school. A steadying hand on his shoulder that felt fraternal.
At the same time, though, it pulled him forward, allowing him no
escape from the thin blade that raced up to meet his main artery.
They'd demonstrated the technique quite thoroughly in school,

using hapless political prisoners as teaching dummies. We timed our success based on how quickly they bled out. I'd received praise for how quickly I'd mastered the move and earned more than a few points for my Family, making me quite popular.

Once he obliged me by bleeding out fully, I had a mess to clean. I tucked him tightly into my bed, with the curtain carefully in place. A quick note in my chart ensured the next attendants would allow him to sleep off a sedative for a few hours.

The dossier was my passport to receiving my pack horses. I found them well watered and fed, and properly exercised. We would make good time.

The blind attendants sent me on my way with many offerings of blessing and health. I was rather terser than they, but I think they were used to patients being eager to return to their lives.

I headed due south, and as soon as we were out of sight of that tall tower, I let the horses run flat out toward the Capital.

24

Cera

FOR DAYS LEADING up to the Dissertation, the shop was flooded with heavy-set Domestics to carry out all of Vincius's equipment and displays. Piece by piece, they moved everything out of Vincius's lab until the space echoed eerily with our voices.

Eva remained out of sight, scrubbing floors in the kitchen. To the casual observer, she was just another anonymous Domestic in her shawl. I spent most of my time with her, careful not to be seen and recognized by anyone in the work detail.

The night before the Dissertation, Vincius paced the hallways, rehearsing the findings of his work. Unable to sleep, I joined him in the shop as he continued to pace. He let me pose questions that the judges might ask so he could practise fielding the answers.

"What was the inquiry of your Dissertation?" I asked.

"Say it like I asked."

I cleared my throat. "Honoured supplicant. What is the inquiry of your Dissertation?"

"Honoured judges," he said, "the point of my inquiry was to ask: is there a means to make man, without needing Unmales." I looked up at him, and he stumbled for a moment. I had never heard him articulate it this way.

He continued, "The focus of my work is twofold. First, to attempt to combine sexual cells from men and the medium they grow in, from Unmales, and foster them to combine and grow in a vial. Second, to discover if there is a way to do without the Unmale contribution — the medium they provide, and the space to incubate the Male."

"Sexual cells come only from men?" I asked. "There isn't a female half?"

"This is what Orthodoxy teaches," he responded. But I pressed on.

"I know it isn't the same as all you have learned, but the Hedgerow Mams, the old ones who teach Domestics, say it takes two people — one Male and one Unmale — to make a baby. That each child is half of each of its parents."

Vincius came close to whisper to me. "Everything about Orthodoxy is repugnant to me. And I am not alone in this. There are others. Men and *women*" — he emphasized the forbidden word — "who desperately want things to return to how they were, hundreds of years ago. But technology marches on. And technology has to make sense of the fact that we don't call the female 'contribution' a cell. We don't call it that. We call it something else so the Autokracy is mollified. But of course, many Toolists know how cell division and replication works. Mankind reproduces sexually. But I was approached, some years ago, with a letter from the Autokrator Himself to pursue the idea that perhaps reproduction could be done without Unmales. And to present what I found."

He showed me one of the many vials we kept in storage, in freezing cold cases.

"This here, this is life. Suspended. I am, we in this workshop are, I believe, the first to have successfully combined them outside the body. But it does require a male cell and a female ... contribution. No matter how they try to force it, I can't make Toolism bend to Orthodoxy." My mouth felt dry, considering what we had wrought.

"But, Vincius? Is it a good idea to do this?"

"My role isn't to question what the Autokrator wants. My role is to find out if it can be done."

The next morning, the three of us left, Vincius in his best clothes, Nelius up early and in a lighter mood for a change. Streams of people were en route to the Capital for the Dissertation. Toolists came from across the land to gather for adjudication — and to compete for funding and the few coveted spaces working under Imperial guidance.

The route took us through the old town, over an ancient bridge, and through the triumphal arch of the Autokrators of old. The bridge gave way to a steep incline worn smooth by the feet of men over the millennia and flanked by the flags of the noble Families.

The thick, listing walls that encircled the oldest part of the city depicted the warring of the earliest Families. They marched along the walls, thirty feet high or more at points, their outlines carved deep into the rock in stylized profile. The walls had withstood armies and never once been broached.

Under the crushing bare feet of the ithyphallic early Autokrators writhed their myriad conquered enemies — foreigners from beyond the Autokracy and errant Domestics alike. Each noble face showed a stern profile with his wide eye fixed on a brilliant future, while his feet crushed and his hands severed heads, sexes, and limbs.

Under the heavy load of equipment, the Domestics struggled as the incline grew steeper. They leaned deeper into their burdens, shouldering the yokes, while the overseers directed them up and onward with heavy hands and sharp threats.

All of a sudden, the Palace loomed above us, spilling over the edge of tall cliffs and buffeted by chilly winds coming off the wide river below. At the crest of the hill, rows of soldiers flanked a passageway under a tower. They stared sightlessly at us while we marched to the inner ceremonial hall of the Autokrators. Of course, I'd seen it all before — but only ever through the mesh strands of my shawl, and never through the front doorway, with my head up.

Long tables filled the massive hall with vaulted ceilings held up with towering stone columns. The tables were organized by the area of science they represented. The various doctrines of Toolists and their assistants set up equipment and displays. Chaotic bleating indicators, spinning motors, and labouring fans made a busy noise.

Vincius guided us to the Medical and Human Sciences section. Specializing in reproductive technologies, he was part of a proud tradition. Earlier men had had quaint ideas of sperm as germs or seeds. In the old Orthodox thinking, these germs were tiny homunculi that swelled until they were infants, children, men. Vincius was part of the early push to explore the deeper intricacies of how traits and strengths passed from father to son and how this process unfolded within Unmale bodies. After we were done setting up our technical demonstration and data displays, we settled in for the long wait to present.

A blast of trumpets announced the entrance of the Autokrator. Stiff in his ceremonial cladding, he moved forward with tiny, stilting steps, leading a long parade of hangers-on. His head was high, face covered by a golden mask held in place by handlers. Through the cutouts of his golden mask, you could see his sharp, wrinkled eyes gazing into the bright future like his ancestors once had. Below the mask, his beard, under waxy daubs of gold, was greying. He walked beneath canopies of beaten gold wherever he went, splendid, shielded.

The Consort followed behind him, wearing a gaudy painted face and the exaggerated lines of his traditional women's weeds. I knew his face better without makeup. Instinctively, my eyes darted away, and I ducked slightly even though it was unlikely that he could identify me at this distance. Behind him, still young enough to be carried in his gilt sedan chair, sat the darling Kratorling. My child. I felt a strange pinch in my belly. I had not hoped to see him so soon. I had not rehearsed how I might feel or act.

I had a wild thought to seize him right then and there. To pull him out of that sedan and run. How quickly would they be upon me? Would surprise give me a few extra seconds to get away? Would his weight be too much? Would I make it to the front door? Would they try to kill me with my arms wrapped around the Child? Might he be harmed in the attempt? Would he ever know whose blood they wiped off him?

As was traditional, the Triumvirate was attended by a gaggle of Portfolio Ministers and handlers who followed closely. A herald shouted their names and positions so they could be applauded by all those in attendance.

"Ferrius, Imperial Toolist!" The man himself was unremarkable, rotund and sandy-haired, but I recognized him immediately. This was the Toolist who'd stopped me Below to inspect my nethers after I gave birth. The memory made my skin crawl. It was a strange peccadillo, touring below to grope Domestics. Though nothing Males did Above or Below shocked any of us.

A thin man of slight build stood behind Ferrius. He wore his bright red hair cut close to his scalp and was clean-shaven. He had spidery fingers and limbs, but his robe was cut with exaggerated shoulders and collar, as if to make up for his slightness. He paused in the doorway with an air of self-importance, fingers poised dramatically.

"Tiresius, Imperial Treasurer!" The red-haired man inclined his head slightly as his name was announced, the very picture of self-aware humility. He floated close behind the Imperial Toolist and the Triumvirate.

Only the Ministers spoke to the common Toolists who had gathered for adjudication. The Ministers relayed questions whispered stiffly into their ears by the Autokrator and Consort and then ferried back the answers from the common Toolists. The Triumvirate remained waxen-faced except the Child, who shrieked with delight at some toy in his hands.

The Triumvirate wound their way through the endless rows of displays, leaving behind a gold coin with Toolists who made presentations of merit. What they all sought, though, was one of three Beneficences given each year. A Beneficence would guarantee a man's station for life.

Vincius paced while Nelius lolled, crude and insouciant. I wondered sometimes if Vincius noticed the boy's eye rolls and exasperated sighs or if he'd grown immune to them.

As soon as the Triumvirate approached our row, Vincius cuffed Nelius to stand at attention. Vincius's face glowed with a sheen of sweat. I expected it was social unease, since the science behind the presentation was firm and irrefutable. My own unease made me nearly sick. The only thing that gave me courage was the sheer incredibility of an Unmale masquerading as a man. The audacity lent me greater cover; most people see what they expect to see.

For forty-five minutes, we stood waiting. I pressed myself as far back as possible, almost out of sight. My role was to turn the levers of our scientific dumb show, to roll out the process of experimentation and result. Nelius was to stand by to hand over vials, specimens, and placards as needed. Vincius was to be the sole point of contact with the Imperial presence.

Finally, they approached us. The golden mask was lowered. It was a re-enactment of the Autokrator's descent from Heaven to the realm of the mortals. The Autokrator, with his pan-shaped face and his weak chin, cast his eyes over Vincius's work. Vincius kept his jaw and fingers clenched. From my vantage point, I could see the muscle in his cheek flex like a beating heart as he bore down on his teeth. Finally, the Autokrator made the slightest inclination, and a lesser Minister bent his ear to the holy mouth.

"Present this item," ordered the Minister. He pointed, and Nelius fetched the vial in question. The Treasurer, the red-haired man, lingered over the august shoulder of the Autokrator. He gazed at the vial, but I could see his interest was feigned. His real interest was clearly following the changing interests of the Autokrator.

"Explain your findings!" barked the Treasurer, taking over from the other Minister, who shrank back.

"May it please the Autokrator," began Vincius shakily, "our work is in the area of reproduction. We sought to find a way to enhance and expedite the human gestation period. We also sought to find a way to reverse and correct development, should it present as Unmale in the embryonic stage."

A very slight nod. It was impossible to say if it was of comprehension or approval.

"We have work to do yet, as we fell short of our goal." The air slumped a little with the open admission of failure. "B-but we came across an unexpected victory."

Again the slight flicker of a nod.

"Our work points to the viability of a human life gestated inside a vial."

"Solely in a vial?" demanded the Treasurer quietly. The Autokrator and the entire retinue stood mute while Vincius nodded furiously.

Ferrius the Toolist bustled over, joining the Triumvirate.

"I know this Family," he boomed enthusiastically. "This is Vincius and his lad Nelius. I've had my eye on these two." He laid a finger on his cheek, pointing to his eye.

"Let me see. Let me see." I noticed a scowl cross over Tiresius's face. Ferrius seized the vial for himself.

"Life in a glass!" he exclaimed.

"We are confident we can extend it, with the right conditions and research. Perhaps all the way to the point of viability," Vincius offered while the Imperial Toolist nodded appreciatively.

The Autokrator gazed at the two men. A moment lapsed. With the softest of sounds, he clapped his gloved hands together three times, a signal to the entire gathering to applaud.

"Gentlemen, the Autokrator has selected the Prime Dissertation!"

Vincius nearly fainted at that moment. Nelius ran to hold him up. In the ensuing fray, the Autokrator stood to one side, circled by Ministers.

Officials hovered near Tiresius, who carried the golden key to the Treasury chest that was carried along with the whole procession. He removed the gold medal from the ornate chest with extreme ceremony and turned to present it to Vincius. The medal was purely for show. The real prize was the money and the access to Imperial laboratories.

The Consort stepped forward to handle the vial. With all the attendants busy aiding the Autokrator, no one was left to attend the Consort but me. He handled the vial in his long, feminine gloves, peering at the contents curiously. I stood with my back to the wall, head down.

"This was life in here?" He'd asked me directly, and my breath caught. The Consort was never to directly address a commoner.

I nodded and whispered discreetly, "We suspended the process with chemicals to preserve the appearance at the moment we detected the failure."

He seemed to appreciate the information, though he paid scant attention to me.

"Incredible. Life in a glass. The wonders that men can accomplish," he murmured. For a moment, his eyes, dark and frank, met mine. I felt faint under the sheer amount of power the man exuded. "Have we met?" Memories flooded me. My throat swelled.

I shrank within myself and shook my head, terrified that he might recognize me by voice. I felt any word I might utter would lead to perdition. But the moment passed, and he moved away into the crowds at the behest of a Minister. Sometimes the eye does not see what is right before it.

At a word from a conductor, brass horns sounded a blast, and Vincius was called forward to accept his Beneficence.

In the very next moment, it was Nelius's voice that echoed through the chamber. "Honoured Triumvirate. I demand my accusation be heard."

The great room fell into a shocked silence. This was very irregular.

Nelius's words invoked a formal charge. He savoured the attention and milked the moment, sucking on his cheek. Once all heads swivelled around to him, he pointed a theatrical finger at Vincius.

Vincius lost his colour and stood, slightly stooped. No doubt he'd expected this day to come, just not today.

"I charge Vincius, my pater, blood of my Family, of gender crime."

25

Tiresius

THE WEEKS I spent riding to the Capital and escaping from my Family were the last real days of my youth. Everything that came afterward was toil.

After many days of dusty travel and saddle sores, I came at last to the so-called Golden Bowl.

This was the most fertile and prosperous valley in the whole country. All streams flowed here, those of water *and* money. All roads led here too. The glittering Imperial buildings lay just past the Golden Bowl, but I was still a few days out from the sight of their spires.

Money pooled here and was interbred, giving birth to taxes, interest, bribes. It amassed in the coffers of the Autokrator and flowed back out on a nod of his head to men and travails he found worthy. Many men flocked here like birds to a berry bush, hoping to feed.

I recognized the insignia of different Families on men I passed on the high road. I even fell in beside a military school group on an outing. Their chants and measured footsteps made me a little nostalgic for those old days.

The road became finer and smoother as I approached. Close

to the city, the large paving stones were set so close you couldn't have fit a piece of paper between them. They glowed white and hot in the mid-morning sun, polished by the transit of many feet. The closer I came to the city, the more people thronged the road, chattering tediously. By the time I'd reached the massive ornamental gates, I was surrounded by a press of people surging forward to engage in the many enterprises of the city.

As I passed through the gates, I craned my neck up to gawk at them. They were hewn from black stone, inlaid with semiprecious metals and layered with gilded floral and military elements. Autokrators of old with stern, farseeing eyes and heroic phalli pointed the way forward to the centre of the kingdom. The place I intended to mark as my own.

The next several months of my life were tedious, proving my worth against Autokracy-sanctioned academic entry papers. They were progressively difficult, but there were insultingly simple ones that had to be filled out first. I sneered at the questions, wishing for a way to speed through the process.

While I took the seemingly endless tests, I found a garret apartment where I could read books I'd hefted from the library. I studied laws and treaties and contracts. I sat for more monotonous exams. I was always the first to leave — catching antagonistic looks from other students still bent over their work.

I kept to myself, spending my free time in cafés frequented by older, endlessly yammering scholars rather than the loud gaming places people my age usually went. I always kept a pen and a notepad at hand. I grew fat with knowledge even as my funds grew thin. However, I did keep some in reserve. I knew there would be unpredictable expenses.

One expense was essential to my survival. Every man in the Autokracy was required to make his deposit at least once in a Public Consiliorum. The Autokracy needed Males, and Males were made by the seed of men planted in the dumb incubators of women. Sooner or later, I would have to provide proof of my deposit.

However, anything can be bought. I bought a clever Toolist and a willing donor, handsomely paid, of course. It wouldn't be hard to orchestrate; I wasn't the only man with such an affliction. Seed could be bought if you knew where to go.

The day the guards stopped me to ask for my papers and noted that I was derelict in my civic duty in the Public Consiliorum, I was unperturbed. I told them I'd been so busy with my studies it had completely slipped my mind. They steered me straight to the gates of the place to make sure I would fulfill my duty right then and there. I wasn't even bothered when I descended the steps of that rank-smelling place. I fingered what I'd long kept secretly in my pocket and felt secure.

At the gate, they took my information, and I was guided through a maze of cubicles to a stall with low walls. I was pushed into a change room where an overseer handed me a utilitarian towel. From there I was herded into an open stall and barricaded inside. I had not expected it to seem like a prison. Handling the towel, I was offended by how rough the cloth was. Even at school, they'd given us finer. I could hear muffled grunts and breathing all around. I waited on an uncomfortable bench. Not long after the door slid shut, a young Domestic, all but naked, came in through a low door in the back wall. This part I did not relish, but I had prepared for it.

I made a little circle with my finger, which she understood to mean "turn around." I fumbled around at her nether parts. Oddly, I was put off by the dim light in the place. Everything was so dark. But I could tell where the outer labia were easily enough. I worked her flesh, moving my fingers about to gain entry, and with my other hand, I extracted the vial I had in my pocket. One sharp squeeze of the finger-sized device, and the semen I'd purchased burst out of its hermetic seal and onto the tip of my prosthetic piece. I kept my eyes on the Domestic, but she remained immobile. Still, I sweated, fearing that I would be seen. As quickly as I could, I pulled my clothes aside, and I worked my prosthetic piece in. She made an involuntary noise that froze my insides. I gave some plausible thrusts, made a show of enjoying myself, and then pushed her away from me and raised my hand up above the low wall to be let out.

I scowled imperiously at the guard as he let me out.

"You should treat men better than this. This is ... animalistic."

He shrugged.

They would test her later to know that I'd left a deposit. For now, I'd have a record of performance.

I left two steps at a time, anxious to get back to my books. I did wonder if the hermetic seal was as good as the Toolist who'd wrought it for me had said it would be. Trafficking in human semen was a crime. Posing as a man was a crime. Being a man and not supplying the Autokracy with semen was a crime. The various binds I was in gave me a bit of a thrill when I realized there was a slim possibility that I could be the first Unmale in the Autokracy to become a pater.

26

Cera

NELIUS LOOKED AT his father with a twisted kind of victory painted on his features. Vincius looked furious.

"Boy, how could you? After all I have done for you?" he hissed at Nelius.

"Raised me in filthy Unorthodoxy, you mean?" sneered Nelius. "All you've done is make me long to live in a Clean household. You've poisoned my childhood with Unmales." He turned to address the crowd. "Vincius has been unlawfully living with an Unmale for many years." The hall had erupted around us.

A surge of men surrounded Vincius and held him in place. Tiresius was close at hand and seized the gold medal from around Vincius's neck.

"Congratulations on your exquisite work, but I don't think you'll be able to make use of this anymore."

Nelius was still yelling. I was sure that he was outing me as well, but I couldn't hear him over the din. Terrified, I looked for a way out of the chaos. There wasn't one. Men were crowded belly to back in the room. The Triumvirate were bustled out within a protective circle of armed guards. I saw a captain point at Vincius and then at me. Before I could even try to dart away, I was grabbed by strong hands and ferried off my feet through the room.

Nelius, Vincius, and I were paraded through the streets, while onlookers paused and gathered. It was starting to look like a Process — the walk of shame taken by those about to be executed. Men jostled along with us, roughhousing and shouting our crimes to bystanders. The crowd jeered back. Soon, they were throwing things at us. Nelius caught a stone in the temple.

Finally, we were thrust into a tiny, hot, airless room. There was barely enough space for the three of us.

On the other side of the door, men continued to surge and shout.

"What is this place?" I whispered to Vincius.

"This is where we meet judgment," said Vincius bitterly.

"Well, what do you expect, choosing to live together with a filthy Domestic, you hypocrite!" From the tone of his voice, Nelius was enjoying hearing the slur sink into Vincius.

"I should have sent you to the Consiliorum, boy. I didn't want to compound the crime of loving Eva with the crime of keeping our child at home. I only kept you back because your mother begged me to do it! And what thanks does either of us get?"

"I wish you had sent me! Do you know what it's like to have to keep a filthy secret like this? I wish I were a Consiliorum boy with a proper pater and no filthy incubos hanging about to contaminate me! What were you thinking, old man? Not only did you take one Unmale into your home to live and breed with — you let her bring in another one! And you let her do thinking work! No one in their right mind would go against Doctrine like that. It's disgusting. You're an abomination."

"An Unmale who outstrips your thinking at every turn."

"My way of thinking will prevail, Pater." Nelius spat it out. I felt the stiffness in Vincius's body as he contained his anger, but to his credit, he said nothing more.

27

Tiresius

"TIRESIUS OF THE Family Marnius, you are invested as Treasury Apprentice in the Imperial Treasury of the Supreme Autokrator. You hereby give your seal as a man to serve the Autokrator, your peers, and your countrymen to your very death."

Treasury Apprentice was a dreary thing to aspire to. It promised a life of anonymous labour in measly departments like Clerk of Chicken Feed for Imperial Flocks. To oversee clerks who oversaw clerks was no great accomplishment. The majority of those I'd graduated with were in flashy fields like military, law, science — anything but clerk. Not I. For me, the path was clear. The quiet, innocuous number-totter who one day holds the key to the kingdom.

The first year I spent at the Palace was as a Page. I learned the intricate network of pathways by running from wing to wing, carrying purses to those who had merited them or fetching the receipts of various lords. When I wasn't running around, I was reading the promissory notes I carried. I opened them all, devoured their contents, and squirrelled the information away for later use.

I avoided my peers and their pastimes — gambling, smoking, intercourse, etc. These pursuits were not for me. My counterparts knew me as an ascetic man who had no passions beyond work.

They tried to jostle me into friendships but soon left me to my own devices, finding me to be far too dry for their tastes.

Though it seemed like I was doomed to wallow in the lower rungs of the Treasury forever, I did rise by being as helpful and invisible as possible. I was an encyclopedia of information, whispering facts, numbers, and names into my masters' ears so it seemed they came out of their own heads.

I fanned my masters with admiration and coaxed them to become dependent on me. They could rest while I listened in chambers and read any documents that required their attention, summarizing what they needed to know. I made sure to be in the sphere of the Consort of the day, Gentius. As he rose in rank, I had my own smaller rise.

It was an eventful time to be in the Capital. The succession of Gentius was approaching. The entire Autokracy was about to shift. When it did, the chessboard of alliances would be thrown into the air and the whole game reset.

As a Consort waxes in influence, an Autokrator often wanes. His bills were passed less frequently, his favourite dishes were in shorter supply, his rooms were dustier, and his garments had a tinge of decades ago. Once upon a time, he had been lauded for being combative and insistent, a man of simple taste. Now he was considered argumentative and shrill but dull-witted.

When Gentius was still Consort, he was known to be deeply conservative, a man who lived fully within the bounds of Orthodoxy. He felt the Autokracy had strayed from its former purity. Increasingly, his star rose in the firmament. His witticisms grew funnier, and his observations elicited agreement. He was impatient to rule, as all Consorts are at the end of their ceremonial role. He couldn't wait to cast aside his women's weeds and take on the mantle of Patriarch.

By contrast, his son, Caelius, Kratorling of the day, was an unknown. It was whispered that he already seemed too rebellious to play the subservient role of Consort, to quietly bide his time at the sleeve of his Autokrator until his own Ascension came. Such rebellion was dangerous. Consorts had been replaced plenty of times throughout history. Sometimes, they were replaced in their beds as they slept. One Consort went to bed and a different one was there the next morning. Of course, in the heady old days of the Autokracy, they were just murdered and a quick replacement "found."

The pundits had opined that Caelius's career would be a wreck. He was one to watch carefully, I thought. At that time, his day was still more than twenty-five years in the future, and I had a lifetime to accomplish before then.

I found ways to give the up-and-coming Gentius access to revenue. Able to shower the men about him with gifts, he became wildly popular. This, in turn, sapped the Autokrator's popularity even further. It paved the way for my ascension handsomely. On Ascension Day, when Gentius of the Family Evander formally divested himself of women's weeds, dressed in his paternal regalia, and took up his sacred staff, becoming the sixty-sixth Autokrator, I stood behind him, holding a scroll naming me Imperial Treasurer. It was the second most powerful role in the Autokracy.

Gentius, in his fiftieth year, was tending to fatness. A good decade younger than him, I could have been mistaken for a far younger man. There was a decent chance I could outlive Gentius and automatically serve the incoming Autokrator. At the time, the years of power that lay ahead of us seemed like an eternity. How fast that time went.

When I imagined the Ascension and my role beforehand, I burst with strange pride, felt tears prickling in my eyes at the magnitude of it. On the day, it all felt appropriate. This was what I was built for. It was only afterward that I realized my original gender hadn't even occurred to me as I stood there surrounded by men. I had quite forgotten the temporary inconvenience of my birth. I was the Treasurer and keeper of the Autokrator's purse, and I planned to make the most of it.

28

Cera

IN THE DARKNESS of the cell, I kept my face pressed to the stone wall, taking slow breaths to calm myself. If I'd had my pocket goddess with me, I would have been turning her over and over in my fingers for comfort.

With the three of us crammed inside, the tiny space grew hot. Nelius was shouting demands that he be released since he was the accuser. Vincius hissed at him to keep quiet. Everything we said was being monitored. Everything could be used against us.

"Just wait for the outcome."

After a time, a clanging sound vibrated through the cell. They were banging on the metal door with spears.

A door flew open, revealing a lit corridor. The new light blinded us as we were dragged into it.

They chained us together with handcuffs and then hurried us down a low, pitched hallway that led up to a pen. A short stage, decorated with carved motifs of Fallos, heroes, and kings, stood behind us. Before us was an angry crowd of men, perhaps two hundred, tiered in raked seating. A harsh, thick beam of light hit us from an oculus above.

A judge appeared on the stage, to raucous applause. He sat on a small throne, meant to be a replica of the Autokrator's. His garb exaggerated his shoulders and arms, making him appear like a titan, though he was clearly aged. Directly over his heart, he wore a shiny medallion depicting the Autokrator's face.

"There has been a charge of Unorthodoxy, in extremis," he declaimed theatrically. This pleased the crowd. Nelius had his face beatifically turned up to the judge. He held his breath in rapture. "For which there must always be punishment to satisfy the will of the Autokrator and this realm." More cries from the audience.

"There is no defence to be mounted. The accusation of a free man against another is enough. But I am ordained by his Imperial Majesty, who derives his power from Bartolius the Just and from Fallos Himself, to whom we are all subject."

He stood and strode to the edge of the stage. From our vantage point, his belly protruded from under his embossed breastplate. He pointed at Vincius, imperious.

"Vincius, you stand accused by another man of Unorthodoxy. You are accused by your own son, which is grave indeed. You will be executed. But let me hear the words of the accuser so that I may determine the fate of your apprentice."

The crowd continued jeering, drowning out Nelius's statement. Nelius spoke louder and louder, until they yielded.

"August judge, I long to tell you everything! I wish to be clean of this Unorthodoxy!" The judge looked down on him. I noticed that under his beard, he too wore a black kerchief. He looked down on Nelius with a warm expression. Like a father might.

"Speak, boy."

29

Tiresius

OVER THE MANY years I'd acted as Imperial Treasurer, I always made a point of visiting the courts. It was important to know who had been accused of crimes and which crimes were wont to be pursued. After the madness of the Dissertation and the explosive accusations against the winning Toolist, I wanted to know more about this Vincius.

Men from any class were welcome to attend the courts, and they could appear as rough or well dressed as they pleased. I enjoyed the spectacle of such places. I mainly enjoyed it because I never missed an opportunity to show off my robes and station in public.

The courtroom was arranged like a theatre. It was an august space with wonderful acoustics, plush seats, and masterful paintings of the old Autokrators on the ceiling.

Onstage, a lone judge wore the insignia of the Autokrator over his heart to suggest that his power came directly from the leader, and he had an expression that said his life was an endless tedium. It was cultivated, I suppose, because what played out here was always a passion play. And the results were almost universally the same. Prisoners who entered through an iron door and stood in the glare of an oculus in the centre of the stage were thought to be doomed. The audience could see through the gnashing of teeth and pleading that came after judgment. People laid wagers on which response was likely. A lot of money changed hands in those seats.

As pleasurable as court was, I had serious work there too. I had to keep an eye on the changing whims of the citizenry. Something about this trio of unfortunates intrigued me. This obsession of the Autokrator's had started to blot out everything else, siphoning influence and resources in a perturbing way.

This Nelius lad simmered with hatred. And what cheek! To turn in his own pater! Vincius was intriguing, as well. He stood in his chains with a vacant, resigned expression. He knew what fate was ahead for him. A real shame for a man on the cusp of such achievement to be snuffed out. But such was the will of an Autokrator whose rule had to be followed.

What was more, I felt something was strange about that apprentice they had. Too scrawny and young, too scraping and shy. Something was off about him. How could such a socially inept lout be useful to an important Toolist? Unless the boy had colluded in the Unorthodoxy. I settled in my seat and pressed my fingers together, eager to learn more. The older boy was speaking.

"August judge, I am a sworn adherent of Fallos." Nelius clapped his hand to his breast. Others in the audience did so automatically. "I have been made to suffer the Unorthodoxy of my pater these many years. And only now, on reaching the age of reason, may I finally make the charge. May I finally be Clean. I beg that all of you good men gathered here today will follow my example. Pray earnestly to Fallos that the many wrongs we see being perpetrated are put right. Pray for the return of Bartolius to punish the wicked. Pray for the final extermination of Unmales, that we can do away with all Unorthodoxy once and for all and live as brothers in glory and peace!"

There was a pause. No one in the audience made a sound. The judge put his thumbs in his belt and sucked in a deep breath.

"Lad, you are the future we all aspire to. You shall go free." As he continued speaking, guards came at once and released Nelius. They led him away. For a moment, he looked back at his pater, maybe only then registering what he had done. But he turned, wordless, and went through a hallway out into the light of the street.

"Vincius, you will be executed in three days' time. Meditate on your sins until you are destroyed. And this boy. Does he have anything to add?"

The scrawny boy just shook his head and kept his eyes cast down.

"Very well, you shall go with your master. This is the Autokrator's justice."

I waited for the crowd to disperse. There would be new prisoners shortly. The Autokracy never ran out of those. I watched them lead the condemned away. There would be more to come with those two.

I planned it.

30

Cera

THE HEAVY DOOR they shoved us through shut out the clamour of the court.

We were led down one long hall, away from the courtroom. Out of the corner of my eye, I watched Vincius. He looked defeated. The floor sloped steeply down around sharp curves. These were the switchbacks that led to the prison levels.

The prisons housed many enemies of the Autokrator. Underneath the prison was the world of Below, where the Unmales lived. The proximity was by design. It reminded men that anyone who displeased the Autokrator could be relieved of their rights.

Few Domestics entered this place. A handful hauled away soiled linens, entering through the usual hidden passageways, but there were no Domestic doors, lest anyone try to escape.

Several levels down, we came to a row of iron doors. The guards picked one and forced us in.

The door slammed.

The moment we were alone, Vincius cried aloud, "I should never have raised him!" Veins stood out along his neck and temple. His skin flushed to the roots.

A sharp blow fell on the little window in the door. I drew my knees up protectively.

"Quiet in there! Or you'll be gagged."

"I stood on the brink of achievement, only to be thrown down by my own son."

Vincius drooped in his restraints.

"Vincius, I have helped bring this upon you. Nelius disliked me from the first."

"It is hardly to do with you. You heard what he said. He's planned this a long time." Vincius heaved a breath. "With me executed, he gets my shop. He gets his freedom. He's planned this since he was young. Against his own mother, even."

The alien word hung in the chamber and seemed to echo.

"Everything I've done has ruined everything for her. They'll search the house, oust her. Execute her. And our baby with her. Even if she were to escape them, where could she go?"

I looked up. Their baby?

Vincius smiled kindly. "I thought she would have told you. She's known some months. All in vain, now."

I swallowed this new information. "Many Domestics carry children during their work. The state always has use for another soldier or Domestic. Chances are, she could escape their notice and carry the child to term. If she can get Below before they find her."

"What happens to those children when they are born?"

"They are separated by gender. The boys are sent to nurseries. The girls ..." I wasn't sure how much I should share, but it seemed pointless to worry about it now. "While they are very young, the girls stay Below with us. A Domestic can do her work and leave her young with other Domestics. When the children are little older, Mams look after groups. At four, they are put to work."

"And you — have you had a child who was taken away to work?"

I grimaced. A smile full of regret.

"My only child was taken too. But earlier, and for a different calling."

"A soldier then?"

"We try very hard not to think about what becomes of them."

He nodded and fell silent, though I knew he wanted more. It wasn't personal interest in me, of course; he wanted to know what might become of his child with Eva.

My thoughts were interrupted by a fierce pounding on the door.

"Vincius!" Down the hall, guards were calling his name. His eyes filled with fear as the door scraped open. Two armed guards entered.

"Vincius," demanded one of the guards.

Vincius nodded curtly. One guard seized him, while the other read from a written charge. "You stand accused of gender crimes against the Autokracy."

"I do." Vincius was defiantly curt.

The soldiers grabbed Vincius under his arms and hauled him away, dragging his toes along the floor.

"Good luck to you, Dominius," he called out. Using my male name was his parting gift to me. It bought me a little more time.

31

Cera

I MARKED TIME in the cell by following the sounds outside. Food came at regular intervals. And a whistling guard with a lopsided gait walked past every twenty minutes most days. There were regular beatings in what I came to associate with morning. I listened keenly when I heard someone new being shown to their place, for these sounds were unexpected. I knew when to expect the door to open and a pathetic offering of stale bread to fall to the floor. I wondered who was making the rolls for the Domestics and the prisons, now that I was gone.

When my door opened, I immediately felt a mix of fear and interest. It could mean an extra beating or a new cellmate. Or death. They say danger and opportunity are close neighbours. Two guards heaved their bulk into the room and stood over me with weapons pointed, which seemed silly given my shackles.

"Give me a moment alone." A confident voice entered the cell from the hallway outside. A slight man entered the cell.

"I am Tiresius, Imperial Treasurer."

I blinked at him, unable to understand why a man of his station would be in my cell.

He waited with a serene expression as the guards clanked out. He stood with folded hands, looking like archaic portraits of the old religious leaders.

"Tell me, boy, how long exactly have you been an apprentice in the house of Vincius the Toolist?" He lingered on the word *boy* in a way that made my mouth dry.

"Is this to be my interrogation?"

"Since you are being questioned, it follows this is an inter-rogation." There was a haughtiness in the response. "I am the questioner. Answer: how long?"

"Perhaps six months."

"So not very long at all. Little enough time that you mightn't, nay, couldn't have known anything about Vincius's depraved Unorthodoxy at all. As a mere boy, in fact, you would have feared for your own life had you spoken up about his criminal actions."

"As you say." I hoped it sounded certain. But I had the feeling he didn't need my input.

"You're very fortunate. Once you'd graduated from your apprenticeship under Vincius, and the law is very clear here, you would have been compelled by the Law of the Autokrator to expose his crime."

I nodded.

"Before your apprenticeship, I assume you were a Public Con-siliorum child? Plucked out by Master Vincius to get your degree in his workshop?"

I considered giving myself a greater lineage, a child from the Imperial Consiliorum. But I felt embellishing the lie further wouldn't help me, and I nodded.

"Standard state education, leading to a Toolism degree."

He eyed me closely. "Do you have anything else you want to tell me about yourself? Anything at all about you, in particular, that you think I might find … interesting?"

I forced myself to meet his eyes. It was no mean feat, given a lifetime of being forbidden to look at men directly.

"Nothing at all, my lord."

"What impresses me, in fact," he said, a little conspiratorially, "is that you did hold your tongue. Tell me why."

I was being tested, for a purpose I knew nothing about. I assumed that the questions were related to whatever death sentence would be read out against me.

"Loyalty to Vincius, who took me in and taught me."

"Loyalty." He lingered over the word. "Very good, very good. Tell me, is there something special about Vincius the Toolist that requires loyalty, or is it a reflection of your character?"

"I would have to say a measure of both."

"How novel. You don't, I notice, offer Vincius up as a sacrifice and beg me to spare you because you were misled, tell me how corrupt he was, or how little power you had. In fact, you admit you adhered to a course of action of your own volition."

"I do."

"You have a narrow choice before you, young man. One of two options. The first, as you know, is very bleak: death. The other will have a measure of bleakness, and will inevitably end the same way, but could last quite a bit longer." He looked at me archly. He appeared to be checking to see if I might guess what my second option was. But my stubborn ignorance was my failing, and I saw a hot current of anger flash over his features. He quelled it right away, restoring his placid mask.

"You clearly have no idea, so I will be kind and tell you. You may be executed immediately, or you may choose to bind yourself to me and be my unquestioning assistant. Before you answer, know that I may well set you tasks that could kill you."

"I choose to serve you."

He put his waxen, hairless face close to mine.

"Good. Dominius, is it? Let us say from now that you are of the Family Marnius — my own Family. You're my charge. You're keen on entering the Treasury. Your time with Vincius we can keep between us. Complete secrecy and loyalty to me is your only path to survival. I've paid for your freedom out of my purse, and I can throw you back in here on a whim. I do not give second chances."

He rapped on the door, and guards came to release me from the wall. He marched ahead of me out the cell door and up the hall, the hem of his fine garment trailing over the stained floor.

We rose up the dark, sloping walkways until we came to a level with a window, and I saw the sky for the first time in ages. Outside, I limped to keep up as he forged ahead. We threaded through gracious parks and courtyards. Delicate bridges spanned staggering heights between hilltop estates.

At last, our path took us through massive, bronze double doors. Tiresius slid past armed soldiers stationed at each gateway, needing no more than his face to permit our passage. The guards shot suspicious glances at me as I scurried past.

On the other side of the bronze doors was an endlessly long hallway of smooth, blond wood. Arched windows stretched floor to ceiling, dappling the floor with buttery gold afternoon light. Opposite the windows I saw salon after salon after salon where cushioned seats and fireplaces beckoned. These were the private rooms of the Triumvirate. They were accessible only to the Autokrator, the Consort, and the Kratorling. And, apparently, the Imperial Treasurer, who led me still further.

32

Cera

I HURRIED BEHIND Tiresius as he swept through the maze of hallways. He cast a glance back at me as he ducked through a door near the top of a narrow tower. He kicked open another door that led to a series of rooms lined with books. Worktables overflowed with manuscript rolls.

He set a match to a table flame to heat water. He thumbed through a pile of sealed documents that had gathered under a slot in his door, then poured the boiling water into two cups. I stood at the window, where a slight breeze slipped through a crack between the panes. How sweet the air was up here, far from the fetid humours of the prisons. I lifted my face to the warm sunlight.

"A pretty view in the warm months," the Treasurer noted, throwing open the casement. "But a wicked wind blows cold through the windows in winter. I like to look down on the pageantry below, see who is walking with whom on the way to the Parliament. Wave down from my lofty tower. They know I'm a heartless bastard up here with my cold rooms and my frugality. It means few people come begging frivolity." He smiled at me indulgently, as though I understood everything he'd said. He'd gestured to one of the hot beverages he'd just made, in a flat-bottomed vessel. I frowned at it before picking it up.

"I have very little time for Domestics and am disinterested in being waited on hand and foot. Besides, I'm of the mind that even Domestics can be spies, with training. Imagine, with a little work, what you could get them to remember? Everything they hear and see while just standing there, holding beakers of wine for men who sit about, getting drunk, flapping their lips. No, sir, no wine for me. I keep more secrets here by making my own beverages and food, and with these cups that hold themselves up."

I kept my lips tight on my own views of Domestics, of course.

"Please, sit." He gestured to a leather stool. It was much lower than his own, I noted. Luckily, I'd had practice sitting with men. Lucky too that I had practice being subservient.

"Where is my companion?" I blurted. I reddened when I saw that his mouth was open, just about to speak.

He smiled that slow smile at me. One that I would learn meant he was being incredibly indulgent. He led me back to the window and sat easily on the edge, his drink steaming in the spring air. He patted the ledge near him. He swung one foot rapidly, as though he burned with unspent energy. I sat near him, balancing my own drink.

"I had hoped you might tell me that. It so annoys me when things happen that I am unaware of. You must learn to work hard to find out things that I can't. Sometimes people are inclined to hold their tongues around me, knowing exactly who I am. But around an unimportant young Page like yourself? Men love to talk about themselves. Their hopes and dreams. How they would have done things. How they plan to do things. I'm hoping you will learn to make yourself very useful in this respect." He crooked a finger at me in a paternal gesture I was sure would soon be repeated. "Now tell me," he asked, leaning close, "how is your numeracy?" He unfurled a scroll of confusing sums.

"I do not have a good understanding of sums."

"The numbers are merely a ruse."

"A ruse?"

"Numbers are comforting when they tally up the right way. And with a little sleight of accounting, they always tally the right way, no matter who's had their way with them." He set the scroll aside. "Aside from the numbers themselves, the Palace is a busy place. And I can only be in so many places at once. I'm invested with the Treasury, but the real currency here" — he stood and swept his arm over the vista below, populated with important men huddled in earnest groups — "is information. And who better to help me than a young lad already at risk of losing his life?"

He stood suddenly, leaning hard against me so the window casement pressed into the backs of my thighs. I struggled for my balance, and my cup careened down and smashed on the pavement below.

"Careful," he said casually. I think he smirked. "You're my protegé now. I will school you to be a broker of our chosen currency. Pay me handsomely and you live." Over the rim of his beverage, he smiled at me again.

Before retiring that night, he produced a small roll from under a table. By this I was to understand that my "bedroom" was a chilly corner of his library, crammed partially under a desk.

"I rise at five a.m.," he told me. "You will learn to keep my hours. Be sure, if you're gone for too long on an errand, that I'll find you. I have many eyes who will know where you are Above. If you are gone too long, I'll know you've tried to escape Below. And then woe to any Unmales you meet down there."

I digested this carefully. Was he suggesting he knew what I was already? Or that he thought me callow enough to hide in the Domestics' quarters?

His hours proved to be arduous. He rose and began work in his nightclothes, taking no food until hours later. He ate a pauper's breakfast — water and a bit of coarse gruel. After this, he dressed meticulously. I would even say obsessively. I made sure to remain unseen, but I couldn't help pausing to watch the slow, deliberate way he pulled on his trousers, fixed his buttons, arranged his scarf and robe. He would pick and pick at it all, folding, peering in the mirror at the effects, standing back, undoing and redoing the whole affair.

He was the first to appear at audiences, debates, the Parliament, or any other governmental event, arriving before nine in the morning. He worked all the rooms of the Capital, appearing everywhere he could. He worked in the Treasury itself for at least three more hours, then returned to his quarters to make notes on all the things he'd seen and done, which kept him occupied until past 11:00 p.m.

Years of baker's hours meant I, too, rose early, and the adrenaline of landing in his lair kept me breathless and watchful between flimsy snatches of sleep.

The first order of business the next day seemed it would mark the end of my very short career as a Toolist's apprentice. I was to be outfitted as Tiresius's Page, and this required what might as well be nudity. A Domestic arrived, laden with heaps of velvet and the tools of a tailor. Tiresius sat nearby at one of his several desks, nose already deep in ledgers.

"See to it you have a bath. The odour of the prison clings about you."

I panicked.

The Domestic gestured for me to disrobe, with eyes averted. I shook as I reached for the buttons that fastened my jacket, still alien to me, and worried at them without actually undoing anything.

"Get on with it," Tiresius called over his shoulder.

I sank to the floor; my legs didn't seem to be working anymore. Had I escaped from prison only to be exposed as a fraud and a criminal a day later? Tiresius looked at me through a pair of thick glasses he was using for reading. He pulled them off, annoyed.

"Let the damn creature do the work for you and get on with it." I cowered back, shaking my head slightly. I tried to come up with a plausible excuse. Nothing came to mind. "Do you think I don't know exactly what you are?"

"I ... my ... excuse me?" I stammered. Tears sprung to my eyes.

He marched over to me, robes swirling around him. His expression was tight. With a sharp motion, he wrenched off my jacket. I tried to keep it on by closing my arms around myself, but it was no use. He grabbed one of my wrists and pinned it in an awkward hold, faster than I could react. He ripped at the neck of my shirt and pulled it open, baring my chest.

"I know what parts you have under those clothes. Why do you think I chose you? Your 'disguise' is barely passable. As long as I choose to keep your secret, you'll work hard for me. Let the Domestic do the work, and we'll see that we make a better cover for you."

The Domestic reached bony, arthritic fingers up to receive the garments. She brushed the fingers of one hand against her palm, making the sign that she begged permission to touch a man, to touch me. I waved her sign away in acceptance, and then wondered at it. Not long ago, I'd had to make it myself. Now I brushed her off as insignificant.

As her hands passed over me, I wondered what she thought. For one moment, our eyes made contact. She knew what I was. Did she wonder how I'd gotten myself there? Was she jealous? Might she out me?

Down below, I might have taken instruction from her as a Mam. I might have confided in her about the men Above and their abuses during my workday. She kept her secrets to herself. I wondered if there had been many others before me.

I sat in my britches, reading ledgers and accounts, feeling self-conscious while the Domestic cut and sewed. Those gnarled fingers flew over the fabric, making fully formed pieces of clothing appear. A cap that would identify me as a Page with the Treasury. It had a band on it that gave my status as a neophyte, not that I understood it then. Key among my garments were a snug vest with extra reinforcement across the chest to hide my breasts and a long-sleeved shirt, likewise reinforced, and padded to give me a slightly burlier appearance. And, finally, breeches. They hung a little heavy in the front. I felt about the enclosure and found that a modest oblong beanbag had been sewn into the front to fill the breeches out.

I looked at myself in the mirror and found the Lord's eyes curiously fixed on me. It went beyond appraisal. He rose from his desk to stand behind me. In the mirror, I watched him smooth my epaulets and arrange the jacket, lingering on my arms.

"That band will get you entry to almost any room in the Capital. Dressed this way, you appear to be a young lad with no mind of your own ... Ah, to be young and anonymous. You hear so many interesting things when people don't think you've got any stake in them. Keep your eyes and ears open."

I waited until he was asleep to make use of my new "key" to the Capital. I slipped on my clothes, pulled my cap low, and slid out the door. I had to go Below and find news of Eva. Then, perhaps, I could try to find a way to get closer to the Child.

33

Tiresius

I REQUESTED A private audience with Gentius. We had become close enough over the years that, while behind closed doors, I was the sole person permitted to call him by his given name. It was an honour to be permitted such an intimacy.

The burden of leadership hung heavily on Gentius. While he had gotten fatter over the years, his temper and good humour had thinned. He suspected everyone in the Palace of conspiring against him. As a constantly soothing voice in his ear, I had always felt I enjoyed immunity from his suspicions. He was right, of course — many in his Cabinet were plotting against him. That was the price of absolute power.

I myself had wondered what twists of fate it might take for me to discover myself wearing the crown. I had to be careful about such thoughts. Being near to power is intoxicating and warps one's mind.

As I settled myself on a bench outside Gentius's apartments, I heard unmistakably, from within, the roaring of laughter.

"Just so, Gentius, just so. You hit it exactly."

Gentius? I could feel an angry blush heating my head and was forced to quickly compose myself. By the time the door opened, they found me sitting serenely, hands folded in my lap.

It was Ferrius who was being flagrantly familiar with the Autokrator. And the Autokrator was slapping him on his back. With them, too, was that boy of Vincius's, handsomely clad all in black. Nelius. Now he was wearing a Toolist scarf together with the cult of Fallos kerchief. I thought his look was inelegant. Why would these two be together, I wondered. Why was Ferrius scooping up bootlickers like this? It was unseemly.

Ferrius cast me a look as he exited with Nelius. Clearly, he felt crowded by my arrival. Nelius cut a bow, but the smirk on his face did away with any pleasantness.

"Nelius! Come." Ferrius had an edge to his voice.

"In time, Master Toolist." Nelius's drawl spoke volumes. He seemed to chafe at being bridled. He would not heel for long.

I heard the clink of gold in Ferrius's pouch as he walked away, and I had no doubt that this had been some sort of cabal between the three men.

"Tiresius!" crowed the Autokrator when I rose and bowed. "Good to see you."

"I am honoured to see Your Grace, Autokrator."

"Easy now." He closed the door on Nelius, leaving us alone. "We are old friends, are we not? Here you may be a little less formal. Now, there's some unpleasant business going around. I'm told that Fallos statues everywhere are having their erections lopped off by wicked vandals, and the cult enthusiasts are up in arms. We must make sure not to lose their love for us, old friend. Let us put our heads together about it."

I smiled in the sunlight of this cheerful thought. But my mind was dark: Ferrius and Nelius were weeds. Growing too fast. And too close.

34

Cera

I FOUND A Domestic hole fairly quickly. It was cunningly veiled with a leather curtain painted to make it blend with the stone wall. When I pushed on the curtain, a dank waft of air breathed out of the dark hole. I'd become so used to light that I felt a prickle in my throat at the thought of entering the darkness again. But I pushed through anyway.

It was awkward and painful to creep along the murky corridors. Twice, I walked into the low stone rafters. A Domestic had to keep her head down and feel her way along with outstretched hands. Tiresius's quarters were high up, so I followed the slant in the floor downward, spiralling with the tower's central staircase.

To get my bearings, I made my way to the Kratorling's wing. I knew the paths that led down from his quarters better than any others, and I had to find Eva as quickly as possible. But as I passed beneath his quarters, I felt a cutting yearning for the child. I pushed it away. I could not let my softness for him cloud what I needed to do first.

In time, my eyes adjusted to the dark, and I picked up my pace. The smell changed from merely dank to a chaotic mess of unwashed skin, baking bread, and the subterranean water that came from my old quarters. The smell of home.

I found Eva tallying the loaves in her kitchen, surrounded by ovens full of bread. She was round in the belly, beautifully bursting with life. My throat ached with the relief at seeing her again. What dark thoughts she must have had all these days with no word from me, from Vincius.

Upon seeing me, she fell to the floor, silent, awaiting instruction. I had forgotten my appearance. I crouched down and peered under her shawl.

"Eva, it's me." I pulled off my cap and opened my arms. She looked up, her eyes glinting wet with relief.

She stood, and I could see she was overwhelmed with too many things to say. She put both her hands against the small of her back, leaning into them.

"You're pregnant."

She nodded. Her eyes looked into mine, pleading, searching.

"They arrested Vincius."

She nodded again, her eyes brimming with tears. This was the news she'd expected. "Do you know what they —"

"I was with him in a cell. They took him. I don't know where."

She buried her face against my shoulder and sobbed.

"He'll be gone, then. Long gone." Her voice was unrecognizably hoarse.

I held her in my arms. Many nearby Domestics watched us, but I wasn't worried. They wouldn't question what a man was doing in a lower bakery.

When Eva had collected herself a little, she drew out a spare shawl for me to wear so we could speak without notice. We crouched near the light of an oven where we could see each other's expressions as we talked.

She grabbed both my hands and pressed them to her face.

"I can't believe you're here. How did you come to be free?"

"Free is not the word for it. I've been apprenticed again, in a way."

"Dressed as Male? Hiding in plain sight?"

"To a strange lord whom I fear. But somehow, I feel that he won't harm me. At least not yet."

"Oh God, Cera. Can't you get away?"

"He seems to have spies everywhere. You found out about Vincius's arrest soon enough?" She nodded.

"Some Domestics were serving at the Dissertation," she said. "They rushed Below after they saw everything. If they hadn't, I would have gone back without even knowing … back home …" She faltered on the last word.

"You're lucky, Eva. They took Nelius too."

"I know. I can't say I'm surprised. Sometimes I would see him skulking about when I was doing my predawn shopping. He was always with other Fallos cult boys. Loud and drunk. I thought they were just being young and stupid, but he must have been involved in something else. His pater told me not to worry. I can't understand it, Cera. My little child! I nursed him myself. His hatred toward his own parents seemed to grow as he quickly as he grew in size and strength." She shook her head. "My own boy reviles me. The looks he gives me …"

"I've seen those looks, Eva. He resented the secret."

"Even though he is my own son, and I love him, he has always hated me. When he was twelve, he began beating me and telling me I was a filthy incubo. Vincius never knew. I told him I was beaten at work. Maybe the Autokracy was right to take babes from mothers all along. Maybe the only good that comes out of a mother's love for her child is a selfish want in herself. Nelius could have had a happy life, but I made him live with us." She looked up at me, letting her hands fall uselessly to her lap. I sat with her and this grief for a moment. I couldn't imagine the pain. But neither could I imagine the luxury of having my own child close. She peered around her, looking for anyone who might overhear, and whispered, "There are even more gone since you left."

I looked at her blankly. "More?"

"Domestics. I think it must at least sixty ..."

"Sixty?"

"Shh. Yes. Things have fallen apart. We're working double shifts, some of the oldest of us doing work they don't have the strength for. We've lost a few of them to the sheer exhaustion. I've asked for new hands, but no one listens. They've searched several times in the last few weeks — roused everyone from their beds, counted heads, read arm tattoos. They wouldn't believe that we are losing Domestics, but I think they may be forced to now. We're all stretched so thin."

"I think they could stand to see more of it."

"Wouldn't that be sweet." We both smiled at the deliciousness of this thought. Leaving the men to stew in their own filth, empty bellied, like helpless babes.

"And you needing to slow down and rest," I said. "It is Vincius's child?"

"There's been no one else, thank god."

"Do you wonder why they haven't rooted you out?"

"And executed me?" She laughed bitterly. "I dream about it almost every time I close my eyes. In every dream" — she lowered her voice — "my one goal is to try to find a way to be delivered of this child before they kill me."

I put my hand on her belly. "May it not be Unmale."

"Poor little thing. May it not. I never really thought it would last with Vincius. It was too tenuous, too impossible. But I loved the idea that we could have one house, all of us together. That I could come visit the little thing. Almost every day like I did with Nelius. Imagine! It was a sinful thought to indulge in."

We were all guilty of wanting sinful things.

"But you!" She grabbed my hands, grown smooth since I had begun my new life. "Living free Above. What a thing."

"Not free," I assured her. "And I can't stay long. I don't want my new master to know where I am."

"Your new master?"

"Tiresius, the Imperial Treasurer. He is ... odd. Odder still, he knows what I am." She squinted at me, not following.

"What I really am."

"Of course. How stupid of me. The thought of you in his service makes me fearful, Cera. Stay down here. Leave the city tonight. Dressed like this, imagine how far you could go."

"It makes *you* fearful? I chose it over death. Maybe I chose badly. He says he has spies everywhere. Maybe even Below." She clasped my hand. I clenched hers back. "I'll leave whatever food and supplies I can come by inside the domestic door near his quarters," I promised her. "Spread the word." She nodded. Unexpected contraband could make an enormous difference if one were nursing, injured, or desperate enough to seek a permanent way to leave Below and servitude.

I made my way back up, toward the light, heavy with worry for Eva. For myself. For all of us. Even so, I had to scramble quickly to get back before Tiresius noticed my absence.

I was jolted from my thoughts by a finger jabbing into my eye socket. I heard a low shriek. I had stumbled into another Domestic. Neither of us could see in the dark.

Her thick fingers felt outwards in the familiar, wordless greeting that Domestics had for each other. But my clothes immediately identified me as a man, and the hands shrank back.

I was about to whisper that I was no man, but I stopped myself just in time. "Who's this, then?" A light was struck and went aloft in a fat cupped hand. It was no Domestic. It was Ferrius.

It took everything I had not to gasp. He grunted at me. "Clear the way, lad, I'm on Capital business, can't be interfered with. Bloody whelping Domestics wasting my time. Few enough of them where they are needed, as it is."

I doffed my cap and shrank back against the tunnel wall to let him push his girth past before I started upward once more.

"Out of my way, incubo lover." I froze back against the wall. Another man had pushed past me. Nelius's voice was unmistakable, as was one of his favourite curses. But him following the Imperial Toolist about? Below? Why?

35

Tiresius

THE MASSIVE DOUBLE doors of the throne room stayed shut unless the Autokrator Himself entered or exited. Today, they were open, signalling his presence. It was a tall, gilded room with a forest of phallic columns holding up a deeply coffered roof. Every surface was made of polished ebony. Incense drifted in a thick haze near the ceiling. Near the throne, a locked wrought iron gate was all that separated the Autokrator from stacks of gold in his vast Treasury.

"Tiresius, Imperial Treasurer," an aide announced at my arrival.

I gave my customary deep bow, priding myself on its grace. I knew for a fact that the Autokrator despised personal clumsiness. Gentius sat on a vast gilded chair under a golden canopy.

The Consort's smaller chair was empty. The Kratorling was there, however, playing in his seat at the feet of the Autokrator, oblivious to the world. Part of the Child's conditioning was to spend hours in these dour environments so he would eventually sop up the air of ceremony and gravitas expected of him.

The Autokrator looked perturbed. Out of the corner of my eye, I noticed my new Page advancing too far forward for propriety. I tried to stop the ignorant creature with a low gesture. Too late.

"Who is this you bring, Tiresius? Someone new. Are they known to us?" The Autokrator's ever-growing suspicion was evident.

"Truly, no one, Autokrator." While I smiled generously at him, behind my back I made a vicious hand gesture at my Page, bidding her stop. Melt back. Become invisible. Was I the only one who understood the value of invisibility? "You called for me, Autokrator."

"The Imperial Toolist is pressing again for funds. Why must we have to hurry you along to tend to these important matters, Tiresius?"

"Yes, Autokrator. Were it only a matter of hurrying, I assure you, everything would be done already. There are processes to follow before disbursing such vast sums to the Toolists. Besides which, I disbursed three cases of gold to the Imperial Toolist only a month ago, and these, at your urging, were struck from the records." I spoke from a bow and hoped I'd sufficiently disguised my contempt. Many other demands were made of the Treasury. Lately, none of them seemed as important to the Autokrator as his pet project with Ferrius. I noted the peevish look on his face.

"Perhaps I can offer an advance on the sum, here today, to appease him and ease your mind."

The Autokrator slumped over the side of his chair like a sullen child. Slightly less perturbed but still unwilling to let it go. But he opened a drawer in the arm of his throne and presented me his key to the filigreed gate. I took it, along with my own key, which I always kept on a long chain around my neck. I inserted both keys and turned them in opposite directions. As I selected a dozen wafers of gold, I was careful to let one slip into my sleeve as had been my custom these last five years. The tall stacks that remained were not noticeably diminished. I noted the official withdrawal on the huge ledger by the gate.

"I wonder when we might get a progress report on the Toolist's efforts, Autokrator? We are such benefactors to him. Benefactors are usually permitted a glance at the work in progress."

The Autokrator allowed himself an eye roll and accepted the wafers from his Page. He clinked them idly with his bulbous fingernails.

"He is ever evasive. This is a special project of Ours, Tiresius, and a great one ... Our Great Undertaking. And We assure you, you will celebrate its early successes with Us. Hopefully for years to come, old servant." I inclined my head as he glanced about the heights of the room. "We find Ourselves unwilling to leave Our position of service to the realm just yet."

"You are in perfect health and power, Autokrator. And many long years lie ahead."

"Don't you think, Tiresius, that a life is a very short time? Look how fast the last five years have fled. Imagine the things you could accomplish as Treasurer were We to stretch Our reign longer?"

"I confess, I do have an extraordinary imagination when it comes to such things." I had to be careful with my answer. What the Autokrator was suggesting was treason, even for him. To extend their reigns had been the heart's wish of countless foolish Autokrators before him. And those wishes had been met with blood, steel, and contempt. The reigns were not extended.

He smiled wanly at my reply. "We are gifted with the most imaginative Treasurer in history, then."

I bowed and took my leave, shuffling backward. One never turned one's back on the Autokrator. I was careful to look that my Page did the same. The fool was standing there, slack-jawed. The space was imposing. But it was the Child that the incubo stared at. She had even leaned forward a little, craning toward it. Inwardly, I was disgusted by the lack of focus.

I pinched her ear and towed her out the door with me, breaking whatever insipid reverie she indulged in.

Our first order of business was discovering what this money was for. Too many payments had been made without my knowledge. Worse, the Autokrator's circumspection of me was new and unwelcome. I would need to find out who had his ear now. And teach my new mouse how to listen.

36

Cera

THERE WERE FEW rooms in the entire Palace complex that weren't accessible by Domestic paths. The throne room was one of them. Following behind Tiresius, I stepped over the threshold into the grand space for the first time in my life. I was surprised to learn how familiar he was with the Autokrator. It seemed incredible to me that a man as well connected as the Treasurer would suffer my presence. It also seemed odd that a man of such power and access to wealth would have such mean habits such as making his own breakfast or living like a seedy hermit.

But what truly stole my attention in that hallowed place was the Child.

My child.

He had sat at the feet of the Autokrator, playing with a variety of toys. It was a chilly room, and he wore only a thin jacket. I wondered if he weren't cold. No one paid him the least mind. What if the Child was cold, I wondered. What if he was hungry?

I brought my attention back when saw Tiresius's hand angrily pointing at me behind his back. He was cautioning me. I forced myself to pay attention to what the men talked about. The Imperial Toolist. The money he required. Beyond that, I didn't know what he was talking about. I forced myself to remember the number of gold pieces. The way the keys worked. But my eyes strayed back to the Kratorling.

He was why I stood here in the first place. It seemed worth it, somehow, to live on the edge of discovery, risking death, to have a chance meeting like this. There could be more like this for me if I continued to live Above. I could find ways to be close to him over time. Watch over him. Care for him, help shape his life ...

I marked the deep annoyance that Tiresius expressed over the Imperial Toolist. It seemed almost as if Tiresius thought the money in the Treasury his own.

While the men concluded their business, a soldier fetched the Child and carried him away. I made the mistake of turning my back on the Autokrator and was rewarded with a cuff. Tiresius dragged me out by my ear. After seeing the Child, none of it mattered to me.

We returned to Tiresius's rooms. He took a meal standing up, drinking a beverage in one long draught. While I bent over my own food, he pulled a thick tome from the bookcase. I saw a glint out of the corner of my eye as he slipped a thin wafer of Imperial gold out of his sleeve. I lowered my head, taking exaggerated bites and watching through my lashes as he slipped the piece inside the book. There was a barely audible clink. He made a show of reading something from a back page and reshelved the book before hauling me off by the ear for more rounds of spying and networking through the Capital.

37

Tiresius

FOR DECADES, THE key to my plans had been to become the first Treasurer chosen by two successive Autokrators. This was no mean feat; new Autokrators always reshuffled their Cabinet Ministers. But I was also the youngest to ever serve the Autokrator. I was a careful accountant and, due to my squirrelling away funds, could offer substantial gifts to buy the love of the incoming Autokrator.

After my inconclusive audience with the Autokrator, I wrapped a gold wafer in an archery glove and carried it at my side down the west tower. Outside, after a nod to a nearby guard, a shiny autokinetic appeared, gaudy with silver filigree and emblazoned with the Imperial seal. Its pneumatic wheels glided noiselessly on the cobblestones. The Page gaped at its appearance, of course. I never used the privilege of a horseless conveyance lightly. Few people besides the Autokrator, the Consort, and the Kratorling were entitled to use them. Orthodoxy warned that if everyone were to have an autokinetic or easy access to computing devices, electro-currents, or running water, the hardworking fabric of our society would unravel. It would beget idle Domestics, unproductive farmers, and unmotivated merchants.

Of course, certain vital needs might qualify for mechanical transport — medical equipment, for example. But luxuries like allowing goods to flow in mechanical vehicles would throw too many Domestics out of useful activity.

We drove out the main gate and down the verdant slopes on the other side of the river that belted the city. The archery range was too damn far from the Capital to get there and back efficiently without using the autokinetic. Besides which, I felt taking carriages like common men was beneath me.

My Page sat on the low bench provided for a servant, gripping a handrail, eyes wide. I would have ascribed it to fear in others, but this was astonishment.

"We're meeting with the Consort. He is at the archery range today, with his bosom companions, his personal guard." I thought I noticed a nervous start at my announcement, but I continued the briefing anyway. "Remember, your name is Dominius. You are of Family Marnius — my own Family. They are a good, old Family. You failed as a Toolist, and you have no physical skill. It will make sense you came to me for training to eventually take Treasury exams. You are a Public Consiliorum boy, never met your pater, and have limited schooling. That will explain your general ignorance of the world."

"I have been taught some of the old poets."

This caught me off guard.

"When or why would a Domestic be taught such things?" I demanded, partly incredulous, partly jealous. It was *I* who had transcended my sex to achieve things. It took the shine off me if others had too. I mastered my petty thoughts to hear her answer.

"It was oral, of course. I couldn't read then."

"No. There is absolutely no need of the old poets. Hopefully, with all the other things you've learned, you know to keep your mouth shut. You will be mostly silent, charming when called upon, and you will listen. That is all."

Dominius nodded.

Watching through the curtains over the twenty-minute drive, I saw men stop to observe our passage, as they always did when I took out the autokinetic.

Fields rolled beyond the Capital enclosure. Close to the Capital, an astonishing acreage was kept clipped by flocks of sheep. Beyond, well out of sight of the Capital, the meadow gave way to farmland and, beyond that, wilds. Today, the fields were dotted with the men of the Consort's dedicated regiment. They milled over the archery grounds, at ease. Some were even shirtless in the brisk spring air, exercising, sunbathing. They wore their ever-present scarves, though, proud of their lifelong commitment to the Consort, ready to die for him over a trifle if necessary. They would follow him through his coronation and guard him as Autokrator, one day.

The Consort was a stark contrast to the bare-chested men. He was clad all in black. His long, hooped skirts bunched in the wind, and a tall, stiff lace collar framed his face. He was mid-aim, pulling an arrow back to his ear, squinting at a distant target. I wondered that the ruff didn't interfere. His concentration was spectacular.

Caelius was widely thought to be insubstantial. Men in Capital circles with their endless opinions on all things conjectured he would make a poor Autokrator. He was thought weak-willed, eager to please. Slow to anger but slow to action too. But these attributes made him an ideal Autokrator for Ministers like me with ambition: he was impressionable.

For some reason, he was wildly popular with his men, and due to their fanatic devotion, he was a kind of poppet for the military. They liked to see him wear their colours, as he did today. He wore a regimental jacket, cut to fit with his women's weeds, but in the bright red and deep blue the officers wore. In deference to him, his men chose to wear short skirts in solidarity with his weeds. Each Consort's regiment created their own uniform. When he Ascended, they, like him, would be thankful to dress fully as men again.

Here on the archery field, the Consort was jostled and cajoled and thumped, body to body, by muscled men. They communicated in grunts. The whole thing was tedious. I wondered why they didn't just bypass the archery field and fornicate instead.

"Consort, how good to see you taking activity with the men in this fresh air! Your men certainly seem to like it …" I gestured to them, oiling and flexing in the sun like a flock of popinjays.

"The air does me good when I feel poorly."

"Consort, you must watch your diet. I have a man who picks me fruits and meats from the same farms that supply the Autokrator. Nothing but the best. And you know: Strong body. Strong mind." I enjoyed the feeling of largesse. I liked to think I was known for my exquisite taste and my ability to bring in delicacies. And the state purse, of course.

He smiled broadly to see me. My gifts had become very welcome over the years. I slipped the golden wafer into his grip when we shook hands, and he embraced me. He never questioned my generosity. Those in power never question the many small gifts they receive. One gets used to being given everything very quickly.

My Page dawdled nearby, and the Consort pointed.

"You've got a new one, Tiresius." He squinted. "You seem to go through them quickly enough. Whatever do you do to them?" We both laughed.

"Dominius." I pushed him forward a little.

"Dominius," said the Consort. "How old are you, lad?"

Wisely, no answer was given.

"He is seventeen, Consort." Dominius made a decent bow. The Consort frowned then, looking hard at the Page, who stared at the ground. I found it curious; I hadn't seen overt displays of introversion before. This seemed more like avoidance.

"He is small for his age." The Consort peered closely. "Have we met?"

"I was an apprentice Toolist, Consort. I attended the Dissertation. But I was let go from my post. There was ... trouble."

"Of course. I remember that. I like to think I never forget a face, but God knows I see enough of them every day. Still, it seems more than that ..." He paused, looking a bit closer. He grabbed Dominius's chin. She stiffened but met his eye. "Are you from Family Briar?" That someone of his stature would guess one of the most venerable Families of all should have been understood as a great compliment.

"Yes, in fact."

She took the compliment in stride, rolling it seamlessly into her backstory. I masked my astonishment that she would flout me so casually. And that she did understand the significance of the compliment he'd paid her.

"Thought so. You remind me of someone I knew. You've got the old bearing. Here. Would you like to try?"

We both looked at the bow he offered, made expressly for a Consort. It was a menacing thing, strung taut, sleek and compact, matte black.

Dominius fumbled with it, holding it all wrong. I was embarrassed but said nothing, allowing the Consort room to react.

"A little higher. Grip it here, turn your wrist. Firm but flexible. Your other hand here." His instructions were sound, but the draw was weak and useless. The arrow flew wildly off to one side, well short of the mark. The Consort laughed, and so we could too, relieved. The Consort took the bow back, drew, and dispatched several arrows. They flew straight and true, the work of an experienced marksman. "I might dress like a woman, but I keep myself fit under all the frills." He winked.

This, here, was the laxity I disliked in him. Winking at a common Page. It was unseemly. I'd have to inure myself to it when he became Autokrator. At his gesture, someone came running with a smaller bow for the Page. It looked like something a child might use. Her second attempt was better.

"It's no good, a young lad like this being inept at the bow, Tiresius. Every man in the kingdom should know his way around one."

I inclined my head. "I know I could still take up a weapon if the Autokracy needed it, thanks to my schooling." It was true. I fastidiously kept up my own training.

"Exactly." He turned back to Dominius. The affection was clear. "Shall we continue? We could have you in the regiment, if your master would allow the time."

"I left my bow in the car. If you don't mind?" I said, making up excuses. Excuses to allow the chemistry to continue. I left the Page with the Consort. My level look at her said: Listen. Learn. And report back.

38

Cera

AS UNEASY AS the Treasurer made me, I was more uncomfortable alone with the Consort. I feared I would misstep at any moment. Saying as close to nothing as possible as I attempted to aim the bow was my only cover. Tiresius had marked it when the Consort said I looked familiar to him. How well I knew the Consort — the shape of the inside of his elbow, the heat at the nape of his neck, the crest of his hip bones.

Memories of him were one thing. His presence in broad daylight was agonizing. The shape of his eyes when he smiled. The sweep of his eyebrow. The way he leaned in as he grew interested. I felt all the old warmth. I needed to look away.

I turned, pretending to watch Tiresius walk to the autokinetic, and suddenly, the Consort put his hand on my shoulder and leaned heavily upon me. I had to tense myself to stand up under the pressure. I looked up at him and saw his eyes were closed tight.

"My apologies. I have these ... moments ... Feel like everything ... is upside ... down."

I looked at him. He seemed suddenly pale, almost translucent against the vibrant green meadow. He opened his eyes, blinking rapidly. His own Page rushed up, and the Consort asked him for a vial. I noticed some Domestics squatting nearby, almost camouflaged against the grass. One hurried over with a beverage. After a few moments, he breathed deeply, stood, and we resumed the practice. Once again, he released a volley of arrows, competently finding his mark.

"Tell me, what manner of man do you think your master, Dominius?" he asked casually as he aimed.

"A remarkable one. Brilliant. Disciplined."

"But a strange one, no? I'm not one to talk," said the Consort. "A man condemned to decades in Unmale clothes. It's so silly when you really think about it. Who could have invented such a thing?"

The words came out of his mouth so casually it almost didn't seem Unorthodox. But to suggest that hundreds of years of tradition was "silly" was blasphemy, wasn't it?

"There are days I want to pitch the whole thing. Let someone else be Consort. Let someone else be Autokrator. I'd rather be running around in the grass and the muck in the company of some good men, rather than all this frippery." He tossed his empty quiver on a table nearby and drew off his long kid gloves.

"Have you lived that thought through in your mind, Consort? Give up all this?" He looked surprised to hear me speak again.

"I have. That's no crime. Thinking it through."

"I mean no offence. I've met people who have done even more than that."

"None taken. Are you saying you consort with criminals, young Dominius?" His tone was playful.

"I've known criminals. I believe we all have."

"They say one in fifteen men keeps an Unmale at home, you know." He said it with a kind of delicious glee.

I looked at him and kept my face blank. "Perhaps even more, I've heard."

"I wonder sometimes if the early Paters got it wrong when they set things up this way. Didn't they know the more they force people into a mould, the more they would squeeze out around the edges?" The Consort was asking me to defend the system that had enslaved my gender. I swallowed.

"I don't think they thought people would fight Orthodoxy," I said quietly.

"Why, Tiresius! You're back!" I jumped, hearing Tiresius's name. "Your Dominius has shown some small amount of improvement. You'll bring him again?"

"As you wish, Consort."

My odd master hurried me away to the vehicle and peppered me with questions the moment the door was shut.

"What did he talk about?" Tiresius was greedy for information.

"The Founding Paters' wisdom. Or lack of it."

"In what sense?"

"Making things the way they are. Forcing people into moulds. He chafes at his station."

"Seditious. He should be more careful. What else?"

"He wishes he were not in women's weeds. Or in line for the throne."

"How do you know?"

"He spoke of being condemned."

"Anything else?"

"He felt unwell."

"How so?"

"Dizzy? Faint?"

Tiresius lapsed into silence. As we pulled away from the range, I could see the Consort being helped onto a horse, his skirts in the way. Doing my master's work meant that I had also done the Consort a wrong. I regretted it. I wanted things to be as they had been. When it was just us, alone in a room.

As Tiresius pondered, I looked about the vehicle. How many women had ever ridden in one of these remarkable machines? Looking at the countryside passing by so quickly outside made me queasy. Inside, it was richly finished. The tinted windows allowed us to see out but protected us from view.

There were bins filled with fruits, biscuits, and candies. Tiresius saw me eyeing them and gestured I should take some. I filled the deep pockets of my Page jacket. Eva and others Below would give anything for such delicate morsels. I would hide them inside the Domestic door as I'd promised her.

The autokinetic laboured up the incline to the massive bronze gates of the city. The immense arched phalli cast a long shadow in the late afternoon light. Foot traffic choked our passage. Men walked freely, alone and in groups, while Domestics crowded against the walls, trying not to touch them. A line of naked men and Domestics were driven down the centre of the road by the whips of burly guards. The prisoners were chained one to the next with heavy irons on their necks and hands. They were flanked in the procession by soldiers.

Tiresius looked up mildly at the commotion, arching an eyebrow.

"They've not done a Process for a while. High time for one." Processes were the dire final march of condemned criminals. "I suppose that could quite easily have been you among them."

I looked out the window, desperately. Were there were any familiar faces among the condemned? I expected Vincius to be among them, but I didn't see his tall, sloping frame. I did see a slight, rounded woman with wavy, light-brown hair. My heart froze.

The figure turned. It was not Eva, and I could breathe again, though I felt wracked with guilt that some other woman's horrible fate was my relief.

These unfortunates were guilty of various kinds of Unorthodoxy. Their sins were written on their flesh: Unmales disguised as men; men choosing to pass as Unmales; worse still, men and Unmales who chose to consort with one another outside of Imperial Mandate, like Vincius and Eva. It was always shocking to see both men and Unmales publicly unrobed, heads fully visible. Both genders looked pathetic without their vestments, stripped of identity, value, and status.

A few men, fully clothed, were tacked onto the end of the line. These were the political prisoners, also headed to execution.

The rest of the roiling in my gut was caused by the knowledge that at any moment, my master could send me to the same fate. Even if I were able to escape him, it seemed inevitable.

For some reason, this brought me back to thoughts of the Child. I cursed myself for thinking of him at all. I cursed the events that had driven me out from Below. I could still be kneading bread down there. In darkness with my own kind. In relative peace.

The brown-haired woman looked my way again, her face collapsing under the weight of her despair. I looked away, scorched by the sight of so much suffering.

Ahead of us, a large, black conveyance rolled along, horseless like the one we rode in. It was caught in the same gaggle of onlookers. It was sleek, with impenetrable metal sides and curtained windows. I couldn't imagine what dark purpose it must be for.

Our vehicle came to a sudden stop, blocked by the Process, along with the black caravan just ahead. I watched as the soldiers herded the prisoners into a tight circle. A scaffold stood ready. There were crowds choking the streets of the city in anticipation of the Process.

The door of the van burst open, and a black-clad youth stood up to shout at the Process participants for blocking his path. No one paid him any mind. After standing and glaring, he flopped back down sullenly and slammed his door shut.

In quick order, the political prisoners were walked up the squeaky wooden steps. The executioner bounded up behind them. Judging by the way he was greeted by the crowd, he was well known. The blocked van partially obscured our view, but the sound was clear enough. The scaffold creaked when a Male prisoner came forward. He gave a sharp cry as he was pushed to his knees. The executioner bent his head forcibly over a stump and raised his cleaver. He struck with a meaty thud. The head fell, knocking against the boards and then thudding wetly onto the cobbles below. The work moved quickly; the sounds repeated. As the last of the four men fell, the black caravan was finally able to move, as could we.

The remaining Unorthodox were flagellated down the street. Their path was long, allowing plenty of just Males to cast jeers and insults. The spectacle continued with the shearing and ritual burning of their sexual organs before the roaring crowd while public denouncements rained down. Only then were they be beheaded. The momentary shame of public denouncement followed so swiftly by eternal death made it seem a waste of time for the guilty.

The van turned to the left, its path frustrated by the crowds. The driver nosed forward, but too many people clogged the area. A fistfight broke out amongst a group of men. Sticks and bottles followed fists, and guards raced in from every side to beat down the brawlers. One guard gave the van a sideways glance and slammed his sword hilt into the hood, leaving a satisfying dent, but our autokinetic was able to slip by on the right.

The gates leading up to the Palace were swung open by unseen Domestics, and the autokinetic glided inside to peace and safety.

39

Tiresius

THE FIRST DAY of the Festival of Fallos dawned, a public holiday. As a result, there was no Parliament to attend, no Imperial audiences. Instead, crowds were entertained by the scintillating horrors of another Process. Screams and the smell of blood filled the air. Fallos's Festival was always a heady time.

The Autokrator would be about the city in His sedan, holding the Kratorling for all to see, assuring the world of the ironclad succession. It was a day I always looked forward to. Offerings of coin and written vows were left at the feet of massive ithyphallic depictions of Fallos throughout the country.

The greatest Fallos statue was found at the baths, which were sacred to him. Guards with torches forever stood vigil there. A good thing, because lately Fallos statues were regularly vandalized. The heads and the erections were knocked off. As if this weren't deplorable enough, shrines dedicated to a hideous, squat, fat woman were springing up, even in public quarters. Typically, they were crude paintings or figures made of straw. Crews of Domestics were kept busy destroying these shrines.

Dominius attended me, close by my heels. We were heading somewhere I knew the Consort and his men would go on a holiday. On Feast Days, it was typical to take exercise early, the more vigorous the better, followed by military games and sport. From there, to walk and socialize in public squares, where the air was thick with smoke and roasting meat.

As the day wore on, the parks and squares would empty as men retired to lounges where wine was abundant.

I chose a costly, loose robe suitable for my high position. It broadened my shoulders and accentuated my long legs, which I felt were my best Male features. Beneath the robe, I had a specially fashioned mesh garment, shot through with gold. It masked the scars on my chest and permitted a view of what the doctors had fashioned for me, without spoiling the ruse.

I led Dominius through pleasant, winding garden paths to the baths, following the soothing burble of water fountains and wind in the leaves. The air was scented with a vapour of cedar and salt. Men in robes lounged outside, running fingers through wet hair. Their flesh was hot and their faces red. Men came here to bathe and to fornicate in equal measure.

I led my charge down the wide steps into the winding corridors below. I skirted the ritual bath. Skipping it was Unorthodox, but I was never questioned, nor would I have allowed it. Who was to say I hadn't bathed earlier? The key to getting away with Unorthodox behaviour was wrapping myself in indignation and entitlement. Men were such sheep.

The Page's tread slowed behind me as we passed the pool. It was a shimmering golden basin sunk in an onyx-clad room. The water appeared mysterious, viscous. Men of all types — muscular, rotund, tall, stocky, timid, cocksure, grotesque, and poetic alike — bathed in the water. The light reflecting off their wet flesh made them seem gilded, godlike.

From here, we joined a languorous crowd, moving deeper within the maze of the space. In dim rooms, disrobed men kissed or whispered or wrestled. They drank wine straight from ladles at ornate urns and fornicated on the couches. Against the walls. On the floor. There were Unmales too, naked but hooded. Their presence was tolerated for the sake of those who preferred the Unmale form. The real point here, though, was the glorification of men and the adoration of one another. The early Autokrators believed that the purest love possible was between creatures of rational intellect with a sensitivity to poetry and culture, science and politics. How could Unmales, incubos, be sensitive to such things? Who could possibly love an Unmale? The men who indulged in the oddities of Unmale love for pleasure were thought of as crude throwbacks. Unthinking rubes.

I was not unknown at the baths. My status brought me some renown. I'd come, over the years, to find what pleasure I could — sometimes braving the risk of discovery to feel hot lips on me or to run my hands over strong, beautiful bodies.

I did not love women. I think this was because I shared the contempt Males did. If they couldn't better their situation through willpower, they held no fascination for me. I did not love men either. After a lifetime under their wills, their fists, how could I? Still, something deep within my mangled, edited body responded physically more to the Males than the Unmales. If I was honest with myself, alone in my room I felt more pleasure thinking about channeling power than I did broaching touch or trading fluid. What a mess people are, with their damp spots and trails. Still, some glimmers of desire persisted. I pursued them out of curiosity more than real need.

If I did find myself with a man, I always reached briskly for their groins, which was to keep their wandering hands away from my parts. I brought them to the brink of pleasure with my hands and my mouth and found pleasure sending them into the abyss. Men talk of the power of release, but they seem more helpless than babies in that moment. More vulnerable to attack than at any other time. It occurred to me that the ideal time to assassinate a man would be at the very moment of orgasm.

Still, I did covet that release myself. I wanted my pulse raised, my breath quickened. When I tried, though, my mouth flapped open and closed, and I struggled toward something that crested but would not break. I myself could not open. I tried all the means of release with men, turned over, backside out, upside down ... all intolerable. It put me in mind of the old days before I was Tiresius. In the days when the taste of them in my mouth made me ill. If I could have bought myself a working cock, I would have ridden the biggest of them to the ground, listened as he pleaded and moaned, defiled and diminished under me. That thought sometimes brought me close to something like release.

The fact of my injury was widely known, preceding me everywhere in whispers, as it had my whole life. My partners didn't fight when I stayed their roaming hands. My reassuring bulge was there, if frustratingly inert. Sometimes I couldn't tell if it was more frustrating for them or me. They seemed to understand my coy outfits, which were orchestrated to reveal yet conceal. No doubt they put it down to the shame of my injury. Some scars are heroic. Others invite disgust. I was an unfortunate monster, graced with intellect but doomed never to find pleasure.

There had been companions of various sorts over the years, blurred by frustration. The dalliances were less heady than the thought of pushing an agenda through Parliament or warping the Autokrator to favour some new protegé of mine. I could penetrate my partner after a fashion, but my own false member communicated no pleasure back to me. My original sex, walled up, spoke from within, but in a language I no longer remembered.

Some of my past companions, like my new charge, were those extremely rare Unmales who hid in plain sight. These were favourites of mine, though they were explosively dangerous to cultivate. Either one of us could be found out, which tended to steady the relationship. They were doomed, short affairs, though. I'd sacrifice them in order to pursue my greater goals. Another always seemed to come along, as was the case with Dominius.

My purpose in bringing Dominius to the baths was explicit. I'd chosen her, with her barely passable Male cover, to fascinate the Consort. His proclivities were still a mystery, but I had heard he preferred Unmales.

We found him deep within, lounging on a bench, clad only in a towel, in the Imperial enclave. He was as fine a man as any. It was said he had a great fondness for the baths, where he could shed his women's weeds and the pretense of his position. While he conversed, men from his personal regiment indulged all around him, flesh on flesh, muscle stacked against muscle.

Though my Page hung back, the environment had clearly worked on her senses. There was fear on her face, and curiosity. As I watched, I could see her eyes fall away but then wander back, taking in all the men twining about one another. Maybe her years as a Domestic had not turned her fully against the idea of men?

I turned to face her.

"Are you uneasy?" I ventured. She shook her head, utterly unconvincing. I moved slightly closer, and she stood her ground. "Are you ... moved?" She looked at me. It was a moot concept to her, I suppose. So I ventured further. She fixed me with her eyes and said nothing. She did not approach, nor did she pull away. I leaned in and put my mouth on hers. It was small but plush against my own thin lips. I was hungrier than I expected, so I took more than I shared. Then I stood back to survey the result.

Slight shock. Wariness. No unleashed passion. Well, it had been worth investigating.

"You've brought young Dominius then, Tiresius."

She had shrunk away, spared rejecting me by the intrusion. I was unmoved. Sometimes it was pleasant to pepper the master and protegé relationship. But by no means was it necessary.

The Consort, taller than I by a head, joined us. "Are you two ... joined?"

"Not at all. Dominius is too like an Unmale for me," I assured him. He kissed me perfunctorily on the lips, as men typically did here, in spite of their personal preferences. It was a sign of respect. Faint stubble under his carefully maintained face bristled against my thin flesh.

He stood and turned to the Page. She shrank back, knowing that he would do the same to her. There was a charge in the air between the three of us as the Consort stepped into her space. He tilted his head down and kissed her mouth. A mouth he thought belonged to a boy. They both started back, as though shocked by the shifting energy, and regarded one another. The Consort broke the moment with a hand touched to his mouth, as though it had been burned, and an easy laugh.

"You are my guests," he told us, indicating his personal enclave. He stepped away, a study of ease in his frame, but paused. "Tiresius, I am invited to my pater's table tonight. A small affair. You should join me."

This was a thickly packed offer. First, the Autokrator was having a dinner I didn't know about, when the tradition had distressingly fallen away lately? Second, I had to hear of it from his son? This made my neck prickle with anxiety. But at the same time, his invitation carried weight. As the sun began to set on the Pater, it would rise on the son.

"It would be my honour." The Consort smiled indulgently.

"Don't be too honoured. I don't expect it will be much fun."

He ignored us after that. I could tell, however, that he was tracking us ... tracking *her*.

I removed us with indisputable courtesy. "My lord."

Demonstrating that he could not care less, he barely registered this, which encouraged me greatly.

My plan had succeeded.

40

Cera

I WAS BESIDE myself with worry as we hurried away from the baths. Tides swept in my stomach, my head felt enormous, and I could barely feel my extremities. Only once we'd reached a low hall in the East Wing did I speak.

"My Lord Tiresius, why?" I couldn't conceal my anger. "Do you have a death wish for me? Do you wish to be found Unorthodox? How easily they could have found me out!"

Tiresius put a steadying hand on my shoulder. As the warmth leached through the fabric to my body, I had to contend with the fact of the kiss he had given me. What was the intent? Was my servitude supposed to engender lust? What a thought. As if I'd ever had a choice about it.

"My actions were carefully calculated." A strange look came over him. "And you are as yet too useful to be outed by me."

"Calculated? How easily any man could have grabbed me, even by accident, and quickly discovered —"

"You were under my protection the whole time. No one would dare impose on the Treasurer."

He grabbed my hand, brought it to his pelvis, and pressed it there. "Do you doubt me?" I shook my head.

I froze, unsure of what he wanted. The old habits were still fresh in my brain. Domestics deferred in action and thought to the will of men. I felt myself go limp.

He looked both ways down the hall and pulled open his pants with a clinking of buckles. His robe open, his fingers tore through the golden mesh of his garment. He had a strange, misshapen thing tacked on his body. He ... he? ... grabbed my hand again to feel. The appendage was cool and lifeless. Unlike any I had seen or touched before. He had no testicles ... And the scars on the chest. There were two of them, slanting away from each other, symmetrical. Tiresius replaced the gown over the torn fabric and hoisted his pants back up.

"You're ..." I couldn't say it aloud.

"Unmale? Did you not suspect before? That I am Unmale as you are? Well, not quite." Tiresius seemed gleeful and spoke through bared teeth, like something feral. "Isn't it a delicious slight to all of them? I've lived this way nearly my whole life. Only a few have ever come to suspect me, and those I have dealt with. Very quickly. I know my way around this pit of vipers, and I know how to charm them. As much as I've always wanted to best them at their own games, their own power, I've wanted one other thing besides."

"What else do you want?"

"For someone else to know my secret and marvel with me at the enormity of my ruse. And to mock them for their credulity."

I stared at this strange creature before me. I could tell he wanted something more from me. Adulation. Admiration. I could feel Tiresius willing me to admire him ... Instead, I felt only confusion.

I took a step back, and I felt the charge of the moment fall, like a leaf tumbling to the ground. Something between us snapped, and the fire in Tiresius's eyes died down a little. That cool mask descended as Tiresius methodically clinked his buckles back together.

His mouth wore a slight twist. I felt at once that I had passed a test and failed at something else.

"I dine with the Autokrator tonight," he told me, his waxen face as blank as a statue's. "See that you are back at a decent hour."

Though I remained completely under his … her? … thumb, the admission created a sort of balance between us. From that moment, I could just as easily have outed Tiresius as Tiresius could me. Though with my poor standing, it would be a battle to be heard fairly. In an odd way, I wondered if Tiresius didn't want them to know. Maybe the pretense had grown tiresome?

I wondered how one could live in secret for so many years, avoiding intimacy with anyone for fear of betrayal or misunderstanding. It seemed worse in some ways to be misunderstood. To be betrayed was a simple enough affair: the gnashing of teeth, the weeping, and the execution in relatively short order. But misunderstanding, not to be truly known inside and out by someone else, seemed a greater curse.

I placed my hands on my own belly. I could feel my pulse in the hollow between my hip and the round just below my navel. For the many harsh things that came with being an Unmale, I felt lucky, somehow, that I had once carried a child.

Uncomfortable, drawn out, tedious, and bloated as I had felt for all those months carrying my child, it felt like I'd accomplished something in a life otherwise full of invisible labour. There had been a child. I'd completed something. And then they were done with me. But what I had done had gone on after me. Perhaps to be someone who could change things, make them better.

There could be nothing like this for Tiresius. Though a pregnancy could be passed off under all that cloth, I suppose. But Tiresius seemed even less likely than a Male to be inclined to such messy inconvenience.

My milk had come in shortly after the child was taken, causing my breasts to burn with a fire that overheated my whole body.

Once I was down below, I was relieved to try to nurse another Domestic's child and make use of the milk. The infant struggled to feed. Desperate, and in pain, I coaxed the latch. I grew sore, chapped, delirious, and even bloody. The infant slept and fed while I nursed and wept. But at least the pain in my body numbed the hurt in my heart and mind.

The thought of Tiresius giving over to something like that was laughable. Tiresius had nothing left to spare a growing child.

I fingered the stolen morsels I'd hidden in my pockets, destined for Eva.

I slipped a light shawl over my clothes before leaving the tower room, preferring to be anonymous. It felt too jarring to be in the corridors Below dressed in menswear, and this way, any Domestics I encountered would be more at ease. I felt my way through the lightless, closed paths, but I did not meet anyone. That was strange. Domestics worked late and rose early. This was when the unseen work was carried out. Bedpans and ashes, linens and clothes, dishes and kindling all appeared or disappeared as if by magic.

Only near the kitchens did I begin to see Domestics hurrying about their work. I found Eva moving at a relentless tempo in front of the ovens, wearing a heavy leather apron that ballooned over her growing belly. She bent, opened iron doors, stoked, shovelled fuel, closed, rose, took her baker's peel, shoved, pulled out rolls, twisted, retrieved proofed rolls from a warmer, shoved, and then repeated the whole process at the next fiery maw without stopping.

She was beaming, happy to see me. Her body had grown thicker, and her skin glowed. With two hands, I forced her to sit down on a low stool and wrenched the heavy wooden peel from her grasp. The smooth handle was familiar in my grip. I knew the steps of this dance and soon fell into the rhythm that the heat and the bread demanded.

Only once all the proofed rolls were baked and piled into the distribution bins did I sit. I'd found pauses to shed the layers of my clothes, down to the britches and an undershirt, heedless that any man who might wander down below would have me instantly seized for doing Unmale work and shortly thereafter discover my gender crime. Living in the two worlds at once was beginning to make me reckless.

I sat with Eva and took out the gifts I'd brought. The fruit was bruised and squashed now, the savories stale. But it was more than bread. To incubate a life, she needed nutrients.

We did not speak of Vincius or Nelius or any part of her old life. I would have been happy to listen had she mentioned them, but I knew that skating past the subject would be best for now. Let the dead feed the field, as the Hedgerow Mams would say.

"Where are your helpers?"

"Long gone! We work with ever fewer Domestics. Everyone is exhausted." She rested her hands on the shelf of her belly in a gesture that looked like it had become familiar. "I get a few minutes between the morning rolls and the evening ones — and even then I'm rushing upstairs to do the work for ..." Here she stopped, her face crumpled. "One day they are here, the next they're gone."

"Do you know how many?"

"I think it must be more than a hundred. We need new help; the place is falling apart. The Autokrator Himself found shit in His bedpan. I heard He went into a purple rage to be compelled to see His own shit."

I smiled. "How awful for him. But, of course, being semi-divine, the Autokrator doesn't even have shit. I wonder if they think about how everything would go if we were all gone."

"You know how bad it is. They would have searched for the girl responsible and found her and killed her for not showing up. But, of course, she was gone. They've set a watch now — more guards on some of the main corridors to stop everyone who comes and goes. They still think the reason for the shortage is Domestics are escaping."

"Where would they go? Who would help them? These men are idiots."

"Shh! Cera, you mustn't!"

"It's true. I see it up there. What would they do if we all disappeared, together, at once? Fall apart, that's what."

"They'd freeze their balls off and starve," Eva quipped. We allowed ourselves a little laugh. There wasn't a Domestic alive who hadn't indulged in that particular fantasy.

"You need to get off the line. You can't exhaust yourself like this."

"I'm nearly at the last month. I'll get my lie-in when I'm delivered."

"I will try to come down when I can."

"I wish you wouldn't. We have enough to worry about as it is." She clutched her belly, then she clutched my arm. "Cera, they found Maya. They found her in the middens. Someone ..." She bit her lip before going on. "Someone had cut her. Carved her up like an animal."

"We are nothing more to them than that, Eva. But Maya ... she's past suffering now. She's luckier than the rest of us."

I was surprised by my own response. By the look on her flushed face, so was Eva.

41

Tiresius

THE AUTOKRATOR'S DINING room joined his apartments and was one of the most sumptuous rooms in the entire Palace. It could host hundreds of guests at a series of dining tables that were part of an ingenious winch system allowing Domestics to set them, unseen, with golden plates, shimmering crystal, and heaps of prepared dishes.

At each event, the tables would float down on heavy cables from trapdoors in the ceiling to great fanfare.

This way, the Autokrator could entertain whomever he wished and say whatever he liked in secret. Not without ceremony, though. Nothing ever was. The Autokrator's attendants were always there, holding his golden canopy over him and fanning him to keep him cool.

The dinner parties of the ancient Autokrators were legend. They featured everything from orgies and bloodlettings to garden-variety attempted coups. Some dinners of old were even said to have lasted for several days. Guests took naps between bouts of excess. The dinners featured flat-bottomed cups and Pages serving the plates, so guests didn't have to have their dinner spoiled by the sight of Domestics.

Those days were long gone, though. Gentius's habits were like many of his recent predecessors'. Over time, the guest list shrank. Gentius became surly, and a meal could be a deadly affair. Voicing the wrong opinion or falling out of favour could result in a knife through the throat between courses. In recent years, only one of the dozens of tables floated down when Gentius chose to host a dinner.

Over the years, I had been one of his most frequent guests. Or else the Head Ritualist for Fallos, or very often the Consort. Lately, Gentius preferred to eat his meat alone, while half a dozen attendants listened to him chew in the otherwise silent space.

I knew Gentius had the end of his reign in sight — even though it was still twenty years away — and felt like an old man staring down death. He had started to consolidate power and attempt to convince the Consort to take up His various pet projects. To carry on the legacy of the Autokracy. Of course, like every other Consort in history, Caelius would promise to do so and then promptly carry on as he wished once the old Autokrator was sent away.

I was glad to be invited to dinner. Gentius had wished more than once in my presence that there might be some loophole, some secret combination of events that might allow him to extend his rule. He was up to something, that much was clear. I put on a respectful, happy face and made my way to his apartments in my best gold robes.

I nodded graciously to the guards I passed on my way. Waiting at Gentius's doors, I felt a little burst of pride. I never tired of them being thrown open while the announcement of my arrival echoed off the marble pillars. But I was shocked to see that I was not the first to arrive.

The guests stopped, mid conversation, to look at me. I had to work to repair the expression on my face. The Consort was already seated at the right hand of the Autokrator, in pride of place. Of course, as the one who had invited me, that wasn't a shock, but directly to Gentius's left was Ferrius. At the right of the Consort, wearing black velvet and a Fallos kerchief, was the boy who'd so gleefully sold out his own pater at the Dissertation. I had to admire him a little. If you're going to do it, do it with gusto.

I smiled, but I feared it was a little brittle since all the best places had been taken up already. I would have to make do with sitting to the left of Ferrius, a notoriously uncouth eater, or to the right of that upstart shit with his smug face. My stomach sank. I was not going to enjoy this meal.

The look on the Consort's face lifted my spirits a little. It was clear that he would rather have been anywhere but here. Especially on this Feast night, which was usually supposed to be given over to pleasure. He sat with his arms crossed, refusing plate after plate. He even turned his nose up at the Autokrator's wine. It couldn't be suspicion, since we all drank from the same pitcher — although, one could never rule out a cup being poisoned.

I held my nose and sat by Ferrius. Sitting one person removed from the side of the Autokrator was at least a little better than *two* people removed. I settled my clothes so they'd be as far away from Ferrius as possible.

No one made conversation with me as I sat, another slight I registered with disgust. They were already in a heated debate, and the Autokrator sat back with tense fingers, listening intently. The cult of Fallos boy was shouting, and he had risen in his seat to make his point.

"And I say, you *must*! You *must* make the rites mandatory for all." The Consort scoffed at him. "What harm is there in it? As every man loves the realm, he loves Bartolius's memory and Fallos by extension. There is no separation between love of the realm and love of Fallos."

"Nelius, a man may choose to love Bartolius or Fallos. Only love of the Autokrator is immutable. Otherwise, he is free in his mind to be religious or not. It has always been this way," remarked the Consort.

"And look how things are," muttered Ferrius in dark tones. "Unmale shrines popping up. Protests outside the Parliament. Fallos statues defaced."

"You won't get any more love out of men if you force them to kneel."

"Start with those who already know fealty!" shrieked Nelius.

"Such as?" The Consort played with the rim of his water glass.

"The army, for example." The glass tipped over. An attendant rushed forward with silken cloth to mop it up. There was no mopping up Nelius's comment, though.

"You overstep, sir," the Consort said flatly, pointing straight at the boy.

"I see I have mistakenly come to some kind of dance, if people are overstepping at this rate," I joked. The Consort and the Autokrator laughed politely, which meant Ferrius and Nelius were forced to laugh as well. "Nothing like a good debate to whet the appetite. I congratulate the Autokrator on reviving the old custom of friendly debate."

"Which side do you land on?" demanded Nelius.

"Oh, I think religion spoils the appetite, don't you?" I asked.

"It's time some appetites were curbed, and if swearing belief in Fallos helps, then so be it. I encourage you, Nelius," pronounced Gentius. We all knew what that meant. He disapproved of the Consort and his preference for Domestics over a Male lover. The Consort tossed his napkin down.

"My appetite has been curbed. I am afraid I cannot eat a single bite. Pater." The Consort stood, which was always difficult in his cumbersome hoop skirts. We stood while he made a curt bow.

After he had left and the double doors clicked shut again, Ferrius broke the silence.

"I had hoped he could be brought on side. We would be stronger with his support for many of your Great Undertakings." He appeared to be speaking in code to Gentius, who nodded a little sadly.

"I had hoped he was destined for greatness. Alas, it is a heavy burden to know what is best for all men and to do it alone. He was always willful as a lad. I had hoped he would grow out of his disdain for his women's weeds. Now, I find he is a problem to be managed."

"I fought with my own pater," I suggested. "It is a phase young men go through." Nelius laughed scornfully at me over the rim of his full glass then turned to Gentius.

"Autokrator, you are great. Great by your station, great by your nature. You are so great that compared to you, other men are but insects. When I am bothered by insects, your Grace, I simply swat them away."

Gentius nodded slowly. The rest of the meal continued in this manner, with that little shit pouring obsequious flattery into the Autokrator's ear, while Ferrius beamed and cogs turned in my mind.

42

Tiresius

I HAD AN audience with the Consort the next morning as he dressed. It was a privilege to enter any of the Triumvirate's chambers at any time, but one of the greatest privileges was to attend the morning dress. The greatest fanfare was always around the Autokrator, but as the next in line, the Consort was hotly fawned over too. The Consort had fallen further from favour of late, though, so we arrived to discover my Page and I would be alone in dressing him.

Not a good sign.

I allowed my Page to announce my arrival. The Consort lay yet in bed. I knew it couldn't be drink. He hadn't touched his wine at last night's dinner.

Worse than pale, he was an odd grey colour. I frowned to see him.

"I must look very poorly to get that kind of a face from you, Tiresius."

"Did you enjoy yourself too much on the holiday perhaps? Resin? Boys? Unmales?"

He managed a weak smile.

"No, not overindulgence. It seems for every day I feel well, I have two others I feel ill."

"You certainly didn't indulge last night."

"There was nothing on offer that interested me." Clearly, the Consort was in no mood to ruminate on our odd dinner party. I switched tactics.

"You haven't touched your meal here." I had learned that power brokers enjoyed being coddled. "And where is your Domestic to hold your beverage?"

"None have come." It was one thing for men to abandon the Consort, but Domestics too? It was unheard of.

He sat up, with difficulty. I motioned to Dominius.

"Hold the vial for him," I ordered, taking the thing out of its stand. The Consort threw me a strange look.

"Fastidious Tiresius telling a Male to hold my vial? Why, Treasurer, you constantly shock and surprise me."

"Well, there's no one else about. It's not like men are helpless without Domestics."

"What other Unorthodoxies might you be capable of, I wonder." He swung his legs out. His fit frame made his weakness seem all the more strange.

"If I'm so honoured to be there with you when you Ascend, Consort, rest assured, I will only be capable of the Unorthodoxies that support your rule." I handed him the first of the traditional petticoats that went under the ceremonial garb.

"If you please, those first." He pointed to a chair and a pair of leggings. It was my turn to stare. Far be it from me to question what the Consort wore in his own apartments, illegal or not. He was still my better ... in title at least.

"Dominius is quiet today. Have you been working at your exercises, as I told you?"

This drew a startled look from the Page — an old habit of Domestic life. But I was pleased. Pleased that the Consort had noticed young Dominius. The closer they became, the more I could hope for a relationship to exploit.

"When the Consort is feeling better, perhaps another round of archery practice?"

He waved the thought away.

"Could you lend me Dominius? To read some of the old poets to me?"

This was tricky. I demurred, about to make a noncommittal sound in my throat, until ...

"I have some old lays memorized."

We both looked at Dominius. It was a gamble to say so, one I begrudgingly admired.

"I thought you said your schooling was quite narrow, Dominius." I was hoping the slight edge in my voice would see that the subject was dropped.

"Nevertheless, I learned a few when I was younger."

I wondered how long Dominius could plausibly be useful. There always came a point when a servant knew too much.

"Consort, in what way do you feel unwell?" Dominius plumped a pillow behind him. More falling back into the Domestic ways, but in this case, it was good. Acting like an Unmale might convince the Consort to be even more candid. He might spill information on his plans. I stepped through the strategic outcome of revealing the Page in my mind and filed the branching possibilities away for a future day. It was always good to have options.

I half-listened to the Consort detailing his symptoms. Spells of inexplicable weakness, nausea, vomiting, shortness of breath. It could be many things. Fragility, I thought to myself. I made my excuses and strode from the room.

Of course, I did not leave the Consort and his new favourite completely alone. While the entire point of placing her with him was to have him open up to her, to divulge the opinions and secret plans that he would never share with me, I suspected Dominius would become loath to share everything with me freely.

Fortunately, the Consort's apartment housed a number of places to look and listen in secrecy. Except for the Autokrator's own apartments, virtually every room in the Palace had places to spy. One just had to stoop to the level of taking Domestic passageways to access many of them — a slight inconvenience, but one easily borne.

There was a padded seat behind the wall, with a vantage facing the Consort's bed. I wondered how many spies had sat in this seat over the years, mapping the pillow talk of Consorts on the cusp of their Ascensions. How many secret liaisons had toppled men who were just about to rise to their power? How many assassinations had been planned from this little peephole? Through it, I could see the length of the main room of his apartment and easily hear the conversation taking place.

Dominius betrayed the secret of her gender with virtually every word and gesture. In the absence of available Domestics, she automatically fell into the role herself. It was hard to tell if he noted it, but I suppose a guilty mind sees things an innocent one does not.

He lay with closed eyes while she recited poetry. All her selections were of the old masters on the subjects of love, pleasure, duty to the Autokracy, fecundity. Strange choices, I thought. I'd have chosen martial subjects: leadership, rallying. The stuff that stirred men into battle.

He found it strange too, for he seized her hand at one line in particular and asked her to repeat it. She did, haltingly.

"We've met before." The statement caught her off guard.

"Of course, Consort. At the archery range, and the baths. We've often met, with my Master Tiresius."

The Consort shook his head slowly and spoke with conviction.

"Before that, and you know it. I know your voice. And don't" — he lowered his voice — "tell me it was at the Dissertation with all that business with the Toolist. I've been considering it for months. We met long before that." I strained closer to hear Dominius's reply. She removed the Page cap and softened her speech a little.

"We have, Consort."

Caelius held her chin in that way I'd noted before.

"The Imperial Consiliorum." I couldn't parse his expression as he looked at her.

"Yes." She looked up at him, and they held the moment, while I held my breath. Then they both laughed out loud and embraced.

"I wondered if you recognized me."

"Of course I did. But how could I call you out with so many eyes around? For all I knew, you had been placed there to out me as Unorthodox!" He hung back a little. "Maybe you *were* placed here to out me as Unorthodox."

She seized him by the shoulders and pressed herself to him, as if to let him know that wasn't the case.

Not even I had expected this. I kept my composure, though. The situation would have to be managed, but information was neither good nor bad. It was simply currency.

I gathered my things. Among them was the Consort's beverage vial, which I'd taken on the way out, and his chamber pot.

43

Cera

"REPEAT THAT PHRASE."

It was a passage about migratory birds and the way they would go from branch to branch with one eye cast back over their shoulder, looking for their nest mate. It had been a little inside joke between us. *He* was the bird, forever looking over his shoulder to see me.

"We've met before." I felt a chill at those words. He'd ruled out the recent meetings; he knew it was something else.

"The Imperial Consiliorum."

His eyes flashed with relief at the connection, and he drew me to him. I wondered how I appeared to him now. In those days, I'd been coiffed, perfumed, perfunctorily robed per my role.

"No wonder you were so bad with the bow." He laughed. "Cera," he murmured into my hair. "I wondered what became of you."

Parroting the poems of Old Masters was expected in the old days. The poems were meant to help the Consort to get into the mood. But he had always wanted to know what I thought. It was what I thought about things that drew him to me. And when we'd exhausted all talk ranging from low to high, profane, cultural, and even Imperial … when words ran together so much that it was hard to say who had said what first, that was when touch followed.

Two blind people in a dark box, easily reading each other's movements. And the fact that we were simply meant to carry out our duty to the state didn't even cross our minds. We did what we did for our own pleasure, and for that reason, it was sinful, Unorthodox. It was a crime against the Autokracy.

Shy in the unyielding light, shy due to the years that had passed, we found each other's arms again and sinned against the Autokracy until we were faint with exhaustion.

Lying there, on his massive bed, I wondered how many years had passed since I'd been with him. The Kratorling was perhaps five. The Caelius before me now was a different man. He was leaner, his face pinched. And he had an almost ethereal quality, as though he was less of this world than he had been when we'd been lovers. I wondered how the years had made me look to him and felt suddenly shy about my face, my skin, the shape of my body. Did the Page uniform affect his regard of me?

"Does Tiresius know?" he asked.

"My … gender?"

He nodded.

"Tiresius knows." I was careful to use no pronoun. I feared revealing Tiresius's own secrets. "But I've not told Tiresius about the Consiliorum. I was afraid what that might mean for me."

"How are you here?"

"I came to look for … our child because I am an idiot who doesn't know her place." It came out with a great deal more bitterness than I'd expected. And I stuttered over the word *our*. It felt presumptuous.

"And you were caught by Tiresius?"

"Plucked from a cell by him. To work. He gathers information."

"He believes he does. He is as misinformed as anyone else, though richer. Are you not in danger?"

I laughed a little. "I was born a Domestic. There is no other way for me to exist."

"Yes, of course." He shooed the idea away, obvious as it was, sheltered by his innate right to safety. "I meant of being exposed."

"Constantly. And now, more so." I looked at my hands, which he took in his.

"If I can do anything about it, I will. I can have you assigned to me. I can take you out of Tiresius's reach." He seemed to have an idea. "Do you want to ... see the Kratorling? Our child?"

A wave of need and nausea rolled through me at the prospect. I wanted it too much, and now it was within reach. But it could be a trap. I pushed the unwelcome thought down.

"I can't. I mean, I don't think I can ..." He gave me an encouraging look that warmed me.

"Look who you are with! The Consort does as he pleases! Mostly."

But suddenly, a wash of grey passed over his features, and he doubled over. He was abruptly sick all over the ornate covers.

"I'm sorry. I'm sorry," he kept saying, mortified by the vomit. Males were trained to think themselves above and beyond all the fluids of the body, save one.

Concern for him prickled at me. I busied myself bustling linens to and from the Domestic door, helping him rinse his mouth, and brushing his hair out of the way.

It was dark when I left him sleeping soundly. I returned to the tower to find that Tiresius had left me instructions to attend the Parliament the next day. I was to take careful notes of all I saw and to give him an accounting of all that had happened between me and the Consort.

A wave of fear washed over me. I would have to tread lightly. Tiresius knew me to be Unmale, and he'd left me with the Consort on purpose. I would detail our intercourse for him, I decided, but nothing more.

I left the next morning to attend the Parliament. It was connected to the main throne room of the Old Palace by an ornate hallway. Early each morning, Portfolios and their assistants began to gather in groups, seeking to convince one another to act this or that way.

Soldiers opened the great double doors to Parliament, their presence a reminder that the Autokrator's rule was absolute and Parliament was merely a nicety. Sunlight flooded into the room from the wide oculus overhead as we took our seats. I sat in one of the galleries, high above the floor.

At precisely one quarter after the first hour of the day, the Autokrator appeared at the mouth of his personal hallway to the Parliament with the usual fanfare. He stood under his Imperial canopy, his august face behind a mask of beaten gold held up by his attendants.

The Leader of Parliament shuffled into view between the doors, on his knees. The earliest Autokrators had liked to see bruised kneecaps as a show of fealty, but it had become tradition over recent years to pad the knees of his garment to ease the discomfort.

"Do you swear to serve the will of the Autokrator?" recited the Sergeant at Arms in an ancient dialogue.

"Faithfully, loyally, preferring death to disgrace," came the Parliamentary Leader's rote response.

"Is he to be granted access?" the Seargeant at Arms asked the Autokrator.

"He may enter." The room was hushed so the Autokrator did not have to raise his voice.

Tiresius had a place next to the throne. It was one of honour, which he was entitled to occupy at any time. The Treasurer was not permitted to participate in debate on the floor, but Tiresius

had schooled me in how to follow the measures taken in the Parliament and to watch for signals from the Autokrator. Tiresius
was in attendance today himself, but increasingly, he relied on me
to take notes while he attended to mysterious matters elsewhere.
I was to pay particular attention to who rallied behind or against
decrees, and how the Autokrator reacted to the support — or lack
thereof.

The Autokrator sat, and the golden mask was laid aside. He
delivered the words to open the session, his disdain for the entire
undertaking clear.

He began by reading from a recent decree but was interrupted
by a commotion outside.

"What is all that?" he asked with annoyance. A guard ran to
a narrow window in the gallery across from me. After peering
down, he shouted down into the bowl of the chamber.

"The Autokrator's guard is in arms against a protest ... two
protests."

"Two?"

"A group of men, with weapons. And ... Unmales."

"*Unmales.*" The Autokrator sneered in disbelief.

"What do the men want?"

A Page, tasked with answering the question, sprinted out the
doors. The room filled with muffled speech as Portfolios began to
gossip. The Page returned, slightly winded.

"The protestors want an audience with the Autokrator to beg
that He lower their taxes." The Autokrator rolled his eyes. "And
the Unmales have been surrounded by soldiers. They number
thirty."

"Cover the Unmales with pitch and set them alight." The Autokrator moved to continue reading his decree, but Tiresius whispered
quietly to him.

"Have the men rounded up," the Autokrator added. "And
put their heads on pikes outside the city as a message to all who

would question the will of the Autokrator." He unfurled the decree again and read in monotone, "It is Our will to move sums from the Treasury for use by the Imperial Toolists of the Palace for the creation of conduits and tunnels ..."

I noted that a sizeable faction of Portfolios raised their hands to support a smaller disbursement. A few of them spoke on the matter, and the Autokrator looked to Tiresius, who nodded his approval of the notion.

"We are stretched across many Portfolios. These new disbursements upset the balance."

The Autokrator nodded slowly, as though taking in this wise advice.

"The decree stands as I will it. Disburse the funds."

Tiresius bowed, showing his total submission.

Following this, Ferrius rose to make a point about Domestics going missing. At times, he was forced to yell over the din of the guards rounding up the protesters. We could hear the sound of metal on metal as guards clashed against them. Before continuing, Ferrius coughed a little; the smoke from the burning pitch had filtered into the chamber through the open windows.

"Honoured members," he began in the collegial tone he always used, "some of you by now will have become aware of a dip in the levels of service by Domestics." He was met with bored, loud groans. "Please, I beg you to hear me out. We are in fact reaching crisis levels of missing Domestics from throughout the Capital. Manufacture and labour sectors are suffering greatly." The groans intensified.

"August lords, even hygienic needs are not being met. I ask only that" — his voice rose even louder to overcome the distracted chatter of the Portfolios who could not rouse themselves to care about the plight of Domestics — "some study be done to account for the low levels, and that fresh Domestics be procured from elsewhere and brought to the Capital, if only as a temporary measure.

The Consiliora, in particular, are experiencing grave shortages of Domestics. It is our responsibility to ensure the steady supply of young boys who form our armies of Toolists, teachers and scribes, politicians and militia. We must protect the futures of these vital lines of work until such time as we can find some healthier, cleaner way of gestating Male babies. Autokrator, I put forth a request that we ensure the number of Domestics remains adequate to the needs of the Capital!"

While the Autokrator had listened intently to the Imperial Toolist through this speech, his eyes darted about the Parliament as though he too were taking stock of the reaction. Despite the speech, the Parliament voted against ordering more Domestics. I wondered how many pots full of shit would have to turn up before the group acted.

The most remarkable decree of the day, in my opinion, came sandwiched between others on sanitation and the acquisition of new buckles for the military. The Autokrator had voiced a decree suggesting the automatic deposing of the Consort in the event that the Consort was too ill to perform his duties over the course of several months. The Autokrator would absorb the Consort's duties.

Men leapt to their feet, begging the Autokrator to reconsider. Their words echoed all across the great round chamber; the Consort was more popular than the Autokrator had bargained for.

The Leader of Parliament looked anxious and sought a response from the sullen-looking Autokrator. He knitted his brows, chewed on his lower lip, and then nodded.

"The decree is withdrawn."

A hush returned to the Parliament. It was very seldom that that many men spoke in unity against the Autokrator. It was even more seldom that a decree was withdrawn.

The Autokrator was angry. It was easy to tell this was a serious matter. As I scanned the room, noting the expressions of each

Portfolio, I was seized by a sharp pang of fear. Nelius, dressed head to toe in black, was watching the proceedings like a hawk.

To escape Nelius's notice, I waited until all the men had filtered slowly out of the Parliament and scurried toward the nearest Domestic hole. I crawled inside only to discover a chaotic mess of brooms, broken chairs, and dirty drinking vials. Tiresius had ordered me to go back to the tower and write down what I'd seen, but there was something else I needed to do first.

I was shaking a little as I walked down the dimly lit passage, thinking about Nelius.

All this time, I'd wondered what had become of him. Now he wore those black clothes I'd seen on the other young men from the resin dens Nelius had brought me to all that time ago. Or the driver of the caravan during that Process. It was possible Nelius was his own man now, though that hardly seemed likely. Without passing his Toolist apprenticeship, he was nothing. No man got a career without entering a guild of some sort. He would have to belong to something or someone else now.

The floor began its familiar slant down. I regretted that I hadn't thought to bring fruit from one of the stands near the doors of the Parliament, but that could wait. I needed to know something else.

I entered the sleeping area I used to share with several other Domestics. I had to cover my nose and mouth. The smell of the earth overcame all the other smells of life down here — the bread, the water, the body odour, all were secondary to the earthy, musty smell of dirt.

My niche was at the bottom, dug into the soft earth of the far wall. I got on my hands and knees to crawl into the small, grave-like pocket where I used to sleep. I elbowed into the darkness, choking a little on the smell. I reached forward with apprehensive fingers until they touched the cool wall.

There was my calendar, row on row on row. We all kept calendars, in our own ways. It helped us anticipate our monthlies and avoid pregnancies, if we could. Some of my ticks were upright, others were sideways, a few each month. My blood days. I knew to add some five months from where I'd left off. I ran my fingertips over the divots, silently counting ...

How many years? They bled into one another, and it seemed incredible that I'd worked with Eva for so long. I counted the divots, did my calculations. Four. Five. And a half. The child should be about five.

Eva would know if my count was right. She'd been here when I arrived, weak and exhausted from giving birth.

I crawled back out, conscious of the Domestics who were asleep in the bunks — they needed their rest. I headed toward the ovens. They were only a few twists and turns away.

I could see Eva in her heavy leather apron, swaying to the rhythm the bread beat out of her. A shove into the oven. A twist to knock the litter of fresh buns into a bin. And a direct look at me with her shawl pushed back just enough to see me. But it wasn't Eva. Eva was nowhere to be seen.

44

Tiresius

I YANKED A Domestic off floor polishing duty and ordered her to follow me with the items I'd taken from the Consort's apartments covered in a barrow. I was irritated at having to waste precious time searching for a Domestic to use. My patience, like the number of available Domestics, was in short supply these days.

The Domestic struggled to keep up as I moved quickly along the main hallway that allowed Portfolios to flow between the Imperial rooms and their own. The oldest section was built from wood timbers with creaky, wide-planked floors. Mosaics and paintings of Autokrators were here as everywhere. As I rushed along, their watchful eyes followed me.

In the newest sections of the hallway, harsh planes of concrete gave way to a glass tube suspended over a ravine some half an hour's walk from the Imperial rooms. The sudden blast of sunlight after the dim, claustrophobic halls seemed garish and unreal. Soon enough, I was in the Toolists' sector, at the furthest reach of the Capital. They would have gone even further out had I allowed the disbursement of the funds. But neither I nor the Autokrator favoured the idea of the Toolists holing away in some distant lab.

Infuriatingly, the doors leading to the Toolists' quarter were shut. My status gave me access to every quarter in the Capital. In the country, for that matter. But here, Ferrius had instituted security at the gates to "protect" Imperial technology from the wrong people.

So today, I stood before locked doors with a crouching Domestic, a covered barrow, and an official look of plausible openness on my face. The Toolists had devised some pneumatic opening, which was crude and more comical than useful. It was also Unorthodox. Doors should be opened by mute Domestics. So it had always been. The more doors, the more Domestics, the greater the glory of the Autokracy. Automation would be the downfall of the Autokracy.

Despite my status, I was ushered suspiciously from antechamber to antechamber, and once I was as geographically far in as I could go, Ferrius still insisted on communicating with me via speaking tubes, his face refracted through a series of mirrors mounted to a wall.

His expression was pinched and pained. I intended to change it.

"I'm a painfully busy man. Why are you here, Tiresius?"

"It has come to my attention that some papers have been sitting with the Autokrator these past months, esteemed brother."

"What papers?"

"Ones of interest to you, I would think. Rather large disbursements. I know how many mouths you have to feed." There was no such stack of unattended papers. Nothing like that circulated without my express knowledge and permission. "I would be happy to jog some things along, perhaps even circumvent some of the usual routes in the interest of expediency."

"You would?"

"Yes, of course, and for very little in return."

"I don't have time for your sideways talk. What do you want?"

"Some analysis. Such as your most junior Toolists might do."

I pulled back the cover on the barrow and tilted the mirror so he might catch a glimpse of the chamber pot. He wore a furrowed, impatient look.

"Send the Domestic through with the items so I can take a look."

"Do take care they don't become … compromised." I was instantly angry with myself for the show of concern.

"We are all Toolists here, Tiresius. Fighting contamination and compromise are the cornerstones of our guild. Send it through."

With a worried glance, the Domestic paused. At a prod from my foot, though, she poked through the nearest hole to ferry the items through their secret channels.

I waited in the antechamber, facing a blank mirror. The narrow oblongs of light thrown by the meagre windows crept across the length of the floor. I stood, gathering my robes. I had a certainty in my gut that I was being watched. My patience was wearing thin once again. A moment later, a junior Toolist's face appeared in the mirror.

"The analysis is complete." He spoke with full deference but still managed a look of complete contempt.

"And the results?"

"The Imperial Toolist requires knowledge of the provenance of these items before relaying the information. He feels it may be a matter of Imperial security."

"Everything is a matter of security to this fanatic," I muttered under my breath. Then, louder, "Alas, I shall be detained in providing that, and certain other things we talked about, as a result."

The face in the mirror clouded and then disappeared. A moment later, the frame refilled with Ferrius himself.

"I will send a messenger with the details. And I will watch events closely to know more about your motives, Tiresius."

I cut a neat bow, choreographed to show the absolute minimum of respect. On my way back across the glass bridge, my mind returned to the Toolist's response. It spoke volumes about his analysis. Had it been nothing, he would have handed over the compound list and been done with it. The noxious items they had to have found confirmed what I'd suspected. The Consort was frequently sickly because it was very much in someone's interest that he be sick.

I had to admire the slow artfulness of it; he'd been sickly since I could remember. This was an act of delicate patience. The steps of a man with deep vision. How could I not be impressed?

45

Cera

I WONDERED AT first if Eva was off relieving herself. She was in the late stages of her pregnancy, after all. The stone-faced Domestic who moved the bread in and out of the oven would not speak to me, let alone meet my eye. I thought her unfriendly until I remembered I was wearing my Page clothes. She was terrified of me. I left the kitchen, searching for Eva.

Eva's bunk was full, but it was another Domestic who lay there, blissfully unconscious. I kept moving. I told myself not to panic. Eva would have reassigned her market duties after Vincius was arrested.

She might have gone to the Mams to be delivered, as Domestics did when they carried children they wanted to hide. It was early, but the strain she'd experienced could have hastened her time. I hurried through the passageways, hoping to find her in labour, or perhaps already delivered.

The sanctum Domestics used to give birth was usually warm and humid. Today, it was colder than I'd ever experienced it. The place was almost empty. My stomach lurched. I had hoped she was here. I had convinced myself she was. Now my thoughts churned, and panic started to choke me. I darted about the room, looking into each cubby, each nest. Other than a few Mams, there were no women. No babes.

I turned and ran, without any idea of where to go. I darted along Domestic paths, scuttled across the polished hallways of men and back down another tunnel, hands splayed out in front of me.

"Eva?" I hissed frantically at every Domestic I met. I could feel them shaking their heads. Refusing. Terrified. I kept running.

My feet finally took me to Vincius's house. The doors and windows stood ajar. The place smelled of emptiness. No one had been here for a long time.

I rummaged through a desk drawer where Vincius kept odds and ends, where I found my pocket goddess shoved under some papers. Holding her tight in my palm, I ran out.

I didn't know where else to look. I numbly gravitated back toward the Palace. The afternoon crowds were thicker. People of all sorts filled the streets, skiving off the end of their workday. My attention was caught by an Imperial autokinetic that honked imperiously at the heavy pedestrian traffic. When the crowds didn't move, armed guards slashed at them, but the way remained blocked. Ahead of the autokinetic and the crowd, a black caravan was angled thoughtlessly in front of an iron gate. It had a small insignia bearing the Toolist mark near one of the windows.

Nelius swaggered into view from the other side of the caravan. My pulse raced as he cast a look over one shoulder and got into the vehicle. The driver rammed forward, pushing like a bull.

"Get out of the way!" Nelius stuck his head out the window to shout at the cluster of people. "Imperial business. Move, or I'll mow you down." The engine revved menacingly, and the caravan rocked on its wheels. Finally, the crowd dissipated, and the van swept down the service tunnel to the left.

Two miserable-looking Domestics hauled on pulleys to close the iron gates. I strode up the middle of the road, looking at neither woman. The gates shut behind me. The Domestics resumed squatting on the ground as I continued on, following Nelius into the tunnel, into the dark.

46

Tiresius

MY NEXT AUDIENCE was with the Autokrator. He was floating in his enormous copper bath like some kind of pale garden grub. I smirked inwardly. Here was the Male form in all its power and glory ... hams for legs, swollen arms, a belly that folded over itself, and tiny genitals that seemed to have gone into retirement. All these appendages looked nearly phosphorescent in the bathwater.

"So? Out with it." His voice ricocheted off the hard surfaces of the room. He was always ill-tempered these days. Constantly turning over real and perceived plots against him in his mind.

"I have reason to believe the Imperial Toolist is holding onto secret information regarding the Consort."

"What sort of information?" he asked with noticeable caginess. I hated the old goat for thinking he was so clever.

"I believe that the Consort is being poisoned."

"Oh ... that ... well ..." For a moment, Gentius's composure slipped. He struggled to find words, but he quickly settled on outraged deflection. "Who would do such a monstrous thing!"

"It is unthinkable, Autokrator."

"Indeed. We must investigate this at once." He hauled himself out of the tub while water sloughed off his hanging flesh. "We must call an emergency Parliament. You call the Portfolio heads. Say, after supper?"

The Autokrator was buying himself the rest of the day to obfuscate.

"Perhaps we two could have an audience with the Imperial Toolist?"

"Impossible. He is busy with Imperial work and must not be disturbed. I will speak to him myself and relay his words back to you."

This didn't come as a surprise, but it still rankled that the Autokrator had been triangulating between us like this for years now. Despite dripping disbursements out to the Toolist and offering the odd gift, the gates remained shut to me. A churlish, infantile means of exercising power. Moreover, the Autokrator's solution was unseemly. Running about like an errand boy? If that was the way the supreme leader wished to carry himself ...

"At the Parliament then, tonight." I backed out of the room with my head down, perturbed that I'd had to witness his rolls of loose, glistening flesh.

47

Cera

I KEPT THE van at a safe distance as I followed it down a spiralling road leading to the lower levels. Even if it rounded a corner and left my sight, I could still hear the tires on the cobbles. It drove slowly enough that a brisk walk allowed me to keep pace. At an abrupt fork, I nearly missed the steep turn it took, for fear of being seen by its occupants.

This was a newer tunnel; the earth had been clumsily shored up with metal braces. A mass of ugly conduits crept along the walls like vines. I could hear the hissing of gas and the rush of fluid. Steam vents spewed gas into the tunnel at various junctures, choking the air with foul smells and obscuring my sight until they dissipated.

The van crept toward the base of a ravine. A bedraggled line of Domestics filed out of a hole cut into the side of the tunnel. They were a filthy work detail, balancing heavy barrows along the edge of the tunnel. They left a trail of viscous drips.

I pushed rudely into their line, knowing that any other behaviour from a "man" would be suspicious. Like dumb animals, they paused, averted their eyes, and allowed me to pass before them.

244 EMILY A. WEEDON

This tunnel was new construction, and the muddy floor had not yet been tamped down by the passing of many women's feet. I had to skirt barrow after barrow, the Domestics shrinking back against the walls while tilting their heavy loads away to allow me passage. One after another they came, plodding like pack animals. Thankfully, the tunnel spanned only the breadth of the ravine.

On the other side, the Domestic tunnel rejoined the driveway. The caravan idled at a gate blocking its passage. I hid in the mouth of the tunnel while a guard checked the driver and let them pass. As the gate squeaked closed, I heard a high-pitched sound from somewhere deep. It was unmistakably a cry of anguish. A woman's cry.

I was overcome with a nameless horror. I ran from that place, all the way back up the winding tunnel, until my breath was raw inside my throat and my legs quivered. I staggered back to the world of men, free.

I returned to Tiresius's keep with mud still clinging to my shoes. I couldn't remember the last time I had eaten. Tiresius seized me by my collar roughly.

"How long have you been gone?"

"A few hours, I think."

"A few hours? Hardly. I expected to find you waiting for me."

"I saw Nelius." Tiresius frowned at me. "The son of the Toolist arrested for Unorthodoxy."

"I see. I think you need reminding that you are under my orders, not your own. Your position can easily be terminated."

"Will you groom someone else to get close to the Consort then?"

A little light came into Tiresius's eyes, a very slight, very grudging respect.

"Were you planning on telling me about the Imperial Consiliorum, Dominius?"

"I didn't feel it was important enough to share."

Tiresius allowed a reluctant smile.

"There are times I doubt you will survive long enough to understand that, in this life, everything is important at some point. So, to be clear, you have lain with the Consort."

"Yes, Tiresius."

"How was it?"

This took me completely aback. "What?"

"It's widely known that the Consort prefers women. Can you corroborate this? Did he enjoy it? Was he vigorous?"

"Enough to climax, so I suppose."

"You are being purposely vague. Did he linger? Did he appear ... attached?"

"It was not done with quickly, if that is what you mean. We talked. We joked."

"Joked? With a Domestic? Good. This is very good. What did you speak of?

"The nature of men. And Unmales."

"Delving into Unorthodoxy. Excellent!"

"Why is it excellent?"

"His behaviour is sinful. That could be useful. And isn't your concern."

"We also talked about the possibility of fate or its complete absence."

"Did you indeed? I believe there is no such thing as fate. It's a security blanket for fools. But to discuss such concepts with a Domestic? It is too good! Enough. You'll tell me more later, but other matters press. I have discovered that the Consort is being poisoned, slowly, subtly, since some time ago ..."

My ears started to ring, and I lost the thread of what Tiresius was saying for a few confused moments. Poisoned? How long did he have, when I had just found him? Though my head swam, and I clutched a chair to keep standing, I had to keep my senses sharp. Tiresius continued.

"You're not to tell him anything, of course. This is a very useful development. It could be useful if he dies. It could also be useful if he lives, and I saved him. Dominius, you're filthy. Clean up. The Parliament is assembling again. The Autokrator has been backed into a corner, and something interesting is bound to happen." Tiresius paused. "Tell me, did you risk coming out from Below because of your love for the Consort?"

I looked down. I hated for Tiresius to know anything more about me, less still about my child, but I didn't think I could avoid it any longer. "I did not."

"Then why?"

"I left the Consiliorum after I ... conceived."

"After you incubated! Oh, Dominius. You disappoint me. I thought you had some interest in bettering yourself. In enjoying some of the delights that the men keep for themselves. But you left merely to chase after some infant? To what end? To raise it yourself in some fairytale land where men and women live together and lovingly raise children?" Tiresius shook his head slowly.

In those words, my connection to the child did indeed seem ludicrous. I wasn't going to share exactly who the child was, though. Tiresius could never know that.

"In any case, you will lay with the Consort again. We can have him cornered too, once we accomplish that."

"You think it's so easily done?"

"It's widely known that men like him seem to lack some self-control. You will do this for your sake, and mine. Now, hurry. Get yourself presentable."

I closed my mouth. I had been ready to tell him of the curious black caravan and its descent below the Capital, of the Domestics with their barrows. But now I felt I could trust no one, least of all him. I vowed then and there to give Tiresius less and less information.

48

Tiresius

THE AUTOKRATOR SAT taller in his chair this evening. He was prac-tically vibrating with energy. A Page knelt near him with sheaves of paper, ready to take notes. The Leader of Parliament began with the usual call for submissions but was cut short when the Autokrator stood.

"Ask yourselves, dear members of the Parliament, where is the Consort?" The Autokrator's voice was arrogant as he swept his hand out to indicate the Consort's empty seat. It was ridiculous — the Consort was not expected at these types of Parliamentary sessions, and every man knew it. However, it was the job of all men to agree with the Autokrator. And so a murmur of outrage began to swell in the room.

I could see Dominius up in the gallery, frantically writing notes. I appreciated the rededication to diligence.

"We reintroduce a decree put down earlier by this Parliament that makes a provision for the Autokrator to take over the duties of the Consort should he be indisposed ..." He held out an impe-rious hand for the next sheaf.

"Furthermore, we move to decree that, from this moment, the Consort is to be put under house arrest for committing various acts of Unorthodoxy. This decree is irrevocable without Our consent and is made law from this moment, superseding argument from Parliament upon Our word. The charges are written in Our own hand and may be viewed in the Imperial library after the session closes." He sat heavily, self-satisfied.

I was surprised that the Autokrator had roused himself to act this boldly. Only a few times in the history of the Autokracy had anyone ever moved to imprison the Consort. And none of those times had boded well for the Autokrator. Typically, their power moves ended in bloodshed. But those were the machinations of simpler, more brutal men — not ethical men of argument and enlightenment as Gentius styled himself. It was possible the Autokrator could pull off a bloodless coup.

A tedious period of assent followed where every man in the room had to stand, state his full name and station, and vow that he stood by the sterling word of the Autokrator. I found myself wondering if it would yet come to bloodshed.

The Autokrator had been a functional ruler for five years, moving through the rituals, seemingly above the politics. His only interest was science, his little pet project with the Toolist. He hadn't even shown interest in the Consort over the years, although previous Autokrators had often bonded closely with them. There were even scandalous whispers that some had been lovers, despite being related.

I'd thought there would be quite a few more years to weave allegiance between the old man and the Heir, but now I wondered how quickly I would have to ally myself fully with one or the other. There was, of course, a third choice: the Child. I had paid only passing attention to the Kratorling since he was as yet so unformed. I made a mental note to send a basket of treats and playthings to the Kratorling's apartments. I sat back, stifling a yawn, knowing full well the call for assent would take hours.

49

Cera

AS SOON AS the murmur died down a little, I crept out of the gallery and sprinted for the nearest Domestic hole. The crisscrossing paths would connect me to my destination faster than any aboveground route through the dizzying Capital ever could. I ran, still holding my unfinished notes in one hand. I didn't think through where I was going. I just had to go to him.

I burst out into the Consort's private antechamber, surprising a Domestic. She actually looked at me as I passed. I thought little of it in the moment; I kept forgetting I was dressed like a man. I reacted to her as the Unmale I remained under the disguise.

I ran through the Consort's rooms until I found him at his dressing table. He wore his trousers and half of his ceremonial garb. His hair was plaited, but his makeup had not yet been applied. He stood to greet me.

"I came straight from the Parliament! You are to be put under house arrest! On the Autokrator's decree!"

He took my hands in his. He seemed oddly unperturbed by the news.

"I know. I have favourites among my Domestics. You should know, word travels fast underground."

I felt an odd twinge. Of course, he would have favourites. Preferring women to men meant a lifetime of clandestine enjoyment with Domestics. I wondered how many of them were meaningful to him. How many others recited poetry for him?

"Cera. I missed you, making do with only Domestics to nurse me. Domestics who don't know old literature."

"You seem better today."

His colour was good, and he sat upright.

"After a few days without food, I always feel better." His mouth formed the words, but his eyes, the tilt of his head, showed his thoughts were elsewhere.

"Tiresius suspects you are being poisoned."

"And he hadn't thought to tell me. How unkind of him."

He picked at a fastening on his garment. "I've often wondered how hard it would be to get a body to match mine. A dead one to leave in my bed, so I could disappear." He paused. "House arrest. It just means my circuit grows smaller." He indicated the grand room, which seemed to diminish a little. I hadn't noticed before, but not one wall looked out into the world. Not one ray of real sunlight was permitted.

"I know ways you could disappear ... down Be—"

"No, no. Without a believable substitute to bury, they'd be after me in a moment. Then I'd be dead for certain. Don't think I haven't thought about it. It would be an adventurous way to commit suicide, at least. I like the idea of going down in a commotion. That way, maybe one day I'll be immortalized in a fresco. Imagine!" he crowed and stood to his full height, holding his arms out as though imagining himself surrounded by flames. He was enjoying this. "What about you? Why haven't you disappeared?"

"There is nowhere an Unmale could hide for any amount of time outside. Other Domestics would eventually give me up if I remained Below. They could earn retirement. And if I went out like this, someone would soon spot my true nature. I've only gotten this far because Tiresius lends me credibility and protection."

I wanted to tell him, then and there, what Tiresius really was. But even though I had a reckless desire to aid the Consort, I felt strangely incapable of betraying Tiresius's great lie.

The Consort sat and looked at himself in the mirror, his face long. There were circles under his eyes that I hadn't noticed.

"They will be some time counting names in the Parliament," he said.

"A few hours. Not that much time."

"There never is. Will you drink with me until they come?"

"Drink?"

"Does that seem reckless?"

I had to smile. "Odd, I suppose."

"Did they give you drink before, when we first met?" No one gave things to Domestics, so I couldn't help my laugh. "Ah, poor you. You had to meet me sober then."

"*Meet*," I teased. "As though I had any other choice."

"Would you have? Chosen otherwise?"

I held his look.

"I would not."

"I wonder what I might have been, in a different life from this," he pondered as the Domestic approached with a vial for each of us. "My only role in life seems to have been waiting to do as I was told. I imagine you can understand that."

I nodded. I took a deep drink of sour wine. It tasted awful, but I liked the warmth it spread in my face and my throat, the lightness in the front of my forehead. I sat cross-legged facing him on the couch.

"The thing is," he said as he accepted a refill from the Domestic, "I've never liked doing what I was told. I think I would make the worst Autokrator ever. I'd much rather live an anonymous life, alone, someplace far away from here."

"You should have been a Domestic. You'd find that anonymous enough."

He laughed at my treasonous idea. "Please. I would look terrible in that godawful shawl."

"No one looks good in it. That's the point."

"It is, I admit. I always preferred seeing you in the Consiliorum garments." He squinted at me in my Page uniform and smiled. "I have some of that picture of you now. Though I'd prefer fewer clothes."

The wine and the notion made me flush.

"I wondered if you had thoughts like that about me."

"You weren't supposed to be thinking such things." He was teasing.

"Most of a Domestic's life is spinning between what we aren't supposed to do and what we have to do."

"But you sometimes chose what you wanted to do."

"Inside our prisons, we all find ways to stay free in our minds."

"If they knew how much rebellion was brewing inside the minds of Domestics, I think the men would be quite fearful. You'll think it strange, but I've been remembering all the times I visited you in the Consiliorum. Those late talks. You even made me laugh. It was a secret world, where things could be different."

"I've thought about it too, over the years." My voice felt small when I told him that, strangled by too much longing. He raised his vial to the Domestic, who scurried forward to take it, along with mine. Then she melted away. I looked at my empty hands and then picked up one of his long, dark plaits. It was heavy. Not because of the gold wire securing it, but the hair itself. Thick and dark, like finely made rope. But it was this step that led to our mouths on each other, and all the Unorthodox things that followed. It was unceremonial and utterly sinful.

I took his face in my hands and put my lips to his. He took me in gratefully and yielded everything to that kiss, to the moment. We pulled off our garments and, with them, our prescribed roles. Naked, we placed our hearts together, separated only by our skin.

In the moment, it wasn't sin. It was selfish, the most selfish thing either of us had ever done.

We slept for a little while. When we woke, he found the bottle of wine, and we drank straight from it. We fell together again, marvelling at the many ways we fit together. My head lay under his chin, his throat sharp against my cheekbone. I didn't care. I would remember this better; too much comfort would have been my ruin.

As we lay, staining the fine brocade with our sweat, a booming knock came at the door to his apartments.

I scurried naked for the nearest Domestic hole while he readied himself. I glanced back as I went and saw that he stood proud, with shoulders back, ready for whatever was about to come. The booming knocks pounded harder.

At the hole, I grabbed a spare shawl hanging on a hook. I had meant to keep my cap, but it fell as I pulled the shawl over my head. I cast a look back at him as I fled. Perhaps my last.

Through the fringe of the shawl, I saw him triumphantly throw open the great doors and stand before them, half-dressed in pants. The pants alone were cause enough for his arrest. I plunged Below, wondering what could possibly come next for him. Despite myself, I meditated on the worst possible outcomes.

Strident voices faded behind me as I felt my way through the tunnels. I wasn't sure where I could go now. Tiresius would have seen me leave the Parliament and be out of patience entirely. After today, our alliance was at an end. A bloody one for me if I didn't think quickly.

I entertained the wild notion of pretending to be Eva, returned from an unsuccessful pregnancy, finishing my days in front of the ovens. Maybe I could stay in the tunnel near the Consort's apartment — perhaps he would smuggle food to me. I almost laughed at how wild my thoughts ran.

At a juncture where a Domestic hole led to an outside path, I came across the same Domestic I'd seen on the way into the

Consort's apartment. She had to be part of his personal house detail. She grabbed my wrist with an unshakable hand and pulled back the hood of my shawl.

"I keep seeing you creeping about. Who the hell are you?" she hissed into my face, setting fear coiling in the pit of my stomach. It was incredible she had the wherewithal to ask. But she abruptly let go. She had been seized by the throat and pulled off her feet. One hand clamped on her mouth, and another pulled her up out of the hole.

My first instinct was to reach for her flailing legs as she resisted being hauled up and out, but she caught me in the face with them, and I saw stars. I heaved forward dimly, fumbling for her ankles. But someone else pried me off. There were others down here. Men.

Like the other woman, I twisted, I kicked, I tried to shout over the hands that covered my mouth and squeezed my neck. My shawl was over my face, so all I could see were the rudimentary shapes of men.

I felt my feet leave the ground and then felt myself being tipped upside down. I heard a metallic noise first. A click. Then rolling. I fell heavily, cheek laid against a cold, corrugated floor.

The other woman sobbed nearby. Then I heard the rolling again. Through the floor, I could feel the vibration of a motor. Every bump in the road below jostled my body from side to side. This was the black caravan I'd seen before. They had wrapped a biting cord around my wrists, and I could feel my swollen fingers growing numb.

We had to be headed underground, where I'd followed before. We tipped toward one side, listing so far that gravity pressed the other woman's body against my flank. I pictured the descent of that spiralling tunnel. I listened for the point where the road branched off, expecting the surface below to sound different. The swaying and lurching swamped me with nausea. I was losing my sense of time and direction. The trip seemed to go on and on. I heard the other woman groan and was elated that there was an annoyed anger in her tone. If she had fully given in to panic at that moment, I might have too. Her anger gave me strength.

I tried to pull myself upright, despite my bound hands. I had to push down with my chin and fight against the swaying of the van. My ribs strained until I was up. But the hood of my shawl was over my face, and there was no way to clear the drooping thing from my sight.

The caravan finally lurched to a stop. Light pierced the weave of my shawl as the door opened, but not enough to give me a proper view. Someone laughed. I wasn't sure why.

I was seized and flipped upside down again. I feared they would drop me. The top of my head prickled, anticipating the pain of hitting the ground. Someone else took my feet, and I was carried like a carcass for some distance. I heard doors swish. Sound hushed as we entered smaller spaces. The air was foul with something I couldn't identify.

At last, we stopped. I was flipped again and dropped hard. I could feel other bodies on all sides. I heard others breathing. Some were sobbing. It was damp. I felt claustrophobic with the strange pressing of flesh all around me.

I did not know how long I was there, arms aching, legs crossed. To my shame, eventually, I urinated right where I sat. It came out hot, spreading warmth through my shawl, but it quickly turned cold and clammy. My stomach churned with nausea and hunger by turns. At some point, I was the one sobbing softly. None of us spoke. I fell into tiny sleeps, waking myself violently when I inevitably tipped sideways into someone else's shoulder or head. But eventually, another body made a counterweight against me, and we both succumbed to exhaustion.

50

Tiresius

I SUFFERED THROUGH those few hours in the Parliament with my head supported on my arm. Only when the Autokrator's wax Seal was applied to the final decrees could I stand and join the mob that formed, heading for the Consort's apartments. Join. I should say, lead.

"Hold." I spoke forcefully, and the soldiers froze at my command. I strode to the gleaming double doors. It was necessary for the historical record to reflect me being present in this group. Many others would claim to have been here, but my name should go down in the official history. The arrest itself was a formality in my mind. What mattered most was what came next.

If I was too friendly with the Consort when the Autokrator completed his coup, I would spend the rest of my career digging myself out. If I was too friendly with the Autokrator, should the Consort find some way to prevail, the outlook was grim. Either possibility led, in only a few stumbling missteps, to death. But I had spent a lifetime outmanoeuvring death. I needed only a few moments more now.

The soldiers pounded at the doors with their long staffs. I thought it wry that he left the rabble waiting. There was something bred into you, some contempt for the lives of common men, that allowed such a pause. As the infernal pounding carried on, I began to wonder if the Consort had taken a coward's path out of his apartments.

The doors were flung open.

He stood there, his face unmade, his chin up, and his pants visible to the crowd, which would not aid his case at all. His lip was curled, and he showed his teeth. He seemed fearless. I admit, I took a slight step back. Hopefully, the scribes didn't notice. A Page nearby wrote hastily, capturing the Consort's stance. My own chin was high and my expression inscrutable, which I knew the Page would capture as well, though I doubted with much panache. No matter: I was in the habit of editing records after the fact to make sure that history received a fitting report.

"Consort Caelius, of Family Evander, you stand accused of high treason, Unorthodoxy, and sedition. You are, by the direct order of the Autokrator — your own benevolent pater, and the Pater of all — to remain under house arrest until such time as you are brought to answer for your crimes in full."

The Consort reached out and swept the decree out of the herald's hand. It skittered across the floor. With this, soldiers swarmed into the room. They brushed curtly past him and seized anything of value and anything that might help him break out. Once that was done, the rabble dispersed. I noticed, though, through sideways glances from some of the men, that they looked apologetic.

I faced the Consort, keeping my eyes on his. As the doors swung shut behind the soldiers, I lowered my chin slightly and lifted my eyebrows. "I have not abandoned you, Consort."

I have to admit, I admired the composure he showed in the face of his uncertain future. Maybe, having been born to power, he didn't crave it the way I did. I felt a kinship with him. His time in women's weeds had not been good to him, and he might never get to play the part of the active ruler. Having been both master and slave, I could identify.

"I can't be abandoned by anyone, Tiresius. I have always been alone, and always will be. That is the true cost of leadership. So forgive me if I don't feel comforted by your ... ministrations."

Feeling dismissed, I walked away. The doors shut him from my view. I recognized several men from his personal detail posted outside. Their expressions toward me were not friendly.

I wondered if the Consort would ever pass alive through those doors again. The key to knowing that was uncovering what it was the Autokrator was secretly doing with Ferrius the Imperial Toolist, once and for all.

51

Cera

I DIDN'T SLEEP long. I tried to stretch my cramped legs out a little but was kneed in the back and elbowed in the stomach. The entire room heaved with the small, pathetic movements of women.

I whispered to the woman I had leaned against, startling her awake. "Could you help me pull off my shawl? I want to see."

"My hands are tied," she hissed back.

"Your teeth?" I ventured. She struggled for a bit but eventually pulled the hood back. I blinked in strong, greenish light. There was a hair from my shawl still stuck to my eye, making it water. I tried to wipe it off on my shoulder, with no success. But I did see why the other woman had urged me to stay blind.

There were at least twenty women in the small enclosure. Those of us in the middle were pressed to one another, while those around us had body parts spilling through the bars on all sides. The floor was slimy and wet. Most of the women wore shawls, some still hooded as I had been. Some huddled naked. Many were filthy, smeared with blood and other fluids. At least one appeared to be dead, and the realization made me retch.

Ours was only one of many cells. No matter which way I turned, there were more, row upon row, separated by wide pathways. Across the way, one of the cells appeared to hold only pregnant women, many of whom lay on their sides in similar states of distress. My heart sank in my chest, and my head spun. I rubbed my bound fingertips against the rough, wet floor, trying to focus on the pebbly feeling to ground myself. As I did, I realized that this must be where all the missing women had gone.

The thought made me dizzy once more. I had imagined those missing women somewhere dark, somewhere alone. I'd even pictured them in forests, ravines, meadows, running away whilst hunted. But this, the scale of this, was beyond my comprehension. It seemed so strangely wasteful. What could the purpose of it all possibly be?

Maybe Eva was here as well. Perhaps she lived. I clung to the thought with desperate hope.

I craned my neck as best I could to see if she was among the pregnant women nearby. If she was, I couldn't see her.

A commotion broke through the low murmur of sighs I had grown accustomed to.

Toolists appeared, hauling a woman haphazardly. She made a hoarse cawing sound from inside her throat. She appeared to be drooling. They opened the door to a cage already teeming with bodies and tossed her in roughly. She curled like a fetus, clutching her hands to her middle. They were bloody.

All of the women looked up at the men, frozen with fear. I could have guessed what happened next — they grabbed another woman, seemingly at random, and took her, writhing and screaming, back the way they had come.

Only when they were gone did the other women attempt to help the newcomer. The woman was retching now, a miserable huddle. She was barely recognizable as human, and she fought off the soothing hands like a wild animal pushing away an attacker.

As a knot of women surrounded her shuddering body, I heard a word I didn't comprehend. Several of the women were quietly chanting it together. One was crooning to the poor creature huddled on the floor. They drew closer together. And then the word landed. *Sleep*. Their knot grew even closer to the poor woman. All I could hear was laboured breathing.

After a minute or two, the women dispersed, leaving a slight space around the still body. Someone had smoothed her hair behind her ears and closed her mouth. With her hands now resting near her face, I could see that her lower belly was a wide-open wound.

52

Tiresius

I MADE MY way to the shelves in the gloomy, soaring library where the recordings of the Parliament were kept. Paperwork littered the tables. It came in Pages' hands, in sheaves and scrolls, bound in boxes and leather. It arrived faster than the doddering archivists could catalogue it. I rifled through various decrees looking for disbursements to the Imperial Toolist. I needed something that would give me insight to the Autokrator's plan. I intended to remain installed as his Treasurer if he prevailed. But, should there be a reversal of fortune, I also had plans to see the head groom of the Imperial stables. I wanted to make sure packed bags and a strong horse were kept ready for me.

The library was empty save a few bent men who carried paperwork with shaking fingers. Their skin was almost as translucent as the parchments they painstakingly sorted through. I made my way to the central stack, where I found the scroll I sought. It was massive, and handsomely finished with gold braid and handles made of black lacquered wood. I slid the long nail of my index finger through the wax seal bearing the Autokrator's mark. The writing, in the Autokrator's own hand, was hasty. The space where the Treasurer's name and stamp should be was empty. My eyes flew over the words.

Our Great Undertaking ...

What was this nonsense? I wondered. And then I froze.

I could hear whispers coming from the Imperial carrel — the Autokrator's desk within the library. It was sort of a room within a room that allowed him privacy should he need it while poring over books and scrolls.

I tiptoed toward it, crouching down to listen.

"... once he either expires or is taken out by the crowd, then what?" Ferrius asked.

"He should have expired by now!" I recognized the peevish tone of the Autokrator. So he *was* colluding with the Toolist.

"We have to proceed carefully. I've continued to work on the timeline you requested. Don't let impatience be the downfall —"

"You dare to lecture me?" A small noise of acquiescence followed. "What will come after?" demanded the Autokrator.

"A suitable time of mourning. An emergency Parliament. An early investiture."

"You really think he has the stamina?" wondered the Autokrator.

"Who can say? We can use one of the others. In a pinch. I worry about the long term, though." Ferrius sounded like he was buying time for himself.

"You should. It's what you've been paid handsomely for all this time. Just assure me that we have enough to cover the succession and any unforeseen sickness. And what about the Great Undertaking?"

"I have new accomplishments to show you, at your convenience. The additional men you gave us have helped us make such strides! We've compounded our knowledge, deepened our understanding. We will not fail in Your Great Undertaking."

"It is my legacy I care about, more than the extra time as ruler. This is my gift to all mankind."

"Just so. And you will live on eternally in the history books for it."

I heard a rustling of stiff cloth. It was the Imperial Toolist's traditional papery garb. He was getting up. I gathered my own robes as quickly and neatly as I could and retreated, hiding behind the nearest stack.

The Autokrator remained in his carrel for some time, letting out weighted sighs. I didn't begrudge him keeping me there. I was too busy turning their conversation over in my head.

That they spoke of the demise of the Consort was simple enough, and their words confirmed he'd been fed a subtle poison for many years. But the talk of stamina made no sense to me; the Consort had long been noted for his lack of it. Even if the Consort might somehow prevail in the short term, his health would undermine him in the long. In any case, without important allies, he was less likely to succeed. It made more sense for me to side with the current Autokrator, the known entity. At my heart, I suppose I was a traditionalist. Conservative, even.

What I had to do immediately, though, was access the Imperial Toolist's lab. Too many resources had gone there, and too many secrets between the Imperial Toolist and the Autokrator were housed there.

53

Cera

AFTER A DOZE filled with chaotic dreams, I woke to the sound of metal wheels screeching right by my ear. Domestics wearing especially filthy shawls shuffled through the aisles pushing those ubiquitous barrows. I realized with a lurch what it was they were carrying. They moved from cell to cell collecting the dead, piling them like rags into their barrows. Some were long gone, others only recently untethered from life.

Two men threw open the door to our cage and waded inside. Women skittered out of their way. With a sinking feeling, I realized that they were headed for me. I was seized under my elbows and turned over. They dragged me out backward so I could see the fearful eyes of the others watching me go.

The rough, pebbled floor was cold under my bare feet. They dragged me to a small, tiled room where they tore off my shawl and hosed me down with freezing water. I would have given anything to drink it instead. While I was still dripping wet, they marched me down a hall snaked with hissing black pipes.

Through my sopping hair, I could see rooms on either side. Each one appeared to house a strange, subterranean crop, fed by the network of pipes. Translucent pouches and glass tanks hovered in the air, full of a dark, pulsing liquid. Pale, amphibious shapes bowed and bent with the curve of the glass as we passed by, frustrating my view of what was inside. I feared those pouches with the wrenching fear of a rabbit in the teeth of a wolf.

I tried to pull away, but it was pointless. Their gloved hands were strong. They dragged me to an open area filled with metal tables. Many of them were already occupied by women strapped down with thick leather cuffs. Some of the women sweated in active childbirth. We passed one who was hoarsely begging for water, but the Toolists working nearby ignored her.

I was tossed onto one of the cold tabletops and strapped down with rough hands. They bound me at my wrists, upper arms, pelvis, knees, ankles, and neck. They swabbed my belly, and, without warning, a Toolist sliced into me with a knife, bringing a bitter, expansive pain. I shook so violently that other men came to steady me under the blade. It felt as though they had cut open my entire midsection — though later I learned it was only the right side, close to my pelvic bone.

I arched my back up from the table and slammed it down, trying uselessly to avoid their cuts. As they sliced deeper and deeper, I wondered if they meant to cut through to my spine. My screams joined with those of the other women in the room.

Out of the corner of my eye, I could see my own blood rippling toward a drain in the floor.

"Will you go out of the city for the holiday?" I heard one of the men ask in a jovial tone. The man bent over me smirked a little.

"You know I will." He laughed as he worked. "You're just fishing for an invitation. Let me get through my work today and we'll see." The other man responded with a light laugh.

I wished I could say the pain dulled my senses or that I fainted, but I remained horrifically present. I could even hear the scraping sound of the knife.

"Almost done?" someone passing by called out to them.

"Almost," came the reply of my tormentor.

"Hmm. Can you take these to the administrator?"

"Now?"

"I'll finish up for you."

"All right. Appreciated. You mind cleaning up?"

"Not at all."

The new man leaned over me. His face filled my entire field of vision, but by now, I saw without seeing.

"Wheel this one to my office," he said. "I'll finish her up there."

The wheeled table began to move, and my view of the ceiling shifted. He walked along beside me with confidence in his step. He glanced down at me and hissed, "Be still and say nothing."

It was Vincius.

Was this a trick of the pain? Was I hallucinating?

"Vincius?" I mumbled. I wanted so badly for it to be him, to leap with full faith into the hope that he might take me away from this place. At the same time, experience cautioned me to trust nothing and no one. Not even myself.

54

Cera

"BY FALLOS, CERA," he said. "I thought you were dead." He had brought me to a dim, domed room and was viciously scrubbing his hands at a small sink.

"Your colleagues ... did their ... best." I had to force the words out. "Are you ... going ... to finish me ... off?"

"Rest easy. No such thing. They only harvested from one side. I'll stitch you up. You will live."

He began swabbing me, which made me cry out. Had I been able to move, I would have curled into a tight ball.

"Quiet! Relax. Breathe. This will numb you."

I looked at him through streaming eyes. His face was lined and harsh. He was alarmingly distant as though his mind, his soul, was absent.

"They are harvesting non-vital organs and eggs for experimentation. They've taken your right ovary. I have to try to get you back before anyone else comes."

I felt the tug of needle and thread pulling at my skin as he worked. The numbness was a mercy.

"What *is* this place?"

Vincius looked through a magnifying lens at the sutures he'd made and shook his head as though in dismay or confusion. I knew then, because of him, I had been spared something. There was no telling how much more the Toolists would have taken had Vincius not intervened.

"Shh. Don't move. I'm almost through. We work for the glory of the Autokracy. We work for the Great Undertaking. Some of us by choice, others by force."

"You've been here since the prison?"

"I was given a choice: work in my professed field without compensation until I die or immediate death. I chose to continue the work they admired so much. It's not much of a life, of course, but I am alive. I've continued the work you were doing with us. Finding a way to duplicate children. To create souls at will, for the glory of the Autokracy. I've made a lot of progress since coming here."

Incredibly, he sounded proud, though there was also horror in his eyes. My head reeled to think of it. He was working with them, butchering and killing Unmales. Then a terrible thought crossed my mind.

"Have you seen Eva?" I asked. I feared his answer.

He stopped working and looked at me severely. "Eva is gone." There was an edge of accusation in his tone, as though I had made it so. Horror sank through me. Was I partly responsible? I should have taken her away somehow. Gotten out, somehow.

"Her baby?" It was a hollow question. Just glancing around this lab, I could see what had become of so many innocents.

Now he only looked at me, his eyes wide and deep.

"Vincius," I croaked, "please tell me. What is happening here? What are they doing?"

He slumped heavily onto a metal stool, his back curved like an old man.

"Death," he said. "And life. Sometimes life. But mostly death."

"Did Eva die?"

"She is still with our child. And she is as precious to me as ever." His words confused and chilled me.

He finished up the last stitches and, with a clatter, threw the equipment into a metal sink. He undid my bindings, and I sat up, wincing. I cradled the wound.

"Don't touch it. You risk sickness if you transfer dirt to the wound. You're at risk as it is — they never clean the instruments. Animals."

Vincius walked to a tall series of drawers that ran floor to ceiling. He pulled at the handle of one, and it ran smoothly out on silent castors. A mass of black tubes fed into racks of glass vials. In each tube, little coiled embryos were suspended in solution. Vincius looked them over with a great sadness.

"It's hard to fathom the sheer amount of failure necessary to get it right. Look at this one. Up until a little while ago, five weeks was the longest we could hope to keep an embryo viable outside the womb.

"Ever since they took me, I've been here. The Autokrator and the Imperial Toolist were keen to make use of my work. Extension of life, for work with cells. Isolating cells. Keeping cells alive in glass jars. Duplicating cells.

"But cells are one thing. Cells are hardy. People are another thing altogether. Bodies are huge, complex collections of many cells ... bodies can only take so many insults." I wondered at his words.

He rose, stiffly, and dipped his hands in a bowl of fresh water. He worked the stains of blood on his flesh so hard his knuckles cracked. With his back to me, he resumed speaking.

"I'd been here for perhaps a few weeks when Eva came. She caused quite a commotion. Ferrius gets most excited when we get the pregnant ones.

"It wasn't her time, but you see, that is ideal for his purposes. This is what he's hoping for. He wants the ones that aren't quite done yet — halfway through are the best. They live longer out-side, and they provide a gaudy little puppet show for the Autokrator because they make it seem like we're making progress here." His voice cracked a little. "It's a ruse, of course. Ferrius would have the Autokrator believe that we've already taken eggs and mixed them with the Autokrator's own seed to grow perfect Male chil-dren nearly to the point of viability. It's nonsense, though. We ha-ven't grown a damn thing. We've just taken them out and passed them off as though we made them."

I looked back at the vials. The odd embryo flickered slightly, but the majority were completely still.

"Vincius, did you find Eva the way you found me?"

"As you? Oh ho, no! No, Eva was special. They wanted to see me practise my craft. They brought Eva to me as a special project. Keep this one alive, they told me, and you'll live. Of course, had it been a girl, it would have been no good. We don't keep those. But it was a boy, so I cut him out of his snug little shell. I dragged him into this world before he was ready. Eva died cursing me. And my ... little ... son ..." He stopped for a moment.

"Cera, the punishment for my gender crime was to kill the woman I love and sacrifice my own child. My little son was pre-sented to the Autokrator Himself. Passed off as if he was one of His royal seed. We swapped umbilical cords and veins for tubes and wires. He lives yet, after a fashion. Though he won't grow, damn it. He's willful. He must have his mother in him. He wants to be with her, of course. A sac and tubes are a sorry replacement for the warm belly of a loving mother.

"I have no interest in making the Autokrator's plans work. I'd as soon help every one of these godforsaken unborn die. But my son? I know I should pull out the tubes and unplug the wires, but I can't. As long as my little son lives, somehow Eva does too. And I might be able to beg forgiveness if he can live long enough to understand my sin."

I hugged myself, my flesh rough with goosebumps. When I moved, a sharp stab spoke from my belly. Vincius had walked away from me, toward a panel on the wall.

"Look!" he instructed as he flicked lights on. Bright shafts picked out a gleaming shape in the centre of the room. "All my efforts these many, many years have led me here, where I finally have unlimited funds to experiment, to build exactly as I like. The irony is that every step I've taken drew me closer to the moment I would have to cut my own child out of the person I loved the most. To prove my worth and save my own sorry life. For this!"

He gestured at the looming shape. A round globe of glass was held up by a dark copper base studded with pipes. It was like an altar of sorts. Infernally wrought and yet strangely beautiful.

"The Autokrator is certain that this will start working soon. That all we need to do is inject His seed into this cloud of non-sense and cleanly plant it into an artificial egg. His hope is that here" — he patted the domed glass — "all the future lives of the Autokracy will grow, without ever needing to contaminate the process by using an Unmale body." He stalked a little closer to me. "You know, the Autokrator seems to have a fear of flesh. We've come so much nearer to success by using uteruses taken from sheep and pigs than by using this abomination, but the Autokrator prefers that we find a way to do it with metal and glass instead. He feels that it's so much … cleaner."

He came back to where I sat reeling on the table. He put his hand on my knee. He was so much warmer than I that his touch seemed to burn.

"Have you not come to rue your entry to the world of men?"

"You speak as if I had a choice."

"Yes, of course. It's inescapable." Vincius seemed weary now. "You know Nelius has finally found his calling? He was a miserable Toolist, but he's shown a remarkable talent for mayhem within the field. Ferrius admires his ideas for the large-scale collection of

Unmales yet to come."

"They mean to take some more?"

"Oh!" He laughed bitterly, a tear shining in the corner of his eye. "Some? No, no. They mean to take them all. And harvest all their eggs, and one glorious day in the future, they will see to it that no Unmales are ever brought into the world again."

"But that's impossible!"

"For now, yes, certainly. But one day, we will have the means to make eggs without women. We will close the loop on the entire process. And you will have played your part in bringing it all to be. Who knows, if I make a note of it in my journals, perhaps you'll even enter history as a footnote. It's a shame, your being an Unmale. I could have put you to good use. I imagine you might have ideas about how to make this all work that wouldn't even occur to a man."

He paced in circles about the room. And he kept talking. I recognized the tone that had crept into his voice. This was Vincius at work now, allowing himself to be excited by methods and processes. I imagined it was the only way he could continue down this gruesome path.

He worked a console, and enormous rolling racks slid silently from holding bays around the room. They were filled with pouches. Inside the pouches were embryos and fetuses of varying sizes, suspended in different coloured liquids and glowing slightly. Some flexed impossibly small fingers toward unknown goals. Some shivered in unimaginable dreams. I staggered off the slab and walked to the rows, drawn to them, repulsed by them, horrified by them. Very few of them quickened with life.

"At the most, we keep them for a month. Many live only a few days or hours. The embryos harvested early survive the transplant — their will to grow is strong, but only to a point. The ones we harvest later seem strong at first, seem too advanced to fail. But fail they do. Only the ones harvested late in the third trimester, all but ready to be born, have been successful. Ah, here he is." Vincius had stopped in front of a pouch. "May I present to you my own son."

There was no way this child would live. Despite the advanced development of its face and limbs, it was clear from its pallor and feeble size that this child of Vincius's was doomed. One tepid jerk of his arm indicated that there was barely any life force in him at all. But Vincius appeared blind to his child's shortcomings.

"See! There! A fighter!"

"What do you feed them? What do they swim in?"

"Ah, you see, an Unmale would think of such things right away. Of course. The growing life needs nourishment. Despite the Autokrator's wishes, what the mother supplies can't be left out. They need the serum that can only be found in the womb. In utero, they need food. After birth, they need milk. I've spent a long time puzzling it out, looking for substitutes, alternatives. And I alone, of all the Toolists here, have had the greatest successes. My son receives a special cocktail that no others do. Look!"

I drew closer to the rack he indicated. It was marked with crabbed notes and calculations and thrummed with the flow of liquids. The pipes here were turgid and spat in rhythmic bursts. Nothing else about the liquid in these pouches seemed remarkable, but there was no question that this rack had the most active, healthy-looking little bodies out of all of them. The fetuses turned and swam and hiccupped and kicked at the thick bags they lay coiled in.

"Look!" cooed Vincius in a way that made me doubt his sanity. He pointed, and I followed his finger up to the source of all those pipes. Horrified, I glanced back at Vincius's face. He pressed a conspiratorial finger against his lips.

"My solution. My genius solution is the only thing to work so far. A shame it's a ruse. But don't tell, will you? Or the Autokrator would have me killed!"

Suspended above the twitching little bodies in their clear sacs hung the bodies of half-dead women, each one pierced by tubes that snaked down to feed these lives. The women were inert beings, slowly being leeched of their lifeblood to feed the brood below. I had to cover my eyes and hide from that horror. I pressed my knuckles into the sockets until I saw stars. Ever after, I thought I saw Eva's face suspended among the others.

"He can do away with Unmales, I suppose. But none of us as yet has any idea how the Autokracy could possibly do away with mothers."

"Vincius!" My voice was shrill. "Please help me leave this place. Please!"

He looked at me with compassion. "You need to be patient yet. We need a plan, Cera. But in the meantime, a visitor is coming — an important one. And you need to be completely still."

He helped me back up on the table and covered my naked body with a paper sheet. "Not too long now." He covered my mouth with thick tape and patted my knee absently. I felt constraints close once more around my wrists and ankles. He looked at me with compassionate eyes, as though he felt my pain deeply. But it seemed to me that any expression he wore now was a lie painted over madness.

I heard the door behind him open and the sound of several men's footsteps. Vincius stepped back and bowed deeply. The Autokrator entered, followed closely by Ferrius in his Toolist smock and Nelius behind them.

Ferrius strode up to me and whisked back the paper sheet. He tsked at the sutures he saw on my belly and pressed his fingers roughly against the wound.

"What is this, Vincius? Sutures? I can't say I approve of this time wasting."

Ferrius looked more like a butcher than a Toolist. His shock of thick hair swept up from a high forehead, making a second dome shape above it. His head was nearly a perfect orb, the flesh thick on the bone. It was the face of a dullard. But his eyes were quick and incisive. I wished I could forget his fingers inside me.

"No, no, we have to let this man do his work in his own way." The Autokrator had pushed forward but looked past me as though I didn't exist. "We allow Vincius his little pleasures and pursuits because he brings all his energy to Our pursuits. I always say, Ferrius, let a man work in his own way and you will get twice as much work from him when he is good. Tell me, Vincius, how is Our son today?"

I winced at the royal "Our," knowing what he did not.

The Autokrator swept over to the pouch that held the frail infant floating inside.

"I think he is bigger. Is he not, Vincius? Does he not thrive?"

"Oh, to be sure a little bigger today," Vincius lied. The child seemed anything but healthy.

The Autokrator hung over the pouch, rapt in awe.

"To think, We come yet a little closer to the Great Undertaking and my legacy," he said gleefully.

"More time yet, please, Highness," soothed Vincius.

"And more money, Highness," agreed Ferrius.

"Show me my other son, Vincius. I want to see how far we've come." There was a slight tremor in his voice when he spoke.

Vincius seemed reluctant to carry out the order, but Ferrius gave a firm nod.

A finger on a button brought a pneumatic hiss, and one of the cabinets slid itself out.

Four thick glass cylinders were revealed, suspended between the floor and the ceiling. They bore gilded detailing, denoting that something was special about these. Only two of the cylinders were filled.

One housed a fully grown man. Though his body was slack in the eddying movement of the liquid, it was clear he had been healthy at the time he had stopped breathing.

It was the Consort.

And in the other cylinder, unmistakably, was my son.

55

Tiresius

I BROUGHT SEVERAL soldiers with me to Ferrius's lab. Commandeering a troop of them for my personal use raised some eyebrows, but like good soldiers, they fell to when I used firm words. I watched calmly while they dismantled the doors to the Toolist enclave with weapons and tools. As we marched through the labs, the soldiers satisfyingly sent both tables and people flying. Once the way was clear, I strolled through the settling dust, my robes trailing behind.

Several uniformed Toolists — low-level functionaries by the colour of their scarves — made a limp attempt at stopping our passage. A raised hand was enough to still most of them. The rest scurried back and forth. I supposed they were hiding things or informing others. Once the din of their rushing around quieted, I became aware of the moaning and suffering on all sides. Glancing about, I could see Unmale wretches moaning and writhing in filthy cages or lying on tables, cleaved wide open like meat.

I pointed at a Toolist.

"Bring me someone who will explain all … this."

He scurried away.

I had not been expecting to find a laboratory of horror. I was no more prepared for what greeted me when the doors to the inner lab swung open. Before me was Ferrius, all belly and wringing hands, his lackey Nelius, and the Autokrator Himself, looking flaccidly surprised. I bowed deeply as though this was all in a normal day's course.

"Your Highness, what a surprise to find you here. I've only just become aware of the ... scope of Ferrius's work."

The Autokrator looked perturbed. He scuttled sideways, as though to obscure my view of the Consort floating stone dead in a tube. His round form did nothing to hide it.

"Tiresius, do not be quick to judge what you cannot comprehend."

I gave myself a moment before speaking. A lack of composure at this point would only terrify the other two men.

"Highness, about the Consort — I tried to warn you he was in danger ..."

"And you have my thanks. Everything remains in hand. There are simply things afoot that are outside your ... perspective."

His cavalier reply confirmed what I had heard in the library. He had ordered the poisoning of the Consort. I felt vertigo. My grasp on the situation was slipping. My main task at the moment was to appear as though I was still as much in control as I had ever been.

"Highness, I have served you for many years. I beg that you burden me with anything you need me to undertake. Anything at all. You know you have my undying loyalty."

Though the Toolist regarded me with slitted eyes, the Autokrator seemed to soften a little.

"The time will come for you, Tiresius. Many pieces that have been in movement for many, many years are only now coming together for Our Great Undertaking." There was that term again. How long had I been hoodwinked? "Trust your dear leader to tell you what you need to know and rest assured that all your loyalty will come to bear when the time is right. Your silence is your greatest service at the moment. Vincius, We take Our leave. Take care of all the little ones. Take care, most of all, of Our little son."

Son?

They left, the Toolist casting a scowl at me. This sat like thorns in my breast. No one in the kingdom dared give me those looks. But worse than this was the shooing away. I had been exiled to a cold place far from the warm flame of knowledge.

I was left with this tweedy, bearded Toolist and the naked woman on the table. By the time her face came into focus, the surprise was far less than the rest of the chaos around me. For the moment, I let her be. She certainly didn't look as though she was going anywhere in a hurry.

I regarded the macabre floating figure in the giant glass beaker. At least he was at peace.

"I suppose it is futile to ask you what has happened to the Consort? What your role in all of this was?"

"I am a poor man, my lord. I have but one thing to bargain with — my secrecy for my life. This business with the Consort is that of His Imperial Self alone. I cannot speak on it."

"Good man. You know what side your bread is buttered on. Perhaps when I am the one with bread to offer, you'll reconsider."

I turned to the woman on the table.

"So. Dominius no more. You've come down a peg in the world, I'd say."

Naked, bound, bloodied, and silenced. It could hardly have been worse. Though, somehow, the eyes that met mine were admirably defiant. "You have managed to find a fate even worse than serving me. I wish you luck with whatever you have left of your life."

Outside, for all I knew, the Autokrator and the Toolist plotted my assassination. I had to think of my own next steps.

"Do you know this Unmale?" asked Vincius.

"We've met," I told him and turned on my heel.

56

Cera

VINCIUS WHEELED ME from his office to another room. It was another cell, but one with walls. He passed a device over my belly. The glow on its hand-sized screen lit up his face as he frowned.

"The implantation took," he told me. "But something is wrong. No, not wrong. Unexpected." I heard the words, but I didn't make the connection right away.

He put the device away and looked at me.

"We harvested one of your ovaries. We deposited as well. You are carrying two children. But one was there before the implantation. Several weeks in fact. I hope both come to term. It would be a great disappointment to lose the new life after all that's happened." He said it as though he was the one who had been farmed, who had been violated.

I was still haunted by the sight of that lovely child floating in the water. Now I also had to contend with new life in me. The Consort's child. And this alien one foisted on me.

He left the room and didn't return. It took me a long time to notice that he'd left the door ajar. Surely that was on purpose. By painfully slow degrees, I stood up and shuffled over to it. I was met by a Domestic with a barrow.

She saw me weaving and caught me in her strong arms. I remember thinking, *This is what lying in a mother's embrace must feel like.*

She laid me in the barrow with my feet draped over the side and threw a cloth over me. It smelled foul, but it blocked the harsh lights of that evil place. After everything I'd seen, I would have gladly curled up and died at that moment. But I wasn't given the chance.

The wheel at the front made a high-pitched squeal, and the barrow swayed with the Domestic's gait, like a cradle. I counted the hiss of doors for a time, and then I lost track. I was a little delirious.

I slept for a while and woke only when my head bumped against the front of the barrow. We were on a downward trajectory; my entire body had slid to the front. She pulled the cloth up, but it was still dark. A familiar dark. We must be Below.

I sat up a little, unfamiliar with these paths.

"You should rest," said the woman. "We have many levels to go."

I did as I was told. I laid my head down again, my cheek against the curve of the barrow as she steered me to the depths.

When I woke again, I found my rescuer nearby, squatting with her back against a wall, tallow light dancing over her dark face. She was eating bread ravenously.

"You slept a long time. Almost a whole day." She flashed me a little smile and brought me some fresh water to drink. She gave me bread. I wondered who made it now that Eva was gone. She watched me eat, endlessly patient.

"You rescued me."

"Me?" I was dumbfounded.

"Yes!"

"But you're the one who took me out of the lab."

"Yes, but I've been working in that evil place for years now. Once they find you, they don't let you leave alive. That Toolist was the one who told me to take you away. So it was really you who rescued me."

I wondered what price Vincius would pay for it.

I stood up slowly, still feeling weak. There was a familiar tautness in my innards. I recognized that feeling from my first child. I felt a pang for that poor little body floating alone in that tube. At least he wasn't suffering, I thought, as tears slipped down my face.

The Domestic shuffled over to me and took me in her arms. She didn't ask what made me weep. She simply held me to her broad chest and stroked my filthy hair as grief flowed from me.

I wept for myself. For the child. For the years without him. For Eva. For the mother I never knew. For the permeability of my flesh and the chafing of forced compliance in every breath I'd taken since the day I was put to work.

I wept for the Consort, wondering how he had met his end. I wished, somehow, I could have been there, and I felt strangely hallowed by the last embrace we'd shared. It was a futile thought, but I wanted him with me now, greedily, selfishly. I wanted the shape of him to lie up against. I wanted the sound of his voice rumbling against my back. I wanted simple days back when we were just voices in a lightless room together.

I wept until none of my wandering thoughts dredged up a new well of tears, until I felt flat, depleted, and weightless. I lay still, recalling that I had been held like this before. Long ago by a nameless Mam. After a time, my thoughts drained away, and neither of us moved. The only sound was the earth swallowing my tears.

57

Tiresius

I HURRIED AFTER the Autokrator and his hangers-on with full speed, keeping my ears open. I caught up to them quickly. They were too corpulent to have much speed.

"We should have sliced that meddler up when we had the chance!" I had to admire Nelius. He acted decisively.

"Your Highness, forgive the boy for speaking above his place. We could not have known which way Tiresius would go, and we needed allies."

"We don't mind the boy speaking. He is full of vigour. We are sure he understands his place, beneath Us."

"And beneath me."

The Autokrator stopped, and I had to freeze as well, hiding behind a corner to listen.

"Is he, though, Ferrius?" I could hear the Master Toolist gulping to answer while the Autokrator continued. "Have we not been patient these many years? Waiting for you to bring Us real results? Yet Nelius here, building on the work of his unfortunate pater, brings us more results than you. More would-be sons of the Autokracy. More babes in beakers, ready to be born, free of the stain of Unmales."

"Sire, we are yet years away! What they showed in the lab is just trickery. Those babies will not be born. They're unstable. It's a gimmick put on to mollify you."

Peering around the corner, I saw Nelius step forward. He forced fat old Ferrius against a wall.

"Do you declare the chosen son of the Autokrator dead?" Nelius asked threateningly.

"The technology is not viable. It is a fantasy!"

"Ferrius, you wound Us with your lack of faith!" cried the Autokrator, stricken. Nelius leaned his thumbs into Ferrius's throat.

"It is Unorthodox to say such things," Nelius growled. "It is treason to wish the Autokrator's chosen heir dead."

"I wish nothing but His happiness! But you yourself know the Toolism isn't ready. Admit it!" Ferrius squealed through a closing windpipe. "Your Grace ... it has been the way for years ... to choose twins for Kratorling. To keep the second child in case of trouble. We are decades away from knowing how to truly duplicate men, let alone create them outside of Unmale incubators!"

"I know what I saw!" screeched the Autokrator, forgetting his august plural. "You know there remain fewer than twenty more years. Without the power to give this gift to my people, I cannot hope to extend my reign rightfully. I need to continue My Great Undertaking." He stepped forward. "Would you really stand in the way of the entire Autokracy's happiness?"

Nelius glanced over his shoulder at the Autokrator, who looked on, quaking with displeasure.

"Ferrius does not know what I know, thanks to my pater, your Grace. I alone can give you the technology you seek. Ferrius is nothing more than a dead weight."

For a moment, there was nothing but the sound of three men breathing. The Autokrator jerked his head sharply.

"By your Grace's will," whispered Nelius with appetite as he leaned into his thumbs. The pressure squeezed a strangled noise from Ferrius.

"So be it," said Gentius levelly, sentencing Ferrius.

Nelius pressed all his muscle into the flab of that throat. I pulled back from the corner and listened to Ferrius fight for air. I heard him slump down the wall.

"Come, boy. We can move faster now that we have less standing in our way." The Autokrator padded away with Nelius at his side. I stepped out once they had rounded a corner.

Ferrius was a sorry puddle on the floor. I prodded him with my toe.

"So good of you to be an enemy of my enemy, Ferrius," I told him. But, as his eyes were glassy, I feared he was too long gone to hear my thanks.

58

Cera

I WAS FEELING about for the tallow lamp when I found bony, ice-cold fingers instead. I started back. For all I knew, they belonged to a corpse.

But a moment later, a thick light sprang from the lamp. An old Mam looked at me across its flame.

"They told me you would be awake now. You have been up and down, Cera. Up and down and all around."

"Who are you?"

"I'm one of those old ones they forget about. I live in the shadows now."

"I don't understand."

She touched my arm gently and brushed away a strand of my hair. Then she pointed to my belly. She wanted to feel. I nodded.

She prodded about, expertly, and this touch, like the feeling inside me, was familiar.

"You were in the Imperial Consiliorum," she said, still poking at my belly between navel and pubic bone. When she finished, she patted my cheek with an unfamiliar softness that nearly broke me.

"I saw many things there. Long before your time." She sat back on her haunches, looking at me through tufted eyebrows.

She had that hardened, canny look that most Mams did. But there was also a warm glint in her eye.

"Forgive me, Mam. I have nothing to offer to you."

She smiled and shook her head. "Another time, you can find a way to make good for me. You did the unthinkable. You went looking for your child."

"I had to."

"And what did you find?"

"I thought I found him. In the labs. But it couldn't be him."

"But he looked like him?"

"He did!"

"He was a lovely baby. Such a grip in his fingers." She drew up her knees and looked off, into her memory. "I was there the day he was born from you. I had a feeling about him. I knew he'd be handed up Above. And sure enough ..." She took my hand. "You mustn't blame yourself. The child you saw could never have survived what they did to him."

"What do you mean? They would never hurt him!"

"The Autokrator has been trying to become master of life for years. And many Autokrators before him too. They wanted copies of the children to safeguard the future. Their future, anyway."

"Copies?"

"The copy of a man. A particular man. You already know so much about cells, Cera — in Vincius's shop, you learned how they join, how they divide. This division has become very important to the Autokracy. Perhaps with the right division, they won't need Unmales anymore."

"They copied my child? I don't understand."

"Your children, Cera. There were two boys. The boy who lives, and the boy who died. They tried to copy the poor thing with their experiments. But they failed. They've tried taking blood and running it through their machines. They harvested parts from women. They farmed our bodies like fields. But they always run into trouble. There's always sickness." I felt hollow inside. I wanted to stay hidden in this room forever and never again look at the faces of men.

"But why, Mam?"

"Men are not connected to their future as we are." She pulled up her shawl and showed me her folded navel. "Look — this is the connection — each one of us connected to our mothers, like links of a chain, back through time to the first Mam. We are fed by our Mam; we share our blood with them. We breathe with them. And then they let us go. But we remain connected through time, one mother to another. The men are outside this chain. They are unlinked. And this, they fear. They want to break our chains. They want to forge the chains for themselves. If they can cast copies of themselves, I think they believe they can live forever."

"The child — the Kratorling — he lives?"

The Mam nodded.

"There have long been copies in the Imperial Consiliorum. They choose the daughters of mothers who had two or more babes that were the same. This way, they can play their games of Heir in the world Above. A bad copy won't obey his father, but maybe a good copy will. The Consiliorum Domestic we know as Cera had not one but two children." She took my hand and chafed it. "One of these they tried to copy. The copy died."

"The Consort — was he poisoned?"

"For many years, many, many years, Cera. They have wanted to break the chains for many years."

"So the Consort isn't dead?"

"The father of your child is not dead, so far as the Domestics in his wing report. At least not for the time being. Here." She motioned for me to put out my hand. When I did, she placed something in my palm. A plump little idol with a tiny face. The spitting image of my own pocket goddess.

"I was there."

"When my child was born?"

"Yes," she said, smoothing my hair. Her eyes were moist and full of care. "And I was there when you were too."

59

Tiresius

UPON RE-ENTERING THE main buildings of the Capital, I came across a puzzle. Though I had seen the Consort dead, a guard remained on duty in front of his doors.

"Does the Consort remain within?" I asked the guard on duty, in all innocence.

"The doors are locked and guarded until further notice!"

Guarding what, I wondered. Everything until now had been about the day he might take power, and his death would leave a hole. It could only be covered up for so long.

I hurried up to my tower and was pleased to find that I hadn't been locked out of my own quarters as yet.

I paced around my rooms, mind racing. A coup was underway, that was clear. The Autokrator had assassinated the Consort. And his pet Ferrius not long after. Doubtless the guard remained so no one would be the wiser. And doubtless the Autokrator was biding his time now — waiting to see if I would act on my discovery. The only course of action for the moment was to do nothing but wait.

After a while, I sent a boy down to the stables with some bags. Money, food, clothing, and identity papers — everything needed to get me outside the Capital doors in a hurry.

I found myself thinking of Dominius. I wondered if I should have done something more for her, based on our shared gender. But I shrugged off the thought. She had always been the master of her own destiny, so she should forge her own way, if she could.

I would need to get a new mouse. And soon. All the old doorways were closing, and the only way to get news was by listening at the keyholes.

I made my way to the library to seek clues in the archives. I wanted a second look at the disbursements that had been made using my seal. There they were, ink on parchment. Transactions in the minutes from the Parliament, as well as records of visits to the Treasury. I continued rifling through the scrolls. This was curious. There was an order from the Treasurer, dated a few days earlier, to release funds for the immediate mobilization of the entire Imperial army. An order I had never made.

I scoffed to myself. It was not nearly enough of a disbursement. Not if the entire army would need to be lodged, fed and watered, and liquored. The funds released might pay for them to all arrive, but they would hardly pay for them to be well taken care of for any amount of time. They would be unpaid and idle. Which, historically, was a poor state for a roused army to be in.

With a squeeze of panic, my next thought was that, if the Autokrator were comfortable signing my name for me, he could hardly have much respect for my person. Or my person staying alive. Did he know my secret? Impossible. He would never suffer such an abomination for long. There must yet be some value to my being alive if he was forging my name instead of ordering my assassination.

I thought it prudent to liberate a few extra wafers from the Treasury for my own immediate needs. Then I would set out to revisit Vincius. Perhaps I could buy his way out of the Toolist lab, and maybe he'd throw whatever he knew in with the bargain.

60

Cera

THE OLD MAM walked me back Above after I'd rested some more. I had never before seen the section of Domestic's tunnels she took me through. The going was slow, with her gait and the havoc that had been wreaked on my body. Pain from the incisions shot through me with each step, but my mind still raced. What had happened for the Consort to come to be in the labs? What would happen? What would become of me?

Finally, the Mam led me to a juncture I recognized. From this point, I could have gone directly up to Tiresius's tower alone. It was a place I meant to go eventually. But first, I had another destination. I kissed her forehead, and she mine.

It didn't occur to me that I was filthy and ragged until I was already through the leather Domestic door of the Consort's exquisitely spotless apartments. I was dressed in a borrowed shawl but still covered with scabs and sores and my own blood.

Even with the hood of the shawl thrown back, it took him a moment to register that it was me. He stood, dropping the book he had been reading. I was too grateful that he was alive to do anything but drink in the sight of him.

"My god. Cera." He shooed away the Domestics.

"I thought you were dead!" I blurted.

His fingers seized mine, and he frantically touched me everywhere, as though to be sure I was really alive.

"What have they done to you?" His face, paler than usual, creased with anxiety.

"They mean to kill us all."

"They? Kill who?"

"The Toolists. The Autokrator. I don't know who else. Kill the Unmales. The women." I used the word recklessly. "And you. I saw you!" I grasped him by the collar, frantic. "I saw you dead — I thought. I was certain of it."

"Not yet." He crushed my head to his hard breastplate, pinching my cheek. But I did not pull back. Until I remembered my foul state. Then I pushed him away.

"My skin is crawling," I told him, covering the lower half of my face with filthy fingers. "I want to be clean."

He led me to his bath, a long, deep pool set into the floor and surrounded by thick textiles. I shed my shawl and kicked it away from me. He called for a Domestic to bring hot water, and he sat me in the tub, pouring bucket after bucket over me himself. His fingers shook when they passed near my wounds. When his grip on the bucket faltered, I saw that he was himself weak. A strong Domestic's hand took the bucket from him, and she continued the task herself while he smoothed the waters down my back.

"There is another you. Or there was," I told him bluntly. My mind was too dull to think of a more elegant way to say it.

"Another me? What can you mean?"

"I saw you, the very likeness of you — a beautiful man, floating dead in a tube filled with fluid. Like a keepsake. And our child. They had him too." My mouth buckled with grief, so it was hard to speak the words. "Dead! Who could do such a thing to a little child? Monsters!" I cried, horrified. The enormity of it was still coming into focus for me. I grabbed his hand and held it to my forehead, as though I could press the reality of him being still alive into my comprehension.

After my sobs calmed, he continued smoothing the water down my back until he had to stifle a fierce cough coming from deep inside his chest. I looked down at the water swirling around my knees and ankles, dizzy with the unreality.

"You left something here." He rose for a moment and returned with something wrapped in a little silk cloth. He pulled out a fine gold chain with a small clay pocket goddess dangling from it.

"My idol!" I exclaimed. He dropped her into my cupped hands. The smooth contours of her round figure soaked into my skin. In this moment, she was my mother. She was him, soothing me. She was comfort after grief. I rubbed her against my cheek, my mouth, my forehead.

He rose and paced stiffly, face warped by incredulity. His hands shook slightly.

"A hidden copy of me? A twin? And dead? To what end?" I could see his mind was racing with the news. "Perhaps there are others as well." I nodded numbly.

"You need to leave this place. Or I do believe they will kill you," I told him.

"I think everyone should leave this place. Sack it. Burn the whole thing to the ground."

"Or change it," I said, looking up at him.

He smiled, a little distantly. "Soldiers are gathering. I'm told by the guards that you can see them camped on the hills outside the city. The Autokrator has called them all home."

"He's already tried to have your succession ended in the Parliament. Perhaps he's going to try another way." I paused. "The guards told you?"

"Yes, they seem quite happy to tell me things through the slot in my door. Treasonously happy."

"You have their support. They would fight for you. To a man, I bet."

He chuckled. "Perhaps."

"If I could find a way for you to go, would you try something else?"

"What do you suggest, Cera?"

"Change." Then, thinking better of it, I said, "Change of Autokrator."

There came an insistent rapping at his doors.

61

Tiresius

I KEPT THINKING about Dominius. The image of her lying on the table, marred and mute, her eyes boring into me with hatred and accusation, had been burned into my mind.

I tried to swat it away. There was always collateral damage on the way to achieving a goal. I couldn't understand why this turn of events would be any different for me. It pricked at my thoughts until I thought I was slightly mad.

And then there was the Consort, floating in that monstrous beaker. What had they done?

I thought I might go to the Autokrator, ask him what was to be done. I could act as though everything would go on as normal. The Consort needed funeral rites even if the Autokrator thought him treasonous enough to murder. I could convince him that appearances had to be kept up even at a time like this. But when I tried to enter his rooms, I found the doors barred to me, with no explanation. My mind raced with the possibilities. Might Dominius have told my secrets while under the knife? Even if she had, it was unlikely anyone would believe the ravings of a Domestic.

But what if they had?

I had only myself to blame if she'd betrayed me. Would I have done any different in her place? Had I given her a reason — aside from fear — to do my bidding? Was there a chance to undo some of what I'd done? But what was done was done. By now, she would be lying on some refuse pile, food for crows.

As I soon would be too, if I didn't carefully plan my next move. So I left the Autokrator's apartments and paced the hallways, realizing that I might have been saved from putting my foot in it by demanding a funeral.

Instead, I sent one of my runners to give word to the Court Ritualists that they should seek a body in Ferrius's lab. There was nothing that stopped me from seeing to the burial myself. I would need to acquire black crepe and dark flowers. Mourners. Funeral musicians. I saw myself at the head of a dour procession, carrying the noble body. I would walk the corridors of the Imperial Palace, tears streaming down my own ennobled face. Courtiers and Portfolios would bow with reverence. I would eventually come upon the Autokrator Himself, who would have no choice but to embrace me in fraternal grief and then assume his place at the head of the procession. The Consort would be put in the ground with the right honours, and I would be seen honouring him. As the plan took hold in my mind, I began to feel better about the path that lay ahead.

I steered myself toward the Consort's apartments. The insignia of his station would ride atop the bier and cause men to fall still, in awe that a great man had passed. The details of how or by whom could wait for another day. Another plan.

The closed doors to the Consort's apartments did not perturb me. But the presence of guards did. The Autokrator had an exaggerated fear of a man who was stone dead.

"No one passes," barked one of the guards.

But one of the men loyal to me was stationed some distance away and whispered, "Knock on the door, my lord. The decree doesn't say you can't still have a chat with the man."

Did he expect me to use a spirit medium? I took my bafflement in stride and knocked. A window in the door slid open, and another guard's face filled the square.

"The Consort is not disposed to talk."

"I should think not, since he is dead. Let me pass. We have a funeral to plan. Have some respect."

The man pulled away and slid the window shut.

A moment later, it reopened. This time, the face in the square was the Consort's. And he was very much alive.

Again, I had to temper my bafflement. Something more infernal than a simple murder was afoot.

"Whose funeral?" he asked.

"Consort, I am surprised to see you."

"What do you want?"

"Only to tell you that, as a friend, I think you should take whatever steps you can to safeguard your life." One of the guards next to me bristled. "I can't safely say more right now. But take it under advisement." I took my leave, a little disappointed to have to scrap the moving and impressive funeral plans I'd made.

62

Cera

I SCURRIED OUT the Domestic door of the Consort's apartments, clad in the Page clothes I'd left there. My heart was in my mouth remembering the last time that I'd left that way. But I pushed past the irrational fear I could be taken again and went on. The low tunnel forked. One way led back Below, the other out to the service hallways in front of the Consort's door. Careful not to be seen by the men stationed outside, I became an imposter in the world of men once more. I doubled back down the gleaming onyx floors, the torches of the guard detail reflected in them at the Consort's doorway.

I found a seat on a bench there and took out some grapes I'd wrapped in a cloth, hoping they would notice me.

"What have you got there?" ventured one, looking at me past his spear.

"Western grapes." I hopped down, a spry lad. "Want some?" They were the best grapes to be had — and normally reserved for the Triumvirate.

After a moment's hesitation, he helped himself.

"Aren't you that boy of the Treasurer's?"

"Dominius."

"Dominius. That's it. You're the one who can't shoot for shit."

"That's me." I grinned. We bonded over his mockery of me.

"We figured you to be Tiresius's bed boy."

"Ah. The Treasurer is not my type. I far prefer the Consort."

"Oh ho, do you now! Set your sights high? Good on you, lad." He took some more grapes. "Can't blame you. You have taste, at least. The Consort's a decent one. More of a straight shooter than that Tiresius. Still, stick with your master, lad. You serve him, and he's bound to look after you."

"Must be strange to be guarding your master in there."

"Orders are orders. But I don't have to like them."

"Still."

"'Course no one likes it. He's one of ours. Wears our colours when he rides. He knows we love him."

"It so happens that I know he wonders lately just *how* much he is truly loved. Locked away as he is, while the Autokrator is making decrees to pass him over."

"Pass him over? That's Unorthodox. Give your head a shake."

"I heard the Autokrator read it out Himself, in the Parliament. In case of sickness, pass over the Consort altogether."

"What, before he even gets a chance to get out of his women's weeds? That's not right."

I played with the stem of the grapes.

"From what I can tell, before he gets a chance to draw many more breaths."

He leaned in to me. "Are you suggesting that the Autokrator is planning to do away with His successor?" His voice was a growl that made my insides liquid. It was treason for me to say so. But I kept myself level.

"I've seen the plans of it myself." He stared me down. I could feel other guards standing close behind me. They'd been listening in to the whole conversation, as I'd hoped. "I think the Consort hopes that maybe he can get out of his women's weeds a little sooner than he otherwise might. To give himself a fighting chance."

"That's something I'd want to see."

A few moments later, the guards used their spears to pry off the metal bar that held the immense doors closed. They swung open on their noiseless bronze hinges to reveal the Consort standing there dressed in the manner and colours of a soldier of his own regiment: breastplate, epaulets, shin guards, and, most notably, leggings.

He held aloft the long, ceremonial plait of his hair and threw it down to the ground with derision. Normally, this happened when the Consort was elevated at last to the role of Autokrator. The retiring Autokrator helped remove his women's weeds piece by piece, culminating in shearing off and burning the ceremonial plait. Seeing the thick braid tossed away and the Consort newly shorn with a soldier's cut, the guards cheered and slammed their spears against their shields in approval.

The Consort walked into the throng of men and was heartily clapped on the back. Though I could see he was still pale, a look of pride and happiness made him smile in their midst.

"Who shall be the rightful Autokrator?" I shouted behind them, my voice barely cutting through their din. For a moment they all turned to me, quiet. And then, one by one, they began crowding closer to him, proclaiming his name over and over.

"Caelius! Caelius! Sixty-seventh Autokrator!"

63

Tiresius

WORD ABOUT THE Consort's arrest had been spreading for days. Now, whispers of his death poured from the Palace and through the streets like water running downhill. As I hurried through various wings on my way back to that infernal lab, I saw plumes of smoke and heard men's voices and weapons clashing. I was not anxious about this. The city was studded with guards and soldiers at all times. The Palace was nestled high above the embrace of the city walls, where no martial strife had ever penetrated.

I needed to know exactly who it was I'd seen in that beaker and put a stop to the funeral I'd started. The resemblance to the Consort was more than passing. It was something that could exploited in many sinister ways. But I arrived in the labs to find a confused muddle of ritualists and other officials standing around helplessly. Pages had begun to assemble a funerary bier while the ritualists stood idly by, twirling their beards, afraid of leaving empty-handed.

"Where is the body?"

"We've been trying to get word to you. The Consort is not dead."

"I know that, you dodderer. But where is the body?"

"Lord Tiresius, there was no body here that met the description we were given. There was only the corpse of Vincius the Toolist, since taken away to the midden."

Someone was steps ahead of me in this forsaken game. I felt like I was walking on dagger points.

I left the labs behind, intent on confronting the Autokrator. I reasoned with myself that I still had a purpose and utility. His activities were so furtive that firm, guiding words from me would be welcome.

I was stopped by an ashen-faced Page.

"They have the body. Outside!" whispered the boy. He pointed out a nearby window.

I rushed over to see.

I was met with the sight of a black autokinetic caravan heading toward the square in front of the Palace. The back doors hung wide open. It was full of whooping Toolists, Fallos boys, and other men. Some rode on top of the van, and dragging along on the ground behind was the body of that unfortunate drowned creature from the labs. They had tied rope around its ankles.

Nelius stood at the back, holding onto the roof with one hand and waving a massive black flag.

"We demand answers!" he screamed over the roar of the caravan. "Why does this man look like the Consort? Who is Consort? We demand to know!"

I strode to the nearest guard and snapped my fingers before his dozing face.

"Come! The Autokracy needs you. And you, boy." The petrified boy and the sleepy guard fell in behind me. We gathered others along the way, and I raced out the nearest door, down the ramparts to the square.

By the time I reached it, Nelius and the van were already there. Heaped on top of the autokinetic, they formed a spiky group in the centre of the plaza. They had drawn the corpse up with them, jeering, waving its hands.

"The succession has been compromised!" Nelius screamed, inflaming the growing crowds. "We demand that the Autokrator be granted powers to extend His rule!"

So this was the plot Nelius must have concocted with the Autokrator. Throw the succession into disarray. Re-consolidate power. Crude. Uncouth. And effective.

I recognized some of the Consort's own guard among the stony-faced bystanders. They were unmoved by the mania of these Fallos boys. I directed the two dozen people I had collected on my way to stand shoulder to shoulder with them.

"The Consort is alive and well," shouted a stout fellow with a clear voice and a disdainful look.

"Lies!" shrieked Nelius, and the word was parroted by his followers in a frenzy.

"I served him his breakfast with my own two hands just this morning," the stout fellow shot back.

"Lies and untruths. This is the Consort. Look at his braid. His face! The Imperial chain." Now the man grew angry.

"You call *me* a liar?"

The braid and the chain could be faked. What was harder to disprove was that face, which, despite being slack and bloated, was exactly like the Consort's. But I myself knew what I had seen.

"Everyone knows perfectly well that the Consort is under house arrest in his apartments," I shouted, afraid the general noise would drown me out and weaken my authority. But it was loud enough for Nelius to hear it.

"More lies! A puppet is inside those apartments. This is the Consort. We demand an extension of the Autokrator's powers."

I wondered which window the Autokrator watched this passion play from. I could imagine him pacing back and forth, wringing his hands. Nelius was pouring his heart and soul into the role. I turned to the stout soldier.

"Go up to the Consort and bid him to show himself from the balcony. Let's put an end to this nonsense." He grinned and loped off.

Though the number of followers around Nelius grew, the watching crowd around us grew too. Many faces were pinched with suspicion. Nelius had not won over the mob yet.

A moment later, a gilt stool sailed out of the glass on the balcony doors that led to the Consort's apartment. The Consort himself stepped over the chains and golden locks that had been placed there by Imperial decree. He tore his shirt loose from the jagged windowpanes and came to the front of the railing, where he held one fist aloft. The crowd lit up, cheering him on. I imagine whatever window the Autokrator had watched from was abandoned in disgust at this point.

"An imposter!" shouted someone nearby. As I spun to see them, the words were answered by Nelius.

"Yes! Exactly. None should believe their own eyes. Listen to me instead! This is a ruse. A deceit. There are vast lies within the Palace, and only the firm grace of the Autokrator can put things to right."

"He is our new Bartolius!" someone else called from with the crowd. This was taken up by the Fallos boys who rode atop the Autokinetic. I admired their propaganda. It was excellently laid out. Within moments, men all over the plaza were fighting with one another while the fallen corpse lay face down on the cobblestones.

A moment later, the thundering of horse hooves echoed through the space. The crowd scattered. Two riders raced toward the Palace, leading a third horse. As they rode up, the Consort dropped down from his third-floor balcony, dangling off one of the chains from the doors. While the riders approached, he hung suspended some twelve feet above the ground. Guards on the balcony held the other end of the chain and braced his weight against the railing. At a shout from him, they let go, and he dropped to the ground. He landed in a crouch and then sprang up. He walked over to the free horse, mounted it, and rode away down the High Street. At least half the crowd assembled in front of the Palace cheered him as he went.

64

Cera

WORD THAT THE Consort had fled his arrest without drawing a drop of blood soon surged through the Capital.

I made it to the railing on his balcony in time to see him riding away from the city, back straight. He was flanked by soldiers who fell into formation behind him. The ground in their wake was littered with the standards of the old Autokrator, which the men had thrown down and trampled. At the main gates, men willingly opened the way to him, and soon the distance swallowed him up.

I was heartsick that this could be the last time I would see him.

I watched until the last soldier in his wake had slipped from view.

I left the Consort's rooms and took the winding stairs up to the top of Tiresius's tower, but found no sign of him. The place was empty, allowing me to walk freely about the cage I'd occupied for a time. I realized my bondage to Tiresius had only ever existed because I'd had faith in it.

I fingered one of the books I'd seen Tiresius slipping gold wafers into. How many were stowed away here? In other places? I'd only just slid the book I was holding back into its place when the doorway darkened with Tiresius's shape. Any surprise he might have felt at my presence was carefully masked.

"So you've come back Above, have you? Congratulations. I thought perhaps you'd died in the lab. Are you looking for employment again? You weren't the most useful of my informants, you know."

"I come with an offer. You have a narrow choice before you, old man. One of two options. The first, as you know, is very bleak: death. The other will have a measure of bleakness, and will inevitably end the same way, but could last quite a bit longer."

He recognized the words with a faint smile. "I've always prided myself on listening to offers with an open heart."

"The Consort has left the Capital."

"Old news to me."

"He means to overthrow the Autokrator."

"Now that is a daring pursuit. One that I'm sure the Autokrator won't take lying down. Come to think of it, perhaps He will. He does tend to laze about."

"I could give you a place in the new Autokracy."

"Ah! This is a rich idea. An Unmale offering me a place in the future Autokracy? You have balls, Dominius, and I have to admire that. The Toolists must have done terrible things to you to make you so stroppy all of a sudden." Tiresius paced a little, and I realized he was buying time to think.

"In a strange way, you are like a son to me." He laughed at the irony, and I couldn't help but laugh too. I had learned much from his tutelage. "Listen to me: upon hearing the news, the Autokrator will demand an emergency session of the Parliament. With the Consort on the outside and supported by his own men, he is now a real threat to the Autokrator. And a true traitor. Of course, if he prevails, he is Autokrator, and the sitting one is the traitor." Tiresius continued to speak, mulling over the options as if I weren't there. "What I see is a headstrong Consort, weak with mysterious afflictions, being aided and abetted by a renegade Unmale, a gender criminal. His guard might love him, but do you think he can possibly prevail against hundreds of years of tradition? I think it more likely the people will rally to the existing Autokrator. I could remain loyal at His side, if only to live to see the end of His rule." He turned to face me. "I think it most likely that *you* will find yourself quartered and thrown on a refuse pile and burned. Soon."

"Then I am finished here. You've made your choice. And we can see what history does with you."

"Hold — I've made no choice. But I make a counteroffer. Send me word of the Consort's movements. If enough men amass behind him, and they are ready to pounce, I will consider opening the gates to them. If I see that you have no support, I will inform the Autokrator of your treachery and your gender crime, and you and the Consort will be hunted down."

Keeping my eye on him, I made a bow to Tiresius, guarding my pant leg and my hidden treasure as I did.

He did not return my bow.

I made my way down the main steps and through hallways below. I walked carefully so as not to attract attention — neither in too much of a hurry nor too slow. I was carrying important cargo.

I ducked into a Domestic hole not far from the main doors. From there, I could move as quickly as I needed, clinking and clattering as I went. I raced through the lower halls and then back up again to the streets. I ran past the house that belonged to Eva and Vincius. It stood shuttered and dark, the front windows shattered.

I slipped into the veil of evening crowds only to find myself trapped inside the city's gate. No one could come or go on account of the Consort's escape. I had to find another way out.

I went back Below, still running, now with a stitch in my side and sweat greasing my face. Near the ovens, I grabbed a spare shawl and wound my way to the passage leading to the lower levels.

Following the smell, I found the passage where Domestics trundled garbage out of the Capital in wheelbarrows. I waited for a slow Mam and took the wheelbarrow of putrid cargo from her. The procession crawled at the pace of the utterly defeated, winding along the lightless tunnels. Eventually, I saw a glimmer of evening at the end of the tunnel. We were heading out under the city wall to the garbage heaps, where rotting corpses and refuse mingled together in a great stinking pile.

The death and decay stretched out from the city, hill after hill. I climbed up one and down another, following the silent women before me, listening to the squelch of the ground below and the squeak of the wheels, waiting for the moment guards might look away. Over a third rise, I pitched the barrow and ran, tearing off for a hilltop past the archery fields where I knew the Consort would be waiting for me.

65

Tiresius

THE APPROACHING SESSION of Parliament would be an interesting one. How would one preside over it after trying to arrest one's own son? In more than a thousand years of history, Gentius was the first to attempt it. I waited in the wings of the Parliament as men gathered outside, waiting for the Sergeant at Arms to admit them. Here, at least, was one room still open to me. I planned a serene and imposing entrance after the others had sat, cementing my place in the firmament alongside the Autokrator for the time being. The crowds were more animated than usual as they filtered through the doors and took their places. I watched from a curtained alcove as the Autokrator passed by and brought the Parliament to order.

I was inspecting the pristine cuffs of my robe, about to enter the room, when the Autokrator abruptly opened the Parliament. Some junior Portfolio was jostled to his feet by a guard and made to read a charge from a piece of paper with a quavering voice. The charge was that the Imperial Treasurer should be immediately deposed and removed from his post for incompetence. I was thoroughly annoyed.

Incompetence?

That was the deepest insult they could have levelled at me.

I felt my face redden.

This was not the entrance I had planned.

This junior barely knew me. So, clearly, it was the Autokrator who planned to oust me. I was gratified by the number of voices that shouted down the charge. It was dropped. Many bribes over the years had ensured my survival for one more day.

The sun had fully set on Gentius, but there was still a slim chance to salvage a position for myself. I abruptly turned my back on the Parliament, striding away down the hall. Some steps away, I broke into a run. If the Consort was able to rally men, I resolved I would wait inside and open the gates to the conquering hero. If he didn't ... well that part hadn't been written yet. No point rehearsing the lines until it was.

66

Cera

MEN STOOD WITH horses on a dark hilltop. They lit no fire; they raised no tents. Many of them squatted in circles, speaking in low voices with their weapons close at hand. Others stood restlessly. The Consort was huddled with several others when I arrived. I could hear them discussing tactics.

"Broach the front gates only to die under a hail of arrows and pitch and anything heavy they've got to hand? No, thank you."

"The other option is to attempt to scale the walls and be picked off one at a time while cresting the ramparts. They'll stick swords in the throats of each man coming up the ladder."

Hearing death discussed so frankly made my head feel thick.

As soon as I approached the group, one of the men shoved the point of a spear toward me.

"You dare, incubo!" He was indignant. "Step away from the Consort!"

I stood tall and shed the shawl at spear point, revealing my Page uniform. From one disguise to another.

Men turned and looked at me, shocked. The point of the spear only went down when the Consort himself approached and touched it with light fingers. He greeted me with both hands. The soldier still seemed suspicious. I saw him spit with derision and could easily read his thoughts: No one clean or good would wear a shawl if they were a man.

"The Autokrator has troops gathered all around the city. They have swords sharpened especially for me, your rightful Heir. We stand at a pivotal moment of history when a lawful Heir could be struck down by a power-mad Autokrator. We are pitifully outnumbered, as he has amassed his whole army against us," the Consort told me.

"How many men do you have?"

"Two hundred, or thereabouts. He has thousands." He turned to his soldiers now, addressing them too. "But we have something else. Something no man in this realm would have thought to count. There are others who are willing to die for us. Others who are willing to help, others whose time has come to be counted." He pulled me forward and presented me.

"You see a boy. But this boy is an Unmale." The soldiers bristled. He raised his voice. "And she is an ally. One who wants to see us demolish the traitorous old Autokrator as much as I know you all do." The men's voices rose in a din as they all talked at once.

I pulled something out of my pant leg and placed it in his hand. He laughed, shaking his head in slight disbelief.

"A Domestic saves the entire Autokracy with a gift of gold. Who will believe any of this ever happened?"

His captain came forward and reluctantly gave his hand, in a sign that he would accept this Unorthodoxy.

"Be careful how much you would bend tradition, Consort," he warned. "Bend too far and everything breaks."

The Consort nodded and pressed a hand to his mouth, stifling a sound. Even in the gloom, I could tell he clenched his fist against some unspoken pain.

"Give me your shoulder," I told him.

He leaned on me as he had done before, the weight crushing my shoulder until I found a rock for him to sit on. "I don't know if I have the stamina to lead anyone."

I held his fingers, alarmed.

"But we are here now, and the only way is forward, even if it's the way to death."

"That is my path too."

"I wonder what will they write about this, later. The errant Consort, with an Unmale fighting at his side, slaughtered the Autokrator's forces and threw their bodies into the river? Forgive me." He stopped. "Here I am assuming you will be fighting. You don't have any place in a fight, of course. It is men's business."

"This is my business. Our business."

I could see his eyes glinting at me in the dark. He did not blink. I held onto him and buried my face in his clothes so I could pretend to be safe for the moment.

67

Tiresius

I SHED MY official robes and moved about the Capital wearing a dark, threadbare cloak instead. It very much depressed my spirits to have to mingle with the populace anonymously, with not one single mark to let them know to make way for me. It made me feel naked.

My pulse quickened, and sweat soured in my armpits as I went. But this was not a moment to give in to the frailties of the flesh.

Every doorway closed at dusk now, and there were men stationed at each door to guard them. They were questioning the identity of people moving about inside and out. I heard men talking about me everywhere I went.

"Escaped."

"Treason."

"Warrants issued."

"Selfish fucker."

That last one really stung. I was no more selfish than the next man.

Cast out of favour and away from my tower, I had a card to play yet.

My deep pockets clinked with gold.

If I chose the right path, only ten doorways lay between me and the gates of the Capital. Years of scrupulous accounting had left me with enough to get that far, at least.

68

Cera

I HAD INTENDED to wait for the Consort at the camp while he and the men rode ahead to take the city. What else was I going to do? A lifetime of toiling at Domestic labours had hardly prepared me to pick up armour and weapons. I couldn't bear to see him ride off, but I would be a liability to him, if anything. And I feared death.

He was helped onto a horse, though even in the torchlight, I could see that he resented needing the help. I nodded goodbye to him. It was one of those terse goodbyes that is made with the awful knowledge that later it would be regretted as not enough. He laughed at me and held out his arm.

"You're not staying here!"

So we grasped each other's forearms, and I stuck my right foot in his stirrup. He helped me swing up and onto the hard saddle behind him.

"Couldn't the Consort have a more comfortable seat?" I complained. And he laughed.

We brought three of the Consort's original detail, men who had served him since they were barely out of short pants themselves. They rode ahead of us, waving long white banners. The colour of those banners and the uniforms our men wore were the only thing between us and certain death.

We wound our way along a hilltop to a rough tent where several men in tall headgear waited. I had no idea who they were. It was only later that I learned they were the leaders of each of the battalions of the Autokracy. They'd returned from stations far away from the Capital and had converged here on the Autokrator's order.

The men cheered the sight of the Consort. He'd clad himself in their colours, the green and gold of soldiers down through the ages. Though he could have worn the scarf and braid of an officer, he chose to dress as simply as a rank-and-file soldier. They loved him for it.

They told us that in the Capital the Autokrator had donned his Imperial robes and sat in an emergency Parliament. They pointed out that the ancient beacon that alerted distant towns of trouble in the Capital had been lit.

One of the generals spoke first to the Consort's aide.

"Darius, I served with you when we were younger. I know you. Is this the traitorous Consort who has left the Capital, and not some pretender?"

"I can confirm, this and none other is the one true Consort Caelius of Family Evander. He has been treated wrongly by the Autokrator and seeks only to be reinstated as the rightful Heir."

"I've heard that the Autokrator sought to have him executed for treason."

"In order to extend His own reign, which, if true, would be treason itself." The general nodded thoughtfully. The Consort said nothing, watching.

"It is Unorthodox for the Consort to throw off his women's weeds prematurely."

Now the Consort spoke.

"Less Unorthodox than for a pater to steal the future of his own son's promise. I would happily serve the rest of my time as

Consort to the Autokracy, but circumstances have robbed me of that duty. Just actions have come from the most surprising quarter of all, though." He turned to me, putting his hand out for the pouch of gold I'd brought.

"This is wry; a Domestic offers gold to the commander of the military to overthrow the Autokracy."

"In effect. Think of what a colourful moment it will make for the history books," the Consort told him, and they both chuckled.

"Imagine what a moment it would make if the commander refused the gold."

I heard the Consort's breath catch. As mine did.

The general pulled his sword. Our attempt had failed.

"I will not take gold, and certainly not from some Domestic." He gripped his sword in both hands and thrust the point in the earth at the Consort's feet. "I do not do this for this one's sake." He pointed at me; his inborn disgust of me and my kind was clear. "But I will give you my blood." When he knelt, all the men in the tent did too.

"Long live the Autokracy," he cried. "Long live Caelius Evander, sixty-seventh Autokrator."

The Consort gripped the general's hand on the hilt of the sword and squeezed it hard with his own.

Only then did I find my breath again.

We returned to our camp with raised spirits. Alone in our tent with our heads close together on the same pillow, like they had been so long ago in the Consiliorum, we made plans.

"There's something we need to do," I said. His eyes glittered darkly, picking up the reflection of the fires outside our tent. "There is someone else the people will rally to — someone else who needs to be made safe. The Kratorling." I sat up, my heart bursting to even speak it.

He nodded. "You have to go in disguise — you seem to have picked up a knack for it." He traced my jaw with a soft finger.

"I never quite know who I am going to see every time we meet."

We kissed, and I felt more want for him than I had before. I wanted him to fall into me, needy, hot, senseless. I wanted for a moment to blot out everything that was happening and focus on his kiss opening my lips, tilting my head back. But instead of pressing hot to mine, his kisses were tentative. He broke away, unsealing us to rub his hand across his scratchy stubble. He was far away, distracted by many other things. I felt my heart heave a little, and I placed my mouth softly on his temple, tasting the salt from his skin. He made a distant noise acknowledging me, but still he remained fixed on everything that was in the future.

I left his bed that night while everyone slept. I took a horse and urged it out along paths that picked their way back down toward the Capital.

As much as I felt like I was tugging at a chain between him and me, I could feel the magnetic draw back to my other heart.

I looked at the moon peeking out between the leaves of young trees branching overhead. I imagined that a time might yet come when we could, all of us, stop running, stop being afraid.

A rock skittered onto the path ahead of me, and I saw that several of our soldiers were ahead. A checkpoint barred the way. I slowed my horse to a stop.

One of them stepped forward, small for a soldier. With a gasp, I realized they were not soldiers. They were women. They were all bareheaded women wearing pants or breeches. The first woman who approached was young, a teenager. She had luminous skin and thick, straw-like hair. Her eyes, even in the dark, were a bright blue. She stepped closer and looked up at me with something that seemed like reverence.

"You are Cera."

"I am called that."

She turned to the others, unable to contain herself. "Cera! It's true!" She slapped her hand on my leg. "You're real!"

"Enough, Gaia. Step back." A second woman poked the point of her spear into my leg, catching it on the cloth. "Get down. And we'll be easy with you."

They would be easy with me? I slid down from the horse. My foot caught for a moment in the stirrup, leaving me dangling and vulnerable. Several hands steadied me. But then they gripped me and slung something across my wrists. I turned to face them. They still had their weapons up.

"Don't do anything quickly."

"We've heard you're strong," said Gaia.

"Well, I can't fight like this." I shrugged, and the points lowered a little.

They marched me up a small, rocky footpath between clumps of grass. When I stumbled on rocks, they steadied me. And we marched for the rest of the night.

69

Tiresius

I HAD SOME forty wafers of gold in my pockets and many more gateways to navigate. How much would I have to sustain myself after escaping? Each wafer was worth more than any soldier or guard's salary for an entire year. I was still an accountant, after all, and it pained me to pay too much for anything. But unless I found a way to break the massive Treasury wafers I carried into smaller currency, I would be stuck.

I wandered the streets, wracking my brains. Everywhere I went, men were throwing things or setting random fires. People were shouting for the Autokrator to produce the Consort. Acolytes were leading chants and prayers at the feet of Fallos statues. They looked rather ridiculous with all the brawling and looting going on around them.

I skirted a dozen men wrapped in cloaks warming fingers at a small bonfire. A few wore military-issue sandals under their civilian wraps. With the Consort amassing men and the Autokrator's recall of the entire army, I needed to keep an eye on them. I lingered within earshot.

"More than half of 'em gone over."

"Idiots. They'll get what for. This will blow over."

"And then what? String him up?"

"I wager. Incubo lover that he is."

"I heard they had gold. A good amount."

"Must be nice. We've been on survival rations. Thank Fallos for a furlough and my savings."

"Keep that jug passing, will you? Who knows when we'll get more here."

"What's your bother? There's plenty more."

"Not bloody likely. I heard incubos destroyed all the barrels they had laid up for the year at the Autokrator's vineyard. Whole year. Down the drain."

"Crazy bitches. Why'n't they drink it? Total waste."

"Oy! Watch!" Another scuffle had broken out nearby.

When I had to duck to avoid a stool flying through the air, I decided to find one brawny soldier and pay him to escort me out. I turned on my heel and made for the direction of the main gates.

A firm hand stopped me in my tracks.

"What are you doing skulking around in such shabby dress?"

"Nelius!" I struggled for composure. "My, what strange times afoot." He chortled in response.

"We are blessed to live in interesting times, old friend." I winced inwardly at the familiarity but chose to let it go. "Interesting times that will lead to interesting outcomes. But you haven't answered my question. The Palace is so far from this neighbourhood."

"I'm keeping an eye on matters of state — sounds interesting, but really it's quite dull."

"I think you could do with a jolt of excitement, then. And a chance to make a real difference."

"Your attention to what's best for me is deeply flattering." He was leading me up through winding cobbled streets into the Garden District, known for its parks and churches. It was in the opposite direction of the city gates.

"Have you seen Ferrius lately? I feel recent events have upset all the normal social graces." He didn't know I had seen. How would he spin it?

"I've not needed Ferrius for some time. His importance with the Great Undertaking has ... greatly diminished. But you ... you're an important man, Tiresius. You hold the keys to the Treasury! A very good man to know."

Did he know about the attempt to oust me in the Parliament? Very likely he and Gentius had crafted it together.

He led me up to the stone steps of the oldest Fallos shrine in the city, but I couldn't fathom why. It was at the centre of a lush park, hung with sweeping branches and dark leaves. There was a white Fallos statue heavily protected from meddlers and vandals by a spiky iron fence and alert guards. As with all Fallos shrines, stone steps led down below the statue to the rooms where men collected to praise him.

Nelius threw a hood over my head and ushered me down into a low, dark tunnel punctuated with torches. At the mouth of the tunnel, smoke blended with gusts of acrid sweat and the sound of men's voices. They chanted their adulations.

When we reached the threshold of the place, we stopped, and I heard the ring of spears crossing to block our path.

"No one is allowed in but initiates!" commanded a guard, but Nelius kept two hands on me and steered my faltering steps down more shallow stairs. At each one, my feet sought the ground with panic. I expected to fall at any moment. His voice, quiet behind me, was surprisingly comforting.

"Relax. It is our way. The uninitiated cannot see what we do."

I staggered forward, arms outstretched, and heard laughter all around me. Elbows and fingers ribbed me. I was forced down to my knees. Perspiration streamed under my hood. It was sweltering down there.

"What do these initiates bring?" demanded a booming voice. I was lightly kicked.

"Dig into your pockets, Treasurer." Nelius's voice came from just behind me. I fumbled in my pockets, making a show of looking. I pulled out one wafer.

"I cannot offer everything I have here. I need to break this up."

"Oh ho! This is a healthy offering indeed."

"For Fallos's sake, Nelius, this is my whole salary," I lied. "May I keep back a portion?"

"Easy! We are grateful for any offering, and Fallos wouldn't choose to bankrupt any man. Give what you can."

"Then make it ... half," I stuttered, not expecting I would see a penny back.

He took the wafer from my hand. I did not tell him about the others.

Clusters of men were chanting in a rising pulse around me. I couldn't make out individual words, but I could hear flesh bumping and jostling as though men slammed into one another, and the air was growing thick with heat. Somewhere, further within, a man's voice rose and fell in the cadence of a priest. He was talking to the faithful. He was whipping them into a frenzy.

"The day is nearly come!" He strained to be heard over the chanting. An unintelligible response. "We must be Clean of the stink of decay. We must rise up. We must rid ourselves of contagion!" I risked a glance from under my hood.

The place had a low ceiling and was covered in soot dripping with condensation. It was crammed wall-to-wall with men, many stripped down to their underclothes, sweating, swaying, colliding. It looked like an orgiastic riot.

Beside me, two other hooded men were kneeling. They clasped their hands before themselves.

The circle wound around and around the feet of another Fallos whose head grazed the low ceiling. They were lifted to ride on one another's hands. And when they took a swing around the white marble flanks of their god, they reached up a hand to touch him on his belly, his thighs, his erection. I saw men dropped; I saw men trampled. I thought I could pick out faces of men from the court, but with the dimness and ceaseless movement, who could really tell?

"We will not wait any longer for leaders to do the right thing. We must defeat evil ourselves! We must ferret out the Unmales. Line them up. Let the streets run with their blood. Only then will we see Bartolius return. Only then will we see men's lives improve. Only then will we be righteous." The rotating mass of men cheered.

"Will you be my soldiers? Will you not fall at the feet of Fallos to do this?" His pleas were met with screaming assent. The crowd thrashed against one another, slick with sweat.

Through a break in the crowd, I could see that the man who spoke was Nelius himself. Droplets of sweat hung from the tips of his hair and his nose and fell when he convulsed with shouting. Men clambered toward him, seeking to touch him the way they sought to touch the god.

The other uninitiated and I hung back. But at each rhetorical question, I heard the man beside me grunt and saw him strain forward. He wanted desperately to join the others.

"Who is ready to die for his fellow man? Who is ready to bring in a new age of righteousness? Who is ready to do what it takes to bring back the righteousness of Bartolius, of our Golden Era?"

The man beside me staggered forward, still wearing his hood. Accidentally pummelled by the crowd, he went down and then got back up, riding the crest of their lifting hands.

Nelius and the mob were chanting, "Swear to Fallos! Swear to Fallos!"

I turned, yanked off the hood, and scurried for the doors, ducking under the crossed spears of the surprised guards.

"In the name of Fallos ..." I faltered, but they gave me no resistance. They guarded the entrance, not the exit. I staggered up the tunnel, which I could see was littered with the vomiting bodies of men sporting black eyes, scrapes, and crooked smiles.

I staggered up the stairs, happy for cool air to breathe.

70

Cera

THEY TOOK ME to one of the rocky hilltops overlooking the Capital. The thick walls of the city were sheer and impossibly high. The deep river that flowed around them was ruffled with fast-moving water.

Dawn was breaking as the women led me down a path that disappeared under the long skirts of a grove of massive old cedars. The ground was covered with soft, slippery bracken, and wide branches looped down to the earth like hammocks. The base of one tree was cleft into a ragged niche where it had grown around a rocky opening. At the base of this cleft, the women knelt down and pushed forward one by one, disappearing into a limestone cave. Sandwiched between two women, I knelt too, entering darkness.

The rock quickly became ice cold and slick with moisture. Sometimes, small shafts of light came through from overhead, but other stretches were completely dark. The women guided me with voices: step down up ahead, crouch down here, mind your head. At one point, we had to slither through a narrow space where massive limestone walls nearly touched. I could feel my ribs starting to squeeze as the way grew narrower. Hands pushed me on. I started to panic, feeling certain I would become wedged here.

Finally, I could see light on the other side of the narrow passageway. There was an open cavern carved through stacked up sheets of limestone, disappearing into darkness. Dozens of women — only a few of them wearing shawls — sat in groups, cooked over small fires, sharpened tools and weapons. Some were building rudimentary stools and tables with sticks and twine. They must have hauled everything they had here through that narrow eye.

They'd painted an image of Mother on a niche in the wall. She was nearly life-size, and her curves had been smoothed over with ochre many times. They'd given her a face, shadowy and indistinct, with kohl-ringed almond-shaped eyes. At her feet were candles and offerings of fruit and blossoms. She was covered by the handprints of women who'd paused to mark their reverence with ochre or blood. It made my eyes prickle.

"Hello," I told her, rubbing my own pocket goddess. The way the candlelight danced on the image made it seem as though she recognized me too.

The women showed me to a long table made of planks. They put food in front of me. Real food, not scraps and leavings. Properly cooked greens and stewed meat. Root vegetables. I was grateful.

Many of the women were trying to catch my eye. Some of them seemed awestruck like Gaia had been. Others hid their mouths behind hands, shy and giddy.

"You are celebrated here," said a woman who pulled up a seat right near me. She reached over to tear a piece of bread off my roll and stuffed it in her mouth. Her eyes glinted. She was serious, but a smile played at her mouth. She looked at me like all of this was completely normal. I stared at her in disbelief.

It was Adria.

I embraced her, and she squeezed my head tightly to her shoulder. She smelled of sun and sweat and new wool. She beamed at me when we separated.

"It is good to see you."

"And you. By Mother, it was so awful when you went missing. All of us mourned you."

"I know. I've felt it before. We all have. Hopefully, one day we won't have to anymore. I am one of the lucky few."

"Did you go to *that* place …" I trailed off, shivering.

"Yes, I went there." She tightened her mouth. "But they could not keep me. I kept my wits about me. I watched the comings and goings. I watched the old Domestics with their barrows. When they came into the cell to take the dead out, I crawled in under another woman's corpse. They dumped me out in the refuse heaps on the western side of the city. And here I am. Resurrected from the garbage." She laughed a hollow laugh.

"Did they …"

"What? Did they cut me?" She laughed again, bitterly. She pulled up the shirt and vest she wore. A long scar snaked menacingly from her ribs down to her navel and across to her other hip. It was puckered and purple. "Sewed it up myself. But the yarn I found was none too clean. They put a baby in me. But they only left it there for three months or so. I'd barely started to show. And when they took it out, they took everything else with it. I'm some kind of Unfemale now. Not male. Not female. Something new. I suppose I am myself. I don't bleed anymore. Which I can't say I miss. What about you? Did they grow one in you?"

I touched my belly. I wondered what would come of Vincius's words. That I myself carried a new life.

"They say they put one in me. I don't know if it is true. They harvested my eggs, but I got away too."

"Aha! That's the Cera we've heard so much about. Escaping from the monsters! Passing for a boy, travelling the paths of men, wearing pants, eating like a lord, kissing her lover on the mouth, sleeping in a bed. You've become quite the hero."

"I've been noticing the stares. They all know?"

"You know how quickly word passes along the pathways. I was jealous. I would have loved to walk among them. And then spit in their faces and kick them in their poxy balls. Listen, Cera ..." She leaned close. "I know what they are doing in those labs. They mean to do away with us. A few at first, and then the lot of us if they can. They want to replace us with a device."

"That can't be done."

"Do you think that will stop them? I hear them arguing. That fat fool of an Autokrator thinks that they have already done it. Soon, they will start collecting the women in earnest. I for one don't want to meet that day grovelling on the floor in front of those swine.

"I hid out in these hills and sewed myself up. Ate bugs and sparrows, stealing food when I could. When I happened on other Domestics, I told them my story. I convinced them to come up here with me. Soon they were coming here on their own, looking for the women they had heard were hiding in the hills. Word is spreading. We are organizing. Mams carry messages to and fro in pails and wheelbarrows, and wherever the word goes, your story goes too. It's starting to catch fire for Domestics. Whenever you see a little shrine, that's us. Whenever you see another fucking Fallos with its dick cut off, that's us. We need their anger. We need them to have hope and anger and faith."

"What do we need it for?"

"Revolt, Cera. We are going to take back our place. Take back the place they cast us out of. We have a captain. We have numbers. We have faith. And that faith will carry us through the blood, the pain. The dying."

"We couldn't ask for a better leader than you, Adria. I am so glad you've found your way to this! Think! One moment you're dead to the world, the next you are beginning a revolt that maybe will end all of this." I clasped her hand, and her fingers were strong around mine. "But I have a favour to ask of you. I have a mission of my own. I want — no — I *need* to go back to the Capital. I have a child there. I want to take him away from all of this. I want to raise him myself. And, what's more, I know I have the help of the Consort himself. He wants a better world for our child too. For all children. Perhaps there will be no need in the end for anyone's blood, or revolt. Things are starting to change! I know it."

"And you believe the Consort is of his word? That he holds anything women want or need dear?"

"I do, Adria. With all my heart."

"Then you are an idiot that he has fooled. He doesn't have any interest in helping you. I know the child you speak of is the Kratorling. Let me be the one to tell you. You can't have him. The world that is coming has no room for him."

"Maybe so, but I want to at least try to make a world *for* him. I will take him away if I can."

"I think you misunderstand me, Cera. There is no way I can help you with this business with the Kratorling. Let him survive on his own if he is able. The way forward is women. And the one I want to lead us is you. If not willingly, then I will see to it that you are appropriately martyred. And then, when you are dead, I will kill the Kratorling myself."

71

Cera

I WASN'T EXACTLY a prisoner again. Any women who spoke to me treated me as though I were an honoured guest. But I was never left alone. The narrow pathway out of the cave was the only way out, and it was choked with women coming and going. Adria was ever present. She was there when I ate. She was nearby when I slept. She had a glint in her eye to see me. I was her trophy.

The second time I woke in the cave, she was cross-legged on the floor nearby. Before my eyes were even open, she was talking to me. I rubbed the sleep out, catching up to her words as they hammered at me.

"We need to move quickly. The time is coming. We have numbers, but we need weapons. And we need to bolster these women with the faith to carry us through everything that lies ahead. Let's get you cleaned up. The women are starting to gather."

Adria herself helped dress me and clipped my hair shorter, so I appeared as virtually all of them did — bareheaded and fiercely cropped. She brought out a long bolt of white muslin after I'd pulled my Page gear on. It was oblong and plain, with a hole in the middle. She pulled it over my head and belted it. I understood. She wanted her mascot to be seen, leading everyone in sacrificial white.

"I will tell you what to say. In truth, they only need to see you, Cera. You'll put blood in their veins."

She bade me stay out of sight until she called me. I could hear from the growing chatter that women had indeed begun to gather in greater numbers. Outside Adria's rooms, a step of rock formed a natural balcony. Adria had had them build little pyres on either side, and she took her place between them. The din rose until she lifted her hand, and a hush fell. She had all the bearing of the military captains who served the Consort, even if she didn't have their years of training.

From where I sat off to the side, I could see that every space in the vast cave was taken up with seated women. They had extinguished the other fires in the cave so that the balcony and Adria were the only thing lit by dancing flames.

"May our Mother guide us," she began. The gathered women repeated her words reverentially. "We have waited a long time in the darkness. We were put into the darkness by men. They called us sinful and stripped us of our names, of our place beside them in the world. We have been crushed under their heel, made to wait on them and clean their shit, asking nothing for ourselves. Still, they are not satisfied. They are not satisfied that we live and die under their feet, below their regard. Now they want more. They want, in their madness, to wipe us all out.

"I have been to their darkest places. I have heard their plots. I have seen their foot soldiers of death. They call us incubo because they think our only real service to them is to bear their sons and then be discarded. They have been searching for a way, these many years now, to replace us with infernal machines that will do the job of incubating their sons and copying their seed. So that we are not even incubo to them anymore.

"They are led by madmen! Only fools kill the chicken and wonder where the eggs will come from next. No man is motherless. Yet they presume to find a way to make men without mothers.

We will not stay under their heels anymore. Look!" She pulled up her shift and showed them the ugly scar on her belly.

"They tried to kill me. And they failed!"

A swell of jubilation came from the women whom she held spellbound with her ire. "And look at Cera! You have heard of her. The one who escaped to live among them. Look!" She beckoned me.

I walked out, with faltering steps, to the growing cheers of the women waiting outside. I lifted my hand in a small wave. The din swelled higher.

"Lift your arm high," Adria hissed at me through her teeth. She grabbed my wrist, lifting it high and straight. The room erupted in wild cheers and hoarse calls. When the sound abated a little, Adria continued.

"They took Cera too, as they took so many others. But she survived. By the Mother's Will, by her own wits, here she is, come back to us to guide us against all those that would destroy us. We will take back our place. We will not hide in darkness anymore!"

At these words, women in alcoves high up in the walls of the cave lit pyres. The gathered women rose to their feet and called both our names. They embraced one another in a kind of ecstasy. It was the pent-up fury and energy of hundreds of years of servitude being thrown off, and even I felt myself bursting inside to think that this could be the moment that everything changed.

The crowd began passing out pikes and pitchforks, knives and hammers. The flames glinted off the metal. And then I became afraid. Would there be a place for my child and Caelius after this?

When we emerged from the cave, it was night. No one spoke. They walked on silent feet, the way that had been ingrained in us all those years. The group that had captured me had kept my horse, and Adria lifted me up onto it while women looked on with yearning faces. What they did not see was that Adria had tied my belt to the saddle. Her attention to detail was impressive.

She leapt up behind me.

"I'm going to keep you where I can see you," she murmured in my ear as she clapped her hand to my shoulder in camaraderie. She turned in the saddle and motioned the women forward.

We wordlessly picked our way along hilltop paths until we emerged in a valley where farms and factories were clustered together. At the edge of the brush, where the fields opened up, the women halted. They sat on their haunches, all eyes on Adria.

"This will be the first test," Adria whispered into my ear. Her breath was hot, and her fingers dug into my shoulders.

She kicked my horse forward, and the women ran silently behind us, emerging from the trees. Adria pointed to the right, and I led the horse where she indicated. We jumped a low stone fence and raced into the courtyard of a farm where animals and Domestics alike slumbered. Our women streamed forward and began grabbing every implement they could. There was a forge here, and farming tools.

Domestics began to stir and were shocked to be met with women. Some ran for implements. Some froze in disbelief. I watched a silent struggle as one of Adria's women grabbed at a Domestic's broom. The woman's face was hidden in her shawl, but she resisted. Her attacker paused and looked to us. Adria gave her a sharp nod, and she struck down the Domestic. Her fall made my stomach leap with fear and sickness. Adria felt my response.

"They will join us or they must be dispatched," Adria told me with a steady voice. I bit down on the inside of my cheek to have something else to focus on. The same battle played out again and again until the baying of dogs chased us back into the woods. Some Domestics had ripped off their shawls and joined, but we left many behind, bleeding in the dirt of the courtyard.

72

Tiresius

I CONSIDERED LEAVING the city wearing a shawl and crawling around in the dark with the Domestics, but I had come too far, risen too high to ever allow myself to do such a thing again. Instead, I headed to the markets, which were still limping along despite the fact that fires burned in various districts and groups of people scuttled around breaking into fights and looting from one another. The prices they were charging as a result were outrageous, of course. But it comforted me to know that things remained calm enough that smart men could still turn a profit.

"Low stock today. And I'm getting ready to pack up. What do you want?" asked the broad man I normally got my cheeses and meats from. I pulled back my cowl. "Your lordship. Difficult times. You look a fright." He grasped my arm and I, his. When he pulled away, he was holding one of my precious wafers. "That's quite a sum. What do you need me to get you?"

"Safety," I replied. "I have one more of those if you get me out of the city and over the western ridge."

He had a cart pulled by two stone-faced Domestics and an old cow where he made a nest for me, right under the bench he rode on. I curled up with my arms crossed over my chest and my feet tucked in, and he slung a canvas tarp over the bench. It was passably comfortable, but for the burlap bedding he'd laid down. That was sticky and fetid. I had to cover my nose with my scarf to breathe with any ease. I hoped there would be a bath on the other end of my journey.

I could tell by the halt of the wagon when we passed through gates. Upon seeing a humble merchant and an empty wagon, the guards didn't bother to poke around under the empty baskets and burlap heaps.

Only when we reached the tenth gate did I peel back a little of the tarp to let in some fresher air. I considered pulling it back altogether and climbing up onto the bench once we'd been out of the city for a few hours. I was glad I hadn't.

I heard an Unmale shouting, and the wagon came to an unexpected stop. I couldn't make out the words, but a moment later, I heard the merchant shouting too.

"Get off. Get off of it." There was a strain in his voice. Then, unmistakably, I heard a thud that sounded like he'd been hit with something heavy. I chanced a look. He was fighting with one of the broad, stony Domestics. She was trying to take the reins from him. He shoved her down to the ground.

I sat up a little, trying to peer over the edge of the cart. The Domestic was on her back like a turtle. The other one was running away, head bared. And, astonishingly, the road ahead was choked with an entire herd of Unmales. They forded the road, streaming from one field to the next. Two of them were watching this astride a horse, for all the world like commanders overseeing an army. The rearmost one was a strapping creature with thick arms. She pointed, and a dozen armed Unmales streamed toward the wagon. The one in front turned and faced us.

My page.

She made no motion. But it was clear she sided with the other one who barked orders and had an attitude to rival any general.

I dove back down and covered my head. I heard something connect with the merchant again; this time, he slid off. I felt the wagon shimmy as women swarmed on board. The cow bellowed nearby. And then again at a distance. Then no more. The women shouted to one another. The wagon began to shake from side to side. Its old hinges squealed under the abuse. Then, suddenly, I was upside down, kissing the splintered underside of the bench with my face. I stayed there, still as a mouse, until the women's voices receded. I slowly became aware of hurts from my head to my toes. They appeared like flames, slow, and then burning hotter. But I didn't move until all was quiet and dark.

Then I walked. The merchant lay dead beside the wagon. I liberated my gold and a little more besides from his pouch. The cow was nowhere to be seen. The slightest midsummer brightness showed me the west, and I stumbled over rocks and roots to crest the western ridge. Near the top, I looked back. A few fires burned in courtyards, but for the most part, it was quiet. I wondered if I was doing the right thing in leaving. But the hot memory of "incompetent" came flooding back, and I felt a sour, sickly rage. I turned and bent harder to the climb.

My scarf was enough to gain me entrance when I met sentries, but it was my imperious voice that made the men snap to.

"Parlay. With the Consort."

They put me on a horse with a soldier. Ahead of us, men called softly one to the next, "Parlay!"

The Consort was in a tent with his generals. He seemed oddly happy to see me, in the way that one acts friendly to those they despise when they are the only familiar face at a strange gathering. This was a strange gathering indeed.

"I have other news, my lord, but you should know, I have seen my Page," I told him.

"Alive?" The fear was evident.

"You will not want to hear this." He held his breath. "Very much alive. And leading Unmales in a rampage. They have killed one man that I know of."

He exchanged a look with one of his men. The man's look was an "I told you so." I saw the Consort willing his chin to be steady. His temple bulged as he bore down, clamping his own jaw.

"Trust a woman," said his companion. "Like Bartolius."

"It could be a mistake," the Consort reasoned.

"I am not mistaken. But I have come with money for your troops. And ideas about how to take the Capital."

The Consort sat, heavily. He indicated a seat for me, where I could see the positions they plotted on a chart. By the grief in his expression, this was clearly the one blow he hadn't foreseen. But any man who thinks battles come without betrayal is too optimistic to be in a war.

73

Cera

WE DID NOT stop at the farms. We carried on, arcing widely around the outskirts of the city. I believe Adria's plan was more than simply raiding for weapons. The sleepy farms and factories we pillaged were overrun. She seemed to want to give the women an easy victory. When I looked over my shoulder at her, there was a beatific expression on her face. The blood of these women was up. And Adria's was with them.

After the last farm, she commanded a halt. She shushed, and they fell silent, watching her, panting and ready. She picked up my arm, and they all raised theirs too, some holding weapons, some holding their palms open. There was an air of glee. We were getting away with it.

How many times had I fantasized some such thing? When bent over backbreaking work that would only be scorned or wrecked. When bent under some Male intent on his pleasure not simply at my cost but because of my cost. Cowed, under-rested, underfed, under the feet of men. I had imagined grabbing implements nearby and slashing at every man near me until I, too, went down. I only ever imagined that it would take a moment before my life ended. And since I was a coward, I wanted to keep my life, miserable as it was.

But I had never imagined there would be scores of us grabbing brooms and cutlery and baring our teeth. It was surreal to see women's bare heads, faces streaked with mud and blood. It didn't matter whether I was a coward or not. I was a cork carried on a tide.

A bend in the road brought the Capital in sight. Adria pulled the horse to a stop and jumped down. She yanked me down after her. She pulled on a shawl, and everyone around us did likewise. We shuffled along like a group of Domestics being filed into the city to work. A few women even played the part of drovers, licking at the rest with knotted ropes. Just moving the workforce along.

74

Tiresius

THE CONSORT SETTLED on an unoriginal plan: a march to the gates of the city. He bargained on being welcomed back. Enough men had already rallied to him. I made a case for finding other ways to sneak inside but was overridden. Caelius felt history was being made. Sneaking in was cowardly.

"If you make it safely to the throne, rewrite history as you please!" I told him. "If he kills you at the gates, it will be Gentius writing the history." My advice fell on deaf ears.

We arrived by the main road in an orderly formation of clean, smart-looking troops just in time to witness something remarkable.

The road was unusually busy for nighttime. By torchlight, streams of people were leaving the city, many carrying packs and bundles. Even more people were on their way into the city. Drovers moved columns of wretched Domestics, herding them back to their lives of drudgery. But a curious thing happened.

The Consort was mid-sentence, talking about archery, when the man at the front of our troop cried, "Hold." The halt was immediate and soldierly. Ahead of us was a spectacle of fire and smoke. A lone scout surged forward on a fast mount to survey what was happening.

The columns of Domestics suddenly broke apart and scattered like ants. Torches danced like fireflies. Even at this distance, we heard their screams. Then, the chaotic mill of bodies flowed with purpose into the city. The scout clattered back toward us in excitement.

"Domestics!" he panted. "They are in revolt. Killed the guards at the gate. And now they hold it."

The Consort was taken aback.

"Surprise is their ballast. Who could have imagined that this would happen?"

"I think it will be a short wait," noted the scout. "They're unorganized. They'll be easily beaten."

Around us, there was a quiet rattling of weapons as men stood at ease. Uneasily.

75

Cera

ONCE WE WERE inside the gates, all sense of order was lost. The attacking women were a storm unleashed, running in all directions, slashing at soldiers, at men, and even at other Domestics if they didn't immediately join us. But many did join.

We surged along the winding streets, coiling toward the crown of the hill and the Palace. Domestics dropped their tools as our force approached. At first, they trickled out, and then they poured, racing through the streets to join our mob. They pulled off their shawls, felt the air with their faces.

Throughout the city, we set homes and businesses alight. The men ran out into the streets, chased by flame and pike. They carried their pathetic belongings and tried in vain to escape into the countryside.

A small force of soldiers remained behind to defend the Palace. As the horde of women with torches and sharpened sticks appeared, the soldiers held the gates shut with their bodies.

It took four men to work the mechanism that closed the gate. They hadn't bargained that even more Domestics would come out from the within the Palace. At the gate, the bravest and most foolish women hurled themselves forward. They were easily put down by the small force of well-armed soldiers. But the women's numbers grew and grew and overwhelmed the men.

Once inside the Palace, we headed for the lab. We poured through underground tunnels. We pried the doors to the Toolist enclave open with metal bars.

I wanted to warn the others about what lay ahead, but Adria stopped me. She pressed me against a wall with her elbow, her hand gripped across my mouth.

"We will let them see it for themselves. And we will let the men feel all their fury when they do."

Out of our sight, we heard screams. Not from the women pining for death inside but from their rescuers. And then from the Toolists they found there, still doing their unforgivable work. Some of us set to the task of freeing those who might yet live. Others focused on corralling the jailers and locking them into the cells. Most of the women expected to die but planned for the Toolists to be first.

Adria seemed to forget about me during the scramble. She leapt agilely forward, finding high points on which to stand and urge the rest onward. Her face was alight with passion. A stream of orders came from her lips, directing the women. Search rooms. Seize valuables. Capture men. Force them to their knees. Let blood flow from their veins.

Once the labs were secure, they demanded I show them the way to the Parliament, and then they surged along in the direction I pointed. They broke the doors down. As they streamed down the halls, they gouged the mosaics on the walls with the points of their weapons.

Meek bureaucrats surrendered immediately. They were herded into the middle of the room and tied up with ropes. I thought then that Adria might take the podium, claim the Parliament as hers. But instead, she took a sword from one of her captains so that she had one in each hand. She strode toward the cowering men and began thrusting at them. The rest of the women raced forward and fell upon the men in a fury. I saw a beaming woman hold aloft a nose she'd cut off, blood snaking down her arm. She hurled it and bent back to her work. Shrieks filled the room. Sickened, I tried to creep out.

"Where are you going?" Adria's wrath seemed to fill the doorway behind me.

I could only stammer. She pointed one of her swords at me, hand brown and red with old and new blood. But looking down the point of that sword, I saw I wasn't the target. A man cowered under a table behind me.

"To me!" she roared. But by then, two other men, heavy and well-armed, had shot out, surprising us all, and the man behind me scuttled away. I recognized the Autokrator by the gold in his garments. More men appeared, Nelius among them, fully armed. We were ambushed. Soldiers had lain in wait for us, hiding the Autokrator, and now they began to repulse us.

"Get the Autokrator to safety!" howled Nelius.

Adria stood her ground, snarling. I darted to pass her. Her foot tripped me. But they set upon her before she could haul me back. I wriggled my way along the floor, through the legs of the women trying to help Adria. I found one of the stairway passages leading from the chamber floor up to the soaring galleries. More men appeared from behind the throne and pushed toward the invading women. An organized force, they overlapped shields and pressed forward like a plow, forcing the women back toward the doors. The women were soon tripping on their fallen comrades and were overcome by the men. The doors were forced closed and barred.

Nelius stood at the Autokrator's podium. He grabbed both sides of the slanted desk in gory hands.

"I reclaim this Parliament for Fallos!"

His men cheered. They milled about the floor of the Parliament, clapping one another on the back and kissing cheeks. Nelius remained at the podium, soaking up the atmosphere.

"We need to secure the Kratorling." He spoke in a low voice, but they leapt at his words. "I want four men who can travel quickly." Several men, all wearing Fallos kerchiefs over their uniforms, shot their arms into the air, begging to be chosen. Nelius took his time, savouring the choosing. "Find the Child. Put him in an autokinetic and drive him out past the western hills. A year's salary paid to the man who brings me back his heart."

I clung to the top railing of the gallery as four men jogged out of the room, swords clattering against their armour, sandals slapping against the sleek floors. Nelius still lingered at the podium. He peered up at the gilded canopy overhead, meant to shelter the Autokrator from all harm.

"I could get used to this," he remarked to no one in particular.

But his enjoyment was short-lived. Adria leapt up from between the rows of the gallery a few feet over. She ran toward the front railing. Several other women emerged and followed her. By now, all of them wore trophy armour cobbled together from slain soldiers.

Adria vaulted over the railing, dropping almost two stories down to the dais where Nelius stood. She had followed my secret pathway up into the galleries. Ten other women landed on the platform too. The sound of their bodies landing on the stage was like the deep beats of a hollow drum. They circled Nelius and pounced. Working together, they pinned his arms, and Adria stood behind him with her long blade just below his chin.

"You will give us passage, or we kill him!" she shouted to the men below. They faltered at the sight of their leader in her hands.

"Go ahead," Nelius offered. "They don't need me." The looks on their faces said otherwise. Nelius was the fuse to their powder. The women led him to the lip of the dais, walking crabbed like some strange creature with many legs. As they led him down toward the stairs, the men ebbed backward.

Seeing my chance, I crouched over and ran along the top row of seats. There was a chance I could make it to the Kratorling before the men.

"I see you there, Cera. Don't think I won't come for you and your boy too."

I believed her. And so I ran as fast as I could.

76

Tiresius

WE ENTERED THE city neither by force nor surprise, not strategy nor secrecy. We rode through the main gates after the rampaging women had made their way deep into the city.

From where we stood, at a distance from the gates, we could hear the squeals and racket of the women storming through the city. A great mass of people had poured out of the gates, which the women hadn't bothered to bolt shut. As we rode through, we found the bodies of soldiers and, outnumbering them three to one, slain Domestics.

We took a leisurely pace, marching slowly but surely up the high street. Weapons were sheathed. We were not meant to look like an invading force but rather a returning son's guard. The column of soldiers with us extended out through the gates, across the river, and back out of the city as far as the eye could see.

We were met with a fell sight as we climbed toward the Palace: standing ramshackle in front of the half-closed gates was a hastily erected platform. It was made from carts and wooden steps torn from structures and placed there like a rickety pile of children's toys. The wooden steps were dyed dark red with blood. The women had been hard at work. Even now, more Domestics arrived, carrying more supplies. The ground all around was littered with heads, like a strange crop of unsightly pumpkins. The bodies were stowed in an orderly pile nearby.

Even at a distance, one could hear the squelch of blood that had worked deep into the cushion of the velvet stool they used as a chopping block. They severed heads with rough, rusty implements. They didn't stop at beheading, though. A sorry pile of disembodied male genitals pooled at the base of the platform, adding terror for those who waited their turn. Among these was Nelius. Several women were stoking a fire, which they also fed with body parts.

In their dire labour, the women ignored the overwhelming military force that had walked quietly up to the front door.

"Let us end this!" the Consort called out to them. "It is our will that this insurrection ceases at once. Mercy shall come to those who bend to my will."

"What shall we do with this one?" This was the great, strapping Domestic I'd seen on horseback outside the city. She stood to her full height, her face streaked with filth, her garments shredded and exposing one breast. With the help of a few others, she hauled Nelius up onto her stage. Nelius begged the Consort to free him and the others, but the Consort was unmoved.

"The Autokracy does not recognize traitors."

"Suits me." The Domestic shrugged, and while he was held fast, she gutted Nelius navel to throat, jerking his body with the force of her knife.

There was a blast of horns from our side. Prisoners and torturers alike stared at us. The Consort stood tall in his saddle.

"The authority of Autokrator Gentius is herewith abolished. My Autokracy begins now. And you Domestics will cease this Unorthodoxy."

With all her might, the woman up top hurled the grimacing

head of Nelius toward us. It landed with a thick, wet thud on the cobbles a short distance away.

"You and your army will have to make us," she taunted.

The Consort looked to his generals, who drew arms.

"Right flank!" ordered the lead man, and the mass of soldiers swiftly re-formed, making an advancing crescent that pressed forward to the platform. The women let loose the men they'd taken, but most of them stood their ground. They faced the force that came toward them though outnumbered a hundred to one.

I excused myself to the Consort, but he was focused on the fray. I urged my horse to the far left, skirting the advancing soldiers. I'd have to work my way back over to the right to regain entry to the Palace.

"Stop that one!"

"Stop him! Stop him now."

It took a moment for it to register that they were talking about me. I was too focused on sidestepping the whole mess.

It was the women — pointing at me.

Suddenly, they were leaping on top of my horse and pulling at my robes. Though I held on with knees and hands, gripping the pommel tightly, they wrenched me off the beast and flung me to the ground.

"This one is no man!" shrieked one of them.

"Never has been!" crowed another.

"I knew you back in the dairy, you bitch," snarled yet another at me. "Always thought you were so much better than the rest of us." She punched me in my belly, and others fell to it. I looked around desperately, but the men were all occupied with subduing the women at the execution platform. I would have to deal with this on my own. I was armed with a small boot knife and the harness I'd pulled off the horse with me. Though they got their fingers in my eyes and feet in my ribs, I managed to strike at them long enough for the full force of the Consort's army to overwhelm the square. Several soldiers came to my aid. I was punched, wrenched free, shoved to the ground, booted, hauled up, kicked in the throat, and, finally, shoved to the side. Then I scuttled for the closest door I could find. Had any of the soldiers heard the accusations about me? Was I still safe?

77

Cera

FOR THE FIRST time in my life, I was glad that I had spent years in the darkness, learning my way by touch and smell and changes in the texture of the paths. I moved through them quickly now. From time to time, my throat squeezed almost shut, and I felt a hot prickling at the corners of my eyes to think about seeing him in the flesh. But I had to push the thoughts back down. I had to keep moving.

The tunnels had become a shambles, with confused Domestics rushing back and forth, some determined to join the women's uprising, others senselessly carrying on with their tasks. It came as no shock, when I peered through the cold grate of the Kratorling's room, that the place was a fetid, chaotic mess. I called to him.

I wished I could say that he rushed to me, that my heart was finally able to release the pent-up need for him. But he looked up from some toy with coldness. He did not appear to recognize me.

"Go away," he said. After all the pathways I'd trod, after all the heartbreaks and pitfalls and tears. *Go away.* The words cut a deep wound, but they were not fatal. However, my love for him might eventually be fatal. It did not matter, though. I did not need him to return what I felt. I needed him, and I would risk it all again.

But at this very moment, I could hear armour clinking down the hallway outside the Child's room. Nelius's men were almost here.

"Would you like to play with me?" I asked, making my voice sound as inviting as I could.

"I said go away." His affect was flat. This was a tired child who needed to be fed. Who needed rest. Outside, the voices drew nearer.

I pulled out Mother and rolled her over the cold hearth onto the carpet. She landed with a little thud on the thick pile.

The Child squatted down to pick her up.

"The lady," he said. His fist curled tight about her. Still squatting, he looked at me through the fireplace, across the bed of silky grey ashes.

"What are you doing?" he asked.

"I am hiding," I told him, "from those men outside."

He nodded. "I am good at hiding."

"I don't believe you. This is the best hiding place," I said, desperately hoping to manipulate him. "But I doubt you are clever enough."

"I am. I am clever enough."

The voices were at the door, and their shadows were under it.

"Show me," I said. I don't think he noticed the quaver in my voice.

He bolted toward the fireplace. I clapped my hand over his mouth. He yelped and writhed and kicked. He dug his perfect milky little teeth deep into the meat of my hand. But I did not let go. I dragged him with me, down the winding pathways, putting as many steps as I could between us and those men. Only when we had gone many levels down did I remove my hand, letting him yell and curse at me. And still I went on.

78

Tiresius

THE INTERIOR OF the Palace was desecrated. Statues lay across hallways and doorways like drunken louts, torn down from their pedestals and beheaded or defaced. Unidentifiable liquid pooled on the floors and dripped down walls. Blood and filth, rotten food and shit were smeared across the priceless emblems. Glass crunched underfoot everywhere. Fire. Distant yells. Somewhere, a person played music in a distant room.

The panic at being exposed still clung heavily to me.

I sought the Autokrator. In an emergency, the Autokrator was always to be barricaded in the throne room. My goal now was to encourage him to surrender to the Consort and pave the way to an august retirement. What better way to smooth my transition between outgoing and incoming Autokrator? A peacemaker.

The throne room was locked. But I had a key, the only person outside the Triumvirate to have one. It slid home with a satisfying click, and the door swung open noiselessly. As soon as I entered, guards hurried forward to turn the locks again behind me.

Here, all still looked orderly, and the sounds of strife from outside were muted. Gentius retained a handful of supporters, still bearing the golden canopy above his peerless head. A few dozen of his personal guard lined the room, loyal to the last. Their oath was to stay with him to his demise if necessary, and to end their own lives should they fail him. He was partly curled up on his throne, as much as his own girth would allow, wrapped in a blanket, rocking himself slightly.

When I approached the throne, bowing and full of courtly grace, it was a bit of a tonic to him. He sat up a little. His wispy hair stood about the top of his head. He squinted a little, not recognizing me at first.

"Who is this that comes?"

"Your true Tiresius, whom you would have had dismissed not long ago."

"Not true. We never wanted such a thing. It was the mood around Us."

"Even so, loyal to the last." I bowed with a flourish, knowing how much he needed the soothing of obsequious love.

The Autokrator rose to unsteady feet and tottered toward me. "On one side of the Palace, Unmales are rampantly castrating men — some of them soldiers, even! On the other, some of My soldiers are executing some of My other soldiers. Men fight men." He grasped the collar of my garment for support, and I felt my body bend down under the weight of him. "My son, My own Heir, has abandoned Me!"

"He felt hounded. The imprisonment was perhaps ... ill-timed." He let go of my collar at this. Too much truth annoyed him. I had to be careful. He paced, wringing his hands.

"It's still his place. The pater does as the pater must, and the son must give him loyalty. What are We to do? What will quell all this madness?"

"I urge amnesty. For the Consort. It will soothe your own heart to do so."

"They called for My head! Mine! I am the pater of all. I keep

My head." More pacing. "Nelius. Where has he gone off to? I need a steady hand on the tiller."

"Your Grace, I am here beside you despite trials. I will give you all the counsel you need." I felt he was too frail to hear bad news.

"No! I want Nelius! Bring him to Us! He said he would meet Me in the throne room! He will help Me bring the Consort to heel."

"He is gone."

"Nonsense. He was in the Parliament."

"Gentius, he is dead! I saw him gutted by the women. By now they're eating his liver."

He stopped short when I used his name.

"You dare. Treasurer or no, you do not sully Me with your familiarity. You are no loyalist. You are a snake, Tiresius. I should have done away with you before." He approached me and stabbed me in the chest with a shaking finger. The soldiers about the room all leaned forward, weapons lifted slightly.

From outside the throne room, we heard long brass notes.

"What is that?"

"The Consort."

"What does he want?"

"Your head, I imagine." Now Gentius was angry. He cuffed me with both hands. He pinched my ear and tried to drag me about the room.

"Guards. Take this one. Take him to be executed!"

There was a hammering at the door.

"I demand entry!" The Consort's voice boomed, even through the closed doors.

Now the Autokrator foolishly clutched me to him, as though I could be a shield between him and his son.

"What do I do?"

His assistants and guards were mute. None of them were qualified to give advice to the Autokrator. He screamed in my face. "What do I do now?"

"I demand to enter by divine right of rule!" shouted the Consort again.

Gentius glowered at me.

"How am I to give advice if I am to be executed?" I asked without bothering to hide my sneer. In a panic, Gentius looked back and forth. He went to the first guard he could find.

"Go. Burn the library. You, take Tiresius, take his key, empty the Treasury, and ... and toss the gold in the river. Then execute him. You and you — kill these ones ..." He pointed to several of his own assistants, who backed away, eyes wide and white. "Not you two." He pointed again. "You are my pets. You will help me hide. Come."

No one moved. Fists banged on the door, echoing hollowly through the room. Gentius's eyes darted to and fro. He shook with rage at being ignored.

"Now!" raged Gentius. He quickly moved behind the throne, where there was a iron gate that led to a passageway. It gave access to the Treasury and rooms beyond. I was pushed into the dark. A whole company of us squeezed into the low passage. Someone closed the door and, with it, shut out the light. Behind, the hammering continued. But now it was the sound of a ram, battering down the doors.

By dim candlelight in the cramped passage, I had my last look at Gentius. He stumbled his way to the right, likely to his own chamber. I was prodded by swords to go left, to what I thought would be the Treasury. But these were strange times. The guards moved me not to the Treasury but down. Down to the stony halls of the jail.

In a cell, they used their swords to strip me of my robes. They weren't gentle, and when my clothes were gone, my skin was also in tatters. That was how I was discovered. I sat there, shivering naked in a corner, for some time.

"Look at this abomination!" railed one of the guards. On a day of shocks, this was too much for him. An Unmale, living among them all this time.

There was hasty whispering. The senior guard among them towered over me.

"You're going to write a confession. Detail all of it. Everything you've done. Can't have any of your stink left behind. My god, you've been parading around this whole time as if ..." He couldn't even finish. He pointed at the false member hanging between my legs. Before I could react, they held me, drew their swords on me, and castrated me, cutting the false penis from my body. Real blood gushed out. I heard stifled groans. I thought I saw that some of the guards were discomfited by it as well. They threw it down, where a slow seep of blood stained the grout.

"Confession," the senior guard reiterated over my writhing body.

"That will take quite some time," I remarked.

He smiled. "I have all the time in the world."

79

Cera

SEVERAL LEVELS DOWN Below, I finally rested. Many Domestics had left to join Adria's insurrection or flee the city. The remaining ones sat idle, huddled in groups, whispering uncertainly to one another. Some Mams helped me see to the Child. He needed food and a bath.

I found milk and stale buns, then heated them up into a warm pudding. He ate it without complaint. Then I heated water near the ovens and washed him in one of the massive bins we used to mix dough. We found him a small shawl, since his own fine clothes were hopelessly soiled. He settled down while I wrapped a cloth around my bloodied hand, over his teeth marks. His eyes glittered at me in the darkness, round pools of shining brown set into an impossibly clear white setting. He held the blanket I'd covered him with up to his chin. I watched him while his eyes travelled up and down the room, taking in the low ceiling, the dark, the carvings left by countless Domestics on the walls.

"What is this place?" he asked.

"This is where I used to live."

"Why is it so ugly? And dark?"

"They didn't think to make it nice for us."

"I think they were mad at you and wanted you to feel bad."

"I think so too."

"Why did you come and take me from my nice room? Do you want me to feel bad?"

I crept over to sit closer to him.

"I don't want anyone to feel bad. I wanted you. I wanted you for me."

"Why?"

"Because you are mine. Because I am yours."

"I belong to the Autokrator."

"No, you are mine. I carried you in my stomach. I had you. You were my baby. And now you are my child."

"I am the Kratorling. I came from the Consort. My birth is divine. Everyone knows that."

"Everyone says that, but it isn't true. The Consort couldn't have you like that. He had nowhere in his body to keep you while you grew. But he helped make you."

"Helped who?"

"Me. We made you, together. The same way all children are made. That's why I have this." I showed him my pocket goddess. "To remember we all have a Mother."

"Even you?"

I nodded, but he seemed unconvinced. He took a deep breath, closed his eyes, and turned his face away. I put my hand on his head, felt the heat from his body radiating out through the crown of it. The hair was silky. Beneath it, his head still felt soft. It was unbearable to think about how fragile he still was. Would I ever be able to replace the nonsense he'd been taught with the truth? How are lies, told again and again for a thousand years, ever undone? All I could do was tell him what I knew. Tell him the things I had seen and felt and experienced and hope that the ring of truth would make him believe me.

80

Tiresius

I AM CHAINED to a table, naked. I write holding the manacle with my other hand so it won't chafe unnecessarily at my wrist. They could have told me to write it in my own blood — there is enough of it. And dire as the accommodations are, they are still better than anything down Below. So in that sense, everything tallied: I win. A better prison is sometimes all a prisoner can dream of.

I admit that I've taken my time getting everything down. What wound up on these pages is at times self-indulgent, because each sinful word is as much a purchase of time as it is an admission of my crimes. Other things I knew, even as I scrawled them down, were poorly written, a sketch where an opus should have been. The cruelties I glossed over. The hunger I didn't get into. The thousands of slights that stung at the time and hardened my heart and made me lust for something better than what I had.

So, this is where I lay down my last lines. I can feel the derision of my captors as I finish. They hate the fact that I can write. They hate the fact that I am here, among them. The fact that I am. It brings me great satisfaction. And so, here ends the story of the

Autokracy's most audacious Treasurer, an upstart lord who was never really a lord at all, not even a Male, but who managed, for a time, to flout all of her so-called betters.

I hope for a long, uncomfortable death so that, in dying, I am an inconvenience to them to the very last.

81

Cera

I STOLE A few precious days with him, down Below. I kept him all to myself, knowing that once I brought him back up, we would never again be together the same way. At first, he was distant, pushing my hands away from every attempt to caress him or smooth his hair. He rebelled against my efforts to feed him or lift him, insisting on doing everything clumsily with his own hands, climbing into chairs on his own. But over time, he came to crave being close, sitting on my lap, stroking my hair, playing with the pocket goddess. He fell asleep after I made him dinner, and he let his head lay against my shoulder like a stone. My own body tensed around him, muscles straining to hold him in perfect comfort as he dozed in my arms. I curled my head over his and breathed him in.

Time was closing in on us, but I told the story of my small life. He had to know about his birth. His parents. About the lives of the women I'd lived with Below. He assured me that when he grew up, he would see to it that the women would be allowed to come upstairs and that the men would all have to apologize. I had to smile at this naive notion.

When it was time for us to return, I re-dressed the boy in his now clean clothes. Hesperius. Such a big name for such a small boy. He clambered with me up along the winding pathways, higher and higher toward the clean air and the light.

We emerged in the city itself, some distance from the Palace. I wanted him to see the place where he lived from the outside. I wanted him to see the way the people lived. When I held my hand out to him, he took it gravely and walked at my side, up along the high street, up the hill toward the Palace.

Everywhere we looked, corpses lay bloating in the sun and the heat. The closer we came to the Palace, the greater the numbers of dead. Many of them were men, but most were Domestics, freed from their labours only by death. Among them, I thought I recognized Adria, though her body was twisted and the face was marred in a grimacing death mask. Men and women alike were toiling at the grim task of clearing bodies away. I hurried us along as the boy clutched my fingers tightly.

Soldiers stood at the doorway again, though this time their bodies were lax: they hung on their spears, chatting and joking in the sun. They looked at the boy and recognized the insignia on his clothes. They stood at attention and wiped their faces clean of smiles. They paid no notice to me, walking at his side in a shawl.

Inside, an odour of smoke still hung in the air, and there was a bustle of activity as the people tried to put the Palace to rights. The women I saw all around were idle. And their heads were bare.

It felt odd to walk the wide, smooth hallways, as tarnished as they had become, wearing a shawl and not my Page uniform. I felt even more an interloper now.

I took the boy up to the doors of the throne room. I lifted my hand, made a fist, and knocked. I stepped aside from the boy, releasing his hand as the doors swung open. Even at this distance, I could see the Consort seated on the throne of the Autokrator. He stood when the doors revealed the boy's body. Stiffly, the Child walked forward. They had trained him his whole short life for ceremonial moments such as these.

I turned to leave him to his destiny.

"Stop that one."

The voice echoed across the space, and I was met with the ringing clash of crossed weapons as two guards stopped my exit.

"Who goes there? Who has returned the Kratorling to me?"

The boy turned to me.

"It was Mother," he said.

Centuries of smooth Autokratic succession were brought to a close by the sixty-seventh Autokrator, who ushered in a period of nearly unimaginable strife and upheaval. The remarkable and short coronation and reign of Caelius as the sixty-seventh Autokrator is historical fact memorized by thousands of schoolchildren everywhere. But his reign was so brief that those schoolchildren promptly forget his significance.

Shortly after a brief and bloody coup, the sixty-sixth Autokrator went missing. Searches throughout the Palace ultimately unearthed him in his apartments. Historians tell how he was found locked inside his own rooms, whimpering as he rattled the doorknobs. When the Consort and his men broke into the rooms, he was nowhere to be seen. Ultimately, he was found hiding behind a screen, given away by the glint of his golden sandals peeking out under the base. He was dressed in a Domestic shawl, as though he had intended to steal away in disguise.

He was dragged to the prisons, where the stones of the floor were pried up and a deep hole dug in the earth. He was forced down a ladder and into the hole, without food or water. The ladder was pulled and the stones re-laid, cementing him below.

Gentius's Treasurer outlived the Autokrator by scant days. The self-indulgent "confession" left behind has been widely dismissed as a fiction, as few historians believe any woman could have carried on such a double life for so long without being discovered. It has been suggested the narrative was an apocryphal one, written to cast aspersions on the sixty-eighth Autokracy.

Caelius, the Consort and Heir presumptive, held a hasty coronation, overthrowing centuries of tradition. The greater Unorthodoxy was Caelius's invitation to the Unmale Cera to walk at his side in ceremonial robes.

From the outset, it was clear that he wasn't attempting to win over hearts and minds long accustomed to tradition and conservatism. His short reign is notable for one lasting decree: he assigned Cera as his heir. It was later revealed she was carrying his second child.

Witnesses who recorded the events there wrote that Caelius made this proclamation and then required aid to sit upon the throne. It is said that the room was silent while the new Autokrator laboured for breath on his throne and his new Heir stood quaking before a hushed room of men. It was then that the room was opened to a veritable flood of Domestics from all quarters of the Palace. They nearly created a riot in the august chamber.

It was the personal guard of the new Autokrator who knelt first. They were followed by the various Portfolios and their assistants, acknowledging the new Heir.

The Autokrator Caelius died of unknown complications only a few days later. Cera was appointed successor at his deathbed and became the first female Autokrator.

The coronation lacked pomp or extravagance. The new Autokrator wore a garment modelled on the design of a Domestic shawl but made of fine cloth. Free labour and the use of Unmale as a term were abolished. The words Woman, Women, and Female were added to official parlance. For a time.

Cera's history is nearly as short as that of Caelius the sixty-seventh Autokrator, lasting scant months. The date of her death is unknown, as the entire Autokracy fractured into a bloody upheaval that lasted for generations and begat vicious civil wars.

The Autokratic family, fleeing conflict, was separated. Most historians agree that they were likely put to death upon being found in the wilds outside the Capital, though many pretenders were set on the throne for the next twenty years, some male, some female, as the gender of Cera's children has been obscured by shifting histories. The Domestic insurrection was put down in quick order, due largely to the military disorganization of the women. After their first taste of rebellion, though, unrest continued for many decades.

While women were granted charter status as civilians and permitted to live and work freely above ground with men, pockets of resistance persisted for hundreds of years. Some women refused to join the new world order and sued the Autokracy for the right to live Orthodox lives. Many pro-Male groups, comprised of both genders, practised living the Orthodox ways.

Tiresius was remembered as a hero for a time after the coup. A death mask was cast into a splendid bronze statue that stood in the Capital for a time. It was eventually defaced and torn down, likely made into weapons during the depressions later, when metal was scarce.

There are no known surviving images of Cera, sixty-eighth Autokrator, the first female to rule.

DR. NEREUS GENNADIUS, PROFESSOR OF HISTORICAL POLITICS, HEAD OF THE DEPARTMENT OF HISTORICAL STUDIES, POST-IMPERIAL STUDIES CENTRE
from "Introduction to Global Perspectives on Politics of the Autokracy"

ACKNOWLEDGEMENTS

My deepest thanks and love to Willem Wennekers for being the best friend and confidante a writer could hope for: another writer with a love for the true play of words and worlds and a constant source of inspiration, deep silly laughs. I need to write a new novel to fully capture all I am thankful for and even then, words would fall short.

Thanks to Sarah Cooper for believing in *Autokrator* and championing this book from the start, and me as a writer from before the start of *Autokrator*, when she was my first screenwriting agent — always with a kind word and an esprit de corps and a wonderful conspiring laugh and a whip-smart brain. She told me so, and I am glad for it. To Sarah Jensen for being the next champion and ultimately for becoming my editor, which felt as though it was meant to be. With *Autokrator*, a book is born, a novelist is born, and an editor is born. Sarah guided the work home through waters that became increasingly choppy due to many personal turmoils in 2023. To my first editor before being picked up for publication — Adrienne Kerr, who was the first set of eyes on the nascent work, and an unwavering believer in its content. To Marc Côté for his words of wisdom and bon mots on so many subjects and for taking *Autokrator* on for publication at Cormorant, my deep gratitude. To everyone at Cormorant — the staff have been lovely to work with. To Cormorant sibling writer Lucie Pagé — I hoped we might tour our books together and get drunk in hotel rooms in Sudbury. We can at least still have drinks — here's to second novels. To Sam Hiyate — my globe-trotting agent, for his diligence, insights and encouragement along the way. To Stephanie Hart for her early insightful editorial pass with an eye to Feminist issues not to mention hilarious side comments and general camaraderie. Kennedy Zielke and Kiersten Dee for being early beta readers who gave such warm encouragement and feedback. To Mandy and Lindsay from Holt's at Valmont who were unexpected cheerleaders and pick-me-up captains! To my dear Aunt Jane who was my own personal Eleanor Wachtel after she read the book and gave the best Q and A an author could hope for — and who is the embodiment of my ideal reader — a smart Feminist reader who lives and loves life and loves to ponder and chase threads of meaning. To my darling daughter Ginger who was told many times over twelve years "mummy is writing" and who has always taken it with her unusual good grace. To my mother who passed in the final days of preparing for publication and who tried valiantly to live long enough to see the launch, and to whom I ultimately gave permission to "skip class" after fighting a gruelling battle with cancer. "Un Bel Di" like you said, Mummy. I know we were never as close as a mother and daughter usually are, but I know somewhere inside your love for me was as fierce as mine was for you. Finally, to every woman who has found herself having a thought and having to stifle it because of her gender. Live loud. Live brash. Revel in your good brain the way Tiresius would.

We acknowledge the sacred land on which Cormorant Books operates. It has been a site of human activity for 15,000 years. This land is the territory of the Huron-Wendat and Petun First Nations, the Seneca, and most recently, the Mississaugas of the Credit River. The territory was the subject of the Dish With One Spoon Wampum Belt Covenant, an agreement between the Iroquois Confederacy and Confederacy of the Ojibway and allied nations to peaceably share and steward the resources around the Great Lakes. Today, the meeting place of Toronto is still home to many Indigenous people from across Turtle Island. We are grateful to have the opportunity to work in the community, on this territory.

We are also mindful of broken covenants and the need to strive to make right with all our relations.